"A pretty solid start to a new series. . . . [Chris Marie Green] delivers a lively . . . tale of mystery and betrayal."
—Owlcat Mountain

"If you're dying for a *great* ghost read, look no further than Chris Marie Green's Jensen Murphy, Ghost for Hire series!"
—A Great Read

PRAISE FOR THE
VAMPIRE BABYLON SERIES

"A dark, dramatic, and erotic tone. . . . Fans of Charlaine Harris and Jim Butcher may enjoy."
—*Library Journal*

"An intriguing world that becomes more complex with every turn of the page . . . kick-butt action."
—Huntress Book Reviews

"A book to die for! Dark, mysterious, and edged with humor, this book rocks on every level!"
—Gena Showalter, author of *The Darkest Lie*

"A killer mystery. . . . Bring on book two!"
—Kelley Armstrong, author of *Counterfeit Magic*

"An exciting, action-packed vampire thriller. A fantastic tale that . . . provides book lovers with plenty of adventure and a touch of romance."
—*Midwest Book Review*

ANOTHER ONE BITES THE DUST

JENSEN MURPHY, GHOST FOR HIRE

CHRIS MARIE GREEN

A ROC BOOK

ROC
Published by the Penguin Group
Penguin Group (USA) LLC, 375 Hudson Street,
New York, New York 10014

USA | Canada | UK | Ireland | Australia | New Zealand | India | South Africa | China
penguin.com
A Penguin Random House Company

First published by Roc, an imprint of New American Library,
a division of Penguin Group (USA) LLC

First Printing, November 2014

 REGISTERED TRADEMARK—MARCA REGISTRADA

ISBN 978-0-451-41700-8

Printed in the United States of America
10 9 8 7 6 5 4 3 2 1

To everyone who buys books, whether they are in print or digital—you make every author's world go 'round.

In the Beginning . . .

"I know you have no idea who I am," said the college-aged girl standing on Amanda Lee Minter's porch, "but I really need your help."

The psychic and medium was looking through the peephole at her visitor as the morning sun burnished the girl's straight, dark brown hair. Her eyes were a cherub's blue, and she had on a long-sleeved, baggy gray shirt that covered the top half of her jeans, the light jersey material swallowing her hands. She had a solid form and didn't appear to be a materialized version of one of the invisible spirits who had been knocking on the doors and windows lately.

Spirits who were terribly curious about the woman who had worked with a ghost to bring down a murderer nearly a month ago.

Since Amanda Lee was clearly dealing with a human, she opened the door. The girl hitched in a breath, then launched into an introduction.

"My name's Heidi Schmidt. I'm here because I know Wendy Edgett from some forum boards online—"

"Wendy Edgett?"

Heidi bit her lip, then nodded.

Amanda Lee's hand slid down the door. Fifteen-year-old Wendy Edgett. The last time Amanda Lee had seen her was . . .

Shame breathed over her. It had been the night of the séance in the Edgett mansion—an event that had flushed out a dark spirit that had disappeared and never returned. Not yet, at least.

A chill covered Amanda Lee's shame like a shadow crawling over a patch of heat. She searched her yard—the late spring–leaved trees, the pathway to her house. But everything was as seemingly safe and as perfect as ever, no darkness looming.

"You *are* Ms. Minter, right?" Heidi asked, no doubt wondering why Amanda Lee was acting so strangely. "Because this is really embarrassing if I've got the wrong house. I used a reverse phone number lookup on your address because you haven't been answering my calls, so . . ."

"You have the right one. Did Wendy . . . send you here?" Why would she do that? She had been avoiding Amanda Lee like the pox, in spite of the apologetic phone calls she'd been making, revealing her real identity to Wendy, telling her that she had only wanted to make the world right again by catching a killer during the séance.

Heidi was shaking her head. "Wendy didn't actually send me, Ms. Minter."

"Is she all right?"

"Yes. It's just that she didn't want to come with me."

Heidi shuffled her sneakers. "She's still not up to seeing anyone socially. She said she and her brother moved to one of his other properties, and she's doing schoolwork from home. She doesn't even go on the chat board anymore, but she sends e-mails to me. I think I'm the only one she really talks to. It's the grief, you know? Seeing her sister Farah kill her brother because he knew too much about the murder she committed, then dealing with the knowledge that Farah was evil . . ."

Amanda Lee gripped the edge of the door, her knuckles whitening. "If she didn't send you, then why are you here?"

Heidi pulled at her sleeves. "Over a month ago, Wendy started posting on a social San Diego paranormal chat board I hang out on, too—you know, the kind for fans of reality ghost shows and stuff? Well, back then, she said she couldn't believe it, but she thought there was a spirit in her house. The last time she checked in with us as a group, just before the crap hit the fan with Farah, Wendy said there was a psychic coming over to help make contact and see what the entity wanted. It was all so cool to her."

"You want me to make contact with a spirit, then." Amanda Lee itched to close the door, shut herself in among the antiques and the dusky rooms where the shades were drawn. It was only intuition that had told her to respond to the doorbell, and she always listened to her inner guide, even if it occasionally steered her in odd directions.

Heidi rushed on. "Wendy said that you hang with the ghost who was haunting her old house, and during one of your phone messages, you told her that the ghost is the one who uncovered Wendy's sister as a murderer. This Jensen ghost girl went inside all the suspects' heads and figured them out, then flushed out the true killer. It's true, right? This ghost drove Farah to a confession?"

"Yes," Amanda Lee said, her heartbeat quickening for some reason she couldn't pinpoint yet.

"Wendy . . ." Heidi's face was red. "She said that you would help me because the two of you owe her."

Oh.

Amanda Lee took that in, realizing just how true it was. Obviously, this girl had seen Wendy's ghost adventures on the chat boards, asked for her help, then come here because something was scaring her and she needed Amanda Lee and "her ghost" to intercede.

Was this fate's way of granting absolution for everything Amanda Lee had done wrong with the Edgetts?

All she had wanted was a reckoning for the woman Farah Edgett had killed—Elizabeth Dalton.

God. Her Elizabeth . . .

But there were also many other spirits in need of justice. Jensen, the ghost Heidi had been talking about, was one. Was Heidi leading her to another?

Fear of ruining more lives during an investigation made Amanda Lee's heart beat even faster. Fear in general had been keeping her inside the house, full of doubt, frozen. But at this girl's anxious expression, Amanda Lee stepped outside, feeling the sun on her skin for the first time in weeks. Now that she was closer to Heidi, she could sense the girl's nerves screeching.

"Why is it that you're on edge?" she asked.

Heidi seemed relieved that Amanda Lee wasn't shooing her off. "I'm really worried about someone I care about, and I can't go to the cops about it. And I definitely can't go to my best friend Nichelle because she's the one in trouble, and she won't accept that reality."

Yes. A chance for absolution had arrived on Amanda Lee's doorstep.

Heidi took a deep breath, exhaling harshly. "After I heard what you and your ghost did, I realized that I could use at least one of you to go inside the head of Nichelle's boyfriend to see if he's capable of killing her." She swallowed. "Because I'm pretty sure that's what's going to happen if nobody does anything about it."

To any other person, it would have been a nearly insane request, but Amanda Lee understood perfectly.

She closed the door behind her, then placed her hand on Heidi's shoulder, leading her to the little casita at the side of the bigger house.

When she opened the door and guided Heidi into the antique-rich room, the girl peered around, as if intuiting that something was off about it. As if feeling a coldness that wasn't coming from any air conditioner.

She obviously couldn't see the ghost who'd looked up from her spot near the car battery on a table, getting a charge from it, her normally grayish color high, her energy strong.

"Heidi," Amanda Lee said, her voice more animated than it had been for a while. "Meet Jensen Murphy."

1

When I'd encountered Amanda Lee for the first time a
month and a half ago, I'd already been dead meat for
about thirty years. Supposedly, I'd only gone missing
but . . . nope. It was more like I'd been murdered in the
early eighties after a party up in Elfin Forest in North
County, my killer unknown, my body never found.

But now, as Amanda Lee stood next to this Heidi
girl, giving me the basics about why an unexpected visitor was in my casita, *Amanda Lee* was the one who
came off like the dearly departed, garbed in a dark ruffled skirt and boots, with a matching blouse hanging
limply from her tall frame. Her usually perfect red hair
with the white streaks framing her face was even as
drab as a black-and-white B-horror movie.

And why not, when the woman was as haunted as
anyone I'd ever met?

I could tell Heidi wasn't sensitive enough to see me,
because she kept peering around the room, her eyes
wide. The only humans I knew who could get a lock on
me were Amanda Lee and Wendy Edgett. It's not like I

would've made any kind of awesome impression on Heidi, anyway—I'd died in tennis shoes, jeans, and a pale blue button-down rolled up to my elbows with a white tank underneath. Just your average twenty-three-year-old American girl with my strawberry blond hair, green eyes, and freckles. A Tom Petty song in the flesh . . . or not.

By this point, I had a few questions for Amanda Lee. And, by the way, it's pronounced "A *MAN*daley" with a Southern flair she'd brought with her from Virginia when she was young. Quirky as hell.

"So Wendy's been talking to this chick?" I asked her. I'd mostly been concentrating on the Wendy parts of the story I'd just been told.

"Yes," Amanda Lee said. "They've exchanged e-mails."

"I noticed that Wendy does spend a lot of time on her computer." I'd been watching over her and her older brother Gavin, who I'd nearly driven insane while trying to decide whether he was guilty of killing Elizabeth Dalton. That's mainly why Wendy was pissed off at me, and I didn't know if she was ever going to forgive me. Even so, it was my duty to see that the two of them were okay, that the dark spirit Amanda Lee had summoned during that asinine fake séance was leaving them alone.

I wasn't all that sure it *would* stay away from them since I had a bad feeling that Amanda Lee had accidentally released their very deceased craphead father from wherever naughty people went after they died. Being a ghost, you'd think I'd know exactly where that was, but no. No matter who I asked, no one ever had a good explanation.

Boo World wasn't exactly a place where every question you'd had as a mortal was answered.

Speaking of sketchy things Amanda Lee had done, I should mention that she'd also lied about why she'd recently resurrected me from the residual haunting phase I'd been in for nearly three decades—a time loop where I'd been living my death over and over again because I'd been so traumatized by it. She'd wanted me to haunt the truth out of the man she'd suspected of murdering her lover, Elizabeth Dalton. See, Amanda Lee had told me she didn't know Elizabeth, that she was only seeking justice for a friend. None of that turned out to be true, because Amanda Lee had been very close to the victim, indeed; she'd been manipulating me—the dumb new ghost—the entire time only to make me do her bidding.

Needless to say, trust wasn't exactly high on my Amanda Lee To-Do list.

I float-walked closer to Heidi, and she crossed her arms over her chest, warming herself.

"I meant to ask before," she said to Amanda Lee. "Exactly how much do you charge to help people?"

"Charge?" Amanda Lee and I asked at the same time.

"Yes, I want to hire you."

I didn't need money, and Amanda Lee's spine straightened at the very mention of it because she was what was known as "affluent."

"There'll be no charge," she said.

"Oh. Okay. I only thought . . ."

"No charge," Amanda Lee repeated, and she said it with such dignity that I knew the topic was as dead as disco.

While Amanda Lee was bristling, something caught my attention at the window. Movement, outside. And when I saw an old man's grayish, bearded, ghostly face peering in, I flew over and waved bye-bye.

Dammit, there'd been ghosts swirling around here a lot lately, drawn by all the rumors of what me and Amanda Lee had done with the Edgetts. Apparently, we were high entertainment for the bored denizens of Boo World.

The old man stuck out his tongue and zoomed away. In the meantime, the curtains were stirring with the wind I'd caused. Heidi looked ready to do a Major Tom and shoot into space, fueled by fear.

I have to say that her fear did charge me up a tad.

Amanda Lee strode toward the window. She probably hadn't seen the old man—I was the only ghost she'd ever fully connected with—but she'd noticed my reaction to him, so she could make an educated guess.

She shut those curtains. "That was only Jensen brushing by the window, dear. Don't mind her."

Heidi's voice shook as she continued, but the kid was brave to stay. I'd give her that.

"It's all good, Ms. Minter."

Excellent. Then the girl wouldn't mind a little of *this*.

I turned on the computer by manipulating the electricity in the atmosphere. Ghosts were pure energy, after all.

Heidi made a surprised sound.

With a lowered glance at me, Amanda Lee took the hint, sitting down in front of the computer. "Getting a little pranky, are we, Jensen?"

"Me?" Hmph. I wasn't the pranky type—that was for the ghosts who'd already gotten bored with their existence, looking for stimulation from the responses pranks got from humans.

I wasn't bored. Or maybe I was. After the Edgett situation, I'd been, well, dying to move out of the casita, just to put some space between me and Amanda Lee. But all the annoying ghosts and the threat of the dark spirit had kept me here to watch over her as much as I could.

I'd leave soon, though, I kept telling myself. Someday I'd find an abandoned house that was just right for me.

"What is your friend's name?" Amanda Lee asked Heidi, her fingers poised over the keyboard.

"Nichelle Shaw."

"And her boyfriend?"

"Tim. Tim Knudson."

"Address, please?"

Heidi rattled off a place in Pacific Beach, and Amanda Lee typed it all in. The search engine came up with several links, and she clicked on one of them.

My energy was humming, mostly because I was feeling the growing apprehension in Heidi. "Why does she think he's going to kill Nichelle?" I asked Amanda Lee.

After she translated for Heidi, the girl answered, "It's

just . . . a hunch. I read a book once, and they called this kind of intuition the gift of fear. And that's why I can't go to anyone else, because all I have are creepy suspicions about this guy. He and Nichelle have been with each other for a couple months now. They live together. At first, he was fascinating for Nichelle. She hasn't had a lot of boyfriends, and Tim rides a beat-up motorcycle and has a blue-collar thing going on, so he's edgy and kind of *wow* for her. And he had a steady new job in a department store warehouse, working the swing shift. I found out a week after they were dating that he has a spotty work history, though. When I told her, she asked him about it, and he said that the past didn't matter—he was going to make himself better for her."

Amanda Lee had brought up a profile on that Facebook thingie. Frankly, I couldn't stand the site. It was the type of distraction I would've hated when I was alive, too. I had true, close, dear friends that I used to go out and toke with and drink with every once in a while, face-to-freaking-face. That, and my waitressing gig at Roundtable Pizza, had been enough of a social life for me.

Anyway, Tim's picture showed a handsome guy in his twenties with buzzed sandy hair and a Tom Cruise smile. He was a smaller man. I could tell because he was posing near a bar, and it provided some scale as he toasted the camera with a draft beer.

Amanda Lee said, "He looks harmless enough, but that's always the problem. We know better than anyone that bad people are good at hiding who they really are."

"Let's give him the benefit of the doubt right now," I said. We didn't know Heidi very well, and I was eager to get an empathy reading off her to see if she was on the up-and-up with us. Besides, I didn't need to remind Amanda Lee about Gavin Edgett and how we'd rushed to judgment with him when she'd suspected him of killing Elizabeth.

Just at the thought of Gavin my ghost-heart sank, beating with a longing that was invisible, but real just the same. Regret, attraction, fascination . . . I hadn't expected to feel any of it, being a dead girl and all.

Maybe I was a little obsessed because of my guilt. I'd trespassed into his mind, as well as the heads of other suspects. Sure, I'd been inside of them for good reason—I hadn't taken it lightly because messing with them was hard on their bodies and psyches—but the major fact was that me and Amanda Lee had gone rogue, taking the law into our own hands.

It was just that, when you died a victim like I had, you refuse to live your eternal afterlife as one, too, or to see it happen to others. So I'd become a justice-seeker, just like Amanda Lee. I was even going to solve my own murder someday, as soon as I figured out how to get around the whole lack of witnesses, suspects, and evidence dilemma. There wasn't even blood at my death spot to tip off the authorities to where I'd died, for God's sake. Still, I'd spent the last month collecting data, looking up all my old friends on the computer, hoping to locate them so I could get readings off them and see if they had any clues about what'd happened to me that night.

Heidi was peering over Amanda Lee's shoulder now, hugging herself as she stared at Tim's computerized profile.

"He's very well behaved on this Facebook page," she murmured. "But he's got a temper in real life. Gets in fights at bars and with his so-called friends. One of them even told me that he stole a credit card from a former girlfriend. Nichelle didn't want to believe that, and he told her it was a lie."

Amanda Lee asked, "What is Nichelle like?"

"Strong-willed. Won't take any guff. But she's got a naive side that Tim sensed or something. She thinks she's not very attractive—which isn't true—so she was wide-open to his limited charms."

"Is he outright cruel to her?"

"Well, let's just say that they fight like cats and dogs sometimes. And Nichelle tells me things that he does in private that disturb me." Heidi went back to rubbing her arms. "I thought that maybe a ghost could watch him in those private moments, when he thinks no one is looking. Or a psychic could read him, even if it's just for my own peace of mind."

I got closer to the computer, wanting a better look at Timmy Boy's profile. It fizzed with some screen-snow, but I could still make out that he had been born in Montana and he liked to play guitar. I backed away when Amanda Lee shot me a you're-causing-interference glance.

She asked, "So you think he's violent enough to hurt her badly one day?"

"Yes, and if I'm wrong about that, then I'll lay off

him." Heidi shook her head. "It all sounds so melodramatic, but I swear, it's not. I'm taking general ed classes at SDSU, and one of them is abnormal psych. He's got qualities that point to antisocial behavior."

Okay. Time to see if she was overreacting.

"Amanda Lee," I said. "Ask her if it'd be all right if I did an empathy reading."

"Heidi, would it be fine with you if Jensen read your thoughts?"

"Oh. Sure. Is that safe?"

"Yes. And you'll be cold only for a short time. Jensen won't push it."

If I did, then I'd go farther into her psyche than I needed to, draining her and me more than necessary.

Heidi breathed out, holding her hand up so I could touch it. I took that as an all systems go.

As I made contact with her skin, a shiver zinged through her. It was as if I'd connected with a power outlet while her thoughts slammed into me . . .

Nichelle's voice on the phone. "I can't go to the movies tonight, Heidi, okay? Tim wants to stay in. I know this is the third time I've canceled this week, but maybe tomorrow?"

Walking by Nichelle's bedroom on the way to the bathroom, overhearing Tim's quiet, private-time voice. "This is what you're gonna wear tonight. I'm throwing away that trashy blue dress. It makes you look like a slut."

At lunch with Nichelle. A ringing phone. Tim's voice on the speaker. "Who're you with? Get home, Nich, no ifs, ands, or buts, got it? I want you here, with me."

I unlinked from Heidi, then went to the car battery. Empathizing always took a little juice out of me. Meanwhile, she held a hand over her chest, shivering.

"*Da-mn.*"

Amanda Lee tapped away on the computer, bringing up more information about Tim on that Twitter thing now. "I told you, Heidi. Only a slight chill."

"More than slight. That was . . ." Heidi huddled into herself. "I think I'll sit down."

She walked across the room, pointedly away from my coldness, to a rose-upholstered love seat. She pulled her sleeves all the way over her hands like they were two turtle heads disappearing into shells.

I hoped Heidi would never have to experience a ghost making her hallucinate or going dream-digging if she was asleep. *That* would be intense.

I spoke to Amanda Lee. "I got definite hints about a controlling relationship. Heidi's been around when Tim does things like keeping Nichelle from seeing her friends. It also looks like he checks up on her, chooses her clothes, and seems to get jealous that she wants to spend time with other people."

Amanda Lee turned from the computer to survey Heidi, who still didn't seem comfortable with knowing that a ghost had been inside her.

"She's got a good aura," Amanda Lee said quietly.

"I do?" Heidi asked.

"And good hearing," Amanda Lee said, standing, going to Heidi. She gestured toward the girl's hand. "May I?"

Heidi seemed skeptical, and after the chill of my

touch, I couldn't blame her. Then she pulled the sleeve away from her hand, and Amanda Lee clasped it in her own, closing her eyes, psychically riding the girl's skin while her thoughts were still on Nichelle.

It was over in under a minute.

"So Nichelle really *doesn't* tolerate Tim's behavior," Amanda Lee said. "She stands up for herself, and that seems to frustrate him."

"Right. When they fight, she'll come over to my apartment and sometimes stay while I'm at my classes. But by the time I get home, she's usually gone back to him. I told you—her self-confidence could improve."

"What's that girl even thinking?" I asked Amanda Lee.

"That she has Tim in hand," she said. "And that his good qualities outweigh everything else. It seems like a chemical attraction. You know what love is like."

I didn't want to think about love.

Heidi seemed more desperate to sway us now. "Please, I know all this doesn't sound that dangerous. But I've heard him on the phone with Nichelle when he'll go deathly silent during a fight. I can't help thinking he's going to explode one of these days."

I traded glances with Amanda Lee, seeing that, like me, she would never be able to forgive herself if we ignored this. We had the power to prevent something bad from happening. We also had a responsibility.

We *also* had a hell of a lot to make up for because of how we'd almost ruined Gavin. Not that he was a pristine guy. No way. He had blood on his hands for sure, but in a righteous way since he'd secretly killed his and

Wendy's father, an abusive bastard . . . and, quite possibly, the dark spirit Amanda Lee had unleashed during that séance.

To tell the truth, I was yearning to do some right with my abilities. I'd never done much of anything as a human, and now . . . ?

I could finally be someone who mattered.

Amanda Lee seemed to feel those vibes from me, and she smiled at Heidi. "We'll tell you what we find out soon. Rest easy until then."

Heidi returned Amanda Lee's smile; then, by some miracle, she seemed to find me and give me the same sunny thank-you.

It charged me up better than any battery ever could.

After our business was done with Heidi, I stuck with her until she was safely in her Honda, then watched her drive down the treelined street. The sun was climbing in the sky, bringing a few more curious ghosts along with it since our kind didn't mind the light.

I told them to scram, and they must've seen that I meant it since they gave me no lip. Weird, but I'd never been a tough girl when I was alive. I guess it took a murder or two to sharpen a ghost up.

Back in the casita, Amanda Lee was on the computer again, doing more research on Tim Knudson.

"I guess we've got our work cut out for us," I said, hovering above her, close enough to the computer that the screen danced with interference.

Amanda Lee blinked her eyes, coming out of her myopic online search. Then she said, "You're not angry with me about committing to Heidi before I even asked you, are you?"

"No, but . . ."

She fixed her gray gaze on me. "You don't have to say it. I've felt it for a while. You're not going to be around here much longer for me to bother you."

Having a psychic in your life could be such a bitch. "I've been planning to look for a comfortable, abandoned place. Part of it has to do with all the attention we've been getting from Boo World, with those nosy ghosts hanging around. It shouldn't last much longer because they'll get tired of us soon, but I hate being such a freak show to them."

"You're not the freak show, Jensen. From what you've told me, ghosts are more fascinated with humans who do things such as accidentally opening portals and letting in malevolent entities."

A pall hung over the room, weighed down by Amanda Lee's obvious guilt about what'd happened during the Edgett situation.

"Do you think," I asked, "Wendy was reaching out to us in a way? By sending Heidi here?"

"I wouldn't set my hopes on that."

"You know what I should do? Talk to her. See what she thinks about Heidi since she knows her from online. . . ."

"And how will you manage that? Rap on her window, ask for her forgiveness, then dive right into a relatively normal conversation? We nearly sent her brother into a mental spiral, Jensen."

"But she's thankful for what we did, deep down,

don't you think? We couldn't save Noah from Farah, but Gavin came out all right in the end. So did Wendy herself."

"You can't know what she's thinking by watching her through a window."

True. I didn't want to get too close to Wendy, wanting to respect her by keeping my distance. But I wondered if she'd ever seen me lingering outside her new home, watching over her and Gavin, longing for them to just open a window and let me in.

Amanda Lee had turned to me, her hands folded in her lap. "You realize, of course, that devoting time to this Tim Knudson situation will postpone our investigation into your own killing."

"Oh, you're ready to go forward with that now?" I wasn't being sarcastic. I'd known that Amanda Lee was in no shape to do much but stay in her house, mourning Elizabeth all over again, as well as everything else that had gone wrong during the investigation.

Amanda Lee nodded. "If you're ready."

Hell, yeah, I was. And after I solved my murder, I was also hoping to look up any relatives I had who might be cruising around Boo World. But it wasn't like there was a spook directory that would speed that up or anything. "As far as Tim Knudson goes, it sounds like a pretty easy thing—go to Nichelle's place, observe him, check out what he's all about, then . . ."

"We should talk about the 'then' portion."

"You mean, what will we do if it looks like he's going to beat Nichelle to within an inch of her life someday, after he loses his cool?" I sighed, the sound like a soft cry that skimmed over the walls. "I'll just have to find a way to talk him out of it. I can be pretty persuasive."

Amanda Lee sat back in the chair. "You're rather confident about succeeding in that."

Was I? And why did it sound like Amanda Lee wasn't thrilled about that?

It occurred to me that she might be a little bit bruised by the fact that I was my own ghost now. Without all her lies and manipulations, I was free to make my own decisions. Of course, she was going to help me with my own murder, so she had me by the balls there.

But maybe there were more mediums besides Amanda Lee who could see me and hear me. And, believe me, I needed psychic help, because I was hoping to get some clues from my old friends once I got around to *interviewing* them. Once I had some suspects, I could go into their heads and hearts. But I needed suspects in the first place. A psychic could speed up the process, intuiting details about the night I'd died, giving me a list of people who might've had it out for me, and a medium could communicate all these details to me. Otherwise, it'd be like trying to find a needle in a haystack, sifting through every person in San Diego County, and maybe beyond, to find someone who knew something about my demise.

Amanda Lee was the only person I knew right now who had the power to do all that.

"Anyway," I said, "there'll be enough time for Tim Knudson and everything else." I paused. "I've been planning on visiting Suze soon, too."

"Why haven't you already?"

Because she was my best friend from when I was alive, and every time I dropped by the pub where she worked, I got a little more depressed at seeing how she'd turned out. Lonely, wistful . . . I didn't know if her bright personality had been killed along with me or if life had just been that nasty for her afterward.

"I was only thinking about it," I added, not committing myself.

Amanda Lee stood, straightening her clothes. It was the first sign I'd seen since the Edgett situation that she cared about what she looked like.

"You'll be checking up on Wendy then? Soon?"

"Yeah. I figured I'd see how she's doing before going over to this Tim's house. Heidi said he works the swing shift, so he might be there for me to observe and do an empathy reading."

"I can do one, too. Subtly. Perhaps on any possessions he has outside his home. I'd like to see where he lives, as well, just to get more of a feel for him. We could meet there, say, at three?"

"Let's go for it."

"When you see Wendy," she said, "if you do happen to talk to her, would you tell her I'm sorry?"

Amanda Lee didn't give up. "If she hasn't gotten your flood of apology calls, yes, I will."

She cracked a window, and I floated through the gap, then heard it close behind me.

I avoided the gaggle of ghosts who'd flocked by the sidewalk while I conjured a travel tunnel. As it popped into existence, looking like the inside of an artery, I saluted my comrades.

"Show's over for now, buds."

I shot through the air on a current of electric speed, then heaved out of the tunnel in front of my intended destination.

Wendy and Gavin Edgett's new condo.

2

I whisked to the back of the luxury condo until I came to a small hydrangea-filled courtyard with a running fountain and Italian stone tile. There, as sunlight glistened off Wendy's second-story window above, I found three ghosts hanging out.

Thank God they weren't the lookiloo kind, either.

After I said hey to them, two of them perked up.

"Jen!"

Scott, a fifties teen who wore rolled-up jeans, a flannel shirt over a T-shirt, and slicked dark hair, was sitting with Louis, a black man who eternally wore the World War II–era aircraft factory uniform he'd died in. They were both on an air-conditioning unit and, as the machine worked, the vibrations shuddered their grayish shapes.

There was one more ghost here, too, lounging on the stucco wall that divided the courtyard from beds of flowers, a walking lane, and a statue garden.

Twyla rolled her eyes to greet me, and I ignored her right back. Except it was pretty hard, what, with the way she looked and all. What a total freak, and I mean it: half Robert Smith from The Cure with creepy dark lipstick and teased, inky hair, half Cyndi Lauper with lighter wild hair on the other side. She was all corset, petticoats, fishnet stockings, and Madonna bracelets everywhere else, though.

Basically, she was everything that I'd made fun of while living in the eighties as a SoCal beach girl. Twyla had perished while experimenting with her look, comparing her Goth dye and makeup to her Lauper side when the cord of the hairdryer she'd been using had gone into a full sink of water. So she was doomed to a split fashion personality as long as she roamed the earthly plane. Bummer.

But she was lucky in one way. All of us were, because for some reason no ghost had figured out, we'd been spared having to deal with our death marks, so Twyla hadn't come out of her demise all fried up. I was especially grateful for my circumstances. I mean, it's bad enough having to traipse around for the rest of my existence in some clothes I'd just thrown on that night to hang out with my friends. But according to the little I remembered about my murder, I'd had an ax taken to me by a maniac in the woods wearing a shriveled granny mask.

I *know*. I might've been in Jensen pieces right now if we existed in our death states. Thank God I had erected what Amanda Lee thought was a "fright wall" to spare myself the horrific memories of my murder, too—even the flashes I occasionally had of it were so awful that I wasn't surprised I'd gone into a numbing time loop.

But as more weeks passed, the more I realized I *could* handle knowing how I'd died if I could only recall who'd done it.

You wouldn't ever get justice on someone you couldn't remember, right?

"How's Wendy?" I asked Scott, who was here because he'd volunteered to look after her while I concentrated on Amanda Lee. Most of my ghost friends were on the same shifts, just to help me out.

"She's copacetic." Scott drew his leg up on the air conditioner, bending it and leaning an elbow on his knee. "I know she can see me peeking in her window every so often, but she still refuses to give me a high sign."

Wendy was even more sensitive than Amanda Lee when it came to seeing ghosts. I wasn't sure if that was a good or bad thing.

Glancing up at the second floor, Louis said, "That's because she's still put out with you for being a part of the worst night of her life."

"Gawd," Twyla said. "I don't know what little precious expected us to do. Wave a magic wand and make her sister innocent?"

As always, Twyla was the height of compassion. Ignore, ignore, ignore.

"And Gavin?" I asked, trying not to let my energy go *bzzzt*. Sometimes that happened when I said his name, just like in life, when you'd see or think of any hunky guy. But Gavin was more complex than that. I guess being harassed by a ghost will make anyone complicated and more brooding than usual.

Louis traded a glance with Scott, then said, "He's

still working from home, designing those video games, drawing on his draft board . . ."

Scott cleared his throat, bringing Louis to a stop. From somewhere down the path over the wall, a dog barked at the sounds of us chatting.

Twyla gagged. "Listen to you lame-os. So sweet, beating around the bush and not telling Jen-Jen that Gavin added more pictures of her on his walls. Not very flattering ones, either." She turned to me. "You look like a hellbitch now."

"Oh."

It was true that Gavin had gotten a look at me, not only in some vague pictures Wendy had taken while I was haunting their house, but in his dreams, when I had gone into his sleeping body and straight to his opened psyche. I'd kind of liked how he used to draw me as an angelic image. Now I was a hellbitch though?

"Aw," Twyla said. "Jen is sad."

Scott held back a grin but Louis' tone got stern. "Knock it off, Twyla. There's no need for you to be here, anyway."

"And you? Why're you here?"

I spoke up. "He's taking over for Scott soon."

How else would interactive, intelligent ghosts like us fill the time except for activities like this? We still had personalities and the ability to reason, unlike the sad sacks we knew as noninteractives—the kind who were in time loops or residual hauntings like I'd been. Even anonymous ghosts, who were intelligent but still too afraid to engage with their surroundings, needed stimulation to keep from going back into time loop/imprint mode.

.

The sound of a barking dog grew louder, and I floated up so I could see over the wall Twyla was sitting on.

A poodle had gotten loose from its owner, who was running after it on the flowered path. By now, the dog was at the foot of the wall, yapping its head off at Twyla.

"See," Scott said. "Dogs are even annoyed by you."

"They're, like, generally annoyed by all of us." With a tight grin, Twyla made a gesture, manipulating the energy in the air so that the leash lifted seemingly on its own, then guided the dog away from the wall.

It yelped while its owner froze on the path, her mouth agape as she watched her pet being pulled toward her with the leash raised.

Twyla flicked her wrist, and the leash dropped just before the dog got to its person.

Told you—bored ghosts like to prank, and it could be anytime, anywhere, thanks to the fact that we weren't stuck in the places we'd died. If that was the case, then Scott would still be at the site of the old diner where he'd choked on a chicken bone while on a date with his high school girlfriend. Louis would be wandering the stretch of road where he'd driven into a ditch one dark night, tired from his shift at the factory. I'd still be in Elfin Forest at my own death spot.

But here's the thing: The farther away we travel from our location of death, the weaker we get. We can always charge up with an electrical source, though, or feed on the fear from someone who's scared. It's just that some of us don't like to stay in one place because we've got things to do, people to see. We can also relocate for a change of scenery, getting our jollies that way, because one of the worst things that can happen to a ghost is boredom.

Twyla let out a dramatic sigh, standing on the wall. Or seeming to stand on it, since her ankle boots hovered about an inch above the stucco. She stretched her arms, like she'd finished a tough job and was proud of herself for terrorizing a poodle.

Whatever. I addressed the guys. "Today was interesting."

I could feel the sparks of intrigue from them. Scott and Louis even buzzed.

"Do tell," Twyla said.

"A student from SDSU," I said, "came to Amanda Lee about helping a friend."

"So?"

"Well, her name's Heidi, and she thinks this friend is going to get hurt or killed someday by a guy she's living with. Heidi wants Amanda Lee to psychically see if she's wrong about him. And she wants me to go into him to find the truth, too."

Louis stood from the air conditioner. "How did she know about you?"

I pointed toward the second-story window. Wendy.

I told them the rest: how Wendy and Heidi had met online and become friends, how Wendy had told her that Amanda Lee and I owed her.

Twyla arced down from the wall in a bell of petticoats. "What fun! When do we start?"

"We don't start," I said. "I'm going to look into this

soon enough. It might not amount to anything that'd keep your attention."

Twyla tapped a finger against her darkened lips, then said, "True. Besides, it's Saturday, and there'll be parties all over the place, and you know I never miss a chance to, like, mess with drunk-asses. I love the looks they get on their faces when their cups just happen to flip out of their hands and spill beer all over their tight, hard-body man chests."

Simple tastes for simple minds, I guess.

"If you need any help," Louis said to me, "you remember to give a holler."

Scott was idly making the courtyard light flick on and off. When he saw that it was irritating Louis, he stopped and sent his elder a sheepish grin. "Yeah, man. I'll help, too, Jen."

"You could start by going to Amanda Lee's place and hanging out there until she leaves the house." They'd also been dropping by there, on the lookout for that dark spirit. "I'm meeting her soon to get rolling on Heidi's request."

"Done," Scott said.

Twyla stroll-floated to me. "Aren't you just all over the place, being a helper? Busiest ghost ever."

"I suppose it's the Mello Yello in me." I'd died with a few cans of it my system since I'd been the designated driver at that forest party where everyone else had been wasted before I'd wandered off to pee and never come back. Who knew why the caffeine had carried over into the afterlife, yet there were no ax cuts on me and no blood marks on my death spot?

But maybe the Mello Yello was the reason I didn't sink into boredom as easily as most older ghosts. More important, that time loop in Elfin Forest had been enough of an anesthetic limbo for me, and I wasn't about to slide back into one if I got no stimulation.

"So this boyfriend you're 'investigating' . . ." Twyla said, using finger quotes.

"Don't mock what she's doing," Louis said. "She's accomplishing some good, which is more than I can say for you most times."

"Yes, Daddy." More eye rolling from Twyla. "But I'm only making a point, remembering life and how I had a boyfriend once who liked to fight."

"Did he get violent?" I asked.

"Not in that way." She waggled her eyebrows. "But what if Heidi Ho is totally misinterpreting what's between her friend and her boyfriend? What if they like it rough, and Heidi just doesn't get that? Know what I mean?"

"I'm not sure I do, Twyla."

"You've had boyfriends, Jen. Didn't you ever—"

I cut her off with a raised hand. I'd had one serious boyfriend before I'd died, and he'd never raised his voice to me. That doesn't mean he hadn't broken me in other ways, after he'd left me to go to school across the U.S. Hard times had followed; Dean hadn't been there when my parents had died in a boating accident, hadn't been there when I'd dropped out of college and, really, life itself while I toked and partied too much instead.

The only time *Dean* had come back was recently, when an entity pretending to be him had tried to fool me into staying in this weird star place that'd turned out to be another limbo of sorts. I called him fake Dean, and I hoped to hell I'd never have to see him again. Since he hadn't shown up for a while, I was pretty sure he'd lost interest in me, anyway.

"Oh," said Twyla, batting her eyelashes at me. "I've insulted Jen. Like, gross me out! Barf-o-rama! Rough sex sucks! It should never, ever be mentioned in mixed company."

Louis lifted his chin, above all this.

"We'll see what's what with Heidi's friend soon enough," I said to Twyla. "Meanwhile, once again, you're ragingly out of line."

"And you're such a mega prude." She waved her hand and a travel tunnel appeared above the stucco wall, its innards pink and electric, beating with energy. "Bored now. Later, puritans."

She took a floating run toward the mouth of the tunnel, diving into it. The opening closed behind her with a swishing sound, leaving air.

Louis clicked his tongue. "Why does she always have to be contrary?"

"Because she was a brat when she died and she never grew out of it." Sometimes I couldn't believe that she was only four years younger than I was in human time. I wasn't exactly a paragon of maturity myself, but Twyla was something else.

I rose toward Wendy's window, leaving Louis and Scott below.

Scott called, "She's not going to give you the time of day."

Not even after she'd sent Heidi our way?

I wanted to find out for myself, but I wouldn't bother Wendy if she wasn't ready to face me. Facing me meant she was prepared to deal with the bloodcurdling anguish of the night her sister had gone off the deep end, and that wasn't something that could be forced.

As I peered inside the condo, I was glad to see Wendy had left the curtains all the way open, even though the window itself was shut. Most days and nights, she blocked out us ghosts altogether. She'd never chased us off, though, so that told me she was just as wary of that dark spirit that'd come through her old mansion's portal as I was.

Melancholy music seeped through the window-panes as I saw Wendy lying on her canopied bed, star-ing at the ceiling, her hands clasped over her chest. Her long black hair still had that artistic pink streak run-ning down one side, and she was wearing a long black shirt as a minidress with black-and-white-striped knee socks. She didn't look a thing like Gavin, because she'd been adopted from China years ago.

I tried not to think about where he was in the condo as I gazed at frail Wendy, unable to feel the window-pane as I rested my hand there.

I thought I saw her head turn slightly before she closed her eyes, totally shutting me out.

Ghosts aren't supposed to have hearts, so maybe what I felt was a phantom pain in my chest at being rejected. Didn't she understand that I'd only been try-ing to bring a killer to justice? It'd turned out to be her adopted sister, yeah, but come on—I wasn't the one who'd chosen who Elizabeth Dalton's murderer would be.

Behind me, I heard a travel tunnel pop open, then close. Probably Scott going to Amanda Lee. The clock tower chimes from a nearby shopping center rang out twelve o'clock. Still, I remained at that window.

Wendy must've fallen asleep during that time. I suspected that she was in a battle of wills with me, refusing to look at me or move from the bed, forcing herself to succumb to a nap instead. Stubborn girl.

But I could be just as bullheaded, and if it wasn't for my promise to be at Tim Knudson's house by three to meet Amanda Lee, I would've stayed all damned day.

My persistence did pay off slightly, though, because just as I was getting terribly restless, Wendy's bedroom door eased open.

If I had breath to hold, it'd have been held right then and there as Gavin walked into the room. He wasn't sensitive like Wendy, so he wouldn't be able to see me watching him, my hand against the glass again, as if that was the closest I'd ever get to him.

He was the type of handsome that had a million rough edges to it, with pale blue eyes that looked like they had a tough story for every splinter in his irises. His hair was light brown, cut close to his scalp, because he had other things to worry about than his appearance. His shoulders were broad, a little hunched these days, like a boxer in a ring who didn't have a way out. But his lips . . . They were the softest part of him, shaped like a bow. I'd seen them up close when I'd haunted him.

There was something about Gavin Edgett, a life force that made me quiver. A quality that no other human seemed to have but him.

I didn't realize that Louis was still here until he breezed up to my side. His body buzzed as he watched, too.

"Good thing they still have each other," he said.

"At least there's that, right?"

"You did your best for them both." Louis put a hand on my shoulder, but it passed through with a cold *fzzzt*. "And you'll do your best when you help Heidi with her problem."

"I'm just happy there's not a murder to solve this time."

"Not yet, anyway, according to her."

I smiled slightly at Louis, then, compelled, turned back to look at Gavin.

Soon, he left the room, and shortly after, I heard the electronic drag of a garage door opening below, at the front of the condo.

I started to fly away, but Louis stopped me.

"Where're you off to, Miss . . . Jensen?"

I hated when he tried to address me with the *Miss.* I knew things had been different for black people back in the forties when he'd been alive, but I'd grown up long after that, and it seemed all kinds of wrong, especially since Louis had been educated. The whole *Miss* thing was demeaning for him.

"I thought I'd . . ."

"Tell me you won't be following Gavin around."

What to say? That's exactly what I'd been aching to

do. And I'd gone through with the temptation during this past month a few times, even though Gavin had rarely left the condo for anything but grocery shopping and necessities.

"He's on his way to recovery now," Louis said. "And as soon as we can take care of that dark spirit, we're going to leave these people alone."

"That time hasn't come yet. What if the spirit—?"

"Goes after Gavin when he's outside? I know that Mr. Edgett carries a crucifix and holy water on him, thanks to that cleaner who chased some of the bad energy out of their old mansion. He's a believer now."

Louis' voice had gone soft when he mentioned the haunted house cleaner, a pretty woman who'd caught his eye. Not exactly a romance meant to happen, though.

"Then why're we watching over Wendy, if the Edgetts are armed?" I asked.

But I knew the answer. It was because a few of us felt protective of the young girl who'd been caught in the middle of everything.

The sound of a sports car taking off made me shiver, but I let Gavin go.

Yet, after Louis and I lingered around Wendy's window a bit longer and it was time for me to leave for Tim Knudson's house, I did give in to one last temptation.

I whooshed by Gavin's bedroom window at the front, where the curtains were open, letting in the sun. I looked at his walls: the sketches of angelic me, my arms spread, my hair waving around me as if I was suspended in watery air.

But the newest pictures were in stark contrast to the others. It was the same me, except for the wicked expression I was wearing—devious, nasty, fire-eyed . . . The hellbitch Twyla had mentioned.

I backed away from his window and conjured a travel tunnel before I could start believing I was that ghost.

3

When I busted out of my travel tunnel and onto a Pacific Beach street full of exhausted pastel-painted houses, Amanda Lee's Bentley was nowhere in sight. But that didn't mean she wouldn't arrive soon.

So I brushed along the tops of the palm trees in a neighborhood a few miles from the college bars and the shoreline itself, then lower, looking for the exact address of the house Tim Knudson shared with Nichelle Shaw.

The first hint I had about their lifestyle was that they probably rented their place—I'd noticed on one of Amanda Lee's computer pages that these modest houses near the beach cost a breathtaking amount of money, and unless Nichelle was naturally well-off or Tim was king of all warehouses, I doubted they owned their digs.

The faint scent of brine from the ocean, which I could see in the near distance, was making the air thicker to travel, but I trouped through the atmosphere, finding the address. And what do you know? The first thing I came upon was Mr. Timothy Knudson in his backyard.

He was dressed in long Hawaiian shorts and a sleeveless T-shirt that advertised a bar called Moose McGillycuddy's on the back. Popping what looked to be a breath mint into his mouth, he shoved the roll into his pocket, casually strolling by a peeling white fence and peering between the slats.

As I hovered, I didn't fail to note the brunette on the other side, sunning herself on a lounger, dressed in a bikini. I think most people would call a woman like her a *cougar* these days—clearly older, but very well maintained, and impressively in shape.

So Tim enjoyed spying on the hard-body neighbor. But guys were guys and they had testosterone, so what were you going to do about nature's call?

When I eased down to about five feet away from him, goose bumps rose on his skin. But just as I was going to reach out and touch him for a thought-reading, a female voice sang out from the screen door.

"Hey, baby? What're you doing back there?"

Tim jerked away from the fence—and my invisible hand. He rubbed at his sheared hair and started toward the covered patio, which was strewn with unraveling outdoor furniture and a barbecue.

"Just taking in the sun, Nich," he answered. "It's a beautiful day."

He had a good-natured tone and was as compact as his computer profile had indicated he'd be. Small but fit. But you could tell by the cock-of-the-walk way he moved that he might be compensating for stature.

A dark-haired girl, Heidi's age, with a deep beach-comber's tan had opened the screen door and was facing Tim as he walked toward her. She wore a purple cover-up dress with her bathing suit straps visible, and the skinny thing looked like she'd never hit a 7-Eleven—she sure could've used a burrito or two. She had a face that was pleasant but at the same time a little stern, with a square chin that gave her a harder edge than you'd first expect.

I joined them on the patio, careful to keep my presence on the hush. The trick here was to be very subtle about reading their thoughts, because I didn't exactly want *haunting* to be advertised to them. If a haunted human got spooked, there was always the chance he might call in cleaners or even a bad entity like a demon for help, depending on how savvy or scared they were.

True, no ghost I knew had ever *seen* a demon since those things generally didn't interact much with us. They preferred to slink around humans they could possess, both willingly and unwillingly. Still, careful was the word.

Nichelle had wandered onto the patio, closer to the fence. "Were you frolicking in the sun?"

It looked like Tim wasn't comfortable with where she was heading. "Baby . . ."

She sent a betrayed look over her shoulder at him while she moved to the fence to take a gander. After she peeked at the cougar, she shook her head, then headed back to the house, sliding the door behind her, leaving Tim outside.

I seized my opportunity, slipping over Tim's head before the screen could close all the way. I could've just made my essence skinnier, but it'd take a hellishly long time for me to dribble through one of the tiny openings. And as far as making myself into Jen-suey by trying to move through the screen all at one time?

Ugh, and no, thank you.

"Nich, come on," Tim said from the patio as she headed for the kitchen, with its yellow tiles and a lineup of dried herbs sticking out of jars. I was right on her tail.

Nichelle opened the fridge door, her teeth grinding. I think her pride was wounded but she wasn't about to let him see it.

I took advantage of the refrigerator's chill, touching her upper arm, hopefully going unnoticed, finding a way inside her to get an empathy reading.

With an electric shock, I was in, experiencing her thoughts as they came.

Watching Tim holding a hose in front of the house and watering the lawn, checking out the brown-haired mom two doors down as she washed the car with her kids, laughing, spraying one another until T-shirts stuck to skin . . .

A jump to another image.

Watching Tim lounging in a beach chair at a coastal party, sunglasses dipping down his nose. Brown-haired college girls in the water, dodging the waves, bathing suits small, breasts bouncing.

Perv. Anger hot and red. And he tells me he has eyes only for me. . . .

Another image.

In bed, him facing away. Reaching out to touch his back. "Tim, maybe later we can try again . . . ?" Him shrugging off the sheet, pushing out of bed, leaving—

On a sharp gust, I burst out of Nichelle, heaved across the kitchen, a little weaker than before I started.

I righted myself in time to see her blowing out a breath while shutting the fridge door. Shivering, she put a plastic bottle of diet soda on the counter, her skin still bumped with the chills that she would no doubt think she got from the refrigerator.

By this time, Tim had entered the house, the screen door chopping shut just before he took a stand in the kitchen.

Nichelle gave him a stern why-were-you-ogling-the-neighbor look while fetching a single glass out of the cupboard, then pouring a soda only for herself, clearly making it a point to show Tim that she wasn't about to do the same for him. She maintained steady eye contact and gulped down the drink.

It took a heck of a long, awkward time for her to do that while he just stared at her, like he was daring her to call him on peeping. So I quickly glanced around their place for more details about them: a small house with outdated shag carpeting. Faux leather furniture, the sofa expectorating some stuffing from one arm. A

TV like I used to have back in my day. Truthfully, the most interesting things about their house were:

1) A huge fish tank in back of the sofa, boasting a massive castle as the bubbling centerpiece, and
2) Shelves full of fairy-tale memorabilia. Princess figurines, golden plates, what looked like *Alice in Wonderland* chopsticks, and even cast-iron statuettes of Snow White and her dwarves.

I'd have to stay away from those since touching iron was like poison for a ghost.

A stray thought barged into my mind. You know, I could actually get into someplace like Disneyland for free now. Who'd ever know? And how awesome would it be to relive the good days on stuff like Adventure Thru Inner Space? Ah, days of making out with Dean on that one . . .

Whoa. A little Ghost ADD there?

When Nichelle set her glass on the counter, I came back to attention.

Tim crossed his arms over his chest, still waiting for her to say something.

"I know Mrs. Cavendish is pretty," Nichelle finally said in a firm voice. "But maybe you could refrain from salivating over her in my presence?"

"This again."

"What again?"

"Your jealousy."

"*My* jealousy? My friends," she said, "tell me, 'Nich, he's so possessive and somehow you take it.' 'Nich, he hasn't kept a steady girlfriend in his life. What makes you think you're gonna change him?' It's times like this that I wonder why I'm not listening to them."

Tim looked very collected on the outside, wearing a shit-eating smile that he was probably betting would drive her nuts. But what about inside?

Instead of hearing this argument play out, I knew it was a perfect time to read him while his temper was up.

So I slid in back of him, an inch away from his body, mocking his form with my own essence.

Then I lightly touched his exposed skin and . . .

An older woman's voice. "You're never going to amount to anything, Timothy. You're as useless as your father was, wherever he is."

Nichelle's voice bleeding into the first. "I wonder why I'm not listening to them?"

An image overcoming the thoughts: Nichelle right in front of him, her lips parted as he tore off her shirt. Her gasping as he did the same to her bra. Mouths pressing together, heat, lust . . .

Another image, grinding over the last, different, yet still angry.

Sitting at a bar, watching football with blue and gold Chargers jerseys all around. A man in a Raiders shirt cheering for the other team in the corner. Boos drowning him out.

Anger, churning.

More taunting from the Raider in the corner. Friends on stools close by. "Just ignore him, Tim."

Can't. Won't.

Stepping across the room and, in a flash of fury, fist lashing out, connecting with his nose.

Satisfaction, laughter.

Blood on knuckles . . .

Another scene, like a color slide jamming away the other image.

A warehouse, gray and concrete, boxes, forklifts. Scruffy men eating from brown bags.

"What're you having today, Timbo?" A burly man devouring a burger. "Can't imagine you'd need to eat much of anything to keep that little body in motion." Laughter.

Anger, building . . .

I withdrew from Tim all on my own. Usually the shock of having me inside made a person's body and psyche automatically *want* to get rid of me. But, with Tim, it was almost like I fit. Like I'd quickly become part of the thoughts that'd been flitting through his mind while playing a game of word association, one scene building off the next.

Even odder about Tim? Inside, he almost felt formless, flailing, one emotional image sparring with another, like his spat with Nichelle had forced his thoughts into an angry dog pile.

There hadn't been any indication that he was going

to hurt Nichelle in particular, though. And if I hadn't gotten that vibe from him during a romantic dustup, when would it ever happen?

I needed to go deeper with Tim if I wanted better answers.

As I adjusted to my waning strength, craving an electric charge-up, I saw that Nichelle had walked out of the kitchen with a new soda. From the sound of the back screen door opening and closing, I took an educated guess that she'd gone outside to soak up the sun, just like the cougar next door.

That left me alone with Tim.

He planted his hands on the edge of the tiled counter, pushing back from it, like he was gathering himself. His breath was deep and even, controlled, but the veins in his neck were standing out.

Heidi had been right about his temper.

He stood up, then went to a bedroom like he'd already left the conflict with Nichelle behind. He didn't shut the door as he stripped off his clothes, and I took that moment to float up to a corner and survey my surroundings, which definitely had a womanly touch with its striped wallpaper, ferns, and the lingering scent of honey-laced soap coming from the adjoining bathroom. When I focused on him again, he'd put on a warehouse uniform.

He grabbed a set of keys from the top of an old wicker dresser, not bothering to say good-bye to Nichelle as I followed him outside. There, he climbed onto his seen-better-days motorcycle, pushed on his helmet, then revved up and took off.

I let him go when I saw Amanda Lee's Bentley across the street a few doors down. On the trunk of the sleek car, Scott sat, his hand resting on the contours just like he was feeling up a girl. When he saw me, he snatched his hand away, crossing his arms over his flannel shirt, jerking his chin at me in a hello.

I waved at the greaser, letting him know that I was going to take over Amanda Lee duty, and he pointed at me, grinning, then summoned a travel tunnel and dove into it.

After it swirl-popped back into itself, I went to Amanda Lee, who'd probably sensed Scott but hadn't seen him. But she knew that my friends were usually around her whenever I wasn't.

She rolled down a window, and I slipped inside, taking a seat as she closed the car back up so she could wallow in the low air-conditioning. She'd had the presence of mind to bring another battery pack on the floor, and I clung to it, sighing with pleasure. I'd learned from the Edgett haunting experience to charge up frequently, because I didn't ever want to go back into a time loop after overextending myself.

"You're done for the day?" she asked.

"No. I'll be coming back here after Tim's swing shift, when he's asleep. I got enough out of him to know that it'll be worth the effort."

Tim's dream was bound to give me more information to go on since I could go to a deeper level of consciousness that way. I might be able to see what he was keeping bottled up inside on a more profound level.

"I'm going to meditate on him when I get home,"

Amanda Lee said, pointing to a beer bottle in a drink holder. "This was in the front yard, and I was getting some readings, but they were fuzzy, so I brought it with me to spend more time with it."

"Did you get readings from anything else, like his bike?"

"Not a lot." She started to drive, making it obvious that she'd done all she intended to do at the house for the time being.

"Wait. No neighbors saw you in the driveway or told you to beat it?"

"I merely acted as if I had every right to be there. That's the secret to belonging." She grinned, probably because even she had to realize that hearing Amanda Lee Minter talk about belonging was majorly ironic. She'd confessed before that she'd never had a lot of friends. "None of the neighbors were in their front yards, so I had time to do more than just consult the bike. I was able to get a reading from a towel near the stoop. It belonged to Nichelle, so I received feedback only from her."

"When I empathized with her, I saw that Tim's not the ideal boyfriend, but that only means she should break up with him, not get him put in jail." Content for now, I moved away from the battery pack and hovered above the seat. We'd already gotten on the 5 freeway, where the ocean shimmered alongside us. In the lane next to us, I checked out a guy in a red convertible. Blond, with a surfboard in back. Just my type, if he wasn't so alive.

"What did you get from that towel?" I asked.

"Let's just say I was hearing lyrics from 'Afternoon Delight.'"

At first, I didn't realize that Amanda Lee was being clever. I was literally thinking back to when I used to hear the song on the radio: lyrics about rubbing sticks and stones together, making sparks ignite, then the thought of rubbing someone else getting the singer real excited . . .

"Oh," I said. "I see. So Nichelle was with Tim on that towel?"

Amanda Lee was lifting her eyebrows in a ladylike way. "Yes, with Tim. Up close and personal."

"I had one of those readings, too, except it was from Tim's point of view. Wow, those two are horny." I thought of what Twyla had mentioned about rough sex and arguments as foreplay. Our couple of the moment could very well have *that* process down pat.

What could I say about it, though? I guess some people are like that. Jealousy could even be a sick way of getting turned on.

Were both Nichelle and Tim codependent messes?

"At least she was Afternoon Delighting on the towel with Tim," I said. "I didn't see anything that would indicate she's unfaithful to him. I also didn't get anything telling me that he's stepping out on her. He looks at other women, that's for sure, but I'm not certain he ever acts on his hormones."

I went on to describe my brief tour de la casa for Amanda Lee: the fairy-tale collection, the fish tank, the very ordinariness of everything. "When I go back tonight, I'll take a better look, but dream-digging is my first priority."

Empathy readings could get you only so far because

they were so shallow. I knew that without a doubt, because when I'd gone into Gavin Edgett's dreams, there'd been a crazy world of subconscious clues that Amanda Lee had interpreted and we'd both pieced together, using them to eventually solve Elizabeth's murder. But I needed a suspect to be asleep for that.

At the thought of Gavin again, I started buzzing inside, remembering how I'd finally gotten to speak to him, dream-person to dream-person. It was the closest I would ever get to spending much quality time with him, because materializing only lasted so long and sucked my energy like you wouldn't believe.

Amanda Lee switched lanes as we took a mild curve in the freeway. "What else did you get from Tim? Anything?"

"Just some stuff that we already knew, like he's got a temper that gets him into some scraps. There could be some mommy conflicts, too. She used to tell him he wouldn't amount to anything." I paused. "Tim also hates being teased. There was an incident with a coworker who said something about how short he is, and I could sense rage building up because of it. And there was one scene I saw . . ." I trailed off.

"What?"

It seemed way too private even to share with my partner in crime. Or whatever Amanda Lee was.

But holding back information wasn't an option when you were trying to get someone out of danger. "He was in bed with Nichelle, and I think he might've had an ET Phone Home moment."

"I have no idea what you mean."

Hmm. How to put this delicately. "You know. Shriveled little entity losing its path? Trying to find its way . . . home?"

"Are you saying you saw Tim going flaccid while he was trying to enter Nichelle?"

Wow, that was blunt. "Um, yeah. That was my take on it. And he wasn't happy about losing that momentum, as you can imagine."

"My imagination doesn't quite run that way."

That's right—Amanda Lee didn't care to picture penises.

"I wonder," she said, "if we can also put sexual insecurity on our list of Tim's traits?"

"Sounds possible."

She was silent for a time, the car's tires whirring over pavement, the sun shining through the windshield. I wished I could still feel it on my former skin. I'd even be fine with getting a sunburn if I could still have the rays warming me up again.

But why wish for things you couldn't have? Sunlight and sand on a beach. The taste of pineapple pizza. Gavin Edgett . . .

"I think," Amanda Lee said, interrupting my thoughts, "that we could possibly have an inadequate personality on our hands."

"What's that?"

"We can go online for a precise definition, but, from all the research I did during my time looking into your killing, I know that it's a social disorder."

"I never came across that when I was researching Elizabeth's murder. I'll look it up." I ran my hand just over the leather of the seat, wishing I could feel that, too. "I think, after we hit the computer, it'd be a good idea for me to go up to my death spot to stock up on some real energy for tonight, for when I go digging." I knew that going so deep inside a person's psyche would take a lot out of me.

"Would you like me to come with you to Elfin Forest?" she asked.

Did Amanda Lee sound hopeful that I'd want her company?

"It's okay," I said. "I've got it covered."

A few moments passed by, and when she spoke again, her voice was soft. "How was Wendy when you visited earlier?"

Ah, Wendy of the I-do-not-wish-to-see-you attitude. "She's as stuck in her ways as always. You were right about her not talking to me."

"It could take some time. But I'm starting to have a positive feeling about that and more, Jensen." She smiled, and I was so unused to the gesture that it took me a second to register it.

I wasn't sure if she had more than just a hunch about her positive feelings, but she kept smiling as we drove back to her place, where ghosts were waiting for us on her driveway.

And everywhere else, really.

4

Petty Officer Randy Randall, one of the first ghosts I'd ever met, was sailing around the rest of Amanda Lee's property, shaming a few lookiloos into leaving us alone, making them fly away.

He was just getting them cleared, too, except for a couple of modern male spirits hanging over the driveway.

"Mind yer own businesses!" Randy yelled, veering toward the gray-tinged guys, who were dressed in workout gear like they'd been at the gym lifting weights when they'd died.

"You're just a drunk," one shouted.

Randy nudged his sailor hat back on his head. " 'N' whass yer excuse for bein' a fathead?"

Amanda Lee had rolled down the window upon arrival, so I'd already meandered over, spreading my arms to the gym rats. "Hey, guys."

"Hey," they said, realizing I was the notorious, ballsy, rampaging ghost they'd come to see. Their wide gazes told me so.

I supposed I should exchange death stories with them since that's what ghosts do when they meet someone—like exchanging business cards—but I didn't want them hanging around.

"Getting an eyeful?" I asked.

When they nodded, I leaned forward and whispered, "Great. Because a cleaner is on the way over, and she's real excited about making some ghost foo."

New ghosts—and slow-witted older ones—didn't come with a user manual or anything, so my BS was enough to frighten them off. For all they knew, the human coming up the driveway behind me was the cleaner.

I waved good-bye at the overly muscled Samsons who were probably 'roided out for the rest of eternity . . . or until they decided to go into the *glare* to the real afterlife. Whatever that was.

When they'd disappeared into their travel tunnels, I turned to Randy, smiling. "Looks like you got rid of the ones who were here earlier. There were a bunch of them."

"They musta got bored after Amanda Lee left." He hiccupped. "I only kicked out the few who stayed."

"Surely there's better entertainment in San Diego. Bathing suits at the beach, Sea World . . ."

Randy's grin was large and sloshed. He was a contemporary of Louis', both guys from the 1940s, but young Randy had been passing through San Diego when he'd gotten wasted. In a love-struck mood, he'd wandered over to a bank of rocks in the harbor, mooning over a love letter from his dear girlfriend, Magnolia. He'd lost that letter in the rocks, and while he'd been looking for it, he'd slipped, hit his head, and bled out, leaving another good-looking corpse.

Okay, maybe *good-looking* was optimistic. Even with his electric gray hue, I could see that his hair was light and wavy under his cap, but he also had endearingly crooked teeth and a nose just short of pug. And speaking of short, he was that, too.

He was watching Amanda Lee walk to my casita, her dark skirt flapping in a breeze.

"So she's outta the house now," Randy said. "Scott already told me what precip-dated . . . pre-cip-i . . ."

"Precipitated?"

"Yeah. Scott told me what precipidated yer travel 'fore he left here with Amanda Lee."

Obviously Randy had just dropped by to veg out with us. "A girl might think that you were waiting for us to get back because you're as curious about our doings as those lookiloo ghosts. Scott told you about Tim?"

Before Randy could nod, I made to punch him in the shoulder. He flinched, even though he wouldn't have felt it.

"Lookiloo," I said, waving him toward the casita. "Come on in."

He didn't need to be asked twice, and by the time we got inside my digs, Amanda Lee already had the computer up and running on a page of links.

"Randy's here," I said.

"I thought I sensed him. Hello, Randy."

He gave Amanda Lee a jaunty salute, even though

he had to know she couldn't see it. Then he went to the car battery on a table and draped himself over it. A dopey smile lit his face as he sighed.

I loitered next to a window while Amanda Lee consulted the computer.

"According to *The American Heritage Medical Dictionary*," she said, "an inadequate personality is 'characterized by an inability to cope with the social, emotional, occupational, and intellectual demands of life.'"

I think I knew more than one of these types wandering around the earthly plane. I suspected that Twyla might have even been a good fit if I ever had the chance to do an emotional biopsy on her. Come to think of it, could ghosts empathize with other ghosts or go dreamdigging? I wasn't sure.

Amanda Lee used the mouse to surf to another page. "Heidi was on the right track when she said that Tim fits antisocial markers. We hit a few of them today: Inadequate personalities may not be able to hold down a regular job; they have conflicts with parents, friends, and girlfriends. And, sure enough, there might be insecurity about their sexuality."

On the other side of the room, Randy made a wellhow-about-that face. It was like it wasn't fathomable to him that someone might be insecure in that area.

"This is interesting," Amanda Lee said. "It says that he might need to have the approval of the women in his life, but at the same time, he wants to be in control. A person like this can also alter his personality so it gets him what he needs. He can be grandiose in his feelings, and fights with a girlfriend might make him doubt his manhood at times."

"Maybe we shouldn't go overboard here. We might want to step back and ask ourselves if we're fitting Tim into a mold that Heidi wants him to fit."

"We'll know after you've gotten a feel for his subconscious. It *would* be good if you knew what to look for, though."

True. Tonight, I would keep my eye out for things I hadn't quite seen to my satisfaction already, like grandiose feelings and getting approval from Nichelle.

Randy spoke up. "I don't know much about nothin', but a fellow like this . . . He don't seem like a big bad man. Just . . . confused."

Taken aback by his interest in something other than raiding bars, I told Amanda Lee what he'd said.

She tilted her head and leaned away from the screen, nodding toward Randy. She might've been hearing him but couldn't decipher the sounds he was making. Sometimes I felt like that with him, too, though.

"Not that I'm an expert," she said after I'd finished, "but Randy's right. I know there are different types of deviant behaviors, and what it sometimes boils down to is whether the person has a conscience or not. Some bad people are remorseless. I'm not certain that's who we're dealing with in Tim—if he even has the makeup of a man who'd hurt his girlfriend."

I'd done a bit of criminal research, too, while looking into Gavin, and I'd read about serial offenders, just as Amanda Lee had: There were a certain kind who would never stop committing crimes until *they* were stopped. Those were the ones without a conscience, like the Night Stalker in the 1970s. But deviants who did have a conscience could be driven by very human emotions like greed, jealousy, revenge, profit, anger . . . Their crimes usually stopped when a particular emotional problem was taken care of.

But we were getting ahead of ourselves, jumping to conclusions like we'd done with Gavin. Tim hadn't committed any crimes to judge by.

Randy was scratching his head under his cap. "Back when I was an alive person, I knew a fellow in high school, 'fore I went off to the navy. He didn't care 'bout nothin'. Did what he wanted to, no matter who it hurt. Grabbed girls 'n' kissed 'em on the street, even if they smacked 'im for it. He got into some trouble, put into the slammer once 'cos he knifed a man durin' a fight in back of a moviehouse in Atlanta jus' for fun. I was there. He didn't regret it one bit. Had a smile on his face the whole time. . . ."

I relayed the story to Amanda Lee, then asked, "What happened to him?"

"I heard he got stabbed in the gut one night." Randy shook his head. "But this boy . . . You'da never known the trouble he could get into jus' from talkin' with 'im for an hour. Charmin' as the devil. Picked the right friends who'd get into mischief with 'im. Good at lyin' and tellin' people what they wanted to hear. A bad person on the inside but a winner on the out."

"Tim definitely doesn't seem like that type," I said

after telling Amanda Lee. "He doesn't come off as a winner at all."

Randy lifted a brow, then slurred, "Oh, this boy was real good at that, too. Knew how to win the pity from those who counted. He got away with a whole lot 'cos of pity."

I chewed on that until Amanda Lee gave me an impatient glance and I again filled her in on what Randy had just told me.

Then she said, "There's something other than computer surfing that might help us in this. We still have hours before Tim's shift is over and he's asleep. I know a man who could offer insight into antisocial behavior . . ." Her face went stony.

Right away, I realized this had to do with Elizabeth, but I didn't prompt Amanda Lee to go on. Even Randy knew enough to stay quiet until she was ready.

She swallowed hard, then said, "He investigated Elizabeth's case for me. And yours, Jensen, but I've told you that he worked for her fictional fiancé so you wouldn't ever connect him with me if you bothered to research it."

I could feel a surge of surprised energy from Randy, but my own head was humming. Loud.

Amanda Lee got up from her chair before I could start in on her for keeping this information from me, even after I thought she'd come totally clean about all the lies she'd told me. What the hell? Hadn't she learned a thing?

"I haven't talked to Ruben in a while," she said, lifting her hands to me in a plea. "I hired him to research your case, and the others before you who I couldn't make contact with."

I'd found out that she'd tried to raise other ghosts from their death spots before me to help her with Elizabeth, but I hadn't known that this PI really existed.

"You didn't tell me about him before because you wanted me to concentrate only on Elizabeth and not on my death?" I asked. Manipulated. Controlled by the great Amanda Lee, once again.

I had the overwhelming urge to fly at her, to get into her head once and for all so I could discover everything she'd ever hidden from me, but Amanda Lee . . . she could block like a pro.

"You think now's a good time to tell me about him?" I asked tightly. "Or wait. Maybe over a month ago would've been perfect."

"Yes," she said quietly. "It would've been a perfect time in a less complicated world."

Randy had started to tiptoe toward the door, where he'd be able to slowly seep through a crack.

Amanda Lee said, "I've done psychic readings on this PI without his knowledge, and he's never held back information from me, so I didn't think he'd be—"

"Worthwhile for me to contact. Why didn't you leave that up to me?"

"I wasn't thinking straight. Not after the Edgetts. And you already know why I didn't say anything about him while we were investigating Elizabeth."

Because she'd wanted me all to herself.

I had to get out of here, just like in the past, whenever I'd stumbled over one of her lies. But, dammit, this wasn't actually a lie, just an omission, something fairly innocent, at that. Still. Amanda Lee could've been more of a help to me in finding out how I'd died, and that truth stung.

"I'm going to contact Ruben Diaz today," she said, looking at me as if asking me not to leave yet. "We can pick his brain about criminal pathology. I'm sure he'll help us. He's a kind soul who feels terrible that he never did right by you."

It felt as if my so-called nerve endings were on fire. Talk about a temper—I'm not sure Tim Knudson had anything on me at this point, because my anger was flaring, threatening.

Even though I wasn't human, I still felt like one.

Did we all have the ability to cover up violent thoughts like the ones I was having?

But did having them necessarily mean we'd act on them?

Amanda Lee was writing down an address on a pad of paper by the computer. She straightened her spine, then slid the pad in my direction before walking to the door.

"I didn't keep this information from you on purpose," she said. "If Ruben is open to meeting me in an hour or two, after you recharge at your death spot, this is where I'll be with him."

She went to the door, opened it, then left me with a sorry expression on her face that made me wonder if she felt just as prejudged as Tim.

*   *   *

It was a quick, outrage-fueled trip in my travel tunnel to Elfin Forest, with its gnarled roads and dense trees that clawed out the full sight of the sun.

There were probably as many legends about this place as there were leaves on the oaks—everything from rumors about a White Lady who wandered around, to a band of late-nineteenth-century gypsies who settled in the dark alcoves and got slaughtered because they refused to abandon their homes. It was said that the deaths cursed the area, bringing a ton of paranormal activity.

I hadn't run into any of these spirits yet in the forest, and you can bet I wasn't about to with the way I was canvassing the area now. I'd never seen much of anything here except for the occasional hiker and burned-out remains from fires. Thank God, too, because there was one scary legend that'd always given me the heebie-jeebies, even back when I'd been a premurdered carefree human drinking beer and laughing with my friends in the woods, daring all its urban legends to come and get us.

Even now I was cautious about the witch who was said to haunt the forest. And this was even before that *Blair Witch Project* movie, which I'd seen recently during all the idle time I'd had after the Edgett case. This particular witch was supposed to ride around on a spectral black stallion, cloaked in face and body-shrouding darkness, like one of those Nazgûl characters in *Lord of the Rings*, right? But this witch could intuit whenever someone entered the woods, and she would mark them with a curse that would be activated if you were dumb enough to ever come back. Oh—and you wouldn't ever know that you were marked. Brilliant story to keep the trespassers away if you lived here, huh?

There was also supposed to be an old, burned insane asylum, a religious cult, and ghostly bodies hanging from trees, so you see why this place would be catnip to legend-tripping youngsters. Even forest fires hadn't burned them out.

I flew over charred trees to a part of the woods that hadn't ever been marked by fire damage. I came to the site of my death, drawn to a nearby oak tree and its extended, low branch that rode the ground, curved like a *U*. I got a charge out of just being so close. Some ghosts loved to chill out at the sites of their demises, but not me, uh-uh.

Might as well get this over with.

I stopped at the exact spot where I'd taken my last breath, then laid myself over the dirt at the base of a tree. A sense of mind-scrambling comfort mixed with discomfort swallowed me. It was like the area was embracing me while pushing me away at the same time. But the death energy I was getting . . .

God. It was like nothing else. Bad for me and good for me. Dark and light. Dangerous and safe, just like this was the one place I really did belong.

I absorbed as much as I could before the visions started coming.

Panting, sprinting away from the running footsteps right behind, dogging me, closer, closer, chest hurting, icy, can't breathe—

Just breathe!

Sliding to the bottom of the oak, hiding. Breathing. Trying not to breathe.

It'll hear me if I do.
But what is it?

*No sound. No nothing, except for the hoot of an owl.
A snapping branch.
Then . . .
Mask. Old wrinkled lady, terrifying, a mouth opened like it was laughing. And it was. Laughing.
And it had an ax . . .*

"Stop! Please! Why're you doing this?"

My voice rang out as I pulled back from my death spot. I'd just said my final words out loud, sending a flutter of birds away from the branches above me.

Rising off the dreadful spot, my form sang with energy, stronger than before and, in a way, weaker. So much emotionally weaker because of the repressed memories that wouldn't quite come.

A voice behind me made me startle.

"Ghosts. I don't know if I should be entertained by your predictability or be sad."

My body felt . . . solid. Like it was a real-deal body, with true arms and legs and everything else. And there was only one entity in Boo World who had some kind of weird magic that made that happen whenever he was around.

I tried to keep my words from shaking. "Haven't seen you around lately. I was hoping you'd lost interest in me."

"You've just recently become intriguing again."

Fake Dean was leaning against a tree like a bad boy in school who leaned against a set of lockers, brazenly checking you out as you told yourself not to look. And then you looked.

Whatever this entity was, it wasn't the real Dean. My actual old boyfriend was in his early fifties now, his hairline receding, the father of two kids in suburbia. I knew because I'd watched him soon after being released from my time loop. This Dean, though?

He was like a bright dream with sunny hair that came to a straight edge at his whiskered chin. Tan, surfer-lean, muscled in all the right places. His whiskey-brown eyes and crooked smile both made me feel drunk, and I hated him for that, even though I shouldn't. Not when he'd saved my bacon a month ago, at the end of the Edgett disaster when I'd possessed a willing Gavin's body so that we could prevent Farah from committing suicide. We'd been too late, but the brief possession had fully drained me, dragging me back toward another numb time-loop limbo.

That's when I'd felt something pulling me up and up, and I hadn't known that I'd been taken to fake Dean's star place until I awakened, reenergized by his touch. When I'd seen that the celestial bodies around me were actual glowing *bodies* and not stars at all, I'd realized something about fake Dean.

He was no ghost. At first, I'd thought he was a

reaper, come to take me to the glare. And, indeed, there'd been a powerful light-infused lotus pool in the star place.

But I'd found out from my ghost friends that they'd never met a reaper, or wrangler, like fake Dean.

I did discover something concrete about him, though—he was a "keeper," a collector, and he had a thing for new ghosts who were too naive to avoid him. New ghosts, in particular, who were active and amusing, just like me—Jensen Murphy, solver of a murder. My justice-driven pursuits had entertained him and energized him, so he'd wanted to keep me, thinking I'd be the biggest barrel of laughs ever or something.

I know. Insane. I still hadn't figured him out all the way. I mean, the guy could transform into other bodies, seducing me by using whatever shape he needed, but I think he'd shown me his true face for a millisecond when he'd gotten really pissed at my backtalk.

A wispy beast, roaring.

Not. A. Ghost.

"Let me guess," I said. "I reintrigued you today, when Heidi Schmidt came to me and Amanda Lee for help."

"Bingo."

"So you've still been keeping an eye on me, even after I told you to go lay an egg the last time."

"Just because you say you'll never come to me willingly doesn't mean I've given up. Because I don't give up, Jenny."

For about the hundredth time, I tried to calm myself

when he used the nickname my Dean had called me. There was something about the way he said it, smooth yet gruff, a rasp of need just under the surface.

He noticed my agitation. "Seems there's good reason for me not to give up."

"Eat my shorts." Ugh. That was so Valley, more Twyla than me.

"Is that an invitation?" He eased away from the tree, beginning to walk away in those blue jeans and a T-shirt that only added to his coolness. "Come with."

I barked out a laugh. "Seriously?"

"I'm not going to pull a trick on you."

"Hmm, let me turn this over in my mind. Let's see. Every time I find myself alone with you, I end up in your star place, whether I want to go or not." I weighed my options with my hands. "Believe the bogus jerk? Not believe the bogus jerk? What should it be?"

"What if I told you that I've found you a place all your own—and it's far enough away from Amanda Lee to make you happy? I know you've been thinking of getting one."

I just stared at him. Was he kidding?

"Remember, I've been watching," he said. "I saw the latest stunt she pulled." He crooked his finger at me. "Let's go. It's within walking distance."

"Just tell me where it is and I'll find it myself."

"Nope."

"I have the ability to discover abandoned properties all on my own, you know. It's called initiative."

"Maybe. But you'll never know why it's deserted.

Wouldn't you like to hear whether the owners will ever come back and kick you out? I can tell you anything you want about it."

I hated him. I loved him—or, at least, the part that I still saw as my Dean. The longer I talked to him, the easier it was to believe that he'd never driven away in his Camaro to Columbia University, leaving me behind.

As fake Dean moved through the forest, I followed at a distance, too intrigued to refuse, even if I should've.

5

From the outside, the house made me sigh.

A cottage twenty minutes and a world away from my death spot. It reclined on a small hill in a peaceful, swanky, more residential part of the Elfin Forest area, boasting a private driveway. Quaint primrose paths wound their lazy way toward a porch with an actual old-fashioned swing.

All fairy tales and *Leave It to Beaver* reruns, I thought as I listened to the faint murmur of a creek nearby. The rustle of leaves from the protective oaks that stood over the house only gave it more of a homey feel.

"Somebody has to live here," I said. "This can't be abandoned."

Fake Dean strode right up to the entrance, reached into the porch lantern, took out a key, then unlocked the door and walked inside, just as if he were totally normal.

Not a ghost, I reminded myself. He could unlock doors, touch things.

Then again, I could do the very same activities when I was in his presence, and he could actually touch *me*.

Truly touch—just like *I* was normal. Whoever or whatever he was, he didn't play fair.

But I wasn't about to run away from him like a little
girlie, so I went into the house, too. If this was the star
place he was luring me into, then I'd escape. It was just
such a pain to do that every time.

The minute I saw the inside, I cared a bit less about
being trapped. The cottage still had its furniture, although it was draped by white dustcovers with bows
at the back. Under those, I could see the shapes of sofas,
ottomans, overstuffed chairs, and a piano. To the right,
the open kitchen was one of those paradises that had
an island—be still my beating, wish-I-could-cook
heart!—and a loft rose above everything else in the
main room. There was even a fireplace with the and-
irons still standing.

"Who'd leave a house like this?" I asked.

"It's a vacation home for a snowbird widow from
Minnesota." Fake Dean rested against the back of a
sofa, hooking his thumbs in his belt loops as my Dean
used to. "She won't be back, not even as a ghost."

"How can you be so sure . . ." I stopped when I realized that this was an A1 mysterious entity I was talking
to, a powerful enigma that seemed to see all. A month
ago, this dipthwack could've saved me the trouble of
finding Elizabeth's murderer. He would've even been
able to tell me who had killed *me*. But, to this guy, that'd
be like ruining a sporting event. He took pleasure in
seeing me very active, playing what he considered a
game, just like I was his own investigative gladiator.

He was smiling lackadaisically at my question. "I

know what I know, Jenny. Suffice to say that the owner is going to get into a small plane accident during a trip she takes to wine country this spring instead of coming to this house like she usually does. She won't hang around Boo World long enough to return here, and the daughter who inherits the property will say that she intends to vacation in this darling abode, but she lives in Hawaii, so why would she bother?"

"Then I'm free to put down stakes here."

"Extremely free. There's a caretaker who comes around, but that's it."

A thought occurred to me. "The owner . . . Do you know so much about her because you're going to take her up to your star place, and she'll be hanging around there, like your other collectibles?"

"If that were the case, you know she'd be doing it willingly."

He sent me a slow look that told me he was only beginning to make me willing, too. And someday he knew I would be.

My heartbeat was like the erratic pulsing of a spent neon sign: on, off, bright red, then dark, sputtering back to red again.

Something in the back of my mind said, *You know you like it whenever he touches you—and you're just waiting for that to happen now. It's the best feeling in the world, and it only makes you stronger every time. . . .*

I walked away from him, my sneakers actually sinking into the plush carpet. Everything was so *real* around him. And being in such a cozy home, just like the one I'd lived in as a girl, only multiplied the sensation.

"So what do you think?" he asked.

"I like it. But . . ."

"I promise you, Jenny, this isn't a trap to get you where I want you to be."

"How much is your promise worth?"

He lost his grin. "Everything."

He said it with such seriousness that my newfound heartbeat nearly stopped. Maybe it was the longing in his gaze, too. It's hard not to feel special when you can see naked yearning like that in someone or . . . well, some*thing*.

"You make this so damned hard," I said, touching the counter, loving the slick tile under my fingertips.

"What, trusting me?"

"Yes."

"I know, I really do." He shrugged, standing away from the sofa, coming toward me. "But you're a hard sell, and I've been pushing more with you than with most newbie ghosts. How can I win you over?"

I thought for a moment, and he laughed.

"I guess saving you from a time loop wasn't enough."

"It did go a long way." I really was grateful for that, although I hated to admit it.

And he seemed to catch on to that fact, because he strolled even closer. Crap. Whenever he got near enough for me to smell the beachy salt and the soap on his skin, I heated up that much more.

His voice was soft, alluring. "There was nothing stopping me from just keeping you with all of my stars after I saved you."

Hello? Willingness? "I can't ever see myself agreeing to have something feeding off my happy emotions like they obviously gave you permission to do."

All those comatose bodies, so beautiful, so heavenly, had benefited from this keeper's attentions; he'd planted sublime thoughts inside them so they would never have to think about death or pain. And no matter how much I was resisting, I'd briefly considered going under, myself. Imagine an eternity where I didn't see grotesque granny masks or axes, where I lived every day with my Dean and my parents, who would never have died in the world fake Dean could've given me in the star place.

He braced his hands on the counter—hands that had been all over my body once upon a time. I couldn't look away from them.

"You're not a good liar," he said.

"I'll do better from now on."

"Then start with this." He nodded toward the main room. "Is this the kind of house you always wanted with him?"

With my real Dean.

I opted for the truth here. "We could've ended up somewhere similar. I don't look like I'd ever be a full-time mom or anything, but I seriously thought about that stuff with Dean. You know the rest. After my parents died, I kind of went on a different path."

"The former straight-A student quitting college and losing ambition. Who could blame you? The world had lost its color, its purpose. You needed to regroup."

Why did he have to be the only one around who

totally understood? Even my best alive friend, Suze, hadn't gotten it.

When he sat on a barstool and leaned his muscled forearms on the counter, I saw me and my own Dean utterly belonging here. For a sec, I even gave in to the fantasy of this fake Dean and me, living out the future I could've had.

"There's another plus about this place that I haven't mentioned," he said, grinning again.

"What?" Heart beating. Veins pumping with clipped pulses. Why did I get the feeling that he'd looked right into me and saw my biggest desires?

"We can play house."

Yup. He saw all.

I couldn't help a laugh at how fruitless it was to try to keep anything from him. "Very funny. I wouldn't even know what to say to you when you walk through the door. It sure wouldn't be, 'Honey, you're home!'"

"You could call me honey."

"I don't know *what* to call you."

"Yes, you do."

He wanted me to call him Dean.

Reaching out a hand, he opened his fingers. "Try playing along. Just once."

Trust your Dean. That was what he meant.

Common sense told me not to give in to him, but there was something else whispering to me, and it was saying that he would continue pursuing me until he got what he wanted. And, right now, it seemed like such a good idea to feel someone's human-esque fingers tracing my skin. Especially *his* fingers.

"If you screw me over . . ." I whispered.

"Would I ever do that to you, Jenny?"

Yeah, I thought. *You did it when you left me behind to go to school, saying that you'd see me again.* But it hadn't been the same after that at all.

"Give me another chance," he added.

I realized that the entity had actually taken on the personality of Dean now, trying to seduce me with my old boyfriend's words, not just his image.

And, as usual, it was working.

Locking gazes with him, it was as if I'd been shot through with adrenaline, my heart kicking in earnest now, life breathing through me as I touched his fingertips.

A surge of power almost made my legs fold, and I began to pull my hand away. But he wrapped his fingers around mine, increasing the voltage.

"Don't you miss this?" he asked. "Who has ever made you feel this way besides me?"

I still didn't know if he was pretending to be the real Dean or if he was talking about himself, the entity. The keeper.

"Jenny," he murmured, standing, pulling my hand closer to him.

When he laid my palm flat against his heart, I felt the beat, just as if it were my own.

Ba-bump, ba-bump . . .

It was like being in a bed, under a bundle of covers, when all around, it was cold. It was like being wrapped in cotton, treasured and kept.

Most of all, it was like the moment I'd realized I'd fallen in love with Dean for the very first time.

I didn't pull my hand away. I couldn't, because it was the last thing I wanted to do. My Dean. Everything I'd lost.

"Jenny," he whispered again, making my chest go tight.

If I moved, all of this might disappear.

His voice came on low waves of vibration. "You know I'm the only one who's ever going to make you feel."

I thought of Gavin, and how I wished . . .

"*He* can't do this for you."

Suddenly, the entity's voice wasn't Dean's anymore. It was guttural and velvety at the same time.

I jerked my hand away from him and, for a horrifying flash, I thought I saw a different face on him: misty white. High cheekbones. Bottomless dark eyes.

But just as I took a tripping step away from him, he was back to being Dean, golden and humanlike.

He shook his head.

"You're going to find," he said in the voice I was used to, except tighter now, "that humans will only let you down. Don't ever expect anything from them, especially if you're looking for affection."

It almost sounded like he was . . . jealous of Gavin?

He softly laughed off the moment, his eyes light brown again, just like they'd never changed. As I backed away from him even more, it was like he knew that his whole trust campaign was in jeopardy, and he raised his hands in a type of gunslinger "see, I'm not armed" gesture.

"If you really don't trust me," he said, "all you have

to do is ban me from this house, and I won't be able to come back in."

"Hogwash."

He smiled, walked toward the door, opened it, then left. Just like that.

God, he drove me nuts.

But I wasn't a total dummy, so I whispered, "Okay, you're banned, fake Dean, keeper, collector . . . whatever. You can't come in here anymore."

The door was still open when I went there to see if I'd wished him away by some miracle, but no such luck. He was at the threshold, waiting for me. Then, in that unfortunately hunky way of his, he casually lifted a hand, pressing it to the air in front of him, as if laying it against an invisible layer that was keeping him out of the entryway. He even pushed against it, but the barrier held.

He retreated, shrugging. "See? You've got a place of your own now."

"You don't have a secret way to get inside? Tunnels? Vortexes?"

"Always with the questions. Just *trust* me on this."

For the first time, I really did want to, because I'd never had a safer place to go in my life.

With just a grin, fake Dean showed off his skills and took his leave like he was mocking me with his awesomeness, his body folding into itself like fast origami until there was nothing.

I stood there, bewildered. Not only by our strange encounter, but by the transition my body was making because of his absence. I was becoming less solid, molecule by molecule, each one filling with crackling ghost energy until I was one entire boo girl again.

Now, though, I was brimming with *extreme* Mello Yello energy. I'm talking need-to-run-around-the-earth-three-times hyper. It was because Dean had touched me, and that, multiplied by my recent death-spot visit, clearly equaled major spaz time.

When I turned around to see if he'd lied to me about this house not really being the star place in disguise, I was ready to run if he'd fooled me.

But I was still in the dream house. He'd been straight with me after all.

Huh.

So I darted around the rest of the place, exploring the elegant bedroom with its flat-screen TV, serene blue walls with a couple of waterfallish paintings, and a bedspread with flowery silhouettes over a wide queen mattress. The bathroom had lots of bells and whistles, with two whole sinks and a claw-footed tub that made me go, "Aw."

If fake Dean were around, I'd actually have a body I could bathe.

Then I stopped my thoughts right quick. No baths around *him*. Bad, bad, bad idea.

After I'd seen the other two bedrooms plus the study, I bolted up the chimney, then paused in midair outside, looking down at the roof of my new digs.

Mine! Seriously.

As I wondered if any other spirits were privy to the fact that the owner was never going to be in that house again, I conjured my travel tunnel to zoom to the address Amanda Lee had given me for her PI friend. A couple of hours had surely passed, and she should be there.

I landed in a blocky set of apartments a few miles from the beach in Encinitas. Yellow plank wood and flower boxes prettied up the vague surroundings as I found his apartment, then discovered an open window that I could whisk through.

I heard Amanda Lee's smooth-as-mint-juleps voice first. "Do you ever miss the excitement of getting a new case?"

It sounded like they'd wrapped up a conversation. I couldn't imagine she would've started this meeting with anything other than her questions about Tim's profile, so I'd missed all of that.

"I don't recall what excitement feels like," answered the PI, who had a very slight Spanish accent. He talked so slowly that it even made me bear down while I came around the corner, braking to a complete, shuddering stop in a family room.

I saw a withered man in a plaid recliner, brown-skinned with wisps of gray hair rebelling from his skull. Dressed in a faded striped button-down and kha-kis, his sock-covered feet were up on the raised foot-rest, his hand on his potbelly. Dude had to be at least sixty, but seemed much older. And weak in energy, too.

He coughed, or maybe I should say wheezed, into a fisted hand, and Amanda Lee rose from the couch, go-ing to a table beside him, pouring him a new glass of ice water.

I hated to say it, but it smelled like a sick person in

here, old skin and medicine. The air was also too warm and heavy, as if it'd taken a moody cue from all the dark-wooded furniture and faded family pictures.

I could tell that Amanda Lee knew I was here, but she hadn't let Ruben in on the whole ghost secret. I could also tell that she was expecting me to be a bitch to her because of our spat.

It brought to mind that drawing Gavin had made of me. The hellbitch. And I didn't like it one bit.

I rose to the ceiling, vibrating there, fidgeting while trying to blend.

Ruben's breath was sliced with effort. "I could call in a few favors with some cop friends, just to check this Tim kid out, if you want. I did it with Elizabeth's and all your other cases, and it's no problem now."

As I said, I hadn't been the only dead person Amanda Lee had tried to revitalize in order to get paranormal help on Elizabeth's murder. Someday, she wanted to solve their cases, too.

"That would be wonderful, Ruben, thank you. But you don't have to extend yourself on my behalf."

"Just because I've started looking like the walking dead since the last time you saw me, it doesn't mean I'm at hell's gate just yet." He shivered in his chair. "Whoo. Cooled off, didn't it? A stiff breeze is coming through the window."

As he attempted to rise, Amanda Lee glanced up at me, and I shrugged from my nook in the ceiling corner. So I was too cool for the room. I was what I was.

She headed toward the window. "I've got it."

After shutting it—although she did leave it open a

crack, giving me an easy out—she grabbed a wool blanket from the back of a sofa, spreading it over him.

"*Gracias.* But don't be looking at me like I'm getting sicker before your very eyes."

"You have a rattle in your chest, Ruben. You should see a doctor."

"It's not serious enough to waylay me for good."

She laughed. "You've been shot at, beaten to within an inch of your life, and in a car accident—and none of that even happened while you were a cop or PI. I don't think this is what will end you."

"Flattery. I like it." He started laughing, too, then coughed again.

Amanda Lee lingered on my frown. Or maybe she was only checking out how I couldn't stop being such a mild spaz in my corner or how high my color was. I got this rainbow-y only after seeing fake Dean, and even though I'd been killed while there was a ton of caffeine in me, I'd never put on a talent show quite like this.

Her frown trumped mine.

"Well, then," Ruben said. "I know you came over here for more than just my opinion about a Philip K. Dick story."

"Pardon?" she asked.

"You've never read his work?" He gestured toward his extensive bookcase, which was overflowing with hardboiled novels and sci-fi. "He wrote a short story about psychic mutants who predicted future crimes, and officers would apprehend the could-be perps."

"'The Minority Report,'" I blurted. So I liked my books.

Amanda Lee ignored me and said to Ruben, "That situation sounds ideal."

"You would think. Did it keep society safe? Of course. But is it ethical to point the finger at a person when he has not yet committed a crime? You tell me."

"You're comparing this story to me and the visions I've been getting about Tim Knudson."

Ah. So she hadn't included me in her cover story. Fine by me.

She smoothed down her dark skirt. "I'm not saying this boy is going to be guilty, but what would you do if you saw the potential for a crime before it actually occurred?"

"I might try to stop it, if there was just cause."

Neither of them talked for a moment. I, myself, was hoping Tim's dreams would be full of unicorns and puppy dogs tonight. And not in a psychedelic messed-up Prince music video way, either.

Finally, Ruben muffled a cough and reached for his water, taking a sip. Then he said, "You've been eyeing those files near the kitchen for the last half hour, Amanda Lee. I think that's where you want to be."

I whipped my gaze to the left, where an open box waited on a dining table. My form sizzled. Were those notes about my case?

"You do have the ability to see the truth in people," Amanda Lee said to Ruben as she made her way over to the box.

"Not like you do," he said.

She began pulling out notebooks and manila folders. My energy nearly screamed, I was so excited.

"I dusted those things off after you said you wanted a second look at them," he said. "Can I ask why?"

"There's something that's been bothering me about Jensen's case. It's as if I'm missing a detail I should've seen the first time around."

In other words: *I have a ghost bugging me about her murder, and she's been at me to see you and her file notes.*

"You getting one of your feelings about her disappearance again?" Ruben asked, sitting up a little more in his recliner.

"Perhaps. I'll let you know after I've pawed through these."

He reached over to grab a TV remote from his table. "All right. Then don't mind me if I catch some Padres action while you work. Let me know if you have questions."

"Thank you."

The TV bloomed on, the mellow sounds of baseball in the background while Amanda Lee laid the files open like she was also inviting me over to survey their contents.

I knew she'd seen them before, when she'd hired Ruben all those months ago to look into my disappearance. I'd been the coldest that a case could be, but clearly Ruben had tried to unearth age-old clues to no avail. Even so, Amanda Lee had gleaned just enough information to be successful in pulling me from a residual haunting phase.

After I flew down to her, I didn't bother to whisper, because Ruben obviously wasn't a sensitive who could detect me.

"There's a lot here," I said.

"We'll skim," she whispered under the TV noise. "I remember quite a bit of it, anyway, since it wasn't so long ago Ruben made his reports to me."

I looked at a few typewritten pages as Amanda Lee turned them for me. They said that Ruben had combed the area near the party in the forest for any objects that might've been left years and years after my murder. He'd reinterviewed longtime residents of the area, as well as any surviving friends who'd attended our small party. He'd even talked with the lead investigator on my missing-persons case.

But there was nothing new here. Since there was no proof of a murder, there'd been only speculation anyway, and one of those theories had been that, if I'd been killed, my body might've been moved from the murder site and disposed of elsewhere.

Yet, again, if I'd been killed in my death spot, where had the blood from an ax attack gone?

That also got me to wondering . . . Why wasn't I drawn to the place I was actually buried? *Was* I buried somewhere?

Ugh. It'd be great not to think about my scattered or burned bones.

Amanda Lee had graduated to laying her hands flat on the papers, closing her eyes, meditating and trying to catch psychic vibes from them. But from the frustrated lines etched near her mouth, I could tell she was getting nothing.

Yet she kept going.

And going.

I just kept watching her, my energy leveling out for the time being.

Wow. She did sincerely care about me.

"Thank you, Amanda Lee," I said simply.

She opened her eyes but didn't make eye contact with me. "You're very welcome, Jensen."

I didn't have to say more. I wasn't sure she wanted me to, anyway, because she diligently went back to vibing the pages, like she didn't want to talk about our latest quarrel.

I half smiled to myself, knowing she'd never change. But my smile faded when I realized that I wished I could trust her, even more than I wanted to trust fake Dean. . . .

When she accessed a new folder, I began to read it. Then we went through a few of them, finding nothing earth-shattering.

But then . . .

My energy motored up again as I came to something I'd never known about my murder before.

"Holy crap," I whispered, my voice seeming to rip through me. "There was a main suspect in my disappearance?"

6

Amanda Lee glanced at the page I was reading, then whispered, "I wouldn't call him a main suspect. *Person of interest* is more accurate."

She touched the man's copied picture, which showed a whiskered, bulky, sixtyish guy with a lazy eye and a thing for plaid. "Milo Guttenburg was interviewed right after the disappearance, but I never mentioned him because he didn't pan out as a suspect. Since he passed away nearly thirteen years ago, there won't be any empathy readings or dream-digging from him."

"Maybe he's available in my dimension."

Ruben lowered the TV volume. "What did you say, Amanda Lee?"

She glanced at him. "Just talking to myself. I often do that to sort out my thoughts. It's one of a psychic's prerogatives."

"You know I had a couple of you come to my desk back when I was a cop," he said with a wheezy chuckle. "You're definitely a rare breed." Then he wrapped his blanket tighter around him. "Don't know what it is, but I'm sure feeling jumpy today. And *still* cold."

Amanda Lee looked at me vibrating with soda-pop caffeinated spark next to her. I smiled back innocently.

"It'll pass, Ruben," she said. "Maybe it's something in the air."

He shrugged and turned up the volume again.

I signaled for Amanda Lee to turn the page so I could read more. After I did, I said, "Okay, so Milo was a loner who lived in a cabin near the spot where we held our party. A woodworker who sold his stuff to a boutique in town. A nature man who chopped his own wood, right?"

"At first the investigators thought he'd gotten fed up with all the kids who came to the woods to legend trip," Amanda Lee mumbled, like she was still talking to herself.

"So they theorized that he took an ax out one night and came after the stupid one who had to go and take a pee by herself?" *Hi, me.* "Knowing what I know about my murder, the bastard who came after me had on a scary mask, like he wanted to get his jollies out of frightening me. He was sadistic. I wasn't a crime of opportunity for a crab who flew off the handle and wanted to take care of some bothersome kids who were making too much noise."

"Unless Milo, at first, wanted to scare you off, then took the ax to you."

"You're still self-whispering," Ruben said, shutting off the TV altogether.

Amanda Lee turned around in her chair, facing him.

"What if I were to tell you that, after I had you look into Jensen Murphy's case, I received some pivotal information about what happened that night?"

She was going for it.

"You received information?" Ruben was holding back that smile. It must've cost some effort, because he coughed, his chest rattling. "As in, psychically?"

"Exactly," Amanda Lee said, pointing to Ruben's water, telling him to drink it. He followed orders.

She added, "I'm going back to Jensen's case because I felt for certain that she was killed, and her murderer was wearing a mask. Wouldn't that indicate a planned crime?"

Ruben put down the water. "It could. But we're not sure that was the reality."

"You doubt me, do you?"

"Amanda Lee, when you deal in evidence your whole life, you take nebulous guesses with a grain of salt." Another cough. "I'll tell you, though—I was never sold on Milo Guttenburg as a solid suspect in Jensen's disappearance, either, and the investigators made the right choice in dropping him. They said he'd been agitated by Jensen's group being there, but his usual MO was to pull a shotgun on other trespassers. Plus, he told the sheriff to come inside his home and take a look around to see if he had any missing girls inside. There was no indication that he'd even come within a few feet of Jensen Murphy, much less abducted her."

Hmm. I started thinking about what Milo might have to tell me if I ever found him in Boo World. Had he seen something odd in the forest that night? Something that didn't mean much at the time but could be important, based on what I now knew about my murder?

"I'd think," Amanda Lee said, "that there was a big difference between a man who'd kill with a shotgun and one who'd put on a mask and use an ax."

"Again, going with your view of what you think happened in Jensen's case, yes. An ax is more personal, sadistic."

"Told you," I whispered.

Amanda Lee lifted one eyebrow, giving me credit.

Ruben added, "If what you say about the killing is true, then what we've got is someone who gets off on fear. He'd have a deep-seated need to dominate, to have total control over his victim. This person had probably committed a crime before, based on how clean the scene was. The cop's dogs didn't even lead them to any evidence, because the killer had already gotten good at this, had some practice and refined his technique."

She shuffled through a few folders. "Somewhere in here, I remember you saying that there'd been other disappearances in Southern California during the previous year. Girls in their early twenties, blondes."

"There's always someone missing," he said softly. "And for different reasons."

I shuddered, my electric pulse flaring. I didn't want to say *serial killer*, but . . . Right?

I didn't know if ghosts could get sick, but I was halfway there.

"Some of those missing women," Ruben said, "had bodies that were eventually found. But it turned out that a couple had run away on their own, so they wouldn't relate to Jensen's case."

"Did any of those bodies show signs of being axed?" Amanda Lee asked.

"No."

Well, there went that theory.

But I could tell Amanda Lee had already sunk her teeth into the possibilities, and when that woman bit into something, she didn't let go.

Ruben stared at her. "Just what else did you see in your visions about Jensen?"

She paused, looking up at me, her gaze a sympathetic, watery gray. "She ran from him in those woods as he chased her that night. A long, horrifying chase. Can you imagine being a regular girl one moment, then living a nightmare the next? It wouldn't have seemed real, that mask, that ax."

I looked away, unable to deal. Amanda Lee was a hard-ass, but I couldn't say she didn't feel deeply about the people she got to know.

The room went quiet, and she turned a page to another one, where four color photos were posted.

I ghost-gasped at the sight of my friends who'd been in Elfin Forest with me that night: Patrick McNichol, Andy Grant, Brittany Kirkman, and Lisa Levine. Four smiling early-twenties kids in casual pictures taken long before we'd gone traipsing into hell.

I'd invited my best friend from high school, Suze, to our little party, too, but she didn't like this group I was hanging out with from work. Said they were wastes of life. And Suze, who'd graduated from college a couple of years before and had gotten a decent, upwardly mobile job at a bank, had a point.

Not that I'd listened back then.

Amanda Lee was watching my reaction to the photos, wrinkling her brow, obviously wondering if I was about to crack or something.

"I'm okay," I said. "Turn the page?"

She did, and what followed were notes on the interviews Ruben had conducted with three out of four of the partygoers. Patrick, at the age of fifty-one, had suffered a fatal heart attack and hadn't exactly been available. Amanda Lee had said something about this before, after she'd pulled me out of the time loop, but now that we weren't in the middle of Elizabeth's case, I wondered again if Patrick was around Boo World.

Amanda Lee asked Ruben, "Now that I've got more information about that night, do your investigative instincts make you think that any of the kids at that party were sadistic enough to kill Jensen in the way she died?"

"I didn't get the creepy-crawlies from any of them, no. You know that, years later, they'd forgotten most of the details of that party, anyway, so it was hard to gauge their reactions when they were being interviewed."

"A sociopath would be able to hide his or her true nature in an interview."

"Right. But my instinct is telling me that all of them were just drunk off their asses. It wasn't even until an hour after Jensen went off on her own that any of them even looked for her. They sobered up pretty quick and spent all night searching."

Amanda Lee turned another page. "The authorities didn't do anything right away, either."

"They thought she'd only gone missing. Jensen's friends said she was in a funk, and they brought her out to party because they wanted to cheer her up. She was drying out from a bender from the day before, and she decided to be the designated driver, but she was in a good mood at the start of that night. Who knows what she might've been feeling as the hours wore on, though?"

I knew what I'd been feeling—like I had to pee. That's where the trouble had started.

Ruben added, "I've seen stranger things happen than a young woman running away from her problems."

"You have your evidence and I have mine."

"Tell me about it."

I couldn't stand it anymore. "Amanda Lee, can I just get a read on Ruben? See if there's something going through his mind that might offer a clue that we're not finding in these notes? He could be thinking a bunch of different thoughts, now that he knows how I died, and could be putting things together that he didn't put together before."

She hesitated, then gave me a nod. "Gently," she whispered so only I could hear. "Just do it gently."

A swirling blip traveled through me, but I tamped it down. I wouldn't overload him with my extra energy.

I went to him, being as gentle as possible, giving him the softest of touches on his face. He blinked, his pupils expanding as I encountered a field of zapping welcome.

Then I was inside.

A picture. Long red-blond hair, freckles, green eyes, a summertime smile, a can of Mello Yello in hand, rubber bracelets hugging an arm.

A mass of gray spreading over the picture, blanking out everything.

Sadness. Regret. Sincerity. . . .

I pulled out of Ruben, then went to the sofa, slumping over it, my outline blinkering. He'd been thinking of my picture from the night I'd died: a normal, everyday girl who'd had no idea what was in store for her, just as Amanda Lee had said. He'd wanted to solve my cold case so badly.

Amanda Lee had been telling the truth about Ruben.

I wished I could touch him again, as humans do to make one another feel better, but he was shivering already, and I had the power to only make it worse unless I gave him a peaceful hallucination. I didn't know if his body could take the higher intensity of that.

All I could do was whisper to him. "Thank you, Ruben. I know you did what you could for me."

I'd put enough energy into my words so that he could faintly hear me, and his dark eyes were even wider now, his lips parted.

"Cold," he finally whispered. "Still so cold."

Amanda Lee came over, bending down and putting an arm around him, warming him up. "It's not only the temperature in the room, is it?"

"No."

"There's no reason to feel that way, Ruben. Jensen Murphy is so grateful. She knows that you'd do anything to help if you could."

The tough guy below the sick exterior won out, and Ruben smiled, lifting his chin. "Did she tell you that?"

"She told *you*."

Ruben froze, then glanced around. I thought about materializing for him—Lord knew I had enough energy for it—but then shot that idea down. He'd already had a mild dose of ghost today. I didn't want to push it.

"Tell her," he said, "she's very welcome."

Even though he was playing along, I had the suspicion that he still didn't genuinely believe in ghostus-pocus stuff.

Maybe in time, I thought. Some people needed an opportunity to let it all sink in, and he was a man of fact and evidence who'd stumbled into all this just because he'd been hired by a psychic.

He closed his eyes, resting his head on the recliner. Amanda Lee poured the last of the water from the pitcher into his near-empty glass.

Then he opened his eyes. "Jensen's best friend," he said quickly.

I came to attention. Was he talking about Suze?

"What about her?" Amanda Lee asked, putting down the pitcher.

"Suzanne Field. She didn't go to the party that night.

She and Jensen were going through some girl drama. You know what happens when one feels left behind while the other moves on."

Was he talking about me or Suze?

Amanda Lee said, "It's true they were moving in different directions in life."

"Well, now that we're going over this case again, something she said strikes me. It didn't mean anything at the time, but she mentioned that a party girl—Brittany or Lisa—was wearing Jensen's bracelets in memory of her on an anniversary of the disappearance when Suze saw one of them a couple of years ago."

Embarrassingly, I'd owned some rubber Madonna bracelets. Don't ask why, since I was more into bands like Sonic Youth. Okay, maybe I admired Madonna's I Am Woman attitude. There. But it doesn't excuse the temporary fashion faux pas.

"It's starting to nag at me," Ruben said, "maybe because I was thinking of that picture of Jensen, and she was wearing those bracelets in it."

"Are you thinking of how a killer takes trophies?" Amanda Lee asked.

"I could be."

She was grim. "In my visions, I felt that Jensen lost those bracelets in the woods that night."

And Suze was the one who'd told Ruben about seeing them again on Lisa or Brittany. And I had been putting off seeing her for a while now.

Clearly, it was time for me to stop avoiding my old best friend and actually interact with her, so I could mine more information.

I was already out the window before Amanda Lee could suggest it.

Dusk rolled through the sky, leaving me hours away from my dream-digging appointment with Tim Knudson as I traveled to the Gaslamp Quarter, where good cheer was definitely under way. Revelers strolled the downtown streets, eating and drinking on sidewalk patios, music spilling out of every bar. But the best music was coming out of Flaherty's, an Irish pub on Fourth.

"What Should We Do with the Drunken Sailor" from a Celtic band livened up everything. God, if this had been any other night, I would've called for my buddy Randy to join me. It couldn't get more appropriate than this.

But . . . another time. Because, right now, as I jittered above everyone's heads while they gathered by the long bar, holding beer mugs high and yelling over the band as they tried to chat, I needed to find Suze.

I didn't have to look far. She was behind the bar, wrangling drink orders, her long, curly gray-versus-brown hair pulled back into a chunky barrette, a white "Flaherty's" apron hugging her. She kept yawning, covering her mouth with her hand, shaking off obvious exhaustion.

Maybe she was doing a double shift?

I rose into a pine-wooded corner, just taking her in. Remembering all those years ago when her hair had been a wild, teenaged mess that she'd let go free, when her body had been toned in that take-it-for-granted way only the young have as she'd cheered during football games. I'd been the student council president and homecoming queen, and she'd taken the prom crown. Neither of us had given a shit who would win, just so it was one or the other.

She'd been majorly ambitious back then, so what had happened? Not that being a bartender was a bad job—it just didn't require a college degree. The old Suze wouldn't have been slinging ale to yuppies and tourists.

I waited her out, all the while wondering what the hell she knew about those Madonna bracelets and why Brittany or Lisa hadn't been the ones to let Ruben know about them. I recalled having the jewelry on when that final picture of me had been taken before we'd headed off for the forest—the photo that'd been in all the newspapers and in Ruben's thoughts. But what did I remember *after* the picture . . . ? Nada.

Had I blocked out how I'd lost those bracelets right along with the details of my killing? I'd been swigging soda that night, but I'd been sober, so why wasn't anything registering now?

When Suze was relieved by a cheesy bartender with a raging yellow scarf around one bicep—was it some kind of fashion statement?—she headed for the back of the building.

This was my chance. But I wondered . . .

Well, with everyone else lately, I'd been using empathy, yet that was only because their minds were already on the subjects I needed more information on. How was I gracefully going to get information about those bracelets out of Suze if I couldn't talk to her?

But those bracelets weren't the only reason I was here. They were just the best excuse I could come up with to see her again without feeling bad about her.

Chickenshit Jensen.

I sucked up all my energy—and there was still a lot of it, even if empathy with Ruben had taken the edge off. Then I dove down from the corner, zipping through the bar. Gasps followed in my wake, no doubt at the sudden blast of cold air.

After I slipped through a big crack at the bottom of a door, I saw Suze at a table alone in the back room, her head on the surface, cushioned by her arms. Next to her there was a can of soda pop.

Had she fallen asleep before sitting down to take a drink during a break? She'd definitely looked tired enough in the bar to just crash like this.

I wasn't sure what to do now. I'd never gotten this close to her while I was a ghost before. I'd never seen just how old she looked: over fifty-three, like I would've been.

God, this was like some kind of time warp I'd gone through, where one day I was watching John Travolta in leather singing to Olivia Newton-John, and the next Danny Zuko was playing some horrifying bad Martian dude in a big codpiece and dreadlocks that I'd seen in a clip on the Internet. The future had not turned out right or bright.

Just as I was mulling all that over, Suze dazedly turned her head in her arms, and I was suddenly in her line of sight.

When she lifted her head, my essence hummed. It

was almost like she saw me, but couldn't quite make me out.

"H'lo?" she asked.

I don't know how it happened. Maybe it was my excitement. Maybe it was all that energy jumping through me.

I materialized.

At first, Suze groggily got to her feet, so slumber-addled that she knocked over the soda can. It hit the ground with a clunk and let out a sinister fizz.

"J—Jen??"

I couldn't stop my joy from taking me over, making me glow and lending me more energy. I *bzzzt*ed, taking a step closer to her. "Suze!"

"How . . . ? What . . . ?"

And then she fainted.

I sped forward, electrically shaping my essence into a big hand, pressing under her, being careful not to touch skin, and easing her fall to the cement.

Then I drew away, standing over her, looking at the consequences of my idiot move.

"Crap," I said. "Suze? *Suze?*"

She was lying in a pool of soda, stray curls and her tank top getting soaked.

I hardened my form again, using a phantom limb to lightly slap her face, avoiding any empathy. "Wake up. Come on."

It took a few times, but she finally blinked her eyes open. A moment passed. Then she sucked in a breath, like she was about to scream bloody murder.

"Shhhhhh!" I said, expending myself. Then, pulling

on more power, I materialized again, but I knew I couldn't do it for too long since I had to save up for tonight, no matter how much juice I'd banked today. Dream-digging would be a bitch on consumption. "It's just me, Suze. I know. I know it's a little weird, but I'm not here to hurt you or anything."

"Jen?" she asked again, her teeth chattering.

"Yeah." I tried to smile.

She looked at me like I was an angel, and maybe that's how I appeared. It's how Gavin used to remember me.

When she smiled, I buzzed some more. Suze. Best friends forever.

But then she closed her eyes and pressed her palms over them. "I'm dreaming. I fell asleep because I'm dead on my feet from working last night and all day, and I'm dreaming."

I wanted to hug her, hold her close, remember the days when we'd told everything to each other: how I felt about Dean, how she wished she had someone just like him. We hadn't been as close after my parents had died, but I'd been the one who'd changed, not Suze.

"I'm sorry to scare you," I said. "I wish I wouldn't."

"Yes, definitely a dream."

Okay. If that's what she needed to believe, then I'd go with it. Maybe later we could . . . What—catch up over a brewski?

"I need some questions answered," I said. "Like . . ." Boy, I couldn't just hop into the bracelet stuff. "Like how're you doing, Suze?"

Well, that sure got her. She made a puzzled face,

then gestured to herself, all sticky and rumpled on the floor. "How do you think I'm doing?"

"You don't look so bad to me. For a prom queen."

Her eyes lit up for a moment, and we were back to being bosom buddies. Then she shook her head, like she was remembering this wasn't real.

Shoot.

When she peered at me again, I knew she'd been expecting me to disappear.

She gave in, like she couldn't fight her sleep. "Even if I'm seeing a mirage, I've missed you. It's all I've wanted to tell you for years. There's more than just that, though. I wanted to apologize for not being there that night, because if I had, you wouldn't have gone off into the woods alone. You wouldn't have even gone to that party if I'd asked you not to, but I told you to hang out with your new buddies, have a great time with them, when all the while, I was angry at you for leaving me behind."

"I never meant to leave you."

A tear rolled down her face. She cuffed it away. "You're not a day older than the last time I saw you. God bless dreams, huh?"

"I'm the same because I died that night, and this is how I'm going to be until . . . whenever." Why lie about it?

Her eyes welled up with a *lot* of tears now. "Oh, shit. I didn't want to know that. I always imagined you'd run away to some tropical island, getting your life together."

"I'm afraid not."

"How did you . . . die?"

This, I probably shouldn't go into. "It happened in the forest." Yeah, I was dodging and weaving. "I don't even know who did it, but that's why I'm here, Suze. To see if you can help me."

She pressed her hands against her eyes again, rubbing them. Outside the door, there was a clatter, and I got ready to disappear if someone else came inside.

Didn't happen. When I looked at her again, she was slowly lowering her hands, revealing mascara smears. Was she gradually realizing that this was actually happening?

I think so, because her voice shook. "How do you need my help?"

Here it went. "I was wearing bracelets that night. The sucky Madonna rubber ones?"

She nodded quickly.

"Anyway," I said, handling her with kid gloves, "you told a private investigator that Lisa Levine or Brittany Kirkman has them now, and one of them was wearing the bracelets on the anniversary of my disappearance not long ago."

She only seemed confused.

This was going nowhere, and my spastastic condition made me reach out to her, touching her face to empathize.

Coppertone-skinned Brittany Kirkman, middle-aged with eighties-era bracelets slinking down her arm. In a booth in the pub. Brunch. A random visit on a day that just happened to be the anniversary of Jen's disappearance . . .

Last name Stokley . . . a bottle blonde . . . wearing tennis whites . . .

"I miss her so much, too, Suze. What do you think ever happened to her . . . ?"

Before I withdrew from Suze, I could also feel the love she still had for me, and it hurt too much to stay inside her, so that's why I left. Disengaged.

Disconnected.

Afterward, Suze did as anyone else would do post-empathy—she shivered wildly, got goose bumps, looked at me like she'd just walked out of a showing of *The Shining*.

Then she closed her eyes, laughed once, and started crying.

There was nothing I could do. To think, all the powers I'd gained as a ghost, and here I was, watching her fall apart.

I wasn't sure that I should ever come back to her if this was what was in store. Everything had gone as bad as I'd feared, and I was sorely tempted to give her a serene hallucination to make up for it.

Then she spoke. "I guess it only makes sense that you popped into my dreams. A few months ago, a PI came in here to talk about you, and that stirred up so many emotions in me that I'd thought I put to rest. Then there was that other guy who struck up a conversation with me the other day in here and told me that his parents were good friends with us in high school. Jenna and Jamie. Remember them? He's putting together a bunch of their old pictures and mementos for a reunion and was asking questions about the golden days. He asked a lot about you, though. He was curious about how you disappeared. . . ."

"What guy?" I asked, already getting a bad feeling about this.

She sniffed, frowning, clearly still deciding if she'd gone bat-poo crazy or not. "He was young, handsome in an unconventional way. . . . He said he'd be back some other time for another drink and more talk." She looked at the ceiling, like she was accessing her memory. Then she smiled through her tears.

"I remember now. He said his name was Gavin."

Just as I started gaping at her, the door groaned open, and I rapidly dematerialized, shocked and more confused than ever.

7

After one of Suze's male coworkers barged into the room to announce that her break was over, I stayed invisible, still in a state of fizzling shock. I kept processing what Suze had told me.

"He said his name was Gavin. . . ."

While the aproned waiter grabbed a bag of potato chips from a shelf while complaining about the bar being understaffed, Suze's gaze kept searching me out. She also kept blinking, as if confirming that, yes, she really was awake. Then, after blowing out a mighty breath, she ignored the waiter and grabbed a towel from a counter, her hand trembling as she wet it down with water from a nearby sink and wiped up the soda pop spill. She cleaned herself up, too.

All the while, I just kept thinking about Gavin. My ghost buds hadn't been watching him like they'd been doing for Wendy, so during some trips away from the condo, this was obviously where he'd ended up.

Had it been *the* Gavin, though? It wasn't exactly the most common name, so chances were decent. And if he

had been here, I suspected that he hadn't given Suze
his last name because surely she would've recognized
it from the media attention Farah's death had brought.
Her suicide and the killing of her young brother had
been a top story. Lucky for them, the story had been
limited to that angle; her murder of Elizabeth had been
kept secret so far, because that's what money could do
for a family who had enough of it to cover part of a
coastline.

As far as Amanda Lee went, she'd been vengeful,
yet she hadn't gone to the press or authorities with the
truth, either. She was carrying too much guilt about being wrong about Gavin, so she'd kept mum, too. I
guessed everyone was willing to live with how it'd all
turned out.

Basically.

As for being the son of Jenna and Jamie from high
school . . . well, hello, yearbooks on the Internet. Nothing was private these days, and he'd done his research.

With a wiggin' glance over her shoulder, Suze finally
left the break room, probably wondering why she'd
just had a very immediate psychotic episode.

Poor thing. We really did need to talk more. And
when we did, I was also going to get to the bottom of
what Gavin had asked her about me.

What the hell was he up to?

I drifted out to the bar, my energy slightly lower
than before, thanks to my materializing. So I hung
around Flaherty's as long as I could, hugging the ceiling, watching the crowd to see if Gavin would come in
for that next drink and another conversation with Suze.

No luck. She madly worked the bar, still yawning every once in a while and casting around paranoid glances, probably feeling me nearby.

By the time the bar shut down, I'd decided I would be summoning Sailor Randy to see if he wouldn't mind vegging out here so he could eavesdrop on Gavin's next visit. Asking Randy to keep watch over a bar was like asking Tony Montana if he wanted to hold a machine gun, so I was pretty sure he'd be cool with it.

As I watched Suze go to the backroom and grab her purse, I thought about appearing to her again. But I had a promise to keep to Heidi, so I trailed my old friend to her parked car just to see that she got there safely and then conjured a travel tunnel to Pacific Beach, where Tim should be off his swing shift by now.

His house wasn't far and, better yet, when I got there I saw that someone had made things easy for me by leaving the windows open to let in the night breeze. Even before I slipped in through one of them, I heard a TV on in the family room. Moans, groans.

When I glided there, I got a view of what was making all that noise—porn city. Skin all over the place. Good times on a Saturday night.

Tim was slumped over the cushions in blue sweats, a beer in hand. There were three more bottles collapsed on the glass table in front of him, too, but he was awake, dammit.

If he was an insomniac, I was going to be ticked.

To kill time, I winged through the room and down the hall to the darkened bedroom, where Nichelle's slumbering form huddled under a sheet. The rest of the covers had been kicked off, and there was a pillow in the middle of the bed, like a fluffy fort.

Let me guess—there'd been a lover's quarrel? Tim had been kicked out of bed already?

How had these lovebirds stayed together for even a couple of months?

Well, at least this was a good time to go deep inside of Tim's psyche through his dreams, while his bad mood might still be relatively fresh. But how was I going to do that when the couch potato wasn't even asleep?

When I jetted back out to the family room with all its *ooh*'s and *aah*'s emanating from the TV, I took one look at the fish tank and its peaceful burbling, and I knew.

A hallucination—that was just the thing I needed here. Then I could transition into a dream-dig with Tim since it was similar to a hallucination. The difference was that dream-digging happened when a suspect was asleep and hallucinations happened while he was awake. But, unlike thought-empathy, a hallucination would take more juice from me, not to mention a more intense touch, which would freeze Tim with electricity, supposedly lowering the melatonin level and causing a miniseizure. At least, Amanda Lee thought that's what happens.

All I really knew was that hallucinations melded me with the human's psyche, and I experienced every moment of the visions based on how my suspect's mind reacted to an image that I introduced first. I had no real control over the experience except to give them that first image, and they took it from there.

So, basically the visions could scare me as much as they did my target. Still, I'd found that frightening a murder confession out of people was a pretty damn effective tool.

Even if there hadn't been a murder yet.

Tim's eyes were halfway open, reddened, so I knew he was superrelaxed and I might not need a long hallucination. I didn't pussyfoot around when I pressed my essence against his face, harder than usual, until it almost felt like I was reaching under his skin.

I gave him a thought to concentrate on, something that would get him to sleep: the fish tank, beautiful, blue, bubbling and peaceful. Then I steadied myself as I rolled forward, drawn into him, expanding inside until I felt like I was part of him. Part of his mind's eye . . .

Light. We're so light, suspended in liquid comfort, holding our breath.

Warmth all around us, caressed by water. No worries. Nothing can touch us.

A fish, swimming past, graceful and light . . . so light . . .

Subtly, I pushed my way out of Tim, snapping out into the world again to see that his eyes were only slits now and his mouth was hanging open. The near-empty beer bottle in his hand canted, and I counted the moments until it dropped to the sofa.

Three, two, one . . .

Okay, I was off by about four seconds, but that bottle thudded down to the faux leather soon enough, his fingers loose, his breathing even.

I waited a little longer, all the while inspecting him. Tim's lashes were blond, delicate. Also, he must've shaved after he got off his shift tonight, because his cheeks were smoother than they'd been earlier and he smelled like lathery limes.

A tiny snore came from him, but I wanted to wait until he was deep into dream territory before I went in. His subconscious would tell me so many things that superficial thoughts wouldn't.

I admit it—to pass the time, I watched some of the skin flick. You probably would've had to go to the video store in my day to get this kind of action on TV. But, eventually, enough time passed so that Tim's eyes were sliding back and forth under his lids, and I warmed up, float-hopping up and down like a football player getting ready to go on the field. In dreams, I had even less control of a person's psyche than in a hallucination—I was a watcher in a place so deep inside of them that they owned every move, so I wanted to be on my proverbial toes.

Ready now. So with a hard touch to sleeping Tim's skin, I allowed myself to be sucked in, tumbling like a speck of dust, out of control, through the dark—

I landed with a thud.

Getting my bearings, I saw I was in a basement, and like in all dreams, time seemed to slow to a crawl, the *drip . . . drip . . . drip* from a faucet stretched out, the room drowsily tipping back and forth like I was on a boat.

But I wasn't. Tim was drunk, and this was his mind.

My stomach churned because, in here, I had a body, just like I did whenever I was around fake Dean.

Oh, barf, this wasn't any fun.

I took a few almost never-ending moments to anchor myself by getting to all fours on the concrete floor. In the meantime, I felt a tickle of intuition and turned my head toward the right.

Tim was in here with me, near a furnace where he was quietly picking up broken toys from the ground and placing them in a pile that bent at a strange angle, almost in the shape of a hook. Every time he added a shattered boat, a car, a block, the pile would threaten to spill while the furnace lazily belched fire in its innards, lighting up Tim's stoic face.

He had no idea I was here.

I just watched, waiting as time crawled past and the furnace kept flaring up. He kept reaching for toys, never seeming to run out of them, and the pile never tumbled.

But then he picked up something that wasn't a toy. It was a roll of breath mints, and he casually took one out, tossing it in the air, arcing it toward his mouth. It landed gently on his tongue with floating precision as the room kept swaying, swaying . . .

Stifling a groan, I watched only Tim as his legs started to get longer, making him taller . . . tall enough so that he could stare out a rectangular window that was letting in faint light from near the ceiling. At the same time, the window itself began stretching sideways and downward, mocking the size of a giant television screen, giving me a view of what was enthralling Tim outside.

A brunette in a bikini, lying on a lawn chair, taking in the sun. His older cougar neighbor, from today?

The furnace breathed more fire, and Tim flinched in slow motion, but he didn't look away from his object of fascination.

The brunette reached down and gripped a bottle of suntan oil . . . poured some in her palm . . . spread it over her browned stomach. As she rubbed it in, she shifted her hips, moaning softly.

Tim chewed on his mint, the furnace still bleeding fire.

The woman idly kept caressing herself, the sun gleaming off her slick skin, her lips parting with every turned-on sound she made. She slid her hands upward, over her breasts, then back down until one of them crept into her bikini bottoms.

The faucet dripped . . . dripped . . . dripped . . .

Tim's expression never, ever changed. He grew taller and taller as he watched her pleasure herself, each second a forever.

"Baby," she said in a seductive voice. "What're you doing back there?"

A niggle settled in the depths of my mind, but I didn't know why. Not until Tim reached out, braced both hands at the sides of the window, and pushed it open even more. Just as he started to step through, I remembered.

Nichelle had asked Tim the same question today, when she had caught him peeping at the neighbor. But now, instead of being denied the opportunity to keep looking, he had all the permission in the world. His world.

Something was happening to the brunette, though . . .

As her face seemed to melt, then turn into someone else's, I cringed in my corner.

Heidi. The woman had transformed into brown-haired Heidi, the girl who'd hired Amanda Lee and me today.

"Come to me," she said to Tim, holding out the hand that she wasn't using to stroke herself. "I wouldn't ever refuse you. You can have me as many times as you want, however you want, just come to me."

Drip . . . drip . . . drip . . . went the faucet, the tempo dragging even more than before. The fire in the furnace lagged, too, as Tim moved through the window toward her.

Closer . . . closer while she reached for him.

"Tiiiiimothy!!!"

I hauled in a breath at the screech that'd come from the furnace. Tim had frozen in the window, too.

"Tiiiiimothy!!!" it said again.

He had started to shrink back from the window as it began closing and closing over Heidi's wanton image, shrinking to nothing in the wall. As the room darkened, he was deflated all the way back to his own size.

The furnace cast ponderous, undulating flames onto the bricks.

"You shouldn't be here," Tim said to the screecher, his head down, his hands fisted at his sides.

"Just like your dad," the furnace said, punctuating

each phrase with fire. *"Just like him . . . just like him . . . just like him."*

The pile of toys started nodding, agreeing with the screech. Around us, holes opened up in the walls, joining in the chorus like mouths.

"Just like him . . . just like him . . ."

But the voice had become more familiar. Was it Nichelle now?

Tim covered his ears, sinking to the ground.

As the mouths expanded, teeth glistened in the firelight, yellowed and pointed.

"What're you doing back there . . . ?"

The window resurrected itself on the upper wall, but it was a true television screen this time, black-and-white, square and quaint. Static filled it until Tim raised his head and uncovered his ears.

As he turned to look at it, the screen cleared to show a field with a clump of trees ahead.

The woods, I thought. *Please, not the woods. . . .*

I had seen a few modern horror movies where first-person cameras caught all the action, and this was just like one of them now. Someone was holding a camera and slow-running toward the trees on that screen, where a woman's scream ripped through the air. The unknown cameraman's breath huffed in continual bursts the entire time, competing with the screaming.

Tim merely sat in front of that TV, drawing his legs up and against him like a boy watching a weekend-night movie. The room tilted back, forth. . . .

Just before the camera entered the woods, the lens

slanted down to show that holes were opening in the ground.

And they were yelling.

"What're you doing?"

"Just like your father!"

Somehow, the cameraman wasn't falling into the holes. He kept slowly running, panting with long breaths.

More screaming from the trees. And . . . begging?

The nausea from the drunken tilts had gotten to me bad enough, and now this? I gagged once, trying to be quiet. Trying not to interrupt or catch Tim's attention.

The cameraman changed direction, slothfully chasing down the screams until—

Suddenly, a mouth appeared on the TV, consuming the screen, gaping in a terrible scream that went on and on and on.

Then it was begging, pleading. *"No, please, no . . ."*

It took all I had to listen to it—I was afraid I'd sounded just like that in my own last moments, but I couldn't look away because the cameraman had started to swing the camera at the mouth, using the lens to beat the mouth into submission until the screams became gasps . . . until the gasps became whimpers.

Then he dropped the camera, and it lay on its side on the ground, his eternal breathing filling the room.

Don't breathe, I thought. *Don't move.*

Would Tim turn around and see me now that the show was over?

I held a dream-hand over my mouth, shutting myself up, just as I'd done on the night I'd been killed.

Don't breathe. He might hear you. . . .

But Tim still didn't know I was here as, around us, the walls lightened from black to gray, paling shade by shade until they became a stark white.

The TV disappeared along with the furnace and toys.

Along with everything.

We were left together in a white room, where Tim's back was still turned to me. His sweats had lightened to white, too, the only colors being his blond hair and his flesh.

He breathed in . . . out . . . Torturously. Harrowingly.

Instinct was telling me to leave, but something else kept me kneeling there, waiting. Because he couldn't hurt me in a dream. At least I hadn't been hurt doing this before.

Besides, Tim hadn't hurt anyone in here or out in the world as far as we knew.

When his breath began to quicken, I backed away on hands and knees, my body hitting a wall. The illusion of having no way out made me panic, and I reached behind me, feeling for a door.

All my movement finally caught Tim's attention.

When he rounded on me, it was in fast-forward speed, his eyes bulging, his jaw unhinging and lengthening so that it hit the floor.

He roared at me like a mad thing.

I held up a hand to shield myself from the sight, like that'd help me, but I didn't leave. Not yet.

As he kept roaring, the sound took on a warped, wounded tone, and he began tearing at the air. Even if there was nothing there, blood splattered on the white walls, spraying them with red.

I started screaming as he kept ripping that invisible whatever-it-was apart, blood flying until it was on me, too.

He dropped to the floor, rolling in the crimson, his eyes crazed as he laughed and laughed and bathed himself.

I don't know where my next idea came from—maybe *The Exorcist*?—but I began yelling at him with authority.

"You don't want to hurt anyone, Tim. You're not *going* to hurt anyone. Do you understand me? Stop this—now!"

I didn't know if implanting ideas about nonviolence in his head would do any good, but it made him stop, look at me with curiosity.

"That's right," I said, softer now. "You're calmer now. You're going to be okay. Just . . . calm down."

He kept staring, his jaw on the ground, almost animal-like in his stillness. He stared long enough so that I started preparing to jump out of the dream.

But before that happened, his mouth unhinged even more, his teeth lengthening, spearing out of his mouth.

Long.

Grotesque.

The points headed right for me.

Instead of screaming, I gave a ferocious yell, dodging the blades, crashing to the floor and closing my eyes and willing myself to—

With a banging *pow*, I shot out of that white room,

bursting out of Tim so forcefully that I flew through his family room toward the wall.

Just before I could hit it, I flexed backward, stopping my motion, then falling to just above the floor, where I paused.

As I recovered, my energy felt way lower but not entirely gone. I was learning to monitor myself so that I'd never be in a time-loop situation again, and when Tim jerked awake on the couch with a strangled yell, I float-crawled over to him.

I wanted to empathize now, to see what he was thinking. I had enough juice in me for that . . .

"Baby?"

Nichelle ran out of the hallway, dressed in a long T-shirt that came to her skinny thighs. "What's wrong, baby?"

As she swept him into a cradling hug, Tim opened his eyes wide and—

Oh, God, it was the same gaze I'd seen in that dream, when he'd been rolling in the blood. Crazed.

I jetted at him, stopping just in time to touch his face with a forceful hand. But it wasn't because I intended to empathize.

I made deep contact, entering him again, and since he was awake, I brought up a hallucination, thinking of the fish tank, seeing it through our eyes, making him experience it along with me. . . .

Bobbing in the blue, peace washing through us as we float. There, there, floating, no troubles.

Just water and waves and beauty . . .

I stayed in him awhile, until I was sure the serenity had won him over. And when I eased out of him, he was rag-dolled on the couch, in Nichelle's arms, breathing deeply as the fish tank behind them burbled. She was shivering at the sudden cold.

Dammit. Well, that had gone spectacularly. I was pretty sure I'd exacerbated Tim's emotions when he'd seen me in his dream, escalating all his inner demons. Since I was out now, I trusted the hallucination to keep him relaxed.

But who knew how long that would last?

"It was just a bad dream," Nichelle whispered in his ear while stroking his hair. "Just a bad dream, baby."

Didn't I wish.

8

"So what the hell are we going to do?" I asked Amanda Lee in my casita as I braced myself on the car battery, recharging. "If what I saw tonight in that guy's psyche isn't a raging warning of bad things to come, I don't know what is."

As she merely shook her head, my fellow ghosts who'd gathered here for company seemed just as torn. Louis had one hand in his factory uniform pocket while the other spanned his temples, rubbing. Sailor Randy was faintly bobbing in place. Even Twyla had her hands planted on her petticoat-covered hips.

I'd stayed with Tim and Nichelle through the rest of the night, just to make sure he behaved. She'd taken him to bed and he'd ended up sleeping like a baby, belly-down on the mattress, Nichelle's hand resting on his back. Peace in the House of Blood. This morning, Tim had left early with some softball gear, and I'd followed him to a field, where I presumed he'd be away from Nichelle for a few hours while playing a game with some coworkers, so things were okay. For now.

Finally, Twyla came up with an answer to the Tim problem.

"Let's just, like, kill him."

Everyone but Amanda Lee, who had the fortune of not being able to hear Twyla's ghost voice very well, gawked at her.

Louis said, "We can't kill this man."

Amanda Lee could hear *him*. "Do you have the power to kill directly?"

"Not that I'm aware of, but even so, there's got to be another way," Louis said.

I nodded. "We can protect Nichelle, maybe go into her subconscious and talk to her so she decides to leave Tim before his temper gets really bad . . ."

"Why would Nichelle do that if her friend Heidi can't even sway her?"

"Because we'd go deeper into her head than Heidi can?" I sighed. "Nichelle just has a way of lighting Tim's fire awfully close to his fuse. Maybe she's, literally, Tim's most perfect match. There's no fighting that kind of chemistry with two people, even if it's destructive. There're times when even *smart* people don't listen to what's good for them."

Twyla had been pretending to stick her finger down her throat, telling me what she thought of the idea to persuade Nichelle to leave. When she was done, she said, "What about Tim's next girlfriend? And then, like, the next? Protecting everyone from him isn't going to happen."

The whole time, Louis was conveying the discussion to Amanda Lee, who had her eyes closed. And it wasn't from physical exhaustion. This case was already consuming her.

"Listen," Twyla said, casually going over to an electrical outlet and making her hand into a slim prong that fit into it. As she negligently stuck it in and charged up, her form flashed with dark Goth and light Lauper. The bulbs around us flickered. "I've been a ghostie way longer than Miss Know-It-All Cowabunga Jensen here. So, okay, I party a little. But I also like to spend time watching all the people, you know? I've, like, come to the conclusion that there's some really shitty humans who're still alive while I'm dead. Randomly, grodily *dead*. Slain-by-a-hair-dryer dead. And this killer-in-the-making gets to live while I died early? Whatever."

Louis stopped translating to Amanda Lee. Gently, he said, "Twyla, you don't get to play judge and jury. It's not the place for any of us."

I wanted to ask if he'd wished that there'd been ghost judges and juries while he'd been alive about seventy years ago, having to exist under a system that had valued his life less than others just because of the way he'd been born.

Twyla said, "You know what *is* awesome about being dead? Not having parental units around to boss me."

She stuck her tongue out at Louis and he made a very clear effort not to roll *his* eyes.

I didn't have the strength to care about ghost bickering. Tim's dream had really shaken me. There's nothing like seeing someone rolling in blood to convince you there's something wrong with them. Then there was my own history with violence, which only added to the creep factor.

"We need to do *something*," I said. "Just leaving this alone won't work. If something happens to Nichelle, there'll be blood on *our* hands."

Twyla continued charging up in her corner. "I totally think he'd be better off dead. That's all."

Randy finally interjected. "Y'all've heard that thing 'bout Hitler, right?"

At first, we just looked at him like he should've just said no to drugs. But such an off-base remark could've been the eternal booze in him.

He continued, "It's that ol' chestnut: If ya could go back in time, before Hitler's in power, would ya kill 'im?"

Louis said, "It's a valid question. Would you commit murder to save the eleven million lives that were taken during the Holocaust?"

The Brain speaks. Louis had been a college-educated man who'd worked at a bayside aircraft plant during World War II after they'd exhausted the pool of white workers here. But as a ghost, he'd spent nearly a half century reading over peoples' shoulders in the library.

"Yeah," Randy said. "What Louis said."

Louis continued. "I realize we're not talking about those kinds of numbers with Tim, but there's bad in the boy for certain. We just don't have the benefit of hindsight with him."

"I saw a possible future," I said.

"A possible one." Louis scrubbed a hand over his dark hair, then down over his face.

Amanda Lee watched his moral dilemma with understanding. "When I told my PI friend Ruben about Tim, he agreed that we're dealing with an antisocial person, even before we knew about what is in Tim's subconscious." She exhaled. "Although I'm being cautious because of what happened when I presumed Gavin Edgett guilty, all my instincts are telling me that it's only a matter of time before Tim becomes trouble."

"So," Twyla said, "the easiest way is to kill him . . . indirectly."

Randy flew to her side. "What'f he jus' happened to see 'n image of a woman in a bathin' suit, 'n' she was *jus'* off the edge of a cliff. He sees her, makes a run for her, off the cliff he goes 'n'—"

"Bye-bye, psycho!" Twyla said.

I think she was about to high-five Randy like Lauper would've done with Captain Lou Albano, but Louis' voice put a stop to it.

"There's no glee in this."

Amanda Lee was looking in the direction of his voice. "I vote that we think about everything more before we make any kind of move. In the meantime, if we have any volunteers, we need to ghost watch in a few different places."

I took it up from here. "Right. Scott's at Wendy's right now, so—"

Louis raised a hand. "I'll keep an eye on Tim."

Thank goodness a moron like Twyla hadn't volunteered for that. She looked glum that Louis had spoken first, though.

"Gawd," she said. "What does that leave me with?"

"Amanda Lee could still use someone to fend off the lookiloos and keep an eye out for that dark spirit if it decides to come visit her." I'd almost forgotten about *that* issue because of all the crapola that'd been hitting us.

"Boooring," she muttered.

"Thank you for your willingness, Twyla," I said to spare Amanda Lee's feelings. But from the way the older woman was smiling wryly, I'd bet she knew Twyla wasn't exactly hot to trot for this task.

"Randy," I said. "Could you keep watch on Flaherty's Pub downtown? It seems Gavin Edgett has been taking little trips there to talk with my friend Suze about me."

"Pub? Well, sure."

As Randy was nodding with enthusiasm about his task, Amanda Lee said to me, "You never did get to tell us if there was anything Suze knew about your missing bracelets."

"I read her thoughts, and she revealed that she saw Brittany Kirkman Stokley wearing them."

"I wrote down her address, as well as Lisa Levine's, from Ruben's notes, just in case you would like to pay a visit."

"The psychic strikes again," I said.

Twyla was back on the Suze part. "So Gavin Edgett's been tiptoeing off to this bar, huh? Trying to get Jensen's old best friend to spill info about her. How kink."

"What does that even mean?" I asked. *"Kink."*

"He totally has, like, an obsession for you. That's kink. I bet the attention feels rad."

Ignore.

I addressed Randy. "Can you listen in on any conversations he and Suze might have, if he shows up there again?"

"Yes, indeedy."

"But, Randy," Twyla added, "you must remember that Jen-Jen doesn't want her boyfriend to get too close to any other girls, even her old bud. *She* wants him."

"Bag it, Twyla."

"Bag *you*."

She'd hit a mark in me, and I didn't want her to hit another one. I kept telling myself that I didn't need Suze involved with any of this. Even though Gavin was innocent of Elizabeth Dalton's killing—he'd been her fiancé and we'd thought he'd murdered her in a jealous rage—he'd still killed his father when he'd found out that the old man had been abusing Farah years ago and was about to start with his adopted, oblivious daughter Wendy.

Was I feeling protective of Suze just because I didn't want her with someone capable of that? Or *was* there more?

Twyla unplugged herself from the socket. "I'm going to invite Cassie to hang around during my slog here." She sneered at Amanda Lee. "That way I won't go bonkers in Boresville."

"You do that," I said. Cassie was a seventies housewife, a maternal influence on Twyla. I couldn't argue with the arrangement.

Louis had finished translating for Amanda Lee, and he looked at everyone. "I suppose when it rains, it pours."

Randy bounced around. "I like the activity."

I realized that I sort of did, too. The more I had to do, the more . . . well, alive I felt. The extra electricity running through me these days wasn't exactly like being human, but it was close enough.

Louis had something else to say as he fixed his attention on me. "Are you going to tell us the details of Tim's dream? You weren't too specific."

Oh, how Louis loved this part. He was a regular Freud. So, as the ghosts gathered around me like kids at story time, I launched into the dream details for everyone's consumption: the basement, the furnace, the sunbather on the TV who'd changed into Heidi, and the voices coming from the walls. How the TV had turned into a horror movie in the woods and then the white room with the bloodbath . . .

I shivered, my essence crackling. "Tim's dream wasn't as creative as Gavin's were, but it was vivid enough."

Amanda Lee said, "Gavin is a video game designer, so that only makes sense. Instead of having fantasy landscapes, our workingman, Tim, has a basement."

"The most basic representation of the subconscious," Louis said. "Very primal."

"Thanks, Sigmund," said Twyla. "What about those toys Jen-Jen saw?"

"Sometimes the subconscious stores the things we've put away," Louis said.

Amanda Lee was frowning. "Something Ruben told

me yesterday reminds me . . . He said that a great deal of violent, deviant behavior is rooted in an abusive childhood—physical, verbal, or emotional. The broken toys make me think . . ."

"That Tim's mom literally stuck him in a basement sometimes?" I asked. "God. I mean, the mom's voice was coming from the walls, and she was saying demeaning things to Tim down there. What if that's where she took him when he was being punished, and all he could do was play with toys, look out the window, or watch TV?"

"Maybe that's too literal," Amanda Lee said.

"Maybe," Louis said, "we're dealing with a fairly literal man."

Randy got in there. "Broke toys. Is that—?"

"Duh," Twyla said. "It totally means a bad childhood. The toys were in a leaning pile that's about to fall over, so double duh. He had an unstable time as a kid."

Not bad, I thought.

"Duh yourself," Randy said, floating toward the computer, which had been on the whole time. He manipulated it, surfing the Web as the screen went a bit snowy. "I can guess jus' what that furnace means."

"It's a seething monster of doom," Twyla said, getting cocky. She joined him at the computer.

"No." Randy peered through the screen interference. "This Web shite says a furnace is *power 'n' energy. Duh.*"

I couldn't take it anymore. "Ix-nay the duhs!"

Randy and Twyla both smiled cheekily at me, shrugged at each other, then started whispering about what they were finding on the site.

I got back on track, turning to Louis and Amanda Lee. "I think it's pretty obvious what was going on with Nichelle's voice taking over for his mom's."

"From one dominant woman to another," Amanda Lee said. "He feels as if he's still in that basement, but it's with Nichelle. She's the one who puts him there now, mentally and emotionally."

"But he stays in a relationship with Nichelle," Louis said. "Why would he do that?"

"Because he has a need to control her," I said, "and he's going to try until he finally gets it right. It's a catch-22 for him. A vicious cycle."

"Why does *she* stay with him?" Louis asked again.

"I think, even though she doesn't have much self-esteem, she might like to wear the pants," I said. "She seems pretty dominant in a passive-aggressive way."

Amanda Lee spoke. "It would seem so. As far as Tim goes, though, he's not able to succeed in what he needs, so he's frustrated and angry. That's what you saw when the walls turned white and he was ripping apart that invisible something in his hands, spattering everything with blood."

"Bad tidings," I said.

"Oh-my-*ga*-od!" Twyla, back at the computer. "Farting is in the dream dictionary!"

Randy was laughing as he said, "It means yer passive-aggressive and need to 'xpress yourself 'n a more direct manner! I don't know what *passive-aggressive* means, but thass funny."

Ghost ADD. I'm telling you.

"For real, you guys," I said. "Focus."

"Take a chill pill, we were just looking up *faucet*," Twyla said. "And, lookee here—it symbolizes, like, emotions. And a dripping faucet is . . . Oooo, check it out—sexual problems!"

"Sounds 'bout right to me," Randy said. "Didn't ya say Tim's—"

"Faucet was dripping?" Twyla finished.

"Yeah, I did," I said as they went back to giggling over things like *feces*.

Louis steered us right again. "How about that white room Tim was in?"

"It symbolizes isolation?" Amanda Lee said. "And the blood on the walls . . . I think that's just a pretty clear warning in general."

"Or," Louis said, "again it could be something very literal with Tim. There will be bloodshed."

"Shit," I said. Where were the unicorns and puppy dogs I'd wanted? "And we haven't even gotten to the middle part of the dream. One of the worst things was when he was watching his neighbor through the window. I remember he ate breath mints, just like he did yesterday in the backyard. Actually, there were a lot of callbacks to what happened yesterday as I watched him, like when Nichelle saw him looking through the fence and said, 'What're you doing back there?'"

"What bothers me, too," Amanda Lee said, "was that Dream Neighbor turned into Heidi."

I hesitated, not wanting to say it. But I did.

"This was almost like a fantasy mixed with a dream, you know?"

"His desires could very well be on display for us," Amanda Lee said. "But do you think he's truly attracted to Heidi? Or is she a symbol, as well?"

Louis stuffed his hands into his pockets again. "Either way, it seems to me that he has a real yen for brunettes. Mis— Jensen, you said that, during your empathy reading, his thoughts showed you that he was watching a neighbor down the street, too."

"Another brunette," I said. "And what was interesting was that, when this Dream Heidi was inviting him to come to her during the, uh . . ."

"The part of the dream in which the neighbor was masturbating," Amanda Lee said matter-of-factly.

"Yeah." Wasn't she just a regular Dr. Ruth with the sex talk? "During that portion, Tim started growing taller."

Twyla laughed over at the computer. "You know what that reminds me of?"

"Don't even say *boner*," I told her.

"Naw!" She glanced at me like I was a freak. "I'm talking about *Alice in Wonderland*."

I believe she shocked us all by being more than relevant twice in one day.

Louis was nerding out more than usual now, his words fast and passionate. "Twyla's right. The breath mint's like one of those pills Alice took to grow taller or shorter."

Amanda Lee had understood the *Wonderland* subtext even without Louis' help. "The imagery's interesting, but I think this has more to do with Tim perhaps having some issues with being a small man. He wishes he were bigger. He might even have an easier time impressing the ladies if he were."

"Here's another angle," I said. "What if he's a real Disney fan and the imagery is coming from that? Remember the collection in their family room—the chopsticks and figurines and all that? I know this sounds weird, but what if they're not just Nichelle's, or even hers at all? What if Tim's got fairy tales on the brain?"

Amanda Lee said, "Even if he's merely aware of the collection, the images could have made their way into his head."

Twyla performed a very unsubtle fake yawn. But she still looked proud that she'd contributed beyond the fart trivia.

Louis was running on all cylinders. "How about the part in the woods?"

Amanda Lee gave me a glance, like she was checking up on my state of being. Forests were such a touchy subject around me.

"Again," she said carefully, "the woods could represent Tim's subconscious." She turned to me. "Did you get the feeling he was lost there?"

"Not really. He was chasing that scream. And the woman sounded like she was in pain. And she was begging."

"Because if he *were* lost, that might indicate he's trying to find a new direction in his life. Also, it's interesting that he was watching all this on a television, distant from the action."

I said, "He likes to watch, doesn't he?"

"If you ask me," Louis said, "we're *certainly* seeing some fantasies here, just like you all said. Before falling asleep, he'd been watching TV with all that . . ." He searched for a word.

"Porn," Amanda Lee provided.

"Thank you. Yes." Louis nodded. "With the pornography on it. So that made its way into his dream, too."

I said, "So chasing the scream through the woods? Is that a form of porn?" Hell, I'd seen some of the gnarly scary movies they put out these days. Total horror porn.

Amanda Lee rested a hand near her throat. "That's rather dark, Jensen."

"But a possibility? He's watching very bad things, and he feels guilty about it. That's why his mother's voice was scolding him. Could it be that he doesn't want to displease her with these fantasies?"

"And, at the same time, displease Nichelle?" Amanda Lee asked. "There's the approval we were talking about. He needs those dominant women in his life to give their blessing, but he knows he won't get it, and it's making him very angry at them."

A thought blasted me. "Whoa."

Everyone waited.

"Amanda Lee, did you see on the computer if his mom's still alive?"

"There are a few pictures on Facebook and he mentions her in the present tense a few times. Why?"

"I wondered if he'd . . . you know. Killed her."

While everyone stared, Twyla snorted. "How Norman Bates."

Okay, so it'd been far-fetched. "I wish we could just get him to go to a good shrink."

But I didn't think that was our answer. I didn't know when Tim had started up with these fantasy dreams, but I had the feeling it was back when he was a boy playing with toys. That's a long time for someone to be thinking in these terms, and I'm sure the imagery and anger had been building and building year after year.

So when was the right time for us to slay monsters like the one I'd seen in him tonight, even if he was only a monster down deep?

Louis started flowing to the computer to see what Randy and Twyla were chuckling about now, but as soon as he got near, Twyla started bitching at him because the screen was extra fuzzy with all the ghosts around.

"Guys," I said. "How about giving the computer up to Louis for a while so he can go further with his theories?"

But Amanda Lee came to the rescue. She stood and went to some bookshelves, pulling down a tome and setting it on a table. "Louis, I brought my dream interpretation book over here, since this is where we're doing most of our work, anyway. I can turn the pages as you like."

"Thank you, Mi— Amanda Lee."

"You're very welcome."

They sat down to work, and it was pretty odd to be

in between the kook squad on my right, with their appreciation of the symbolic uses of *burp*, and Team Serious on my left, who was diligently studying in silence.

I moved away from my battery, suddenly feeling useless. I'd been going since yesterday morning, and it'd probably be a good idea to just float now, taking everything in, letting all this information gel.

But the stimulation only made me realize that sitting around really sucked. I wished ghosts could shut down and go to sleep so that awful boredom would never creep in.

Maybe I shouldn't have put my desires out into the world like that, because it was as if the world certainly heard it by sending a sharp rap on the door.

"Gawd!" Twyla said. "If those are lookiloo ghosts, I'm gonna, like, throttle them."

For once, I'd take Twyla up on that.

I flew to the door. "Who is it?"

"Cassie!"

Twyla's good ghost friend. She knew she could slip under the door to enter, but all my Boo World buds respected Amanda Lee, and I guessed me, too much to just zip through a crack between the door and floor. Even Cassie, who hadn't been around all that much.

Once identified, though, she came whizzing through, gathering into full form on our side, light ponytail, seventies paisley-patterned blouse and flare-bottom polyester pants, pale-tinted lipstick and all.

"Jen, you need to come. I tried to yell for you, but you weren't close enough to hear."

Yeah, ghosts could yell for help, too. "What's wrong?"

Already my essence was going, *"Humanah, humanah."*

"It's your friend Wendy," Cassie said, looking around me to the other ghosts, her mascara-framed eyes wide. "Scott's there right now, fending off that dark spirit you've been watching for. Let's *go.*"

After Amanda Lee ran over to open the door, we were off like a hail of invisible shots.

9

We simultaneously busted out of our travel tunnels at Wendy's courtyard.

Me, Randy, Cassie, and . . . Twyla.

When I saw that last one, I didn't have time to ream her out. She was supposed to be with Amanda Lee, and it looked like Louis had stayed instead. But who had time to fuss about that when Scott was tangling with something that looked like a dark stain against the morning-bright sky?

Scott was a whirring tumble of fading flannel and denim as he fended off the spirit, rolling around the air with it, crashing into the condo and not even leaving a mark as they spun away.

I was the first one to zoom toward the dark thing, but instead of cutting through it like it'd done to me when it'd attacked at the séance, something else happened.

It broke into two blobs of anonymous blackness, floating above me and Scott, then spreading its essences out, almost like both creatures had ragged, terrifying wings.

When Twyla, Cassie, and Randy blasted by me, rushing the two shapes, another insane thing happened: The two split up and gushed into three more blobs.

Five against five now.

Twyla and company skidded to a stop, and all of us ghosts just hovered next to one another. Shit. None of us had ever met anything like this before. How many times would this spirit multiply?

Cassie whispered, "It's legion."

"No, it's not," Twyla said. "It's just trying to scare us."

"*We* can't do things like that."

"That's because we weren't, like, pulled from a portal."

Quickly, I scanned Scott, whose form was slowly going paler, bled of energy from the fight.

"You could use more energy," I said out of the corner of my essence as we continued staring down the five. "You need to charge, you know?"

He got a cocky teenage grin on his mouth. "Good idea."

And charge he did, straight at one of the blobs.

It was ready for him, its form fanning out like it was welcoming the assault with open arms . . . or wings . . . or—

It didn't matter what they were, because when tentaclelike arms shot out of it, I yelled, "Scott!"

He veered to the side just in time to avoid the blob's tentacle sharpening like a sword.

From above the thing, Scott zapped out both of *his* arms, making them into sword shapes, too.

Seriously? I guessed if we could form fists to rap against walls, we could do this?

Next to me, the other ghosts did the same, and I followed, just like it was the most natural act.

Zing!

We dived toward the other four shapes, sharpened arms extended. They met us, and I could only focus on my blob, slashing down at it over and over while it avoided every move. Damn, it was good.

But something became obvious: When this thing had attacked me at Amanda Lee's fake séance, it'd stabbed me. It'd been strong. It wasn't so much now, though, after separating into pieces. . . .

As I struck at it again, the blob parried, sparks spitting through the air as I brought up my other arm to slice through it and fend it off. It blocked that attack, too, and the force of this knock sent me spinning away.

But not for long. I flipped around, extending two more sharpened limbs, swirling as I went in again. I was hurricaning out of pure panic.

Yet my hyperactivity was working, because the thing wasn't ready for me, and it weaved out of my reach, twisting upward, trying to get away. As it put some distance between us, I realized that it was trying to lure us away from Wendy's window.

I didn't move from my position, and I could only watch the other ghosts engaged with their own blobs: Twyla was a screaming bunch of sparks as she drove back her guy. Scott was flying through the trees outside of the courtyard wall, giving chase. Randy was tumbling here and there, sloppily but effectively giving his blob fits.

But then there was Cassie, who was down near the fountain, repelling her attacker. When my blob saw an opportunity and bombed downward, exploding into and merging with its other part, its newer, bigger form darkened, growing like a splatter of waving ink.

God, it was stronger now, enough to press its advantage on Cassie, driving her against the marble, spreading her out until she was thinned like a pancake.

The blob perched over her, a tentacle in the air, poised to strike.

Instinct pushed at me to leave Wendy's window, but I'd be playing into this thing's hands. I was her last guard, so all I could do was yell at Cassie to fight harder as the blob speared her with its limb.

I felt what she must've felt, because I'd gone through it before—a stabbing sensation, a bleeding and tearing feeling. But now, when the blob pulled out its limb, I saw a speck of fading essence in its grip.

Part of Cassie?

As the thing plunged her essence into itself, she misted toward the ground, leaching to a dull pale.

Awfully close to a time loop.

Numb, I could only stare at her lying prone, so helpless. *Get to the fuse box,* I thought, like she could hear me or something. But she was just a mass of ghost, and she wouldn't have the strength to harden her form so she could project a limb the ten feet it would take for her to reach the box.

Above her, the blob rotated, fixing its attention on me again, twice as strong as before. There were facial features somewhere in there, but I couldn't make them out.

Almost like the darkest mask imaginable.

I stood my ground, ready, wanting it to come here because it'd gotten to one of my friends. Because it was one of the bad guys, and I was getting sick of them.

Just as it was flexing, preparing to take off toward me, I heard the window behind me crash open, then a familiar voice.

"Stop!"

Wendy?

I whipped around, ready to tell the kid with the pink stripe in her hair to get her ass back inside because she was exposed out here. But then I realized she was holding one of those computer pads in her hands.

Her voice wavered as she read from it.

"Saint Michael the Archangel, defend us in battle! Be our protection against the wickedness and snares of the devil. May God rebuke him, we humbly pray; and do Thou, O Prince of the Heavenly Host—by the Divine Power of God—cast into hell, Satan and all the evil spirits, who roam throughout the world seeking the ruin of souls!"

Whoa.

All of the fighting stopped as the four remaining blobs froze, zeroing in on Wendy.

"Get back inside!" I said, hardening my hand into a fist. I wasn't going to punch her away from the window, but I'd do whatever I could to put a barrier between her and the blobs.

She ignored me, repeating the prayer.

And . . . whoa again. The blobs began to violently shake, almost as if their sort-of heads were about to fall off.

"Amen!" ended Wendy.

All four blobs let out a howl so high-pitched that I vibrated, too.

Twyla, Randy, and Scott began to shrivel into themselves, and I could also feel an inner pull, like the sounds those things were making could shatter glass. Shatter *us*.

But Wendy had started the prayer yet again, louder and more commandingly, and just as a porch light sprayed into pieces down in the courtyard, the dark howls turned to whimpers.

As if compelled, the blobs magnetized toward one another, tendrils of their blackness seeming to claw the air as they were pulled back home.

Wendy's voice grew in volume, and the creatures let out one last howl, then smashed together, becoming a single, darker thing again. Right away, it darted in a trail of pitch tendrils off into the morning, leaving the rustle of tree leaves, singeing the closest ones.

Me and Randy hustled over to them, blowing, putting out any little flames. Meanwhile, Twyla and Scott dashed to Cassie at the fountain.

Wendy leaned out the window and saw our pale friend's sad state as she fizzled on the ground, unable to function, her ponytail curled limply above the ground, her lips even whiter than the lipstick normally made them. She stared at the sky, getting worse every minute.

"I've got this!" Wendy shouted, then pulled shut the window. I saw her running out of her room and, within a minute, she was in the courtyard with her computer pad, setting it in the middle of Cassie's form.

The battery. It would charge her up.

"We need more," I said, floating by a kneeling Wendy, fluttering her dark hair where it slid over her shoulder. "That battery's a good start, but it won't be enough. I should know. I've almost regressed back to a time loop myself before."

As Randy hovered above us, watching for the return of the dark spirit, Wendy ran back into the condo and came out with more battery-operated devices: one of those iPods, two flashlights, and a laptop computer.

"Will this give Cassie enough juice to get to the fuse box and get a real charge?" I asked.

None of us could drag her over there since our "hands" would slide right through her. She was all ghost jelly.

Scott said, "She'll be stronger in a sec." He didn't seem too worried while he gave Wendy the appreciative eye.

I held up my finger to him, telling him to take a red. He shrugged. Clearly, Scott had been feeling his oats during the fight. Even if he didn't have testosterone anymore, he sure acted like it, slicking a hand back over his hair.

Twyla was by Cassie's side, fretting. "Come on, Mama Cass. Absorb everything you can. You can do it. Then you'll get to the box and have a good dose of juice."

Cassie tried to mumble something, but Twyla shushed her. Above us, Randy watched, his usual grin straightened out as he continued to guard.

I tried to make lemons into lemonade. "That thing won't be back for at least a while."

Randy spoke to Wendy. "Thass some prayer, lil' sister."

She was such a sensitive that she could see all of us ghosts. Her skill had taken a little time to develop, but once she'd gotten the hang of it, she'd really gotten the hang.

"I used a prayer to St. Michael," she said, still watching Cassie.

"How did you know you should use it?" I asked.

She deigned to give me a dismissive glance, then turned back to Cassie.

Ah. Still pissed at me. Got it.

I addressed the group. "That dark spirit reached into Cassie and took a handful of something out of her. I don't know how that's even possible, because when we try to touch each other, all we get is electric air."

Twyla didn't take her gaze off Cassie. "Obviously, Jen's never hardened herself when another ghost hardened *itself*."

I looked confused, so Randy came over to me, gesturing to my hand. He hardened his essence, so I did, too, and when he touched me, there was actual contact.

But there was also nothing. No feeling. No nerve endings that made touching nice.

He shrugged with one shoulder. "Now ya know why we don't bother huggin'. Waste of energy, if ya ask me."

A random thought bolted through me as I recalled seeing the spirit reach into Cassie and steal her essence. It hadn't done the same to me when it'd attacked at the séance. Why?

Scott was standing by as Cassie improved to a light gray tone with all the battery help. "That dark spirit doesn't play by our rules, anyway. That's why the prayer fazed him and not us."

Randy nodded. "Our souls ain't stained like that one's."

Stained? I peered at Cassie. Interesting, because she'd died after slitting her wrists. To some people, that was a stain on the soul. I mean, I hadn't been a big churchgoer, but it looked like suicides actually weren't a way into hell for us. Then again, maybe you had to believe that you were going to hell for that to happen. Hard to say when none of us were really sure if there was a hell or purgatory, so what did I know? This plane might even be Cassie's limbo. Or all of ours.

All I was certain about was that Amanda Lee had pulled that dark spirit out of a portal from a place that none of us had ever visited, and it could obviously do things we couldn't . . . or shouldn't.

Wendy's short black skirt spread around her as she sat all the way on the ground. "I can't wait until the neighbors call to complain about the loser teen who yells out prayers from her window. Do you think anyone noticed?"

I was pretty sure she wasn't chatting with me, so I let Randy answer. He hadn't been at her old mansion on the night Twyla and Scott had helped me haunt

Farah into a confession, so she had nothing against him.

"Well," he said, still bobbing above us all, "it seems to me that it's 'bout as quiet as 'n ant pissin' on cotton round here. All the windows are shut, so maybe no one noticed?"

"Thank you, Randy," I said. "That was very colorful."

Scott said, "Maybe they caught on to the shattered glass and the sudden breeze in the trees, though."

We'd see.

It seemed like Wendy was working into saying something else, and she finally came out with it. "I think you guys have been keeping that spirit away until now. I have no idea what it wants from me or Gavin since it was released at the séance, but thanks for being here." She toyed with a loose string on her long-sleeved black shirt. "It's about time I said that."

Another whoa. Even Cassie smiled as her ghost tone improved. She had a way of looking at Wendy that reminded me that Cassie had had children before she'd died, and she'd lived her afterlife regretting the pain she'd put them through with her suicide. She visited them often, even though they were adults now. They were her tether to the earth, and I wondered if she would go into the glare when they were gone.

As we all said a "You're welcome" to Wendy, Cassie's answer came a bit later than the rest.

"Anytime," she said weakly.

"That's a girl," Twyla said. "You just keep soaking all that juice up."

Wendy was smiling down at Cassie. "I'm sorry I took so long with that prayer. I had to go through my files and find the right one. I've been studying. You remember Eileen Perez, the cleaner who chased Jensen Murphy out of my old house?"

So Wendy was using my full name and talking about me like I wasn't around? Maybe she'd start sounding like my mom whenever I would get into trouble and call me "Jensen Mary Murphy! You get over here!" from now on.

The ghosts were all nodding that, yes, they remembered Eileen the cleaner.

"Well," Wendy said, "we've been in touch, and I've been very curious about what she does. She's in a paranormal society, and I think I want to join . . . Probably after I get out of the house more."

Scott hooked his thumbs in the back pockets of his jeans as he said, "As soon as we get done with all this stuff on the front burner, let us know when you're ready to get out. We can guard you from the news people or whoever else bugs you. There're things we can do to fool with them so they won't come around to bother you."

Randy interjected. "Yeah. We can pull hair, scratch, 'n' there're bad smells we can conj-yur . . ."

"Conjure," we all said.

"Conj-yur up to chase 'em off."

"Thanks," Wendy said, smiling tentatively at everyone, tucking a strand of straight hair behind her ear.

I cleared my throat. "About the cleaner—"

Twyla interrupted. "Yeah, Little China Girl. You aren't,

like, using just salt to try and keep that dark spirit out, are you?"

"I've used salt, but—"

"You. Need. More." Twyla shook a finger at her. "Salt doesn't work that great on ghosts unless they're new and stupid, like Jensen used to be. They say salt's, like, really good for demons, but I don't know if that's what our dark dill weed is. Smudging's a good backup, and incantations work only with the ghost you're directing them at. Just so you know."

"I already smudged the condo." You could tell Wendy was taking copious mental notes.

Cassie groaned as she tried to rise, and she made it to a sitting position. As she crawl-floated to the fuse box, Twyla and Randy went with her. I gave Scott a "please join them so I can have some privacy" glance and, with some reluctance, he did.

"A cleaner, huh?" I asked Wendy when we were alone. "Is that your goal in life now?"

She started gathering the battery-operated devices. "Are you talking to me?"

When she headed inside, I went there, too, but the smudging and incantations stopped me cold at the threshold of the French windows.

Fine, then. I levitated to the upper window, which she'd left cracked open ever so slightly in her haste to shut them. Before she could close them on me all the way, I caught the scent of sage.

She saw me floating there expectantly and groaned. "You're not going to let this drop for today? I've already had a lot of excitement."

I ignored the barricading smell. "We've got some issues to work out."

"Okay. Is one of them that I'm studying to be a cleaner? Call TMZ then. I think it's kind of noble to help ghosts cross over, if you ask me. You could say I had a life-changing experience lately that makes me want to find out how to get rid of some of them."

"Cute. And judging from your awesomeness in chasing that dark spirit off, I'd say you found a calling." Her savvy might even go a long way in protecting her, so I didn't have a problem with her paranormal interest.

She seemed taken off balance that I wasn't smarting off right back at her or asking what the hell a TMZ was. Thing was, I already knew about the gossip show, thanks.

Then she returned to being coolly civil to me. "I'm going to uncover who or what that thing is and why it came here. I already know that I sense a male energy to it. You can't stop me from finding out more."

I hadn't told her that I suspected the darkness might be her horrendous father. To do that would reveal that Gavin had killed him, and that would have to be done in his own time.

Maybe it should be soon, though.

At an impasse with me, Wendy shifted her weight from foot to foot as the sheer curtains tickled her arm. Then she sighed, like she was somehow giving in to me, and went to a desk, unplugging one of those devices that some people use to read books now. Space-age, huh? Anyway, she brought it to me, opened the window all the way, and gestured to the reader.

Was she telling me I could use it to charge up some?

I took advantage, connecting with it. "Thanks," I said.

Shrug. But at least a shrug was better than being ignored. I was actually getting juice out of her paying attention to me, to tell the truth.

I said, "Your friend came to see me and Amanda Lee yesterday."

"I got an e-mail from Heidi."

"What's your impression of her?"

"Honestly, you can believe anything she says. I'm pretty good at picking out the liars from the rest."

All right, here it came—the real chiding session.

When Wendy continued, she didn't go quite in the direction I thought she would.

"Heidi's grateful to you and Amanda Lee. She said you and her were looking into her friend's boyfriend for free."

Awesome. Wendy wasn't yelling at me. "Charging her would be wrong."

"I don't know why you wouldn't make her pay something. It's a good chance to take advantage of someone. You guys are really wonderful at that, so why not extend your winning streak?"

It was a late punch, but it still landed.

"All right," I said, "I deserve that. You can be as mad at me and Amanda Lee as you want."

Wendy went to her bed and sank to the mattress. "I'm not"—a huge sigh—"*mad*. Jeez, I'm so tired of it. Even now it's wearing me out."

I let her go on.

"Part of me is thankful that you caught Farah, but part of me wishes that . . . Well, not that she would've gotten away with killing Elizabeth, but . . ."

"That things would've just stayed buried."

"I know that's awful. But I keep telling myself that I didn't mind life as it was . . . until I realize that I'm wrong. Very wrong. But life changed, and not just for me. For Gavin, too. He's not the same as he was before. Ever since you appeared, he's been . . . different. Not a good different, either."

"I'm sorry."

"You can say that all you want, but it's not going to do anything."

"No, it won't."

Her lower lip trembled before she pressed her mouth into a straight line, then said, "Do you have to be so easygoing about this?"

"I can be a huge bitch if it'd make you feel better."

"It wouldn't." She made a thwarted sound. "I don't even blame you, no matter how much I want to. It's just hard to know that someone who was in my family—jeez, I saw Farah almost every day—was messed up. And, yeah, Noah and I fought like beasts, but he was my adopted brother, and when Farah killed him . . ."—she gripped the silken bedspread—"I didn't appreciate him like I should've. We both came into the family together, and there was some kind of adopted-kid bond there. Farah took his life as much as she took Elizabeth's, and all I want to do is think that it was someone else's fault. Someone I didn't know. Someone who didn't fool all of us for years and years."

"I wish it could've turned out differently," I said.

She drew in a sharp breath, on the edge of tears. "Me, too."

She lowered her head, shaking it. Again, I didn't say anything. Probably I'd make things only worse, but I felt her sadness to my very center, and it weighed me down.

Eventually, she got herself together, then peered up at me through her hair, her voice wobbly as she nodded toward the electronic device I was still sucking dry.

"It's like you're a crack addict or something with all the juicing up."

I pulled out of the reader, trying not to think of how I'd been craving more and more stimulation these days. "What can I say? Energy is what keeps me rolling."

She stared at me a little too long, and I knew she was getting her first good look at me since I'd come to the doomed rescue on the night Farah had gone bonkers. She was seeing twenty-three-year-old me, the harmless-looking SoCal girl, but, inside, I was starting to feel so much older and more damaging than that.

"I've been researching you," she said quietly.

Something inside me blipped, but I tried to seem un-affected. "I know that I'm on the Internet. Good stories about me there, huh? Except they all have unhappy endings."

"I can see that you didn't just go missing, like the articles say. What I mean is that you're obviously not alive anymore, hiding out somewhere from drug dealers or whoever might've made you disappear from Elfin Forest."

"And I have no idea who killed me. That's kind of the bummer of my life."

"Truly?" She sat up. "You have no idea?"

I think I'd just given Wendy her next homebound project.

"Truly," I said.

"Because Gavin's been looking into you, too. He could—"

Before she could say *help*, she cut herself off. Then she knit her eyebrows, like she'd said something she shouldn't have.

"Wendy, I know he's visited my old best friend at the bar she works at. He must've looked her up online. It's not a secret that he's doing some detective work of his own."

Another unsure glance, but then Wendy shrugged. "He hired someone to dig up info about you, too. When he found out about Suzanne and how you were friends, he decided he wanted to hear what she had to say about you."

Maybe my brain was bent, but I sizzled at the thought of his interest.

Wendy doused it. "Gavin's more traumatized than I am, I think. He's the type of guy who'd never show it, but what you did to him . . ."

"Really looped him. I know. And that's another thing I'm sorry about."

She gave me a big-brown-eyed puppy look, wet and teary. "Don't get me wrong. He's glad to have closure about Elizabeth. He loved her so much."

Yup. I'd seen it in his thoughts, his dreams. Felt it through and through.

Wendy hesitated, then added, "He does computer searches on you all the time. He even found your high school yearbook pictures, where you were Miss Popular."

"Not in this household."

She didn't address that point. "He also draws sketches of you from those photos I took when you were haunting our house."

"I saw them through his window."

"They've gotten super weird lately."

"Why shouldn't he see me like an angel of death who destroyed his life?"

"It's just his anger coming out at you." Wendy side-smiled. "You're prettier than that, though, and I'm sure he knows it."

He did? I wanted to preen, but stopped myself. Not a good preening time.

I drifted up higher, until my sneakers came to her windowsill. I even dared to take as much of a stand as I could. She didn't tell me to vamoose, so I took that as a good sign.

"Look at me," she said, laughing a little. "Pouring my stupid soul out to you."

"Well, me and my friends did defend you today, so maybe that earned us some goodwill. You could say we've been campaigning for your forgiveness and it finally paid off."

"I really am thankful."

"And I'm glad we got here in time to see you chase that nuisance off."

She smiled carefully at me, and I felt warmth coming from her in waves. Warmth like how the sun used to feel on me.

"Maybe," I said, lightening the mood even more, "you can even help me one day. As a cleaner, I mean."

"Me? How?"

"I've got a spirit of my own who keeps dogging me."

I told her a bit about fake Dean, just to let her know she wasn't the only one being hounded by unwanted beings. By the end, Wendy was on the edge of the mattress.

"Scariness," she whispered.

"Yeah, and all I want is to keep him away. Any suggestions from your studies?"

Even as I said it, I knew that I was exaggerating. Fake Dean maybe wasn't so bad.

"Wow." She got off the bed. "You mean, I'd be a spirit hunter for you? For reals?"

"Don't make a thing of this. I'm only asking for your input." But it was kind of fun to see her brighten up like this.

We truly smiled at each other for the first time in . . . ever?

As that was happening, I heard a car in the near distance, then the sound of the garage door opening.

Wendy gave me a tentative glance.

I didn't move from my spot. My essence was flaring, just knowing Gavin was home.

"Wendy," I said. "This is the first thing we need to work on together. It's time I cleared things up with your brother, too. Can you help me with that?"

She nodded as a door shut downstairs. I burned that much higher, remembering what it used to be like to see someone I really wanted to see, knowing that he was climbing up the stairs, coming closer.

Closer.

But I'd felt that way with fake Dean yesterday, right?

Below me, in the courtyard, I heard Scott shout, "You all right, Jen?"

I gave a thumbs-up, looking down at my friends. Cassie was powered up again, although she seemed to be a shade sicker than usual. She waved to me and, as she took off with Twyla, Scott, and Randy, her ponytail swished behind her.

Scott would be back, I knew. He wasn't about to be deserting Wendy anytime soon.

As I heard footsteps outside her room, she sent me an anxious look. And when Gavin appeared in her doorway, I was the one whose pseudo-nerves were jangling.

Jeans, boots, and a white button-down. Short brown hair. He seemed to fill the room's doorway, and as he slipped off his sunglasses, he revealed those intense pale blue eyes framed by dark lashes. His gaze was enough to pierce.

Wendy pointed to the window, where I knew Gavin couldn't see me.

"There's someone who wants to talk to you," she said.

He bristled, but I didn't shrink or back down.

"I thought I felt some ice in here," he said, frostier than even a ghost could be. "What does the witch want?"

10

Yeah, that hurt. But I guarded my emotions like a pro. Hell, I'd been getting verbal Wendy missiles launched at me earlier, so I was sure as shit ready for this confrontation with her brother.

I took him in: tall, broad, rough on the outside but bruised underneath. His eyes showed the wounds, but his clenched jaw and fists fought them.

Why did his toughness get to me? Just looking at him made my essence tumble, a faint, electric echo of how it used to feel when the alive middle-school Jensen would see a hunky guy walk into a room. Everything around Gavin had color, drawing me, pulling me in with that life force that I felt only from him.

Wendy was suddenly the peacemaker. "It's time to move on, Gav. Jensen and her friends defended me from a crapstorm today, and they wouldn't be doing that if they wanted us to suffer."

"I've done all the suffering I'm going to," he said, sauntering past a palatial vanity table framed by some of Wendy's comic book art. "Just expel that ghost. Or do whatever Eileen is teaching you to do online with her."

As he began to turn his back on me, Wendy raised her voice. "I don't want to."

He slowly faced her, mild astonishment etched on his face. "What was that, Wen?"

"No disrespect but, like I said, some heavy stuff went down today, and Jensen's crew took care of it like bosses. And that's all they were doing with Elizabeth, too—taking care of business." She took a step toward him. "You and I had some time to think about what went down back at the old mansion. We've talked about things to death. Now I just want to get past all of it."

"You want to welcome a destructive ghost into our new home." His lip curled. "A ghost who rifled around in my head more than any other woman I've ever . . ."

He cut himself off, his hands fisting again until the veins in his arms strained.

I wanted him to go on, because he'd called me a woman. Not a spirit. Not a ghoulie or spook.

A woman.

Wendy walked toward him. "You know all the smudging and incantations I did around here to keep ghosts out? Well, one word and I can invalidate its powers and invite Jensen in."

"You really want her in." He chuffed. "That would be a mistake."

"After what she did for me today, I trust her and her friends. She's not the enemy—that dark spirit is. It was here, Gav, for the first time since the séance."

I could see Gavin's body grow even tauter. Was he thinking the spirit was his father, just like I was?

He glanced toward the window, where I was still lounging, but he looked right through me.

Now was my moment. "Wendy, will you translate?"

"Sure."

He talked first, though, and it was to Wendy. "Tell Jensen Murphy thank you for the bodyguard service, but we can take it from here."

"I don't think so," I said.

Wendy ran with that. "She agrees with me—the more defenses we have set up against darkness, the better. Now that I know I'm sensitive to the other side, more ghosts might be coming around to see me, too. This is what my life is now, and it doesn't surprise me, because I've always had an interest in the paranormal. An affinity for it, like Eileen says. It just took today for me to drop my pride and let Jensen in. What's it going to take for you?"

He just stared at the wall, a force field of contained emotion. Didn't he know that, with a touch, I could bring him instant peace? That I could make him see hallucinations with me that could eventually heal and soothe his soul?

None of it would be real, though. I wasn't capable of real anymore.

"Gavin?" Wendy asked.

A few choked beats passed, then he said, "I know you'll do what you want, so she's yours to handle." A muscle ticked in his jaw.

A weight seemed to fall off Wendy's thin shoulders,

but not all the way. She was still carrying too many burdens for someone who was only fifteen. For anyone, really.

"You can come in, Jensen," she said almost triumphantly.

Something vague in the room seemed to break apart, and the smell of sage I'd caught before lightened up. I floated off the sill to hover over the floor. Wendy smiled, maybe because she'd never had much power before, and now it was at her fingertips.

"She's in," she said to Gavin, going over to shut her window.

He began to walk out of the room. "I'm ecstatic for you both."

"Not so fast," I said.

Wendy caught him by the sleeve. "She wants to talk with you. Jensen, what should I say?"

"He's been seeing my friend, Suze."

"Gav, she knows you went to see Suzanne Field."

He let out a short laugh, leaning back against the doorframe, his arms loosely crossed over his chest. "This Jensen really gets around."

"Not nearly as much as he does," I said, wafting over to him. The closer I got, the more I buzzed.

After Wendy repeated what I'd said for his sake, he laughed, but not because he was in good spirits.

Wendy looked exasperated. "I told her that we've been doing research into her past. We're curious about her."

"And what did she say?"

I spoke now. "I said that I understand, because I had

to do my research on you, too, remember?" The empa-thizing, the hallucinations, the dream-digging.

Wendy whispered to me, "Are you sure you want to go with *that*?"

I shrugged, and from the way Gavin was staying here, I guessed that he really did give a fig about what I was telling him.

As I remembered what Twyla said about him being obsessed with me, I shivered. And it wasn't in a bad way, either. Sick.

I was so close to him now that I could see his throat constrict with each swallow, could hear him breathe, could imagine what his Cupid's-bow lips would feel like against me if a dimension wasn't between us.

"She doesn't like me talking with Suzanne, does she?" he asked, like maybe he was content just to rile me up.

Had he been taking some pleasure in contacting Suze, knowing I wouldn't go for it?

"No, I don't like it," I said. "He can ask me any question he wants about the majorly mysterious Jensen Murphy, and I'll answer. But leave Suze out of this."

As Wendy translated, he only smiled that slightly raw smile that made the energy in me dive downward, into my belly area. He clearly couldn't stop remembering how *I'd* crossed a lot of lines with *him*.

"Tell Jensen," he said, "that I'm a stickler for re-search, just like she is."

Wendy shook her head. "Don't talk like that."

"I'm only being honest."

Damn, he was stubborn. "Tell him there's something else I need to talk to him about. In private this time."

"We tell each other everything these days," Wendy said. "That's because we know what happens when you keep secrets."

Poor thing. She was in for another rude awakening someday about her adoptive father.

Gavin seemed to get a hint of what I might be talking about, and his hackles went up. Since he knew I could be a loose cannon, I wasn't surprised when he shot my cold spot a glare and started to leave the room.

"I'm done for the day," he said as he moved down the hallway. I followed.

"She's coming!" Wendy said from her room.

I waved back at her. "I'll deal with him. No translation required."

Her door slammed. Had I pissed her off yet again by shutting her out of this? Teenagers. It hadn't been so long ago that I'd been one but, damn. What a drag.

On the opposite end of the condo, Gavin went into a room with me on his tail. I paused by a drawing board as I entered, my gaze locked on all the sketches of me posted on the walls. The angelic me's with my flowing hair and ethereal form . . . and the hellbitches with the fire eyes and haggy mouths.

Shutting out the disappointment, I found the nearest outlet, made one of my hands into a prong, and plugged in. I hadn't gotten all the juice I probably needed out of the little space-age reader.

Time to get real.

I materialized in front of him, taking perverse delight in how his expression changed at the sight of ghostie me, blinkering around the edges with energy.

Motioning to a hellbitch sketch, I tried to seem flippant. "You got a few of the details wrong."

Even though I could tell he was fascinated, he deliberately turned away from me, pulling keys out of his back jeans pocket, tossing them onto a wide desk, where they slid across half of it before coming to a dead stop.

"Just going off memory," he said.

"I never appeared like that to you—not in a photo and not in your subconscious."

"Sometimes personality overcomes everything else."

The air-conditioning kicked on, taking up the vacuum of silence that'd come between us as he switched on his computer and sat in a leather chair. What, was he going to ignore me and start working?

He sure knew how to push a ghost's nerves.

"Hey," I said, getting his focus again. "I'm using a lot of effort to appear to you right now. Also, I have about a million things to take care of out in the world, and you're wasting my precious time."

"What do we have to discuss? You asked me to stop seeing Suzanne already."

"And I'm sure you'll respect my wishes." The sarcasm might as well have been a Vegas sign flashing *Bullshit!*

"But . . ." I said. "There's something else I want to mention out of Wendy's hearing. It's about that dark spirit from the séance. She doesn't know who it might be, does she?"

He fell back into his chair, an injured expression taking over his face again.

"No," he said.

"You haven't told her?"

"Definitely not."

"When do you plan to?"

"I was hoping on never."

He faced me now, allowing himself to finally get a good look at me. The way his gaze devoured me was reminiscent of how fake Dean didn't hide his interest, either.

Excited, I gave off a mighty *bzzzt*. Embarrassing.

Questions filled Gavin's gaze at my extra weird behavior, but I went on. "Please just hear me out. Lying is not the way to go here. Amanda Lee used a bunch of those on me, just like she did with you. You don't want to keep lying to Wendy when it very well could put her in danger."

"How? That dark spirit is already coming around. How would knowing who it might be make things any better?" He raised a finger at me. "Over four years ago, my goddamned father nearly started putting Wendy through what he put Farah through. But when I found out about his abusive nature, I stopped it. And, you know what? I would kill him again if I had to."

Was that his accelerated heartbeat filling the air? Louder. More forceful. Or maybe it was my imagination.

"Gavin," I said. "You don't know what dark spirits are capable of. I don't even know for sure, but I can make an educated guess. I'm betting they're deceitful, with silver tongues. I suspect, if this one is your father, that he's hanging around Wendy's window because he wants to lure her to him, and if you don't arm her with the truth about who he really was, she'll want to get to the bottom of whatever or whoever he is. You're setting her up as a perfect target."

His gaze blazed through me. He didn't like that the ghost who'd worked him over was giving him advice. Even worse, it was advice that he should be following.

His defenses gave out almost imperceptibly, the chip on his shoulder loosening. "I keep telling myself that she needs a normal life, but it's not happening. I moved us out of that mansion, but the ghosts followed. I told her it was okay to stay in and do her school assignments from home for a while because I thought she needed the space, but all it's done is make her delve deeper into everything I wanted to leave behind. And I've let her do it, because I can't fight any of it."

"There're just some things you have to tolerate," I said. "Like me. I'm going to fight against that dark spirit just as hard as I fought for Elizabeth."

He looked at me, his gaze a melancholy pale. My pseudo-heart broke a bit at the sight, because I'd only made his grief at losing his ex-fiancée worse by haunting him.

But I was sure that, after a month, he was coming around to accepting that I would've haunted anyone who was a suspect in her murder. It'd been about justice.

In the end, I was sure he believed in that just as much as I did.

"You're doing everything you possibly can for Wendy," I said, closing out the discussion. "You're a great big brother."

He must've known that I intended to leave now, because he stood from his chair, and before I could react, he was in front of me.

Tall. At least a foot taller than I was. Big, with that wide chest that held a heartbeat I *could* hear and feel through the air, because it sure wasn't mine.

His life force, I thought. It was all around me.

I wasn't positive about what I saw in his gaze, but it was steady, intense. *Obsession*, Twyla would've said.

And when he reached out to touch my face, I held my ghost breath.

It seemed to take forever for his hand to reach out to me, and I actually waited, waited to feel him against me.

But when he passed through me, I flinched, shocked.

He backed away, too, clenching his hand, probably trying to stop the chills and electricity from crawling up his arm and through the rest of him.

I made everyone so cold, didn't I?

Jerking my hand from the outlet, I disappeared into the air, becoming a nothing to Gavin once again. I rushed downstairs to their fireplace and swept up the chimney. But all the while I kept thinking of the moment before his hand had passed through me and how hopeful I'd been.

And how disappointed I'd ended up.

* * *

I blasted over the courtyard, catching the sight of Scott hunkering on the wall with one knee drawn up like the cool dude he was.

As I wheeled back around, he spotted me, lifting his hand in a wave, so very calm and collected that anyone would've been hard-pressed to remember that he'd been in a knock-down, drag-out fight with a dark spirit recently.

I swooped to him, and he said, "I came back here after I saw you go inside with Wendy. No dark spirits around now."

"Hopefully Wendy's prayer gave it a goose that it didn't like. How's Cassie?"

"Doing fine. She feels a little . . . off, though."

"How?"

Scott idly played with a lace on his high-top sneaker. "Can't say. She says she feels like a part of her is missing."

Yikes. "When I saw that dark spirit reach into her and take out some essence, it shoved the chunk into itself, like it was feeding."

"That ain't good." Scott's big light eyes were wide. "Cassie went with Twyla to Amanda Lee's if you want to give her a holler."

"I'll do that." I needed to touch base with Amanda Lee, anyway, mostly to see that Louis had been allowed to go to Tim Knudson's house to keep watch over *that* problem.

As Louis said, when it rains, it pours.

Scott nodded toward Wendy's window. "You got to go inside?"

"You wouldn't like it. Very girly in her room."

"I've been in some female rooms in my time."

"I don't doubt it, Casanova. This one isn't open to you, though." God, why did ghosts have to be so horny?

He smiled to himself. Then he asked, "Anything exciting happen in there?"

"I made contact with Gavin."

"That's a large charge."

I think that meant it was cool in fifties-speak. "Seems like we're on firmer ground with these two. But we're not all exactly BFFs yet."

"Just give it time. You can work your charm on the wet rag just as easily as you did with Wendy."

"Anyway," I said, "in all the excitement, I haven't thought to ask. . . . I need to find a couple possible ghosts in Boo World fast. Patrick McNichol, one of the kids who was at the Elfin Forest party, and Milo Guttenburg, this crabby person of interest in my case. If they're around, I'd like to ask them about my murder."

"Good luck. You know that ghosts don't have those smartphones these kids walk around with now. We don't even have an official Boo World hangout."

Right. Ghosts kind of pieced everything together, taking what they could get, finding one another as we wandered from one stimulating situation to the next. Sometimes I even wondered if my friends stuck around only because of the excitement me and Amanda Lee provided.

Scott ran a hand through his greased hair. "You just leave it to me. When I get a break, I'll spread the word about your guys and see if anyone has any news about where they are. You might even fly by their death spots to see if they're one of those nerds that like to haunt them."

"Do you think they could also be at their burial spots?" I asked, because, yeah, I'd been wondering.

"Sometimes that happens, like with Old Seth." He was a ghost who was six feet under in an Escondido graveyard, and he liked to attend parties at a haunted house built over it. "But to haunt a burial spot, you've got to have one to go to in the first place. I was cremated, just like lots of others. Some ghosts just don't like to haunt their resting places."

"Let me guess—no action."

"Now you're cookin'."

I smiled. "Thanks for watching over the Edgetts like this."

"Piece of cake. I'm charged and ready to go."

He wasn't the only one.

I brought up a travel tunnel, waved 'bye to him, and plunged into its pink swirling artery, zipping over the electric currents in the air and rolling to a landing at Amanda Lee's house.

There were fewer than usual lookiloos here today, and that was encouraging. Word must've been traveling that some guardian ghosts were surrounding Amanda Lee, and lookilooing just wasn't worth the trouble, anymore.

I herded off the stubborn few who remained, then slipped through the crack in the door to my casita, where Amanda Lee was chatting with Cassie, who'd taken over possession of my car battery.

"Our little ray of sunshine has arrived!" Twyla said when she saw me.

Cassie smiled. When she'd been alive, she'd had her kids early in life, and I could tell she'd been one of those moms who'd felt that she'd missed out on her single years. She and her husband had been to some swinging parties, but they hadn't filled her up in the way she'd been looking for. Death hadn't even satisfied that empty space she'd always had.

"How're you feeling?" I asked.

"Better. Amanda Lee's taking care of me."

"My pleasure," Amanda Lee said. Cassie was one of the ghosts she could hear crystal clear. "Jensen, Cassie was telling me all about the dark spirit."

Twyla butted in. "Totally. We went all Conan on that thing, didn't we?"

Cassie stayed quiet, concentrating on laying her hand on that battery.

I spoke before Twyla could take the conversation over. "I wanted to check Brittany Kirkland Stokley's address before I went over there. Then I should go to Louis at Tim's house. He did make it there, didn't he?"

"After Twyla came back and relieved him."

Twyla got defensive. "Well, excu-o-o-se me for riding off to the, like, rescue at Wendy's and taking Louis' place. I didn't think seniority mattered right then."

Time to do some ego stroking. "Twyla, you were fantastic. Very Conan the Barbarian. I'm glad you came."

Cassie agreed. "You could've taken my dark spirit out, too."

"Hey," I said softly, "you fought it off."

"Fighting's not my thing. Then again, neither was keeping a household, being in the PTA, or carpooling, according to my husband. I know his second wife was good at everything, however."

Twyla went over to Cassie, kneeling and looking up at her with a reassuring smile. She seemed like a daughter to her as the older ghost smiled back.

At the risk of shattering this special moment, I went over to Amanda Lee, whispering. "I made contact with Wendy and Gavin. They still have a ways to go in accepting us, but we're getting there. Wendy's studying online to be a cleaner with that Eileen."

"So I heard."

"And Gavin . . ." Be still my beating heart. "I materialized to him. We needed to talk about that dark spirit. I told him he should tell Wendy who it might be."

"How did that go over?"

"As well as can be expected. He didn't try to stick an iron poker in me or anything, but I think he knows what he has to do."

I left out the part about Gavin trying to touch me. I didn't even want to think about it myself. Too confusing. Too . . . sad.

"So then," Amanda Lee said. "It's off to Brittany Kirkman Stokley to see if she knows more about the old Elfin Forest party and the bracelets than she let on to Ruben. I'd like to come with you, if you don't mind.

Ruben tells me that she spends most mornings at the Oceanside Country Club. That's where he previously met her for an interview, so why don't I call her and see if I can arrange a time to get together there today?"

That worked for me. Amanda Lee could put Brittany's mind on the subjects I needed for her to be thinking about for empathy—especially when it came to those bracelets I'd been wearing.

Twyla had heard Amanda Lee. "Oh, can we go, too? Please please please?"

I didn't think there was any stopping her. "If you goof off, I will kill you all over again."

"And I'll make like Conan the Barbarian and kill you back."

Cassie reclined on the table. "If you don't mind, I'll stay here for a while."

"Are you sure, Cass?" Twyla asked. "It'll be fun."

"I'm sure." She arranged a smile on her mouth, but it didn't ring true.

She was spirit shy, I thought. She was afraid the dark blob was still out there, waiting.

"Cass-ieeeee," Twyla said. "I really want you there."

"But . . ."

Twyla batted her eyelashes. It probably wouldn't have worked on most living or dead things, but Cassie's soft spot responded, and she pushed off the battery.

"All right," she said.

Twyla squealed, skip-floating to the door, where I was already headed. "It's off to Brittany we go!"

And hopefully on to the identity of who'd killed me.

11

When I first saw Brittany Kirkland Stokley climbing out of a golf cart and shaking hands with a silver-haired man on the green, she didn't come off like someone who could've possibly murdered me and taken my bracelets as a trophy. She was more like a total modern-day Dinah Shore: pink pleated skort, white polo, trendy baseball cap, and all.

Twyla, who was hanging outside next to Cassie near the wide windows of the country club's restaurant, couldn't help herself.

"Check it out, Jen-Jen. Unlike you, your friend didn't have to be a ghost to look thirty years younger."

Cassie float-leaned near the window and gave me a maternal grin. "Jensen's much prettier and fresher. You watch—the closer Brittany gets, the more you'll see that she's got a Phyllis Diller face-lift."

"Ooo," Twyla said. "Catty. So glad you came with us, Cass."

Amanda Lee was tuned out of Twyla's convo, seated at a table, drinking a glass of iced tea, and tracking Brittany with her gaze as my old party buddy strutted off the green in our direction. For the interview, Amanda Lee had put on brighter colors—an artistically scalloped long blouse over a layered yellow Native American skirt. She'd even gotten out the turquoise necklaces again, letting her red hair spread over her shoulders in layers with those white streaks in front.

Yup, she looked optimistic enough, maybe because Brittany had agreed to see Amanda Lee after she'd knocked around some balls on the course, doing business with an associate from the mergers and acquisitions company where she worked.

Just think—my fellow pizza joint waitress, a titan of industry. What would I have ended up as? I mean, Brittany partied hard back then, too, so maybe there'd been hope for me.

As Brittany's golf date drove off in his cart behind her, she strolled past the restaurant.

Amanda Lee stood, waving at her. "Excuse me. Brittany Stokley?"

Brittany was stripping off a golf glove, giving Amanda Lee a warm smile. "That would be me."

"Interview alert!" Twyla said, peering over Amanda Lee's shoulder.

Cassie shrugged sweetly as we waited for Brittany to tuck her glove into her back pocket and come to us. It was good to see Cassie in a better mood, and just as long as she kept Twyla in check, life would be grand.

As Brittany approached the table, I marveled at the time-warp effect again. Same old Brittany, right in front of me, but different. She did look very well preserved, in a "Mom, my ponytails are too tight!" way. Cassie had gotten the face-lift right. But Brittany had been born to get cosmetic surgery—she'd been one of those girls who was always too tan, was always wearing too much makeup, and was always a clothes horse.

And look at that, she was clothes-horsing now, slyly inspecting Amanda Lee's wardrobe. She dwelled on the turquoise necklaces, smiling as she probably wondered how much Amanda Lee had paid for the bunch.

When her smile dimmed, I realized that Brittany had priced the jewelry as "quality vintage, but oh-so gauche."

Amanda Lee reached out to shake her hand and introduce herself.

As Brittany greeted her, she said, "You said you and your PI associate have a new lead about Jensen Murphy."

"Yes, and I'm grateful you could take time for some questions about her. I know you're busy."

This was it—the stage was set for some empathy, and I slowly moved forward so as not to disturb the atmosphere.

But just before I got to Brittany, Twyla gave me a sarcastic grin and cut me off, reaching out and making contact with my old friend's skin.

"Hey!" Had that really just happened?

"Oh, my," Cassie said under her breath. "This won't turn out well."

Amanda Lee was just disengaging from Brittany's handshake. The medium in her saw that I wasn't empathizing yet, and since she couldn't detect Twyla, she lifted her brow. Then she carried on with Brittany, making small talk about Ruben for a moment.

"Twyla, you're dead meat," I muttered. But the narbo was already engaged with reading Brittany's thoughts, giving me a view into what a ghost looked like while empathizing. Color was rolling through Twyla in waves as she stared straight ahead, her eyes an airport-light blue, her mouth open and emanating the same color.

Gross. Was that what I looked like when I read thoughts, too?

Goose bumps had spiked Brittany's arms as she shivered a little, then sat, with Twyla still attached to her like a fricking leech.

Cassie leaned over to me and whispered, "Don't take it personally. She only wants in on the action."

"I'll give her some action," I said. But what was I going to do? Start a catfight with Twyla? Classy.

Instead, I glanced at another couple who'd entered the patio. I wanted to see if they were sensitive to ghosts and had spotted us. Nope.

As Amanda Lee gracefully took a seat across from Brittany while the woman ordered an early martini from a waiter, you'd never know she was somewhat of a recluse. She was smiley and open as Brittany laughed.

"Somewhere in the world," she said, "it's happy hour." She hesitated until the waiter left, then added, "So what can I help you with specifically, Ms. Minter? Is there anything I can answer that I didn't before with Ruben?"

"Yes, as a matter of fact, there is." Amanda Lee had

taken out a pad of paper. "And I'm hoping to get in touch with Lisa Levine and Andy Grant to follow up, as well."

While Brittany sat back in her chair, one long, tanned leg crossed over the other, I knew her mind was on Lisa and Andy, my fellow partygoers.

And that meant *Twyla* was probably getting the 411 on them.

Brittany slid off her feminine baseball cap and placed it on her lap, revealing bottle-blond hair. "I know Patrick would've helped you with Jensen, too, if he were only alive."

I hoped that Twyla got a read on where Patrick had died so I could visit his death spot.

During all this, Cassie had meandered off to a different table, her hand over her side, where the dark spirit had ripped something out of her. She seemed pained, and when I sent her an enquiring look, she shook her head, smiling, brushing me off.

Too bad Cassie had left just when Amanda Lee was getting to the meat of the matter. "The night Jensen disappeared," she said to Brittany, her pen over the paper, "she was wearing those black, rubbery bracelets that Madonna made popular. Suzanne Field told us that you had them on when she saw you a couple years ago."

"Oh, everyone had those," Brittany said, laughing again. She was as embarrassed about acknowledging them as I was.

"But you told Suzanne that they were Jensen's, and that you were wearing them for the anniversary of her disappearance that particular day."

"I see." She wrinkled her brow. "Yes, that's right. This was the day I went to brunch with a client. He'd read in a guidebook about the cheese hash browns and roasted tomatoes at Flaherty's, so I accommodated him with a brunch near his hotel. An Irish breakfast, isn't that charming? Unfortunately, the food was rather bland for my tastes."

"What else do you remember about the meeting with Suzanne?"

"I remember Suze was waiting tables, and I barely recognized her. Three decades is a very long time to not see someone, and"—she lowered her voice to a whisper—"I hate to say it, but she hasn't really kept up." She gestured to her face, just to get the point across.

I hated to say it, but at least Suze didn't look like someone had laminated her.

"Go on," Amanda Lee said, totally neutral. She had to see me getting all offended for Suze's sake on my side of the table, though.

"I never knew Suze well, anyway," Brittany said. "She didn't like Lisa, Patrick, Andy, and me very much. She thought she was above us because she had some kind of professional job where she wore Charlotte Russe suits to work."

"And the bracelets?" Amanda Lee asked.

Brittany tapped a long, shiny French-manicured fingernail against her lips, thinking. From behind her, Twyla had a reaction—her color stopped rolling through her essence for a second, then started up again. Did that mean she was getting something from the empathy because of the question Amanda Lee had asked?

"I recall the details now," Brittany said. "I haven't worn those bracelets since that day a couple years ago, so it's been buried in my head. The reason I was wearing them was that I'd seen a newspaper article about Elfin Forest a month or two before Jensen's anniversary. It was one of those color pieces they publish in the local section, and it reminded me of her, so I clipped it out. It put me in a sentimental mood, so I went through my old memory boxes for pictures of us when we worked together. That's where I found those bracelets. I told myself I would remember her on her anniversary, and I did it by wearing the . . . jewelry. Otherwise I wouldn't be caught d—"

She stopped herself before she said *dead*. Then she frowned. "Are you about to tell me they found her remains or . . . ?"

"No," Amanda Lee said.

Then Brittany blew out a breath, recovering. "In any case, those bracelets are not my type of accessory, and I wouldn't have much occasion to wear them at any other time. It was only pure coincidence that I ended up in Suze's pub for her to see me in them."

Again, Twyla's running color paused, then started up again, maybe getting another significant reading.

Even without empathy, I was receiving my own strong feeling that Brittany might be lying. Was Amanda Lee vibing this off her, too, from across the table? Her face was so composed that I couldn't be sure.

Brittany didn't say anything as the waiter brought her cocktail. When he was gone, she waved a careless hand in front of her. "I, of course, mentioned to Suze that the bracelets I was wearing were Jensen's. Looking back, I shouldn't have." Her gaze had a distance to it. "Suze teared up, and another server came to wait on us."

She'd laid her hands on top of her lap, spreading her long fingers over her hat like she was exerting some kind of control over herself. Her voice came out thick, and I realized that she was sad. Or acting like it.

"Jensen Murphy," Brittany said. "I still can't believe it. Gone, just like that. I try not to think about it too hard, because I do feel responsible. Who wouldn't? I'm sure the four of us had to be close to wherever she disappeared from in the forest that night, and we should have heard something, seen something. But we had music playing from a boom box, so if she was screaming while someone took her, we never heard it. And the last thing we were doing was paying attention. Lisa and I were doing a lot of dancing, and the boys . . . ? They didn't mind that a bit."

Dammit, right now, Twyla might be seeing a whole reel of empathic images in Brittany. Could she tell whether she or anyone else at the party had left the group for long enough to kill me?

Twyla just kept reading our interviewee, her gaze blanked, her mouth gaped, both of them still an eerie blue.

Amanda Lee even joined in when Brittany reached for her martini glass to take a drink. Our psychic rested her hand on Brittany's, supposedly comforting her, but actually getting vibes.

"You shouldn't feel badly," Amanda Lee said.

Brittany swallowed, raising her chin. "If you don't mind my asking, why are the bracelets important?"

Amanda Lee smiled. How could she tell Brittany that we were trying to track a murderer without tipping her off that she might be a suspect?

"We'd like to gather everything that Jensen had with her that night, just in case there are some clues we're missing."

"Even if the bracelets were in the car and not in the woods?"

I'd left them in the car?

Amanda Lee cocked her head. "Yes, even if you found them there."

Brittney said, "When I saw Jensen's bracelets there after we'd been looking for her all night, I didn't realize they were very important. You see, I was sure she'd taken them off before we went into the woods because Lisa had been making fun of Madonna during the ride there. Jensen was like that at the time—thin-skinned, emotional—because of her parents' deaths. She was taking a long time to get over their drownings. But she was in a great mood that night, very spirited, dishing out banter just as well as she was taking it. I'm not sure why she took those bracelets off."

This was crazy. Why didn't I even remember putting them there? But a bigger question was why I couldn't recall anything but the mask and the ax and the running and screaming. Yeah, I know—I'd been in shock, traumatized, whatever, and that's what'd sent me into the time loop. But there had to be more answers.

"One more question." From what I could see of Amanda Lee's arm below her pushed-up sleeve, she had maxi goose bumps while touching Brittany. Twyla's energy must've been giving them to her.

Brittany nodded. "Go ahead."

"Why didn't you tell my associate Ruben about the bracelets, or even the cops all those years ago?"

"I . . ." She drew her hand away from Amanda Lee's. "As I said, I didn't think they were all that important. The thought honestly never even crossed my mind after we came out of the forest. The bracelets were only ridiculous pieces of rubber, and I actually forgot I'd even taken them from the car until months later, when I found them in my jacket pocket. Then, it didn't seem to matter because none of the authorities cared about Jensen anymore. What were they going to do with some bracelets that she'd worn?"

Before Amanda Lee could answer, Brittany belted back her martini and stood.

"I'm sorry to rush off, but I have a luncheon to attend," she said. "Is there anything else?"

"No. But if I have more questions, would it be fine if I contacted you?"

"Yes. And if you'd like to have the bracelets, they're yours."

Amanda Lee beamed. "That would be valuable."

Brittany began to rattle off her work address and Amanda Lee wrote it down, then said she would pick the jewelry up tomorrow. Brittany specified that they would be at the lobby desk.

Then she vigorously rubbed her arms, and Twyla's

eyes flashed back to their dark shade as she jerked back from Brittany.

With a good-bye and another rub to her arms, Brittany left, signaling to the lingering waiter, who nodded. He stopped by the table to tell Amanda Lee to enjoy her iced tea, compliments of Ms. Stokley.

Amanda Lee did no such thing. A couple of minutes later, she was out of her chair, striding over the patio and toward the parking lot. She didn't say a word until we got to her Bentley, where she slid inside, waited for us to enter, then slammed the door.

"Jensen, why weren't you empathizing with Brittany?"

I let Twyla take that.

"Sorry," she said so very innocently. "But I've, like, been dying to do something important, Jen. Forgive me?"

Cassie sent her a soft look. *She* would've forgiven Twyla.

I spoke to Amanda Lee. "Twyla says that she wanted to take a crack at the empathy this time, and even though it was, *like, totally rude*, she's going to tell us every single thing Brittany was thinking." To Twyla, "You stayed in there a long time."

"I've gotten pretty tubular at ghost stuff over the years. I've been at it way longer than you, so you can aspire if you want."

No use dwelling on her damage anymore. "So what did you get from Brittany?"

Twyla actually became serious. At least the Robert Smith half of her did.

"Since I don't know what you were talking about while I saw this image, I don't have any . . . What do you call it?"

"Context?" I asked.

"I guess. But I saw that, after you ducked out of the party, not even one of those kids left to take a whiz or anything. The four of them stayed together until they realized you hadn't come back. They wouldn't have had the opportunity to do any killing. Also, they were drunk and ultra-oblivious to everything around them."

I darted a gaze at Amanda Lee. "She says all my friends had an alibi and didn't hear or see anything in the woods."

Amanda Lee closed her eyes like she was trying to tune into Twyla for the very first time.

"An alibi," Twyla said. "That's it. I can tell you how Brittany found your bracelets, too."

"Let me guess. The bracelets were in the car."

"Is that what Britt-Britt told you?"

Alarm bells went off in my essence. Had Twyla gotten different information?

But then she flicked her fingers at my head. "Psych! That's totally what happened. Brittany found them between the two front seats."

I *must* have taken them off. What other explanation was there?

Amanda Lee said, "If Brittany gave all her friends an alibi, where does that leave us?"

Twyla shrugged. "I sure wouldn't waste my time looking up that Lisa chick or Andy Candy. Not if they weren't even at the murder place."

Even the dead-and-gone Patrick McNichol, who might be somewhere here in Boo World, wouldn't be a suspect. And Twyla had verified what Brittany had said about the group being oblivious to any clues around them.

Cassie had already translated, and she added, "You can always try to find that person of interest you were talking about, just to see if he knows anything more. Milo, right? Could he be in our dimension if he hasn't gone to the glare?"

I sank over the front seat. "We could. Otherwise, it sounds like we're back to square one."

That left the car in some awkward silence.

Until, of course, Twyla spoke.

"Why didn't Amanda Lee get a vibe off any of your friends when that PI of yours was investigating?"

Maybe I should've told Twyla the answer later since Amanda Lee was right next to us, but it wasn't like it was a secret that Amanda Lee had hidden things from me.

"She wasn't out to solve my case, necessarily. Not then."

Amanda Lee understood what was going on and finished for me. "I wanted enough information to bring Jensen back to help me and that was the extent of it at the time. My mission was single-minded, and I got what I wanted."

She sent me a sheepish glance, but I figured if Wendy could forgive us for being so hard-core about Farah's investigation, I could forgive Amanda Lee's diligence about Elizabeth.

Twyla was giving *me* a funny look now. "Just so you know, Brittany really was telling the truth about everything. And she was sad about you. I could feel all of it."

Cassie relayed the sentiment to Amanda Lee, who smiled gently at me.

"I can second that, Jensen," she said. "Brittany feels a lot of remorse. It's just that she's usually very proficient at ignoring those feelings. She compartmentalizes, and that's why she's such a successful businesswoman."

As she started the car, I clung to the fact that at least one of my old friends had grown up to be a success. And that I'd been remembered on even one anniversary by her.

Once we got back to her house, Amanda Lee decided to focus on Tim Knudson since my case had just dropped into the shitter. She'd already gotten ahold of Heidi on the car phone to touch base with her and to see if they and Nichelle could get together for what she called an "intervention." Amanda Lee wouldn't reveal her identity to Nichelle at the lunch, but she would be sitting nearby if Heidi needed her.

Even though I didn't think either of them would have any pull with Nichelle in getting her to leave Tim, it was worth a try. And Cassie promised she would stick by Amanda Lee's side as a bodyguard, in case that dark spirit showed. Not that she seemed happy about this.

As for Twyla? She was full of surprises today.

"How about I try to see if that Milo guy is around Boo World?" she asked.

We were floating outside my casita while Cassie and Amanda Lee headed inside. There weren't any lookiloo ghosts around. Maybe they were gone for good.

I cocked an invisible eyebrow at Twyla. "What's the catch?"

"What do you mean?"

"I mean why're you being nice?"

She inspected the dark-painted nails on her Cure side. "Maybe I feel kinda bad about stealing your empathy reading. Or maybe I just think you're a little, like, pathetic."

"Always around to bump up my mood," I said, getting ready to call up a travel tunnel so I could go to Tim's house, where Louis was on duty.

"Oh, barf, you're gonna make me say it, aren't you?"

I paused, then settled into an *I'm waiting* glare. It totally worked.

She let out a dramatic groan. "Gawd, I just wanna be a little awesome, okay? I mean, I never get to do anything, and I saw my chance today. Also, I really did want to help."

Now I felt sort of bad. In all the decades she'd existed, Twyla had never grown out of being a teen, and if I recalled correctly, those weren't exactly supposed to be the best years of most peoples' lives. True—they'd been the best years of mine, but I didn't have much basis for comparison when my post–high school days sucked so bad.

A thought shook me. What if I would've *never* improved throughout life? What if my high school years were the best I would've had?

I imagined Suze at the bar, rubbing her eyes, tired and worn and stooped at the shoulders. Was that how I would've ended up, lonely and overworked?

Wow, I was in a dark mental place. Thank God for that Mello Yello and the good attitude I'd been in before I'd died, because I couldn't imagine being a depressed drag all the time like Brittany had said I normally was.

"You want to find Milo?" I asked Twyla. "Then do it."

"Really?"

"Really."

"Milo Guttenburg or bust!" she said, raising her hands in victory. Then she jittered toward the casita, probably going there to tell Cassie where she was headed. Over her shoulder she said, "I'll take this to the max, Jen. I'll track that mountain man down and come back with something that'll help you. Just see."

She started slimming down and threading through the crack under the door. I turned away, grinning. Twyla was the little sister I never wanted but had somehow ended up with. Might as well make the most of it.

But since I had a little psycho I'd never wanted in *my* life, either, I readied myself to travel to Tim's house.

12

When I slipped through Tim's gaping back porch screen door, I immediately encountered the psycho on the phone, pacing back and forth on the family room floor in a pair of khaki shorts with multiple pockets, bare chested.

"Nich, I want you home. Now!"

I heard her squabbling back at him very clearly since her phone voice was riding the air. Then I glanced over at Louis, who wasn't too far away, hover-sitting over the dining room table with his chin in his hand.

"My very own version of hell," he said.

"Sorry you have to deal with this."

He sat up, waving off the apology. "Nichelle is meeting Heidi for a late lunch after she does some shopping, and Tim's unhappy about it. It's the most riveting thing to happen all day."

"No doubt. As far as lunch goes, Amanda Lee put that together to see if Heidi can at least talk Nichelle out of living with Happy Boy."

"She has time to facilitate meetings?"

"Sure, now that my own case has gone belly-up." I chuffed. "It was a bust with Brittany today. Twyla read her, and she saw that all the kids at the party that night have an alibi. They were also too drunk and loud to hear anything happen to me."

"*I'm* sorry." He frowned. "Why was Twyla reading Brittany instead of you?"

"Long story, but I think I can encapsulate it with one phrase: desperate for something to do." I tilted my head, putting the subject behind me for now. "Do you think that some ghosts, like us, just wear themselves out and that's why they haunt their death spots? A few more weeks like this and I'll need my spot's constant energy just to exist."

He chuckled. "As far as I can remember, I've never been this active, either. Unfortunately, I have no answer for you in the other respect."

When Tim hung up the phone, we both focused on him as he tossed the device onto the counter in disgust. In fact, he did it so pissily that it dropped off the other side, cracking to the kitchen floor. I could sense the rage building in him as he stalked over to get it, slapping it back on the counter.

Whoa, maybe Samsonite made those phones. Tim was handling them like the gorilla used to handle the luggage in commercials when I was little.

He went to shut the sliding glass door, then aimed for the sofa, aggressively plopping down on it.

O-kay. "He's off work today?" I asked.

"That he is." Louis raised a finger. "By the by, do you know Einstein's definition of insanity?"

I shook my head.

"I'll give you a hint. It has to do with experiencing something over and over again and expecting different results."

"Has it been that bad watching him?"

Louis' voice was monotone. "All he does is stay awake, watch TV, and look out the front and back windows. I might need to go out for a stiff drink with Randy soon."

"If only the alcohol stuck with us," I said.

He smiled, and I knew there was no place Louis really wanted to be other than here, where he was needed. Even when I'd first met him at a ghost gathering of sorts, he'd stood aside from everyone else, the biggest nonparty person ever.

I *whoosh*ed to his side at the table. Tim turned around on the sofa midchannel surf, peering at the slight commotion. Narrowing his eyes, he went back to the tube.

"Did you do any empathy on him?" I asked. "Just to see what's going on in there?"

"Yes, I did. It was an intriguing novelty at first, but his mind has been on one thing ever since."

I tried to think of what might be on any guy's mind: boobs, beer, and a good ham sandwich. But this was Tim we were talking about.

"Nichelle," I said. "He's been thinking about her and hasn't been able to stop."

"Smart girl," Louis said warmly.

He almost reminded me of how my dad used to call me that. *Smart girl.* Coming home with a test with a big, bold A on it. Sitting in the family room with my parents when I was in grade school, all of us reading, Dad seeing me nose-deep in *To Kill a Mockingbird*.

Smart girl, he would always say, tweaking my cheek.

I was glad he and Mom hadn't been around to witness their girl go dumb and all waste-of-lifish.

"So," I said. "Have there been any effects from my dream-digging last night? Did you sense that my suggestion of don't-do-violence worked on Tim, or if he gets the feeling something's off with us around?"

"If you're asking whether our boy's got a sense of peace about him, I'd say no. That poor phone on the counter will testify to that. And if you're wondering whether he's catching on to the idea that there are ghosts around him, I can only say that he's either willfully ignoring all the cold air that's suddenly swirling in this place or he's just ignorant, period. He reminds me of a dog I once had, shortly after I got married. You could do back springs in front of that animal and he would sit on the floor, maybe raising his eyebrows every so often at you. Too lazy to acknowledge anything going on around him, that dog. Or maybe he was so caught up with what was going on in his own canine mind that he didn't care." He nodded. "I miss that dog, but I won't miss this one."

Laughing, I gave Louis a long gander. "You never mentioned that you owned a dog."

His eyes were as dark as molasses surrounded by smile crinkles. "It doesn't make me special, Miss—"

"Ah-ah."

"Jensen."

I grinned, then said, "It's just that, out of all the

ghosts I know, you're the most private. Sure, I know how you died, but beyond that? I've got nothing on you."

"You know I went to SDSU."

"But I always wondered why you used your degree for working at that aircraft plant."

"I didn't." His gaze took on the distance of memory. "I was a teacher for a while. High school math outside San Diego, even though this was where I grew up. But then Pearl Harbor was attacked and my patriotic fire was stirred up and I moved my family home to be with my parents."

"You were in the military?"

"They couldn't use me." He put his hand over the area of his heart. "It was bad in here. My heart was too frail to let me fight. So I got a job at the plant when there were openings, after they ran out of white people to hire. Didn't get beyond the cleaning staff, but I was still doing my part for my country."

Something dawned on me. "You didn't get in that car crash because you had a heart attack or anything."

He laughed the fullest laugh I'd ever heard from Louis. "No, sugar. I was overly tired, and one moment, I was driving, the next I saw headlights in front of me, and—"

He smashed his hands together, leaving us in silence. Tim's TV, which was playing some raunchy movie about spring break, droned on.

"If you ask me," Louis said, "I'd gladly take my death over yours any day, so I'm not complaining. It happened quickly. That's all we can ask for."

"What is it that tethers you to earth then, if it's not a burning desire to solve your death or protect a loved one or what-have-you?"

His tone went quiet. "For a while it was my kids, but then they all chose the glare before I could greet them in this dimension. They already had their minds made up, and they had no idea I was waiting here for them. I thought of following them onward, and I was ready to call my wrangler to scoop me up and escort me to the glare. But I realized I might never get to see them again at all, because what if we're in a place where we don't recognize each other? What if we don't end up in the same place at all? At least here, I could stick around to watch over my grandchildren and so on. But there's the rub—no one in my family seems to want to linger here after they pass away. Not like I do." He lost his smile. "These days, my live descendants don't pay much attention to their history. I'm not even sure they know who I was. It's disheartening, and I was just about to open myself to my wrangler again when you walked into that ghost party, talking about Elizabeth Dalton. It inspired me, so I stayed."

You know how, as a human, emotion sticks in your throat? That's pretty much what I was feeling now. I mean, how cool was it that I had someone from a long time ago around to tell me his stories? I might never find my relatives in Boo World—they might've moved on just as Louis' relatives had—but Louis was here instead.

It was especially nice that he felt like he mattered in the scheme of things now, and I suspected he might not have felt that way in life. Kind of like yours truly.

"I'm glad you stayed, Louis," I said.

"Me, too."

We were having a moment, smiling at each other, when Tim jumped off the sofa and made a beeline for the kitchen counter, where he'd left his phone. I guessed he thought he'd missed a nonexistent call from Nichelle. When he checked his screen and didn't like what he saw, he chucked the phone toward the wall.

Crump! After the phone fell, there was a gouge in the wall, and he cursed. Did he ever.

"This is all your fault, you bitch," he said to the small hole. I think he was seeing Nichelle's face there.

"Well, then," I said to Louis. "Sure looks like the seeds of nonviolence I planted in his head last night didn't quite flower."

"I can still picture him ripping an invisible person apart and leaving blood on the walls in his dream, just like you described to us. I don't want to see what might happen when Nichelle gets home today."

Tim went into the kitchen, standing in front of a window by a block of knives, looking out of the glass.

I darted off the table.

"What are you going to do?" Louis asked.

"I know what I *should* do." Because everything I'd tried with Farah in the Elizabeth Dalton case had produced the results I'd been hoping for. A confession. Why couldn't something similar work here, with Tim's bad side coming out for everyone to see? With him facing the consequences for it?

I'd eventually just make sure matters didn't go off the rails this time.

"Maybe," I said, "if I could just plant a few more seeds in Tim about calming down, that would work for now?"

"For how long?" Louis sighed. "But, yes, we could try it."

He paused while the word *we* hung between us.

"We could try something else, too . . ." he said.

"Are you thinking what I'm thinking?"

He nodded, the constant student shining through—the one who always wanted to try new things and gather more information. "If we doubled up, we might suck less energy from both of us. Let's give it a whirl."

Brilliant. "Since Tim's not asleep, we can't plant seeds deep down. But we can sure use a hallucination to get him to back off Nichelle, right?"

"At least for today."

"Awesome," I whispered. It was like I had been driving a compact car this whole time, but now I was about to hop into a double-your-fun Firebird.

As Louis and I put our heads together, Tim wandered to the front window close by us, staring out of it like he could summon Nichelle. I could see his faint reflection in the glass thanks to the angle of the sunlight: There was a scowl. A threatening storm about to emerge if he didn't mellow.

After Louis and I huddled up and made plans, he stationed himself on one side of Tim. I took the other.

I went first, saving the hallucination and starting off slow instead, my gaze directed at our haunt-ee as I summoned the vague scent of a summer night, with fresh-cut grass filling the room. Sweet, nice smells of serenity.

Tim sniffed, then frowned. I hoped he had good memories of fresh-cut grass, because that's what I'd been aiming for. Didn't everyone, though?

Louis took it from there, gearing up to make his voice materialize. We'd decided he'd take this job since he was a male.

"You're starting to go over the edge, Tim," he said conversationally. "Do you realize that?"

Tim turned around, looking where Louis would've been standing if he hadn't been invisible.

"Tim," Louis said. "I'm inside you, telling you to take a good look at yourself. What're you going to do with Nichelle when she gets here? Are you thinking of doing something you'll regret?"

Tim put his hands over his ears, but when he realized what he was doing, he started to laugh.

"That's fucking stupid," he said, going back to the window.

I talked to Louis. "Would a normal person be laughing about this?"

Louis went to Tim, touching his skin, his eyes going blazing blue, the same color shining out of his mouth as he empathized.

He didn't do it for long. "Tim thinks it's just a random thought he had."

I didn't want to drive Tim crazy. We had to be careful and not overdo it. Hopefully he'd keep pegging the voice on his conscience.

Louis tried again, softly saying, "You know you'd never get away with what your anger is telling you to do."

Tim shook his head, each shake harder than the last one, like he was trying to dislodge the thoughts from his brain. Then he laughed again.

"I'm used to being scary," I said. "Not comical."

"He's attempting to laugh the voice away." Louis nodded at me, letting me know I could proceed with my next action.

I concentrated my energy until it was a flaring seethe, then slowly floated up to Tim's bare back, letting my essence shape to his form. Just before I saw the chills on his arms, I leaned into him, hard.

Hallucination hard.

I burst into him, bone deep—no, *brain* deep—and I melded to him, blending with the scene that was already in his head, then getting ready to show him an image that would rock him . . .

We're standing in front of the window, looking out of it. We can barely see our outline in the glass: our short blond hair, our face . . .

The voice in our head is gone. Only the smell of grass is still here. It soothes us after what we just heard. It reminds us of days when we used to get out of the house, away from Mom, to cut grass for a few bucks a shot. The sound of the mower, the lazy rhythm of the blades whipping around, the feeling of getting something accomplished.

Summer grass.

As we remember, we can see ourselves smile in the window reflection. We can see . . .

There's something behind us.

Another . . . face?

Heart slamming, adrenaline rushing—cold, so cold as we whirl around.

Nothing there.

A beat of relief. We laugh. First, there'd been the voice. Now, a face. But the voice had been a part of us, a man's voice, just like ours. The face had been . . .

Unable to remember correctly, we try to call it back up to memory. Delicate features, nice lips . . .

A woman?

Just as we're deciding what it was, it reappears in the window, clarifying every second as it comes closer to our shoulder. Ice chips scrape down our back, and we reach behind us with a hand, trying to feel it.

All air.

Pulse stamping now, we turn around, scanning the room. What was it?

Where is it?

Our breath comes fast, chilling our lungs as we walk away from the window, fast, quiet. We still can't see where it is.

In the background, the TV has gone to static, dead air.

But there's something whispering over the hissing sound.

"Tim . . ."

We look in the direction the voice came from, but there's only a glass-fronted cabinet with dishes, and—

On the glass is the face.

A girl? A woman? We still don't know, but as we try to get away from the cabinet, it shadows our progress.

"Tim," it breathes, stalking us as it floats over the glass, bodiless and pale and blurry. Just a mouth moving, a hole. "Don't make a mistake. Leave Nichelle before it's too late."

We're away from the cabinet, heading for the hall, diving into the bedroom, shutting the door behind us, leaning against it.

Panting, we don't see the figure in the wall mirror until it's too late.

Misty body, a white shadow tracking us as we try to get out of the way again.

"She makes you so angry," it says reasonably. "Why do you stay? Leave before it's too late!"

We pick up a shoe from the floor, throw it at the mirror. It cracks into pieces, but the mist stays.

Now, though, it's pressing up against the glass, like it's trying to get through to us, making scratching noises.

"You'll pay if you don't leave!"

A bolt of true fear struck me inside Tim's body, and it zapped me right out of him. I drift-stumbled backward, weakened. As I went to an outlet, Louis came up to me.

"Look at this," he said, pointing at Tim, who was on the floor and leaning against the bed, sweating and shaking hard.

Success! I hoped.

"Do you think we did any good?" I asked.

"We'll see about that." Louis leaned over to touch Tim's skin, empathizing, but just briefly so we didn't tool with him too badly.

Once again, I got a good view of blank airport-blue eyes and a gaping blue mouth before Louis came out of his trance.

"I think we're getting somewhere," he said.

Relaxing, I let the electricity do its work, juicing me up.

Getting me ready for when Nichelle came home and we could really see if we'd done our job.

She returned a couple of hours later, long after Tim had gotten up from the floor, walked to the bathroom to splash water on his face, then sat in front of the TV again. This time, he watched baseball. 'Twas the season, after all.

When she came through the door, Tim was laid-back. "How was lunch?" he asked.

Nichelle was wary as she set her purse and a couple of small shopping bags on the table. "Great. Thanks?"

He didn't say anything else, just kept watching the zombie box.

She seemed so happy about his submissiveness that she got two glasses out of the cupboard and poured soda for them both, bringing his to him on the sofa. She sat in a nearby chair, grabbing a magazine from a floor rack and paging through it.

"The picture of domestic bliss," I said to Louis as we watched from the dining table.

"I'm sticking around to make sure it stays that way." He braced his forearms on his knees, a sentinel. "You go ahead and do what you need to do."

I thought about Wendy's place, where Scott was on guard. Flaherty's Pub, where Randy was on the lookout for Gavin visiting Suze. Amanda Lee's, where Cassie was keeping her company. Boo World, which Twyla was scouring for Milo Guttenburg, person of interest.

Suddenly, I felt like a fifth wheel. Everyone seemed to be good with where they were.

I guessed I could use a break.

I almost patted Louis on the back in thanks. Old habits died hard. "Don't mind if I kick back then. There's this place in Elfin Forest that I've sort of commandeered . . ."

"There is?" He was all smiles now. "When's the housewarming party?"

I laughed. "It's an abandoned cottage. You're welcome anytime."

"I'll look you up when everything levels out here."

He winked at me, and I winked back. With Nichelle and Tim acting like Mike and Carol Brady in the family room, I was feeling lighthearted.

I left Louis and traveled up to my new pad. I was half expecting the occupants to have returned, breaking my nonexistent heart, half expecting fake Dean to be sprawled on the covered sofa, grinning as I came through the chimney.

But the place was dark and silent except for the night sounds outside: wind nuzzling the tree leaves, frogs croaking from the creek.

I wasn't sure what to do at first. What was this thing called "relaxing"? It was quite the foreign concept now.

I got the hang of it, though, floating to the back porch, listening, allowing myself to veg out.

But, as I said, ghosts don't sleep. We get restless instead and, within a half hour, I was done for. So I retreated to the main bedroom, with its wide-screen TV. Why not? That's how I was slowly becoming a woman of this new world, tele-educating myself in all the new phrases and trends. It was just a bummer that there was so much going on during this era that sometimes I doubted I'd ever catch up.

As I lay on the bed, manipulating the channels on the TV, the room started to feel empty. So did the space beside me. I imagined my old Dean stretched out next to me, his blue-jeaned legs long, his arms folded under his head as he turned to aim that pussy-catcher grin at me.

"Miss me, Jenny?"

I sprang up in bed, my essence sparking. Fake Dean?

But when the image faded and I realized that I didn't have a corporeal body like I always did when fake Dean was around, I lay back down.

Nothing was there in the space next to me. Not even the unreal thing. Damn lonely imagination.

I sighed, hearing the echo of my dissatisfaction through the room. I tried to watch that TV, but I couldn't. I was too wound up, and I shut it off and got out of bed because I couldn't stand the inactivity for a second longer.

So I headed for the forest, partly drawn by my death spot.

Partly giving in to the nature that I was just now realizing I couldn't fight.

13

I hadn't been in the woods at night since me and my human friends had come here to get nice and scared.

Were ghosts allowed to feel that way, too?

Even though I'd never personally encountered huge paranormal activity here besides what I brought to the table, I'd heard that the freaks generally came out at night in Elfin Forest, so, as usual, I kept my eye out for any other weirdos like me.

And I could feel all kinds of gazes watching me right back. Everything in the forest felt somehow . . . well, not alive. Maybe "nocturnally animated" was a better description. Actually, this place was a lot like an enchanted forest at night, where trees were waiting to snatch at me, their branches knotted and long, like the fingers of a sorceress.

Speaking of witches . . . Was that a horse's snort I heard in the near distance? They said the forest witch rode a black, misty stallion . . .

I rushed through the trees toward my death spot,

trying not to feel humiliated that I was a ghost who didn't want to run into another ghost.

Near the twisted, U-shaped oak branch that skimmed the ground and formed a sort of chair, my death spot reached out to me, gnawing through me with its sheer power.

I gravitated toward it. Home sweet home, right?

As I floated down, covering the ground with my essence until I probably looked like a flashing puddle, the death energy droned at high volume, moaning through me. *Now* I could relax, and I tried not to think about everything that had been draining me these past two days: fake Dean, the dark spirit from the Edgett place, Tim Knudson . . .

It was the last one that I truly couldn't let go of, because, seriously, how long could me and Louis continue to assuage Tim with hallucinations or suggestions in his dreams to refrain from violence?

And, as Twyla said, why should we? It might give Nichelle a false sense of security, making her stay because she thought she was safe.

The question harshed my buzz. But I was becoming more realistic by the second, and the more realistic I got, the more Twyla's suggestion about just doing away with Tim came back to me. *Destroy him,* she'd pretty much said. *Take him out and maybe the world will be a better place.*

As my death spot sucked at me and pulsed into me at the same time, the hard-core solution seemed to make great sense. But I was just lucid enough to dizzily wonder if my thoughts were tainted by the spot's energy.

I didn't like the notion one bit, so I forced myself not to think of Tim. Instead, I doubled my efforts to loosen up, to think of my death spot like it was some kind of rejuvenating spa and I was here to get a turbo massage.

A spa. You know who probably went to a lot of spa days? Brittany Kirkman Stokley. She might have even gotten a mani-pedi before her luncheon.

A tiny zap lit through my head at the thought of her. That was weird, so I tried even harder to relax. Like I needed more stress in my life.

But my mind kept going back to Brittany for some reason.

Zap-zap-zap.

It was like a bunch of thoughts were trying to connect in me, like fingers reaching out to touch one another in a dark mass of space.

God, my death spot was really doing some tricks on me tonight.

Then—*zap-zap-zap!*

My essence froze as a thought definitely connected— an image that sent a long, screeching shudder through me.

I saw hands. My hands and arms, and they were in front of my face as I tried to ward off that shriveled, leering granny mask and the ax that was lifted in the air.

"Stop! Please! Why're you doing this?"

Then, Brittany's voice from our interview today. *"I'm not sure why she took those bracelets off. . . ."*

Bracelets. I'd just seen those in the image.

I quickly rolled away from where I'd died, but the

zaps kept coming, each one shredding me with icy heat. They were strong and weak, cold and hot, hitting me so fast that all I saw was the yin and the yang symbol chasing itself until black became white and white became black, one big bewildering blur swimming through my head—

The swirling stopped, and I found myself hovering over that twisted oak tree limb, the forest silent around me until an owl let out an experimental hoot. Had I become like that yin and yang, spinning around in a ghostly smudge until I'd just now solidified?

Damn, did I ever feel strong, though. Even better, I'd gotten another piece to my puzzle.

Those bracelets *had* been on my arm when the killer had attacked. I hadn't taken them off and left them in the car because my other friend Lisa had been making fun of my jewelry's Madonna-ness.

My murderer had to have removed those bracelets from me after I was dead, and he'd gone out of his way to plant them in the car. But why had he left the bracelets behind at all?

Good God, had the sadist been leaving behind a calling card?

The willies racked me, but there was this to consider, too: Did the bracelets have my blood on them since I'd been wearing them while I was killed? Or would they have any traces of *him*?

I knew from watching that *CSI* program a few times that my killer could've very well left a part of himself behind on those bracelets, whether it was a fingerprint or other trace evidence or whatever they called it.

Did I have a fighting chance at solving my own mystery now?

I'd have to tell Amanda Lee about what I'd just discovered, because she was picking those bracelets up tomorrow from Brittany. Ruben would know what to do from there. . . .

I don't know how long I sat there absorbing just what kind of evil freak I'd been up against that night. Because nobody expects the Spanish Inquisition, right? I had ended up face-to-mask with a real live psycho killer, and no matter how many times I saw my death playing out in my mind's eye, I could never quite convince myself that I'd been his victim.

It'd been another Jensen Murphy. Another shit-for-luck girl.

But that avoidance technique wasn't quite working for me anymore. The wall that Amanda Lee had said I'd erected to block out the crime—the same wall that'd probably slammed me into my time loop—was beginning to crumble with the gradual help of my death spot. Questions plugged the places where the bricks had fallen out. For one, I wanted to know what my killer's first murder had been like. Also, what kind of person had he been before he'd committed it? Had he been a mild-mannered guy who worked at a desk job, never giving a hint of the foulness inside? Or had he been more like Tim Knudson, sending off red flags to people like Heidi Schmidt?

As I lingered over that, the back of my essence wavered.

I felt watched again. But in a big way this time.

With a panicked jerk, I turned around, only to exhale out a big unreal breath when I saw that it was only Cassie.

"Sorry, Jensen," she said. "I didn't mean to sneak up and frighten you."

"It's not you. It's this." I gestured to the woods. *Brrr.*

She came forward, her complexion wan, even for a ghost, her paisley blouse dull with lack of color, her flared pants just as bland. "I came from my own death spot in Escondido. Not because I wanted energy. I can't seem to absorb much of it tonight."

"You can't refuel?" There was no way she should be this draggy after pulling from her spot.

"No. That's all right, though—my death spot always helps me to sort through my thoughts. It clarifies them."

"Me, too." Maybe that was another reason some ghosts haunted the places they'd died.

I remembered that she should've been with Amanda Lee right now, and just before I asked about that, she said, "Oh, don't worry. Amanda Lee's in good hands. Old Seth came over to poke around. He said he wanted to see, as he says, 'What was what.'"

I hadn't encountered Old Seth, our nineteenth-century cowboy ghost, in over a month. I didn't know him very well, but the others did, so I was sure he'd take care of Amanda Lee just fine.

Cassie added, "When he arrived, I had the feeling that he'd been hearing about our activity the last two days, and he wanted in. So I asked if he would stay with Amanda Lee. Honestly, I had my doubts about what I could do for her, anyway, if that dark spirit had popped in on her."

"Cassie . . ."

"Please don't give me a false shot of optimism. That spirit got the best of me today. Don't pretend like it didn't."

Wow. The fight had really knocked her down a peg or two. "I still trust you to protect and serve here in Boo World. Don't let one bad encounter bum you out."

She smiled. "Thank you for saying that. Louis tried to bolster me, too. And, yes, before you have to ask, I did go to him at Tim's. I missed you by about a half hour, but he told me you were going to your new house up here. On my way, I saw you hanging around this spot and stopped."

"Is everything okay, Cassie?" I was getting a heavy feeling that it wasn't.

"Everything's just fine." Her tone was lemon-polish smooth, but the look in her eyes wasn't so much that way. There was a cloudiness there that stood out from all the gray in her.

She leaned back her head and watched the sky, like she was listening to the night around us. "I gave a shout for Twyla when I got here because I was hoping she would be looking for Milo Guttenburg at his old cabin, where he died. I also called an old acquaintance who likes these woods. He only haunts outside of them when he watches over his old girlfriend."

"Okay . . ."

Before I could fire more *But are you feeling all right*s at her, she flipped into a different subject, like she knew what I was going to ask and didn't want to talk about it.

"Amanda Lee wanted me to tell you about the lunch with Nichelle and Heidi today. While she tried her best to talk sense into Nichelle, Amanda Lee and I stayed back, listening."

"Did Heidi get anywhere with her?"

"Maybe. Now that you've seen into Tim, Heidi feels justified in coming out with her suspicions to Nichelle. Nichelle told her that she'd noticed his increasing dissatisfaction with life, too. Evidently he's having a hard time at work and she thinks he's taking it out on her."

"That's what she's blaming his attitude on?"

"Yes. Nichelle thinks he'll get over it sooner or later, and she's going to stick by her man, helping him through it."

"That's because she loves him."

"That's what she said." Cassie floated toward an oak, running her hand near the bark. She was paying a lot of attention to the simplest things around her, and that only added to my unsettled feeling. What was going on with her?

She added, "If there's one thing that astounds me about the living, it's how they can't see love for what it is. Or isn't. She's mistaking good sex for emotion. At least, that's the impression I got from what she was saying to Heidi today about Tim." She lowered her hand to her side. "I should know what I'm talking about. During fifteen years of marriage, I never stopped to wonder if I really loved my husband. It wasn't until I was dead that I realized we didn't have what I thought we had. But that's what happens when you marry too young, I suppose."

Gosh, she was getting dolorous. It was like the dark spirit had stolen what little happiness Cassie had died with. I knew that she'd felt big-time satisfaction when she'd taken her life; in that one moment, she'd had some of the control she'd never had when she'd been living. It was just that, in death, the regrets had set in.

She turned to me. "Heidi did suggest seeing a shrink to Nichelle, for Tim's sake. Maybe that'll work out."

"Maybe." Uh-uh.

Cassie's smile was back, sweet and a little sad. "I just want you to know, Jensen—it's been fun having such adventures with you around. You've brought so much activity and brightness."

I frowned, but I didn't get to pursue my own suspicions because I felt another presence nearby.

When a fortyish ghost with scraggly hair, a wild beard, and a definite Jesus vibe showed up carrying a backpack, Cassie clasped her hands.

"Daniel. You came!"

"You called." He nodded at me. "You must be the serial killer chick. I've heard through the ghostvine about you." With a gesture to himself, he said, "I'm Daniel Ashbury."

Cassie interjected. "He was my granddaughter Calliope's boyfriend."

"I'm afraid my story's not half as ear-catching as yours."

"It's made the rounds, huh?" I asked.

"Sure has." He offered up his own death story. Ghost

etiquette, you know? "*I* was just on a hike a few years ago when, apparently, a hidden heart defect got the best of me."

Cassie laughed softly. "I've told him that he should get together with Louis and have some sort of heart-to-heart club."

Daniel grinned, hover-sitting next to me on the curved oak limb. Just as he was probably about to start asking me details about how I was murdered—I mean, he had that ultra-curious gleam in his eyes like everyone gets when they meet me—the sound of a loud "Gawd!" rang through the woods.

Three guesses as to who that was. But Cassie seemed very pleased that Twyla had answered her call, too.

When I heard another voice with her, all deep and growly, I came to attention. Had she found Milo Guttenburg at his old cabin and death spot?

Apparently so, because when Twyla came marching into our view, she had a scruffy, white wire-haired behemoth in plaid air-trudging after her.

"Told you I heard her!" she said, pointing at me. "See, Milo, you didn't have to drag your butt out of the woods after all. Jensen came here, so stop your pissing and moaning. I've been listening to it for what feels like hours."

He grumbled, fixing a lazy eye on me. At his sour mood, I think I might've rather run into the witch of the woods than him.

Eh, maybe not.

Twyla sighed dramatically. "Grumpiest thing I ever met, but when I told him that he's being looked into again for your murder, he wanted to set the record straight with you. *That* got him out of his shithole."

Milo bothered to carefully pronounce his words this time. "I didn't do it."

Still a growl, but very improved.

"Clearly," I said, "I don't have to tell my story to you as a hello."

"Oh, blah-blah-blah," Twyla said. "Let's fast-forward through the etiquette, okay? Like, Milo stroked out and that's how he bit it. Moving on."

"I don't know nothing new about how you died," he said to me, already starting to float away. "So don't come looking for me again."

"You didn't see or hear anything that could help us figure out who might've killed me?"

"Don't know nothing," he said again. "Christ on a cracker, I'd just like a little peace and quiet these days. If a man can't even get it in his own home, then where's it found?"

Twyla rolled her eyes. "That home he's talking about? It's a burned shack that's falling down like a house of toothpicks. Total suckarama."

He'd already gotten good at ignoring Twyla. With another grumble, he said, "Even if the woods get on fire, kids're still coming here, wanting to track down cults or take goddamned pictures of ghosts or find the forest witch. Wish I still had my shotgun."

"So that particular night when me and my friends were here . . . ?" I asked.

"I was in my cabin, listening to you carrying on in the distance with your music and laughing. You just have to be so loud about having fun, don't you? You were lucky that night—I put my Walkman on and finished some woodwork I needed to get done for a shop in town. Otherwise . . ."

Twyla chopped out a groan. "News flash, Milo. She wasn't all that lucky."

He stomped off for good this time, and I called a "Thank you, sir" out after him. He flapped a hand up to me, all "Just bug off."

When he was gone, Twyla said, "I wish I could empathize with that guy. He, like, was the worst interview ever. Humans are way easier because you get to go into them. For being invisible, ghosts sure aren't transparent."

"You tried," I said. "And I appreciate it."

I hadn't even finished my sentence when Twyla started checking out Daniel, and it was obvious from the way he put a couple of inches distance from her that they'd met before.

"Twyla," he said in greeting, keeping it short.

"Hey yourself."

And that was that.

Cassie laughed a little, but the sound died, straying into the night as she lavished a look on Daniel, me, then Twyla.

Something was definitely up.

"Cass," Twyla said, "you're awfully quiet. You have been since this morning."

"I've done some thinking," she said, pushing back her light ponytail, which had flopped over her shoulder. "I've been around Boo World for a long time, Twyla. A very long time, and . . ."

Twyla slowly said, "You say that like you're a thousand years old."

"It really does feel like I've been in this place an eon." Cassie looked upward again, toward the treetops, then directly at me. "I never expected to stay here for this long. When I slit my wrists, I did it because I wanted everything to end. But then I woke up here, in this dimension, and right away, there were ghosts surrounding me. Just before I died, my husband had moved us into a new house. It felt . . . strange. For the month we lived there, I never knew why there were such odd energies, but when I saw everyone around me after I passed on, I realized that the house had been haunted by good spirits. They took me under their wing until, one by one, they went into the glare. By that point, I'd found Twyla, wandering around after her own death, confused and a little off balance. I did for her what those ghosts had done for me."

Daniel said, "You paid it forward. Good karma."

"I was learning the ropes just fine, Cass," Twyla interrupted, but she did it with a tenderness that made it obvious that she was lying about how much Cassie had eased her way into Boo World.

"Of course you were doing fine," Cassie said, smiling. She looked at Daniel. "I'd already realized that I wanted to see my children grow up, then my grandchildren. None of them have died yet, so when my favorite grandchild's boyfriend here passed on, I made sure I was around for him. But there comes a time when you sense that there's more for you, that the glare holds something new and exciting, and you realize that you've been afraid to see what it is this entire time."

Rushing forward, Twyla let off sparks. "No, Cass—"

"Hear me out."

Twyla fell like an autumn leaf toward the ground, fear all over her half-and-half face.

"After this morning," Cassie said, "I want more than anything to go wherever we're meant to go next. When that dark spirit plunged into me, I felt its bleakness. I still feel it, and it reminds me too much of the woman I used to be when I was alive—unhappy, hopeless. But I can make all of that go away."

A sudden sob broke out of her, and none of us moved.

How could you comfort someone who would always be inconsolable? And how could you do it when *you* had no idea how to really feel about almost everything anymore?

Twyla tried her best. I could see her harden her hand, then reach up to touch Cassie. But, as Randy had told me, ghosts didn't feel that very human warmth and pleasure when they touched. So why bother?

Cassie hardened her own hand, anyway, and they made contact, two unfeeling entities, trying so hard to soothe each other. Wanting. Wishing there could be more to it.

When their hands fell away from one another, no one said anything. Not until Daniel came to a stand.

"I get it, Cassie. When Calliope dies, I'm going to move on, too. She's what I'm staying around for. I'm going to miss the hell out of you, though."

Cassie reacted only by smiling at him again, then looking toward the sky. But this time, there was an obvious reason for it.

Something gray and expansive was gently winging down from the treetops, gliding so smoothly that it was enough to take anything's breath away. If they had any.

At first, I thought it might be the dark spirit and the moonlight was playing tricks with its color, but I didn't get a terrible, negative feeling from it. As it skimmed over the ground toward Cassie, swooping to a stand, it slowly took the form of a flowing, lace-torn bride, thickly veiled and covered from neck to toe in a shroud.

So this was it. Cassie had been calling out to everyone she could, just so she could say good-bye to us. Now I realized who her final call had been to.

Her wrangler.

Randy had told me once that every ghost had one, and sometimes they showed up on their own. But not this time.

Cassie beamed at it, her relief a beacon, her eyes filling with the illusion of tears.

Twyla didn't hold back on the weeping, although I'm not sure any tears could come out of her. Daniel only put a hand over his heart in farewell.

When Cassie smiled at me, I felt a shimmer of energy run through me. She was happy, at peace, and ecstatic about the last adventure she'd probably ever take.

"I wish," I said through the tightness of my throat, "you could come back and be the first to report what you find out there."

She laughed. "I'm hoping I'll never want to come back."

The wrangler acted like nobody existed except for Cassie, angling its head as it adored her with its veiled gaze. Then it lifted its hand, resting its gloved fingers on Cassie's face.

She closed her eyes. "This is the first time I've let a wrangler this close. I've always felt it near, aching to take me to a glare spot, but now?" She opened her eyes, looking straight at it. "I'm yours."

With an airy grace, the wrangler lifted its veil only high enough so it could drape the grayness over Cassie. Almost magically, the veil breathed toward the ground, consuming Cassie and erasing her like she'd never existed at all as the flowing material rested against the wrangler once again.

It raised its arms, almost in a beatific way, then lifted off the ground slowly, slowly, until it started moving backward in the exact way it'd come.

Winging.

Flying.

Disappearing above the treetops.

It wasn't until it was gone and I heard the sounds of Twyla crying that I realized I was doing the same thing, even though I couldn't feel any tears on my face.

14

As life went on around us in the forest—with that owl hooting, then the sound of car wheels screeching on a road somewhere in the distance—I thought about how nothing outside of Boo World would ever care about what'd just happened with Cassie. Her kids and grandkids wouldn't know that she'd been near them for so long after her death. She'd been lost in a history that'd never even made it into any books; she'd been here, then gone, leaving no trace of herself in the end.

No trace except for a veiled-phantom memory that still stuck with me with all its awful beauty.

But just as regular life went on, *our* existences continued, even without Cassie here. Daniel the hiker had moseyed back into the woods with a raised hand and a "See you later, Jensen," like he knew I'd be back to visit my death spot sooner rather than later. Twyla, however, had stayed near my death spot and told me to go wherever I was planning to go next without her. I was pretty sure that this place had taken on new meaning for her, because it was Cassie's memorial now, and she wanted to get as much from it as she could.

I really liked the notion of that. Cassie had been completely joyful when she'd taken that final step with the wrangler, and it had brought something new and sublime to the spot where I'd died. When I came back, there'd be extra meaning.

Leaving Twyla by herself, I decided to forget about returning to my new house, because I'd be the only one there, and in this contemplative mood, that wasn't very appealing. Besides, I had to start telling the others about Cassie, and since Scott was one of the ghosts who needed to know about her, I would start at Wendy's, where he was still guarding.

When I arrived, he was outside her window while she sat on the sill, her short black skirt dangling off it while they chatted. It was like the balcony scene from *Romeo and Juliet*, and I had the sneaking suspicion that Scott had starred in similar productions of his own making when he was human.

They'd seen my travel tunnel come and go, so they greeted me casually.

" 'Sup, Jensen?" Wendy asked, fake shooting me with her finger. At least someone was feeling playful tonight.

Scott added his own charming grin. "What's your tale, nightingale?"

Wendy laughed like it was the most original thing she'd ever heard. She really needed to get out of the house more. But the good news was that she'd either forgotten the little fit of temper she'd had earlier, after

I'd followed Gavin into his room for a private discussion, or she hadn't been too angry at me for leaving her out of our conversation in the first place.

It also looked like Gavin hadn't told her about that dark spirit possibly being her adoptive father. She was just too upbeat right now as she smiled at me in welcome.

Damn, I hated to crash the general good mood with my own piece of news. I mean, just because I'd seen how happy Cassie had been in the end, that didn't mean others were going to interpret the circumstances that way, although Daniel had witnessed her euphoria, too, and he'd walked away fine. I'm not sure Twyla had gotten the same message, though.

I must've been terrible at masking my true emotional state, because Scott's grin turned into a frown. "You don't look so up, Jen."

"It's Cassie."

"What about her?"

"She called her wrangler."

Scott looked at me for a second, like he didn't quite hear me. Then he lowered his head, hiding his face, but I could feel his energy dip.

Before I could tell him about Cassie's jubilant exit, Wendy asked, "Scott, are you okay?"

She'd lifted her hand like she was going to touch him. But either she'd already discovered that she couldn't make real contact with a ghost or she was hesitating in the way you hesitate when you haven't yet touched the guy you were flirting with, and you're not sure if you should.

Then she glanced at me, her dark eyes confused.

"Cassie's gone," I said.

She kept looking from me to him. "Did this wrangler take her somewhere?"

"A wrangler is a reaper," Scott said quietly, lifting his head so I could see how tight his jaw was. "It escorts us to a place that ghosts never come back from."

"Oh. Oh, that's horrible." Wendy stood.

There was so much death in this girl's life. I was sorry we'd brought even more to her than she should've been dealing with.

"It's not all that horrible," I said. "Cassie wanted to leave this plane, and she was happy to do it."

Scott was peering up at me. He was one of those guys who basically kept his reactions on an even keel, but his sad gaze couldn't hide everything.

I added, "I've never seen Cassie want to go someplace so badly."

Wendy said, "So she was fine with dying."

That seemed to shake Scott out of his reticence. "She was dead already."

She didn't react to his blunt statement. "I'm just wondering why she can't go into the light herself."

"From what I know," Scott says, "wranglers escort you."

I kept silent, because I'd been close to going into a glare with fake Dean. He'd had one—a glowing lotus pool—in his star place, and he'd told me that he let his collected bodies go into them when they were ready to.

But fake Dean wasn't a wrangler, so why should I trust his word about what that pool was? Maybe it wasn't really a glare at all. Maybe that liquid gathering of light led to something much different. . . .

"I guess," Wendy said, "that it isn't very smart to get attached to ghosts when you guys can disappear on an even more permanent basis than you do when you die." She snuck a glance at Scott, which he didn't notice.

Oh, man. I wanted to let her know she was right about getting attached. I even felt a little protective of her with Scott.

It might be a good idea to get someone else to guard her from now on.

Scott's eyes were pale in the moonlight as he watched me. "What was it like when she went, Jen? I've never seen a ghost taken by a wrangler, even though I know mine comes around every so often, like it's reminding me I can summon it whenever I want."

As I pulled on the memory of Cassie's wrangling, I couldn't keep a note of wonder out of my voice. "This is going to sound strange, but . . . the whole thing was transcendent. There was no fighting or screaming or begging to be left alone from Cassie. She had this look on her face as she went under the wrangler's veil—acceptance. Relief like I've never seen before. Then she disappeared, and it was over. It was almost like . . ."

"What?" he asked.

I smiled. "Almost like the wrangler brought her home." To her own perfect cottage in the woods. To a place she'd been searching for a long, long time but could never find.

"Home," he said, just like he'd forgotten what the

word meant. Then he said, "It makes sense. Cassie was always walking the line between the death we live here in Boo World and the even bigger death. She always said there was a hollowness in her, and I told her that this is just how a ghost is—hollow. She'd answer that I didn't understand, and she wouldn't say anything else. She was right—I never did understand, because I happen to like it here. Always have, always will."

"So sad," Wendy whispered as the night breeze brushed her sheer curtain over her and she idly pushed it away.

Scott watched her in a way that only a ghost could watch a human it was getting attached to.

For some reason, it made me think of Gavin's sketches and how I appeared whenever he saw me through his own warped perception. He had an attachment, but it was far from this kind of innocence that I was seeing with Scott and Wendy.

"Want a break from guard duty?" I asked Scott.

"To do what?" He motioned around, toward the eerily quiet condo landscape. Lights glowed from neighboring windows, some semicovered by grand trellises. Outside the wall of Wendy's courtyard, gas lamps flickered over the paradise-flowered walkways. The splash of the Edgetts' fountain trickled. "This ain't half bad, Jen. It's . . ." He turned to Wendy. "How did you put it before?"

"Like a manufactured Eden," Wendy said. "I was being kind of cynical when I said it, though."

And that's why I liked the girl.

She absently combed her fingers back through her

pink-streaked hair and then wrapped it into a bun. Reaching over to the nearby desk to grab a pencil, she stuck it into her do, securing it. Scott was enthralled.

She didn't notice. But I might've been wrong about that.

"I'd offer you guys a Red Bull," she said, "or some sort of sophisticated cocktail so we could toast Cassie's journey. But Scott showed me how drinks just go right through you."

"Show-off," I murmured to Scott, who'd taken to resting his arms over the sill as he looked up at Wendy. The kid was too cute for his own good.

Did she notice *that*? Probably, but she didn't show it.

We all dawdled for a few seconds more until Scott softly said, "Cheers to Cassie then."

"Cheers," we repeated.

A few seconds went by. It turned into a minute. Then Wendy said, "All right. Since Cassie fought for me today, she would've wanted us to go on with the good fight, right?"

"Right." Scott and I were in stereo now.

She grabbed a computer-printed piece of paper from her desk, like she wanted to show me something on it.

I bit. "What's that?"

"I've been doing more research."

Scott made an aside to me. "And it ain't for the schoolwork that her tutor has her do."

"That's enough from the peanut gallery," she said.

He lifted an eyebrow like he was about to throw a flirt right back at her, and I didn't want to encourage that. Why was I starting to feel like a chaperone?

"What's your research on this time?" I asked.

"Your fake boyfriend."

"Dean-o," Scott said teasingly.

I stopped myself from swatting at him. Suddenly I was a part of the hormone circus around here?

Wendy said, "I couldn't find any literature about what kind of entity he might be. But I did get an e-mail from Eileen about it."

Ah, the paranormal cleaner. "What did she come up with?"

Reading from the paper, Wendy said, "Quote, 'If this entity becomes a severe issue for your ghost, she'll need to redouble her efforts to identify exactly what he is, because one of the only things I can think of that will neutralize a strong spirit like this is another spirit who is even *stronger*. That's why we need to classify him. However, getting ahold of that stronger spirit would require a paranormal expert with abilities far beyond what I can offer.' "

"This is not reassuring," I said.

"Word." Wendy put down the paper. "We might be talking about heavy-duty priest stuff, Jensen."

Oh. Just . . . *oh*. I didn't want to go near that unless it was totally needed. "Fake Dean's backed off me lately, which makes me wonder what he's up to. At least he's kept his word about staying out of my new house, though. Maybe I can put him at arm's distance until he gets ultimately bored of me."

Just saying that made me miss him a little. How had *that* happened?

But I couldn't have him both ways.

Wendy hopped on top of her desk to sit. "If you think that'll work, then do it. But keep in mind that Eileen's hooked up to a sweet network. Someday, I might even be able to do an apprenticeship with her and her peeps." She shrugged with a smile. "Eileen says I'm a rare gem, you know, because I can interact with ghosts. All she can do is intuit your feelings. But I shouldn't act like she got a raw deal, because what she does is valuable. She specializes in helping ghosts cross over to the other side if they need it."

Cassie reentered my mind. She hadn't needed the help.

Scott said, "Not all ghosts are smart enough or think straight enough to call their wranglers." He paused, like the idea that Cassie wasn't here anymore had come back to him, too. "I've also heard of ghosts that are so gung ho about still being in Boo World that they ignore their wranglers. They're ruled by their tethers."

I elaborated for Wendy. "A tether is a reason for staying here."

"Got it," Wendy said. "But as far as the tethered ghosts go, you already said that Cassie called her wrangler, so I kinda guessed that they don't take you by force."

"Only bad humans are taken by force when they die," Scott said. "We can make a good guess about that because . . ."

I subtly widened my eyes at him. Farah Edgett, Wendy's adopted sister, had been the person he was talking about who'd been dragged away by her wrangler after she'd died.

Scott kept his lip zipped.

A thought nudged me. "Do you guys think that the dark spirit we saw today has a wrangler?"

I watched Wendy's face for any sign that Gavin had talked with her about Daddy Most Dangerous, but her expression didn't change. I would've even done some empathy on her if I didn't respect her boundaries. You couldn't just bust into every human on a whim.

"If that dark spirit does have a wrangler," Scott said, "it's doing a punk job."

Our conversation lagged again, until Wendy said, "Cleaners are the most useful when a ghost is too strong to cross over or really doesn't want to leave. Then those spirits have to be expelled. Sometimes they're attached to the property itself, or sometimes they're attached to some*one*."

Like the dark blob is attached to you and Gavin, I thought.

"You know what else is fab, though?" Wendy asked.

Scott was all ears, grinning up at her. "Spill."

"I'm going to learn astral projection soon," Wendy said.

"I read about that somewhere," I said, "back when I was alive. It was in a novel. . . ."

I searched for the story line, then remembered. The book had been about two girls who used astral projection—an out-of-body experience—to switch bodies or something, and one girl turned out to be super-evil, and she tried to keep the other girl's body—

Crap. "Wendy, maybe you want to stay far away from that." God, I wished I could remember the title of the book, but I'd read it when I was a kid.

"Oh, Eileen says astral projection is safe," Wendy said. "Also, I've looked into it, because how amazing-cakes would it be if I could see what it's like in your dimension someday? I think I could do that with astral projection."

"Cool," Scott said.

Of course he liked the idea. But I knew that further pooh-poohing it in front of Wendy might be a bad thing, making her want to try it even more.

It turned out that I didn't have to say a word because there was a knock on her bedroom door.

Even before Wendy called a "Come in," I knew it was Gavin. My essence gave a tiny roar, like it was revving. Scott cracked up a little, giving me a knowing grin.

"Get bent," I said.

After entering the room, Gavin practically bowled me over with his life force; it was amping as he tucked his hands under his armpits and stood with his legs apart. So hunky. And, with that, I officially became the main act in tonight's hormone circus.

"I'm going to guess that you aren't talking to yourself in here," he said to Wendy.

"Scott and Jensen are with me." She was so very good at the whole casual defiance thing with him, checking her nails instead of making eye contact.

"Scott," he said. "He's the hot-rod kid."

What do you know—he made no mention of me. It was like Gavin knew that ignoring me was the surest way to get my goat.

"Did you hear me say that Jensen's here?" Wendy asked.

"Loud and clear."

Scott leaned close enough so that his energy buzzed against mine. "He's still not a fan of yours, huh?"

"Slightly." Then again, there'd been that moment today, when Gavin had tried to touch me, when the look in his eyes had shaken and rattled me until I'd nearly fizzed out. . . .

Was he a fan? Or the complete opposite?

Wendy was on a roll. "The sooner you accept that Jensen's going to be around here a lot, the better off you'll be."

"I'd rather have the other eighties girl around."

Low blow!

"Twyla?" Wendy asked. "Gav, you've never actually met her, so how can you say that?"

"You've told me about all your new friends."

"Then you know that Twyla's such a bitch to me."

Scott and I laughed, and he interjected, "She's like that to everyone, Wen."

"Like, shocker," she said, laughing, too.

Over in Totally Human World, an oblivious Gavin said, "I've asked you not to use that kind of language in the house."

"Yes, Daddy."

He went stiff, lowering his arms to his sides, like he was ready for a fight, but not necessarily with Wendy.

"I've also asked you not to say *that*, even if you're kidding."

Wendy flopped into her desk chair in front of her computer. "Gav, you're the closest I have to a dad. You practically raised me. Plus, you boss me around enough to be one."

Gavin took in a breath, and when his gaze strayed to the window, where Scott and I were still drifting, it was almost like he could see me. Was he wondering if this was the right time to tell Wendy what we believed to be true about the dark spirit?

But he *couldn't* see me, otherwise he would've witnessed my encouraging nod. *Tell her.*

Could he feel my energy reaching out to him? Because he crossed the room in a few slow strides, then as deliberately as a person closes a book after it's finished, he shut the windows on me and Scott.

"Wet rag," Scott said, swirling down to the air-conditioning unit and taking a seat.

I didn't stick around long enough to see Wendy's reaction to his news through the glass window that was now half-covered by curtains . . . and half-covered by Gavin's broad back as he turned away from me once again.

Leaving Scott to guard Wendy for now, I shot over to Amanda Lee's, and what I found there made me hover in the driveway with unexpected hesitation.

Under the closed shutters of the casita's windows, lights were strobing so fast that it looked like stutters of starlight.

The last time I'd seen that was at a ghost party. So what the hell?

I took off toward the door, slipping through the

crack and stretching myself ultrathin so I could get through quickly. I was only halfway inside when I caught sight of the gaggle of ghosts.

Old Seth, with his dusty beard, cowboy hat, gun belt, and boots, was hunkered on top of the love seat, sucking on the end of a wire from a lamp that was flickering. His form was intact, of course, and not the bent and broken shape it'd no doubt been after he was beaten to death in a brawl with a neighbor over a fence line ages ago. A festive group of Mexican women from Old Town, garbed in the long party dresses they'd been wearing when their wagon's horse had been upset by a rattlesnake, flanked Old Seth. They had more cut cords raised to their lips, just like tequila shots. On top of my car battery, Twyla sat, looking exactly like a maudlin half-and-half saloon girl with her corset, petticoats, and crazy hair as she sang "If You Leave Me Now" by Chicago, her voice cracking whenever she got to the high parts. She was holding her hand out toward a wall, where pictures of Cassie were flashing by like they were in a slide show. They were images Twyla was conjuring up and throwing into Boo World, one at a time.

Just grieving for Cassie, I thought. I only wished Twyla didn't sound like a dog with its tail caught in a door.

The room was steeped with dejected energy, and when I found Amanda Lee in a corner seat, leaning her head back, blind to the ghostly slide show, I thought at first that she was one of us.

But she was too solid. And too . . . drinking?

When she saw me, she raised a cut-crystal glass of what look like brandy. "Jen-shen."

"Oh, my God, you sound like Randy."

"To Casshie," she continued, toasting. "I saw 'er dishappear from this plane in a vision."

Everyone in the room lifted their electric devices. Twyla even cut her singing.

"To Cassie," they all said, as sober as when they'd died.

On the wall, pictures of a smiling Cassie with light hair and her pale lipstick loomed.

"Amanda Lee," I said, hovering right in front of her. I wanted to pat her face and sober her up. "You never drink."

"Jush so much death, Jen-shen. Can't get away from the death."

"Cassie wasn't sad." How many times would I have to repeat this because they hadn't been in the forest with us tonight? "She was very happy to go."

I moved away from Amanda Lee and yelled at the room. "She was happy! Can't you guys process that?"

Twyla hung her head, the slide show coming to a stop. From the love seat, Old Seth tipped back his ten-gallon hat.

"This ain't about Cassie, Jensen. It's a time for the rest of us to mourn."

Carlota, who had blooms of red and yellow flowers braided into her hair, all colored up, thanks to the electricity she was sucking, pointed at me with her cord and spoke to me in a deluge of Spanish.

I'd had enough in high school only to get by, but I recognized something about "sad" and "heart."

"Yes," I said. "It's very sad and heartbreaking that we're never going to see her again. Then again, maybe we will, on the other side. But this was what she wanted."

"Suicide," Carlota said, switching to English. "That is what it is when you call your wrangler to you. She took her existence twice, once in life, once in death. She has never minded leaving others behind."

Carlota and the girls, plus Old Seth, had been around for a while—the mid-1800s. They'd hung on because they loved this existence and had a certain point of view because of it. But it didn't mean I agreed with them.

Twyla clearly thought the same. She raised her head and shot a laser gaze at them. "Fuck you. We have every right to call our wranglers to us when we want to."

They all started to squabble while Amanda Lee tipped back her glass and found she didn't have any more booze. She sighed, leaning her head back again.

I didn't engage in the discussion, either. I only listened, being a new girl and all. It was pretty apparent that Old Seth and the senoritas were the type of ghosts that Wendy had been talking about before—the ones who avoided their wranglers and needed cleaners. They were stuck on vendettas, like Old Seth was with the descendants of the neighbor who'd killed him. He loved to haunt those people. Or the girls, who, I'd recently found out, liked to return to the stretch of road, now a freeway, where they'd croaked, looking for rattlesnakes and scaring some of the modern drivers into accidents. All of them fed off the fear from the living, whether that was a secondary motivation or not.

The bottom line was that none of them wanted to leave, but it didn't mean they needed to judge Cassie for calling her wrangler.

When Amanda Lee stood, her glass dropped to the carpet, and she pointed at Old Seth.

"There'll be no dishrespecting Casshie in my home," she said forcefully.

I guessed she could see and hear him, if not the girls.

He made to remove his hat and speak some cowboy justifications to her, but stopped when Amanda Lee barked, "Oooo-uu-t!"

She didn't even have to officially expel them, because when she made her uneven way to the door and opened it, they slid out without another word, all of them seeming confused as to why we didn't understand their reasoning about Cassie.

When they'd left, Amanda Lee went back to her seat, this time smoothing out her skirts with major drunken care.

"I believe," she said, "I just chashed off my bodyguard."

Twyla hopped away from the table. "I'm still here."

I could tell she wanted to be needed, especially tonight, when she'd lost her best pal.

"Twyla's got your back," I said to Amanda Lee.

She looked satisfied, and Twyla bucked up, taking her task seriously, going to a window and stationing herself, peering through the slats.

Reporting for duty hard-core.

As Amanda Lee shut her eyes and started breathing deeply, I didn't rouse her to tell her about the image I'd had in Elfin Forest about my bracelets. Nah, I'd let her know about that tomorrow, before she left for Brittany's office.

Right now, I'd just let her cuddle down in that chair, resting her eyes to get the peace she needed.

At least for tonight.

15

Twyla was so serious about her new duties with Amanda Lee that I left her behind at the casita to guard away to her heart's content.

Besides, I figured that, since Sailor Randy had known Cassie, too, he deserved to personally hear about her wrangling. Too bad I didn't own a telephone shaped like big red lips, like the one I used to have in my bedroom before I'd died; I would've used it to give him an easy ring if that's how things worked here. I could get ahold of a human on their phone by manipulating their cell devices, but ghosts didn't exactly have smartphones.

All I could do with Randy was communicate the ghost way, traveling downtown, where he'd be at the pub with Suze.

Flaherty's was having an off night, with a few barbound customers watching that ESPN sports channel on the corner TVs. Before I located Suze, I spotted Randy in a far seat, eyeing his neighbor's glass of tawny booze.

With his tilted sailor's cap, Randy fit right into a pub. He knew how to take advantage of being there, too, as the inebriated, distracted, muscle-shirted guy next to him droned on about basketball scores with a bearded bartender I hadn't seen before.

Slyly, so as not to create a huge disturbance, Randy gestured toward the man's glass, manipulating the electricity in the air. The glass wobbled. He kept at it, and it wobbled harder. Then it tipped over, pooling scotch on the bar.

The basketball fan pushed away from the spill. "Di' I do that? Rookie move."

As the bartender gave his customer a "no worries" smile and went for a towel, Randy slid over the top of the bar to the other side, where booze trickled to the floor. He caught some in his mouth, and a light stream of sparks cut through him, the liquid running out and to the floor in spite of its delayed journey.

The bartender backed up a step. "Did you see that? Were those little lights in the air?"

All five people sitting at the bar shook their heads, and the server gingerly wiped the surface, then left Randy's area as soon as possible. My ghostly friend licked his lips, hovering in place, gazing at the rows of bottles standing on the mirror-backed shelves like he was contemplating knocking one of them down so it'd break and give him another false rush.

"Prankster," I said, sitting near him at the corner of the bar. "One of these days, some sensitive human is going to see every move you make. Then you'll be as exposed as a *Penthouse* Pet."

He must've looked over a shoulder or two during his ghost time to see nudie pictures, because he just smiled, totally understanding what *Penthouse* was. "Yer friend Suze's in the back, takin' infentery."

Inventory. Got it.

The basketball fan had moved a few chairs down from his former seat. "It's not as cold over here," he said to the bartender.

Randy pointed to a vent above us. "My cover story."

"And a good one." Back to business. "So did Gavin stop in here anytime today?"

"Nah. Lotsa tourists, in 'n' out, some of 'em more interestin' than others. No Gavin, though. Sorry ya came down here for nothin'."

"It wasn't exactly a wasted trip." I wished I could put off the news about Cassie. I couldn't predict how each ghost would handle her final passing, and it was stressing me out a little.

But when I told him about her, his ever-content expression didn't change all that much. He tried to take off his cap in respect, yet it looked attached to him, just as the rest of our clothes were, so he merely bowed his head for a few moments. Then he gestured toward a bottle on the shelves near us, air-flicking it so it crashed to the counter.

At the sudden shatter, the humans around us jumped.

Randy bolted right on over to get him some more liquor. Again, a shimmer of sparks cascaded through him before the drink splashed to the floor.

When he was done, he gave a general salute to the

sky. "If I could hold a glass, I'd raise it to ya, Cassie doll." He motioned me over to join him, but I shook my head.

As the bartender grabbed another rag and rushed to clean up again, Randy jumped butt first on top of the bar, legs dangling. Around us, everyone decided that there must've been a small earthquake. Yeah, that explained why only one bottle had fallen off the shelves.

After that, Randy didn't comment any more on Cassie.

So that was it? He wasn't going to have more of a party for her? There'd be no sodden grief or drawn-out sadness at the fact that she'd ended her time in this dimension?

I tested Randy out. "Old Seth and Carlota didn't take the news about Cassie very well."

"Ol' judgmental farts. I say die 'n' let die."

Just as I was about to ask him to tell me more, Suze walked into the main room. She had reddish smudges beneath her denim-colored eyes, her graying curls springing out of the low ponytail she wore, making her look even more worn-out than yesterday.

Had I given her a sleepless night with my appearance?

After she had a word with the bartender about his shift hours tomorrow, she headed for the back again.

"I'm off to talk to her," I said to Randy.

"I'll hold down the fort."

"No more spilled drinks?"

He gave me a get-outta-here flap of the hand. "I limit myself to two pranks per bartender." Then he glanced around, his gaze landing on a green, clover-painted clock on the wall. "Trouble is, sometimes every second feels like 'n hour. 'Less I'm prankin', that is."

"Behave, Petty Officer."

"Yes, ma'am."

His lopsided smile escorted me out of the bar area until I entered the back hall and found Suze in a different room from the one we'd been in last night. This place was filled with stark wood shelves with boxes labeled NAPKINS and FLATWARE, plus every kind of liquor you could imagine. I was surprised Randy hadn't been back here on a rampage.

As Suze scribbled on a clipboard, I decided to materialize again, but this time with a little more finesse and warning than last night.

Before I gathered my energy to appear, I motioned toward a pile of napkins that had been unpacked from a box on a middle shelf near Suze, and without effort, I pushed one of them off its resting place, letting it coast to the ground like a feather from an angel's wing.

Suze bent down to pick it up.

When she put it back on the shelf, I did it again.

"Are you kidding me?" she asked, bending a second time.

I focused all my energy on materializing, feeling myself burn as my essence folded outward.

And there I was, standing at the foot of the napkin while a squatting Suze gaped at my sneakers, scanned up my jeans, my shirt tied over the tank top, then finally making it to my face.

"Don't freak out," I whispered.

"Shit!" The clipboard smacked the ground, and she scrambled backward until she hit the wall, sliding the rest of the way down. "Oh, God. Oh, my God!"

I gave her a moment to "God" all she wanted, but she just kept shaking her head and saying that word.

Then she went to the questioning stage. "Did I fall asleep again?"

"No. This is for real. It was real last night, too."

She lifted up her hand in front of her face. It was shaking. "Too much coffee. Not enough coffee. I'm not sure which one it is. Does caffeine cause hallucinations like this?" She shook her head again. "Why're you talking to yourself, Suze?"

"You're not," I said. "Also, you have no idea about what a hallucination *really* is."

Ghost inside joke. She didn't laugh.

"Is this thing on?" I asked, tapping at an imaginary microphone.

We used to do dumb stuff like that, and in spite of her confusion, she laughed at me, tremulous, disbelieving, on the edge of crazy.

She would eventually come around, but I couldn't waste a lot of time in material form like this. Not unless I wanted to plug my essence in somewhere.

"Suze, I've got to talk to you."

"You talked last night. At least, I'm pretty sure you did."

She still wasn't absolutely buying into the reality of me. But her cautious bewilderment was better than her being so scared that her heart gave out or something.

Where to start with her, though? I decided to begin where any honest friend would.

"You sure look like crap," I said.

She made what we used to call her "onion face." That's because it looked like she was smelling onions when she exaggerated a "what the hell" expression.

"Nice," she said, still surveying me. "A smart-ass ghost?"

"Not a lot different from the smart-ass human you knew. So have you been burning the candle at both ends lately?"

She gave me an inch of leeway. "The rent's due, my car's been giving me fits, so that means extra hours." Narrowing her eyes, she added, "Plus, I've been having bad dreams on top of it all. Seems my best friend from all those years ago has decided to haunt me in them."

"I'm not haunting you, believe me." Haunting wasn't this gentle, in my book. "Besides, you should know by now that these aren't dreams."

As I kept looking her over—threadbare jeans with a hole eating its way through one knee, a red-and-white checkered blouse that'd faded from too many washings, a Flaherty's apron covering the rest of her—I wondered if a ghost could do something like rob a bank to help out her fellow woman.

But I highly doubted that Suze would take that kind of money, although it might be fun to try to outsmart a bank, now that I could. Maybe.

She'd finished checking me out, and instead of collapsing into tears like last night, she tentatively smiled.

"If this is really you . . ." she said.

"It is."

She choked up a bit. "Then these are the happiest nights of my life. Even happier than my honeymoon, and then the day I signed divorce papers after my husband cheated on me with . . . Oh, you wouldn't know her. You don't even know him."

"I still want to do something mean to him," I said, affronted for Suze's sake. "What a dick."

"I've learned to let it go." She was relaxing more now, one hand on her knee. "I haven't gotten alimony from him in years, so I don't have to associate with him these days. I hated to take his money, anyway. As you can see, I'm a free and independent woman now."

She subtly covered the burgeoning hole in her jeans with that hand.

Ow. How many talks did we used to have about how awesome we were going to be when we grew up? We were going to be Charlie girls—kind of free, kind of wow—just like the perfume commercial's lyrics said when we were kids. We'd carry briefcases down city streets and wear snazzy business suits, wafting along on the scent of success. In high school, Suze had developed a real talent for numbers and I had a thing for Indiana Jones, so she'd be a banker and I'd be an archaeologist someday.

Or none day.

Suze obviously wanted to get off this topic as soon as possible, and she said, "Didn't you mention something about bracelets to me yesterday? I remember that clearly. You talked about Brittany and Lisa and that party on the night you . . ."

"Died." I'd been real vague with her about my death tale last night, and fleshing it out wasn't on my agenda at the moment. "It's a long story, Suze. But you might be interested to know that I paid a visit to Brittany about those bracelets this morning."

"You freaking haunted her?" she said, laughing in more disbelief. But I think she might've been concentrating on my chutzpah this time.

Anyway, I didn't correct her on using the word "haunted" now. It didn't really matter. "Brittany gave up the info I needed about the bracelets. Hey, when you saw her the last time, was she . . . ?"

"A cat lady? Yes. Her face was almost a smear. I'd rather have my wrinkles and gray hair than . . . that."

"I'd rather you had them, too."

She broke into a smile so warm that I could feel a friendly shudder go through me. But before we got all sappy with each other, she said, "If you think Brittany is bad, you should see your old friend Lisa. You can look her up on the Internet under a 'professional name' now."

I wandered over to the nearest plug and started to juice up, knowing—and thanking the stars—that I would be here for a while.

"Do tell, Suze," I said, feeling like nothing had changed between us.

Except maybe for all the things that had.

*   *   *

Suze seemed to eventually forget that I wasn't your average human as we caught up with each other, first
about Lisa Levine, who'd remained a single girl, traveling most days as a beauty spokesperson for an inter-
national cosmetic firm. It felt like old times chatting
with Suze, bringing back our high school days, especially when we would cozy into the Naugahyde sofa
she had in her den after snatching a handful of Otter
Pops from the freezer, sugaring up during extended
girl-talk sessions.

Of course, back then, we'd never dreamed that we'd
be conversing, ghost-to-person, about how Suze's life
had started circling the drain, putting her in a different
existence than she'd ever imagined. Same, same, right?

It wasn't easy to hear her story. After I'd gone missing, she'd spent a long time going door-to-door with
flyers, launching a grassroots campaign in San Diego
County to find me. Beaten down by its failure, Suze
had sunk into a funk, losing her job at the bank because
she'd become undependable. Then she'd met Prince
Charming in a dive bar and life had gotten worse from
there. He'd hidden his cheating for years, and after
she'd found out about it, she hadn't even been able to
conjure enough emotion to care.

She'd let him go and had gotten a job she could take
or leave bartending here at Flaherty's, where career ad-
vancement was capped by a pine-wooded ceiling.

She was just telling me about what a chit the bartender on duty was when I sensed a flow of energy
seeping into the room. When Randy appeared to me,
not bothering to materialize for Suze's sake, I knew by

his expression that something was going down on his watch.

"Is Gavin here?" I asked him.

He nodded, but after I'd said the name, Suze had stood from the spot she'd taken on the floor and begun smoothing back her hair and wiping under her eyes for any stray mascara. My head almost exploded when I saw the look on her face. A turbo blush, a sparkle in her eyes as she straightened her apron.

Whoa. She looked years younger and . . . excited?

"I was out of it last night," she said on a breath, "but I remember we touched on Gavin. Then you left. We never did talk about him beyond that."

We hadn't gotten around to chatting about him tonight, either. "You don't find it strange that he's here asking questions about me?"

"He was doing research for that reunion he's hosting for his parents, and he wanted to know more about what happened to you."

No, not fishy at all. I wanted to tell to Suze to stay frosty with him, but that'd be great advice coming from me, since I was practically humming with his life force, even a room away.

Hell, she was humming, too. But didn't she at least feel weird about the age difference between them? He had to be about twenty years younger. I just hoped she wasn't setting herself up for a disappointment when he never came back after he'd gotten what he wanted from her.

"Suze," I said. "Do you mind if I listen in on your conversation with him since he's looking into me?"

"Sure. Why not?" She sent me an impish smile. "I'd want to hang around him, too, if he was here to talk about *me*."

I laughed, but it wasn't because I found this amusing. "Just don't tell him I'm around, okay?"

"That won't be a problem. Ghosts make some people uncomfortable."

She smiled at me, walking right past invisible Randy, and his gaze stayed glued to her until she walked out the door. Then he inspected me.

"I hate to say it," he slurred, "but Twyla was right when she tol' us ya want Gavin for yourself."

"Not true."

"Jus' look at ya. Ya look like someone ripped a lollipop outta your hand 'n' ran off with it."

"Right, Randy." I flew toward the door Suze had left open. "I wouldn't take Twyla as an authority on anything."

"Maybe jus' this."

I left him in my dust, dematerializing and returning to the main room, where the TVs silently featured men in sports jackets moving their mouths as baseball scores flashed by on the bottoms of the screens. Irish music lulled over the speakers, softer than normal, seeing as the room was only a few people shy of being empty.

The only customer I really saw, though, was at the bar, his shoulders stretching the white linen of his button down, his light brown hair nearly golden under the low illumination from the strategically placed lanterns on the walls.

Suze told the bartender to start closing up, and after

she greeted Gavin, telling him that he was just in time for last call, they lapsed into how-ya-doing talk. I hung back, reading his body language. He leaned his forearms on the bar, his shoulders lacking that steel-beam tension I'd seen on him so many times. And when Suze said something I didn't catch, I knew it was funny, because he laughed.

How often did he do that when I was around?

In the mirror in back of the liquor shelves, I saw his smile, meltingly gorgeous, transforming him from taciturn to . . . Would *bright* be accurate? Because his eyes got these lines that rayed out from them. And he kept smiling at Suze, just like . . .

He was attracted to her?

I would've used some empathy on him, but he was onto my ghost tricks, and he would've known, maybe even blocking me out. Even so, my instincts shivered. *Was* he playing her so that he could get information about me? Or was that smile genuine?

Something small and petty inside me screamed, *Protect your friend. Gavin has killed, and you don't want Suze near him.*

But it could be that I was just full of shit, since I very well knew that he'd killed for good reason. This was more about me and my warped connection with him.

Randy was reclining on the very top of the liquor shelves, all ears as he eavesdropped on Gavin and Suze. I should've been just as tuned in as he was, but I hesitated to get too close. I didn't want to listen in as this obvious chemistry cooked between them. Besides, if I got too close, what would I do? Push Suze away from him like I was some sort of demented, jealous poltergeist?

As I collected myself, a strange sensation took hold of me: my body, solidifying. Becoming *a body*.

I looked behind me to a booth, and lo and behold, what the hell was sitting there? Fake Dean, stretched out over the bench, one knee up with his arm resting on it and hanging over his shin. His back was against the wall as he worked a toothpick in his mouth.

"Heard this was the greatest show in town," he said in that lazy way that made me want to smack him. And do other things to him that'd I'd done only with my real Dean.

I coolly turned back around. Figured he would show up during this incredibly awkward situation. The guy had major Jensen radar.

I checked to see if Suze and Gavin noticed that he'd appeared, or that I had a body now. Was I visible? It didn't seem that way. When I peered in the long mirror over the bar, there wasn't an image there, either.

But Randy was sure staring at me like I was somehow different. And as he eyed Dean behind me, he straightened up on his perch, like a bantam rooster getting ready to dart down for an attack.

I shook my head at him. *Yes, this is the pseudo-wrangler I told you about, but it's cool. For now.*

Randy would have to monitor Suze and Gavin while I took care of this more pressing situation, so I fixed my attention back on fake Dean, who jerked his chin to the other side of the booth, inviting me in.

Like that was going to happen.

He went a step farther, transforming into another identity, a trick he'd pulled on me before.

This time, he impersonated Gavin, with the button-down, jeans, work boots, and a cold smile just for me.

"Cut it out," I said.

"Or would you prefer . . ." He switched into James Dean, in a black jacket, T-shirt, cuffed jeans, greased blond hair, and a burning who-cares attitude.

Still, it wasn't enough to lure me in. "I won't waste my time asking what you're doing here, star boy."

"Why don't you waste your time asking me why Gavin or Suze can't see you right now instead? Because you were wondering. Don't lie."

"Asking would be just as useless."

Yup, he was as entertained by me as always. "I'll remind you that you are a ghost, darlin'. Normal people do not see ghosts."

"Don't talk to me like I'm in second grade."

He took the toothpick out of his mouth. "Why, oh why, do you feel like you have a body when there's none to be seen?"

Rhetorical question. Might as well play along. "Because you have great influence over my state of being, blah-blah-blah. I am how you want me to be—invisible, like I am when I go into human dreams, but solid. The best of both worlds."

"See," he said with that smile. "You're far beyond second-grade reasoning, Jenny. But you forgot one part."

God. "What?"

"You're this way because it's the way I want it. And what I want, I get."

As a combination of hot thrills and cool guardedness ruled me, his gaze went to Gavin and Suze. When he smiled even wider, I couldn't help but give in to my curiosity and see what he was seeing.

For the second time that night, my head almost exploded when I took in the sight of Suze leaning on the bar toward Gavin, both of them laughing.

I expected fake Dean to chuckle, but when I didn't hear it, I wondered why. I found him with a serious look on his face, snapping the toothpick between two fingers.

It felt like the snap that had just happened inside me.

"They move on," he said. "None of us are real to them, even if you spend the energy to materialize and seem real. Suze will always love the memory of you, but when a stud like Gavin comes walking in, paying attention to her in a way that she hasn't had it paid for years, how do you think she's going to react?"

Just like this, I thought as I looked back at them. Suze's blush made her face glow, even if she'd seemed so drawn only an hour ago. I wanted to tell her to watch out, that Gavin had ulterior motives—namely, to get to the bottom of his fascination with me.

I couldn't just stand here anymore, so I walked toward the bar with my Dean-enhanced body, then climbed onto it, sitting Indian style and facing them. I tried not to get so near that Gavin would recognize my coldness and energy—if I was still emanating it with this sort-of body. Bottom line, though? I wasn't about to let Gavin take his obsession with me to this level, roping in my down-on-her-heels friend Suze.

From the booth, fake Dean's low laugh rang across the room, even though I was sure no one but me and Randy heard it.

16

Gavin had obviously made a sobering comment to Suze before I plunked onto the bar. I could tell because her smile had already gentled into that understanding expression she got whenever I used to come to her for sympathy.

"Why'd you get kicked out of the house tonight?" Suze asked.

Ah. This was about Wendy.

"It's my younger sister," Gavin said. "We had an . . . emotional discussion. She needed some space."

So Wendy hadn't handled the news of the dark spirit possibly being her asshole father very well. At least Scott was still around for her to pour her soul out to. But even that didn't make me terribly comfortable.

"So it's your sister you argued with, huh?" Suze asked.

Gavin grinned. Did he know that Suze was fishing for information about a wife or girlfriend?

"I have to tell you," she said, "I wish I had a dime for everyone who came in here saying that they'd been kicked out of their homes and they stopped in to have a drink until things cooled off."

Gavin reached into his back pocket and tossed his fancy leather wallet on the bar, reverting to Mr. Non-chalant Attitude. "You know how suffocating big brothers can be when you're a kid. She hates me right now for not telling her the whole truth about something. I wanted to hang around, just in case she wanted a shoulder to lean on, but"—he chuffed—"turns out she's got that."

Yup, Scott.

"I never had a big brother, or sister. I would've loved either one." Suze backed away from the bar, reaching behind her for some whiskey, vermouth, and bitters. Maybe Gavin had already ordered a drink. Maybe she already knew what he liked. "Hopefully, when you get home, your sis will be asleep, and she'll wake up in the morning ready to talk things out. Then she'll realize how lucky she is."

"She'll have to face me again sometime."

As Suze poured the makings of what I knew was a Manhattan, she lifted her big blue gaze to him. I was torn between congratulating her for having such confidence with a younger guy like Gavin—just like the go-get-'em cheerleader Suze I'd known—and wanting her to be more leery of him.

After she garnished his cocktail with a maraschino cherry, she sent him a shy smile, and he returned it. In back of me, I heard someone clear his throat.

I didn't acknowledge fake Dean because he was only being a too-observant jerk.

Gavin threw some of his drink down the hatch, his throat working with a swallow. Then he said, "It's been a hell of a couple of months in general. Wish I'd found this place a lot sooner."

"So you could drink your cares away? I don't recommend that fix."

"That's not what I meant." He kept his hand on the half-empty glass, his fingers long and sturdy. The hands of a real man who worked for his money, not the kind of rich fraternity cornball he could've been. "Sometimes it's nice to have someplace to go to watch a game or to listen to music."

"You're welcome here anytime."

Gavin's smile was easygoing. It was so simple for Suze to bring that out in him.

Something inside me compressed, building into a frustrating pressure.

The last customers at the bar beckoned her, wanting to cash out, but she was back soon, her skin flushed again. "And how's that reunion of yours going?"

"Right. The reunion." He toyed with his glass. "It's going. But I've gotten sidetracked by all this Jensen Murphy stuff."

In back of me, I could hear fake Dean mutter, "What a smooth operator."

I hated that he was right. But since Suze knew I was still in the pub, I was sure she wouldn't give away too much about her old friend, even if she didn't realize the true reason Gavin was looking into me.

She leaned on the bar again. The apron didn't hide

some impressive cleavage, even for a woman over fifty. Dang, Suze.

"Your interest in Jensen seems to have gone beyond a reunion story," she said.

He leaned a little closer, too. "Just call me curious."

They grinned at each other, and I almost reached forward to brace my arms against both of them, pushing them apart. Above me, Randy floated down from the shelves.

"I can handle this, Jen."

"I'm fine."

From the booth, fake Dean put in his two cents. "Jenny, why in the hell are you putting yourself through this?"

There was such concern in his tone that I couldn't help taking a peek at him: my first love, blond and young and eternal. My first disappointment, but not the last.

My very own facsimile of what used to be.

Gavin asked, "When I read those old newspaper articles about Jensen, it just seemed like there was much more to her than a bunch of words on a page. I tried to track down any family she had left, to see if there'd been any developments on finding her over the years, but no luck there." Almost as an afterthought, he added, "I'm sure everybody at the reunion would love to have closure of some sort."

"Closure would've been nice." A lost curl hung near Suze's cheek. "I get so mad when I see those articles about her. It's as if she became a story, an idea, something that kids tell each other at bonfire parties. But Jen was so much more than that. Her last picture only shows one side of her when there were so many more."

"I've seen other photos. She was really the girl next door, wasn't she?"

And the ghost who'd camped out in his own room when she was haunting him, I thought.

"Right," Suze said. "The girl next door to Animal House."

They laughed together, and I thought I saw a gleam in Gavin's light blue eyes. Was it because of his interest in me? Or was it because he'd finally found someone to share his so-called obsession with?

"I shouldn't say that." Suze tucked that curl behind her ear. "Jen was a sweet girl in school. Not so goody-goody that she was a nerd, but she was someone other kids looked up to. She was on the volleyball team, so the jocks liked her. She led the student council, so that got her the smart kid vote of confidence. And she hung out at the beach whenever she could, sunbathing and surfing, so she had the cool factor going. She used to like how carrying that short board got her more male attention than lipstick or nail polish ever could."

Suze was waxing so everyman-poetic about me that I couldn't stand to hear the bad parts. And I knew they'd be coming up, because after my parents had died I'd changed.

I'd almost forgotten that fake Dean was still around, because when I climbed off the bar, shutting out the murmur of the rest of their conversation, he was standing right in back of Gavin, giving me the chance to see them side by side: one man strung so tightly together by muscle and relaxed tension that it almost seemed like he was going to break after he left this bar. One man loose and carefree, sunny and nearly always smiling like he had a secret he wanted to tell you.

Fake Dean must've felt my emotions, because he sure put them into words.

"Stop torturing yourself," he said, his light brown eyes strangely tender.

"I'm beginning to think that's good advice." So I signaled Randy that I was leaving the pub, and he nodded, taking my place on the bar, a cross-legged sailor with his chin resting on a fist as he monitored Suze and Gavin, who both shifted as if they'd goose bumped with the sudden cold.

I decided that I'd just see Suze another time, when she wasn't so occupied. Meanwhile, there was a whole lot to occupy me, right? But then I remembered how my ghost friends had everything in hand. Randy, Louis, Twyla, Scott . . .

A sense of aimlessness took me over, becoming as much a part of me as it had been in life. A spurt of bummerness consumed me as I walked out the pub door. At least I could enjoy having this body tonight.

Fake Dean was right behind me. "Lesson one for ghosts: You don't have to hang around for every conversation ever spoken, especially if it's about you. Spirits have drawn-out memories, and hurt feelings can last as long as you stick around this dimension."

"That's lesson one?"

"Maybe it's lesson one hundred. But it's a good thing to learn."

We walked past a row of night-lit restaurants that had already closed. Indian, Chinese, Spanish—they'd left traces of curry and noodles and saffron on the air. Then we passed the cars driving down the street, filtering out of downtown after a long night. We passed unsuspecting people with light coats on as they left the more popular closing bars, passed a girl in a pink feather boa and birthday tiara who was weaving down the sidewalk toward me.

At the last second, she bumped me. Or maybe not-bumped is more appropriate, because even though I felt like I had a body, her shoulder still went through me with a dragging fizz.

"I'm freezing!" she yelled to her friend, grabbing for the girl's jacket.

"Isn't everyone," I said.

As we passed a pizza place, the aroma of baking dough made me slow down. I stopped at the window, where the cooks were shutting down for the night in their white, sauce-splotched aprons, and I wallowed in a smell that seemed so much headier in this fake-Dean body than it'd ever been in life.

Dean stood behind me, and I felt him with an electric thrill in my veins, especially when I couldn't see either of us in the window's reflection.

"You miss the smells of a night downtown?" he asked.

"Okay, this is where it starts, isn't it? Next you're going to say that, if I give in to you, I'll be able to smell these pizzas with wonderful human appreciation and hunger for the rest of eternity. I might even be able to have pizza in the coma that you put your stars into. But I only get those benefits if I become one of your collectibles." I turned around, my thigh brushing his knee. A jolt of need pulled through me, warming my belly. "Then you're going to remind me that I could be with my first and only love forever. You. Even though it's not really you."

He traced a finger over my forearm. Goose bumps—oh, how I'd missed them—spiked on my arm, raising the hair. I enjoyed every moment, even if I shouldn't have.

"Why not have a little more fun than usual, at least for tonight?" he said. "This hasn't exactly been the best day of your ghosthood. First off, you had a rough time with that Tim boy. You're on constant watch with him. You ghosts are even starting to realize that there's no hope for him."

"There isn't?"

He smiled down at me with that mouth—soft and kissable. So real right now.

"What do you think?" he asked, true to form. He wasn't going to tell me about anything I couldn't figure out for myself. As this higher being, whatever he was, he didn't believe that enlightening me was necessary . . . or appropriate.

"I think Tim Knudson needs help," I said. "That maybe he's what they call a bad seed, and there's nothing we can do."

"You've debated with the others about terminating him. Taking his existence into your hands like you're gods." He stopped running his fingers up and down my arm. "I don't have to remind you that you aren't even close to that."

His gaze had darkened. Was he about to go all mystery beast on me like he'd done twice before when I'd provoked him?

"It's not up to us to kill him," I said, anticipating what he was going to say next.

"Right. Just because you're beyond death, it doesn't mean you can take life, even indirectly, without consequences. You've dealt with that dark spirit—haven't you learned a lesson from *that*?"

Wait—was he saying that we could kill directly, and the reason ghosts didn't really do that was because of the consequences?

But I needed to know about the dark spirit first. "Are you implying that it killed a human and it got tainted?"

"No, it came out of a portal, thanks to your friend Amanda Lee. But when a ghost feeds on negative energy or even creates chaos, it can become just as black and cursed as this dark spirit that's hanging around. You don't want darkness marking you, Jenny."

This, he wasn't kidding about. "You're telling me that we can still earn our way into heaven or hell as ghosts . . . if those places even exist?"

Fake Dean smiled, and I knew that was all he was going to give me. He'd told me before that he didn't even know what was in store beyond the wranglers. Or, at least, that's what he'd said.

"One more thing," he whispered, stroking my skin again. "You were right about Cassie. She left this plane very happy."

I let him touch me like this, loving the waves of heat that were skimming my flesh, making my libido rise. So easy to give in to him tonight, after seeing Gavin and Suze together. So dangerous.

And so stimulating.

"How did it feel to see her wrangler?" he asked softly.

"Nice."

He traced my wrist, and I bit my lip.

"Just nice?" he asked, chuckling. "You're telling me that the real highlight of the day was scaring the pants off that weenie boy Tim? How did *that* feel?"

"More than nice." And I didn't just mean the rush from the hallucination I'd given him, either. I'd been real pumped up on his fear.

Then I remembered what Dean had said about the dark spirit, and he seemingly understood before I could say anything.

"Don't go too far with absorbing their fear, Jenny," he said. "You can enjoy it. Just don't depend on it for fuel."

"Okay."

He pressed his advantage, coasting his fingertip up my arm, brushing it over the inside of my elbow. I almost sighed but held it back.

"I scare *you* a little, don't I?" he asked.

"Hardly."

He leaned closer as, behind him, humans strolled past, beer-breathed and loud, clumped into social disorder. None of them could see us by the window, and that only added to the burning tumble in my stomach.

"When you were alive," he whispered against my ear, his breath bathing it to tingling awareness, "you never went for the bad boys. Dean was a surfer, a smart guy, a college boy, but there were times you wished . . ."

As fake Dean slid his other hand over my stomach, I ached between my legs. It'd been so long since I'd experienced this immediate, physical desire from anyone else that it felt new again.

He finished his thought. "You wished that he would've had you in unexpected places, even just once. There were times when you'd go for a burger after surfing, and you'd hope that he'd take his hand under the table and touch you where you wanted to be touched."

When I felt him unbutton the snap at the waist of my jeans, I gasped.

Oh, God, what was he doing? What was I *letting* him do? And was it because I was hurt from seeing Gavin with Suze?

The buzz of my zipper coming down made me hold my breath, and now that I *could* be touched, I let it happen. I needed it, wanted it, had already accepted that I couldn't have it as a ghost, and to have it happening right now?

It was more of a turn-on than anything.

Dean kept whispering as he finished with the rest of my zipper. "You wanted to sit in the booth with him, pretending like nothing was going on underneath that table as everyone around you laughed and ate their food, as the waitress came by and brought you sodas. You always wondered what it would feel like to have a little bit of bad in you."

Behind him, the crowd had thickened with college kids, pushing at one another, never noticing the spirits among them. And when Dean slid his fingers into my fly, over my white cotton underwear and over my achiest parts, I reached back with one hand, noiselessly slapping the window with my palm. As I slipped down the window, he stroked me, and I gripped his T-shirt with my other hand.

"That's a bad girl," he said, pressing harder.

I moved my hips with every motion, leaning my head against his shoulder. He smelled so much like Dean, with his clean shirt, his sun-warmed skin. His hair, longish and cut straight near his chin in surfer style, brushed my face like a hundred kisses.

But I knew damned well this wasn't my old Dean. And I still let him go on.

He dug his free hand into my hair, cushioning my head from the window, using his leverage to turn my mouth toward his so he could crush his lips to mine.

I fell against him a little farther, weak-legged, bones of water, lost in dizziness as we kissed and kissed and the humans walked right by us. He ran his hand from out of my jeans and up my belly, over my stomach, pulling up the tank top under my blouse and inching his fingers over my skin until they got to my bra.

When he skimmed his fingers into the cup, making contact with my bare breast, I sucked in oxygen like I'd never experienced breathing before.

His lips stayed on mine as he talked. "You taste like honey," he said. "I knew you would. Strawberries and honey, just like the color of your hair."

Thanking him for the compliment seemed dumb, so I went the wordless route instead. It wasn't like I was able to speak, anyway, especially when he tugged down my bra so he could circle my nipple with his thumb.

I missed this belly-somersault, fuzzy-headed foreplay so much, and he was the only way I'd have this kind of contact with someone again. So big deal if I was enjoying it. How many more chances would I get?

He gave me another slow kiss that made me *feel* like honey while still caressing my breast.

"I was jealous," he murmured against my mouth, "watching you watch Gavin. Seeing how you wanted to touch him."

"You get off on that or something?" I whispered.

"I get angry." He tightened his fingers in my hair. "And then I get what I want."

I get what I want. Just like I was a collectible for sale.

It was then that I fully realized I was standing on a street with people streaming past and fake Dean's hand in my bra. I wasn't on display, but I may as well have been with the vulnerability that suddenly enveloped me.

Bracing an arm against his collarbone, I put some distance between us. He was all too humanlike except for the darkness that was surrounding his light brown irises like rings of black flame.

In a near panic, I pushed back at him with more force. "You can't always get what you want. Ever hear that?"

"I'm making pretty good strides."

I pushed again, and he lifted both hands, backing away from me, that shit-eating grin on his face. The jerk even rubbed his fingers together, like he was letting me know that they'd been caressing a part of me that no one had gotten to touch for well over thirty years.

Zipping up and then putting my bra back into place, I buttoned up all the need and desire, too. What had I been thinking? Or *not* thinking?

"Jenny, Jenny," he said. "You let your emotions get the best of you, don't you? But even if you're angry at yourself for letting this go too far, you still liked it."

I hated when he could see right through me. "You took advantage of me."

"I don't think that's an easy thing to do, darlin'. You've got a strong will. Too bad that's one of the qualities that drew me to you."

"My activity is another quality, I know, I know. But you'll get over it."

"Maybe I will." His grin grew. "Maybe I won't."

I glared. "It was a moment of weakness, okay? And you know that damned well, because you sat there watching me with Gavin. You saw how frustrating that was for me."

Fake Dean hooked his thumbs into his jeans loops. "Go ahead. Tell me all about your tragic feelings for him. You've got a ghost crush, Jenny. That's all it is. And what you refer to as ghost ADD is going to wipe that crush away soon, then you'll be bored and ready for something new—the kind of something you just had."

I laughed. "You know what you sound like? One of

those guys who keeps a harem. 'I promise you riches and love beyond your dreams.' Then there's the part where a girl becomes a part of his collection, forgotten now that the chase is over." I pointed at him. "You like the chase, and after it's done, you put your conquests into storage."

The black flame had receded from his irises, and his hands lowered from that cocky belt-loop stance. "You're wrong, Jenny. So very wrong."

He'd told me how much he cared for every star up in his collection, and if I let myself believe the tenderness in his gaze right now, I'd be a goner.

He said, "You still have such a human conception of love. In my world, it's never-ending. I have the capacity for—"

"Smooth talking." Who was he trying to fool? "And, to think, back in that pub, you called Gavin a smooth operator."

"He is, but not with every woman. He's feeling close to Suze, and you know it."

I shut my mouth. How could I argue with that when I'd felt it with every charged cell in my body?

"You can see it happening before your very eyes," he added, tilting his head, "because Gavin doesn't have anyone to really talk to these days. No one except for her. You're going to end up bringing them together. Ironic, isn't it? Because I know you'd love to keep them apart right now."

"He's not good for her," I said. "He hasn't told her about his past, and when Suze finds out that he's got just as much darkness in him as . . ."

"His father?" Dean sighed. "You know that's not true. Gavin has killed before, but it was out of protective instinct for Wendy and Farah. It wasn't planned."

His father's death had been an accident, yes, but still, his past was something that could very well put a wedge between Suze and Gavin. And if my instincts about their body language and the way they responded to each other were genuine, Suze would need a wedge to avoid another bad relationship.

Dean narrowed his gaze at me. "You'd sabotage your best friend's pursuit of a guy?"

"No." Dammit, did he have to be so all-knowing?

"Your emotions are making you think of doing it. And if you can't admit that, then you need to do a hell of a lot of soul-searching."

I didn't know what to say. He casually returned my stare, then smiled slightly, hooking his thumbs back into his belt loops.

"Ah, parting is such sweet sorrow, isn't it? I should tell you that Louis has been calling on you, so you'd better go to him. After all, who am I to keep you from saving the world?"

"Hey, don't—"

But he did, disappearing into nothing. My temporary body went right back to air and electricity, making me a real ghost again.

Making it real easy to search my soul when that's all there was to me now.

17

Right after I flew in through an open window to Tim's family room, Louis met me, his hands in his factory uniform's pockets.

I said, "I heard you were calling."

"We've got trouble."

He led me to the hallway outside Tim's bedroom, where I could see him and Nichelle sleeping like two larvae, wrapped in their sheets and facing each other on their bed, her arms reaching toward him as he huddled with a pillow.

Louis waved me inside. "On the surface, everything looks hunky-dory, but I've been checking in mentally with Tim since you left, mostly with my empathy."

"And?"

"He's been quiet on that front, mainly thinking about what he just watched on TV, as if he was trying hard to put his mind in the serene state that we wanted him to find in the first place. And I think the hallucination did make him try to behave. But then he fell asleep, and I figured I'd see how he was doing deeper down in the old soul cave."

This sounded ominous, and I didn't know if I was up for it. Dean had left me in a real mood, and all I wanted was for this one thing to go right. But I was getting a bad feeling in the pit of my essence . . .

"Louis, please don't tell me that we made things worse with the hallucination we gave Tim this afternoon."

He moved to the side of the bed, standing over him. "Then I won't tell you that. But I will tell you that what's going on inside of him is uglier than ever."

"Shit." I stared at Tim sleeping peacefully while he cuddled his pillow like it was one of his broken basement toys. Why couldn't he always be so rested and blank? "Did I accelerate the inevitable in him by frightening him to more violence when I took over the haunting?"

"I don't think it has anything to do with you. He might be, as they say, wired this way. Heidi wouldn't have gone to the lengths she did to consult Amanda Lee if there hadn't been something serious she'd noticed in him. He'd gotten to the point where she was already worried." Louis put his hands in his pockets again. "If we can't sway him to the good side by going into his dreams or showing him what kind of harm he can cause, what else can we do?"

Twyla's voice came to me. *Let's just, like, kill him.*

"Louis," I said, "I had a talk with my . . . you know. Fake Dean?"

He looked unsettled as he nodded.

"What Twyla said about just getting rid of people like Tim? It's not an option. It might bring real darkness to us, and there's no telling how we'd have to pay for that in the end."

Maybe that was why some ghosts never called their reapers, I thought. Because they'd done stuff in Boo World that they would need to pay for, and they knew it. The only thing I *wasn't* so worried about was what might happen when a bad seed like Tim made it into Boo World—I didn't think we'd have to deal with him because, from my experience with Farah Edgett, dark forces sucked them out of the dimension right away.

Unless they found their way through a portal . . .

Louis' velvet tone soothed. "Jensen, we can still stop Tim from a bad future. I absolutely believe that, so don't worry about what Twyla says. And don't let this setback with Tim make you feel responsible. We've *got* to be on the right track in helping him."

It was so like Louis to be the optimist. I wanted to believe the same thing.

"Having said that," he said, motioning to Tim, "I think you should give the dreams another try. I'll stay out here to watch over you two and pull you out if I see him getting agitated. He's holding up under our dream-digging and hallucinations better than any human I've heard of, but we still don't want to overdo it."

"We just can't push him too far."

But I was definitely juiced for dream-digging since I'd been in some . . . well, let's just say *heavy-duty con-*

tact with fake Dean recently. I was beyond strong right now and, bless Louis, he'd been kind enough not to mention my super-fantastic ghost coloring so far. Yet I'd have to wait until Tim started his rapid eye movement, so I stood back, still cautious about going in.

But I could see my paranoia reflected in the way Louis was looking at me.

As we waited for Tim's REM, Louis said, "So . . . about Cassie."

"Yeah. Cassie." I tried to gauge him to see what his feelings were on her wrangling. "I know she came over here to talk to you before she . . ."

"Yes, she did." From the way he said it, there was no doubting that he was fine with her choice. I wouldn't put it past Louis to have advised her to do what made her happy in the end.

On the other side of the bed, Nichelle stirred, putting her hands under her chin, like she was cocooning herself in her own light dreams.

That brought us back to current events, and Louis said, "Just so you know, you've become a key player in Tim's psyche. Not *you* you—but he's dwelling on the image he saw of your hallucinatory face today. I would even say that he's *using* it."

"Using?"

"You'll see what I mean." Louis was paying close attention to Tim's sleeping pattern, and the guy wasn't quite where we needed him to be yet. "When I was in him, he was back in that basement of his, with the furnace, the toys. He wasn't looking out a window, though. There was just that big TV, but with a ghostly face on it this time. He screamed and raged and ripped that TV apart until he got to your face, and . . ."

"Let me guess. Was there blood on the walls again when he got to my face?"

Louis nodded. "Worst of all, there's another fine detail I haven't mentioned yet. . . ."

When Tim's eyes began shifting quickly underneath his lids, Louis didn't waste time.

"If there's a way for you to implant placid images in him without him detecting you, that's the way to go, Jensen. You ready?"

I didn't ask him what might happen if Tim spotted me in his subconscious. We didn't know what damage dream-Tim could inflict if he got ahold of a figment in his nightmare—namely, one of us. Could he keep us in the dream? Or, if he had an iron poker—poison to a ghost—in the dream, could he use it on me and make me dissipate? Surely that was possible because my essence was actually in there, right?

I reached out to Tim, but Louis had one last thing to say.

"Careful, sugar."

I smiled at him with a confidence I didn't necessarily feel, but then I pressed my essence to Tim's face, investing myself with everything I had.

A hard touch, a fast rush, under the skin, whooshing into him with electric speed—

My dream-body—so much like the one fake Dean had given me earlier—spun into his psyche. I whirled and whirled until I forced myself to stop.

Inches from the edge of a cliff.

I froze in place as a mournful wind moaned around me, slow and monstrous, draggy and sad. It smelled like peppermint and something else I couldn't identify, but I wasn't going to analyze it when, below me, complete darkness reigned in a fathomless, yawning black canyon.

With my back arched and arms out to balance, I gradually shifted my weight backward until I could crouch on the ground, getting my bearings.

Peppermint, I thought as an unhurried gush of the wind covered me again. The mints Tim sucked on. But what was that other smell?

When I identified blood, I gagged, holding my hand over my mouth, ponderously turning around, taking in my surroundings.

Not a basement this time . . . not even close.

I couldn't process what I was seeing in front of me at first, because it was even more surreal than Tim's original dream: black-and-white squares everywhere, like I was in a checkered tube. Squares up above, on the sides, on the floor.

And huge chess pieces . . .

My hand lowered from my mouth as I opened it in wonder. On the left of this circular tube of a board I saw that an army of white pieces waited, but there were bleeding claw marks on their casings, like nails had gouged the wood. And . . . my God . . .

Almost every piece but the queen had Tim's leering man-boy face on it.

The queen itself had no face, though, only a mouth that kept moving, shrieking like the wind. *"Just like your father . . ."*

But the other side of the board was what made my full-bodied heart pound like it was prey running through a forest: all-red pieces, shining with a coat of fresh blood, little arms sticking out of the sides of the queen and the king and the knights and everyone else, but the arms were only deformed stumps.

And where their faces should've been?

I gagged again, because the faces reflected my own vague, misty, ghostly hallucination demeanor from this afternoon. Worst of all, Tim's imagination had put long brunette hair on every one of me.

That had to be the detail Louis wanted to mention before we'd run out of time in Tim's bedroom—a morbid nuance that put anonymous me in the same category as all the other women Tim watched: the next-door cougar neighbor, Heidi, the neighbor down the street who washed her car in the driveway . . . and even Nichelle.

It seems to me that he has a real yen for brunettes. . . .

I had to get my head together here, because Tim's game obviously had rules of its own: As I processed more, it seemed like the mother queen couldn't move out of her square while his king slid from one space to the next, laughing at the red side the whole time, taunting the opposite pieces while they were mired in bases of thick blood, frozen.

"Just like my father," he said, his voice drowning out his mom's. "I'm just like my father!"

With every passing second, each white, clawed piece on his side was growing in stature, bloating, towering—all except for the queen, who stayed the same. Simultaneously, the red side was shrinking, just like I was doing in the shadows, praying that King Tim wouldn't see me.

How was I going to turn this dreamscape into something peaceful?

With one long, listless slide, Tim's king came toward my queen. Meanwhile, there was a shriek from the white side, where his mother queen was waving her arms, her mouth wiggling like she'd been drawn in a harrowing cartoon.

"Tim . . . !" Her square had opened up beneath her, and she dropped through the floor, screaming just like that woman in the TV had screamed during his first dream.

Begging. Pleading.

"Noooooo!"

Then . . . silence as the square shut itself again. There was only the wind . . . until another sound murmured in the background, rising in volume.

Machinery?

Gradually, the outline of a forklift blackened the middle of the board, just behind Tim as he stood in front of my queen.

A forklift . . . Why had a reference to his warehouse job crept in here?

Tim put on a smile for the red queen, flashing teeth so white that they gleamed like moonlight. "I saw you looking at me from across the room."

As she lifted her misty face to Tim, her features changed from mine to pure blankness. He was looming even larger now, dwarfing her. He touched her brown hair, rubbing the strands between his fingers.

Now words braided through the wind, a woman's voice.

"I could never refuse you . . ." The older neighbor from his first dream?

Her face appeared on the queen now, and Tim cupped her chin in a large hand. "Of course you can't refuse."

When he bent down to kiss her, I held back another gag. What the hell? And when he pulled her against him, her bloody body flowing into his until she pooled against his casing, I closed my dream-body eyes.

I kept myself from seeing what was going on, but I heard it loudly enough: the red queen moaning, enjoying whatever he was doing to her, Tim whispering sweet nothings, the queen breathing faster, faster until she sighed loudly.

I had to see this. That's why I was here. *Suck it up, Jen.*

I opened my eyes to witness her oozing all over the board, a crimson lake seeping over the black-and-white squares.

"I'd like to see you again," he said in a hopeful voice, talking to the blood. "Maybe tomorrow?"

She didn't answer . . . She couldn't.

Her unresponsiveness didn't sit well with Tim. He began shrinking, his face going ruddy.

As the other red chess pieces—all still with my misty

hallucination face—began pulling themselves away from the board with fruitless effort and groaning with fear, Tim slid over to my knight, his hand wrapping around its neck.

"Don't judge me," he said.

The knight's ghostly mouth opened to scream, but no sound came out as it fought Tim, slowly flailing at him with its stumps, brunette mane-hair waving back and forth behind it.

"Shut up," Tim said between clenched teeth. "I don't want to hear it!"

From the other side of the board, voices rose in volume. "What're you doing back there?" all of his white pieces said. Now they were all mouths, no faces.

All accusing him.

Tim let out a heavy yell of such rage that the room rocked. He tore the knight off the board, bloody roots coming from its base, then he spiked it to the ground.

All of the red pieces' heads tumbled off as one, rolling over the bloodied squares, wobbling into their own spaces, their faces growing mouths that echoed what the other pieces were still saying.

"What're you doing back there?"

I huddled as far in the shadows as I could, but I felt Tim's gaze finally discover me, just as surely as I felt the eyes in Elfin Forest every time I went there.

He spoke to me. "What're you doing back there?"

No. Don't see me.

He deliberately slithered over the board, until he was in front of me. I had nowhere to go . . . unless I wanted to jump off the cliff behind me.

His presence was so oppressive that I could feel him shuddering quietly, like every cell in him was screeching with silent fury.

"You," he said. "You came to play, didn't you?"

I hauled my gaze up to his own, wishing, for once, that I didn't have a dream-body. Wishing I were a ghost again so I could fly over the darkness, finding a way out.

"I want to help you, Tim," I said in a last-ditch effort to keep the peace. *Don't be a victim. Not again. Never again.*

He laughed. "Help me?" Then he turned the words over in his mouth. "Help. Me. Why do I need help?"

"I'm afraid you're going to hurt someone someday. You're so full of anger." I thought about getting up from my crouching position, but I didn't want to provoke him. "It doesn't have to be that way, Tim."

When his gaze went teary for an instant, I thought he might break down, admit that he needed help.

But the only reason his eyes had filled up was because of the emerging blood. It pooled in his gaze, slipping down his face like jagged tears or . . . No. Those weren't tears.

It was war paint. And suddenly Tim wasn't a chess piece. He was a death god with those long teeth he'd had before, pointed and yellowed daggers that stuck out of his mouth with lethal arrogance.

Before I could move, one of those teeth zinged out at me, impaling me through the arm.

I screamed, shocked, because it *hurt*.

As he retracted the tooth, blood embraced it, a red

trophy in his mouth. He laughed again, then licked at the color.

"Yum," he said. "Your pain is delicious."

This time, when two teeth came at me, I didn't hesitate—I jumped backward, into the abyss, yelling, wondering if I would ever hit bottom as I fell . . . fell . . .

Tim's voice surrounded me. "But I want to play some more!"

Out of the darkness, one of Tim's broken toy piles swooped after me, and I spun out of the way. Then I saw a giant hand swinging down from the top of the cliff, coming at me to wrap around my throat and—

With a slam, I went busting out of Tim and back into the world, crashing through Louis on my way with a barrage of sparks.

Louis yelled with shock as I tumbled to the floor and scrambled to gain my ground . . . only to find my friend manipulating the energy in the air, throwing a lamp at Tim as he—

Good God—Tim was on the other side of the bed, reaching for Nichelle's throat with that crazed look on his face I'd seen before.

He somehow ducked the lamp as he continued reaching for Nichelle, and even though I was weak, I joined Louis in focusing on a fairy figurine from a dresser and slamming it toward Tim.

He was just starting to clutch Nichelle's neck, waking her up with a jerk as the figurine bashed into his head, hitting him with enough force to make him back off, holding his hand to his temple, moaning.

Nichelle scrambled off the mattress, crawling over

the floor. Her voice was scratchy. "What the fuck, Tim?"

He was rubbing his head, discombobulated.

Louis was hovering over him, ready to throw down again. "He'd just woken up—he was conscious while he was doing it. What happened in there, Jensen?"

"I have no idea!"

As Nichelle got to her feet, grabbing a handful of clothes from the closet and stumbling to the hallway, I looked at my arm.

A chunk of it was missing where dream-Tim had stabbed me with his tooth, and as I bled energy, I heard the front door slam.

I'd gotten to a power outlet before I was drained enough to go into a time loop. I'd been losing energy that fast, but the infusion patched me up.

Still, there was a dull red throb where the gaping wound had been. How long would the healing injury stay? Could it open up again? And what if I wasn't around an energy source when it happened?

"How is it?" Louis asked.

"Still bleeding . . . if that's what you call it."

He glanced at Tim pacing the room, which he'd been doing since Nichelle had left. He was like a coke fiend, extra energized.

Was it because he'd grabbed some of my power inside the dream by taking a bite out of me?

Damn, it really did look like we were susceptible in dreams after all. Not the news flash I'd been hoping for. But at least Nichelle had gotten away, driving off in a squeal of tires, no doubt to Heidi's. I needed to have Amanda Lee call her and explain the situation before Nichelle could, because maybe Heidi could be prepared enough to talk some sense into her friend for good this time.

Meanwhile, Tim paced to his phone again, dialing it, getting Nichelle's voice mail.

"Baby, I'm so sorry. You know I am. I was having a dream—it felt so real—and I didn't mean to hurt you. Please, please, just give me another chance. . . ."

"This is my fault," I said to Louis as we hovered by a window.

"Not merely yours."

Louis was being just as hard on himself, but I wasn't about to shift blame to anyone else. I'd turned all my new friends in this direction, bringing them into my and Amanda Lee's world.

"Why couldn't that figurine have smashed his head when we threw it at him?" I asked. "Then our problems would be over."

"Or just beginning," he said, referring to our earlier talk about killing humans.

Then something hit me. Something I'd read during my dabbling crime research.

"Oh, God, Louis, I'm such an idiot. Violent people have stressors. A situation that makes them snap. It can be a breakup in a relationship, losing a job . . . Did I give Tim one with this dream?"

Louis looked me straight in the eye. "That's the victim in you talking, Jensen—a victim who makes excuses for the bad guys and takes the blame for what happened to her. She asks herself why she wandered into the woods alone and what she could've done to stay alive. She wonders how she could've saved a man from himself when he's prone to violence and on the fast track to destruction. Why're you falling into that trap again?"

Speechless. Nothing to say to that. I thought about how I'd been blaming myself for a lot of things, and realized Louis was dead right.

Don't be a victim, I'd told myself in Tim's dream. But I'd sure come out of it that way.

Louis softened his voice. "If there's a stressor, it's all those fights he has with Nichelle. Think of the good, Jensen. She might have seen the truth about the little bastard this time."

That did make me feel better. Part of what we'd wanted was for Nichelle to wake up, and she had. I hoped permanently.

Tim went to the refrigerator, jarred it open, looking for . . . Of course. Beer. He popped one open and downed it.

"Just playing devil's advocate here," I said. "But could Nichelle's leaving piss Tim off more, make him think that she's declared a kind of war?"

"That remains to be seen."

No more victim, I told myself. But maybe I could be a hero? "I'll ask Randy to come here and help with watching him. If he tries to go somewhere on his motorcycle, we can make sure it doesn't work. We can block his progress to Nichelle with everything we've got. I can even have Amanda Lee ask Ruben if he can go to his cop buddies for advice."

"And they would do something more effective than we can? You know as well as I do that there are thousands of people like Tim out there who skirt the law, and the only time they can be brought in is when they actually cross the line."

"Maybe he crossed it tonight."

We watched Tim drinking his beer and getting another from the fridge, a time bomb on a countdown.

18

By the time I got to Amanda Lee's Mediterranean-style house, gray murk had grasped the morning sky. Heidi's compact car was parked behind a tall hedge of oleanders in the driveway, but even more unexpectedly, there were several lookiloo ghosts hovering near the rose-strewn fence by the herb-and-flower garden and pool.

I found Twyla sitting on the porch steps under an arch, hunched over as she scanned the palm-tree shaded property after my travel tunnel slipped closed. She was sitting up straight, very much on duty, her petticoats spread around her.

I gestured to the property, indicating the lookiloo ghosts, like they were our biggest mystery of the day. "They're back again?"

"Sure. I figured, like, if you can't beat them, make them join." Her eyeliner made her seem extra Goth and eerie right now. She *was* taking her watch duty seriously. "They've sensed a lot of activity here, so they wandered back to check it out. Good thing they were happy-happy-joy-joy to be a part of this when I asked. It's a good distraction for them, and we could use the extra eyes."

Among the lookiloos, I'd seen a couple of Native Americans and a man in a fancy pale suit and straw hat, like the ones you'd see from the turn of the century. And I'm talking about last century, like the 1900s. I kept forgetting we'd passed the twenty-first-century mark. Anyway, those two muscle-head gym rats that Randy had chased away the day before yesterday were here, too, near Amanda Lee's pool. They'd been balancing on top of the white fence and pretending to shoot each other, just like little boys playing soldier. I wasn't sure we could define them as *helpers*, although if you added, *Mama's special* before that, it might work.

"Hey," Twyla said, staring at my wounded arm, which was glowing a faint red color, beating with every passing second. A dull pain throbbed like a slow, growing gnaw. "What trouble did you get into now?"

"I had a run-in with Tim in his psyche. No biggie."

"Wait. He got his hands on you in a dream?"

"It was more like I had a close encounter with his teeth, but it's just a superficial injury. And it feels better every time I juice up, so it should go away soon. But I think Tim got some energy out of it."

"Really? Gawd. I've never been in a dream where someone gets me. The humans spot me in their subconscious sometimes, but I'm out of them before anything comes of it. Also, I stick to normal people when I go in, know what I mean?" Her Goth eyes got thoughtful. "Hey, what if that wound, like, made you go into another time loop and Amanda Lee couldn't pull you out again? Who would I hang with?"

Was she being sarcastic? I didn't think so, and a momentary flash of pity made me smile compassionately at Twyla. She'd lost a good friend last night, and maybe she'd even done some growing up because of Cassie's wrangling. . . .

Then she burped, waving her hand in front of her face. "Taco Bell probably wasn't the most bangin' last meal I could've had." Then she laughed like a hoser.

So much for our moment. I indicated Heidi's car in the driveway. "I see Heidi brought Nichelle here."

"They're inside. There's no way for the dickweed boyfriend to connect Nichelle to Amanda Lee, so this was the first place they came after Nichelle ran to Heidi. They both took the day off their jobs, too, so hopefully Tim won't go to Fashion Valley looking for her. Heidi already warned the Cheesecake Factory and security to be on the scope for Tim."

Nichelle and Heidi both worked at the same restaurant, and calling them was a smart move on Heidi's part. She was no dummy, what with catching on to Tim in the first place and getting the hell out of her own home this morning, where he easily could find her and Nichelle.

Amanda Lee must've heard me outside, because the arched burgundy-colored door opened, and she stepped out. She was dressed in another colorful Southwestern skirt, a pale long-sleeved artist's blouse, and chunky turquoise jewelry, but she moved like a hungover revenant.

"Good, you're here," she said without much verve as she walked past Twyla. She was alert enough to notice my arm right away, though.

Before she could ask, I waved off her oncoming question and repeated, "Superficial wound from a bite Tim gave me in his dream. Doesn't even hurt." Basically.

That wasn't good enough for her. "A wound? From a dream? Jensen, did it occur to you that you're lacking energy because some of your power bled out of you?"

Yup. Next subject, please?

"How's Nichelle?" I asked.

Amanda Lee noticed my blatant attempt at topic switching, and she let it go. "She's asleep now that she's in a safe place. What about Tim? What was going on with him when you left his house?"

"He's being watched carefully. I thought it'd be wise to give Louis some backup, so I went to Flaherty's Pub because I knew Randy would still be there." Even if it was closed. Good old party boy Randy. "He and Louis are going to stop Tim if he tries to leave the house and sets out to find Nichelle. Louis and I also talked about using peaceful hallucinations to calm him, so that should keep him from getting antsy."

Twyla said, "In the short run."

Like we needed the reminder.

Amanda Lee slowly went toward the porch swing and took a seat. "Nichelle did call Tim once to tell him she wasn't at work or at Heidi's and that he shouldn't try to track her down. She hung up before he could start talking back, and then turned off her phone altogether."

"That's good and bad. Letting him know not to bother with those two locations was savvy, but hanging up on him could've made him angrier than he already is."

"Unless he's ghost-medicated with a hallucination," Amanda Lee said, her hand on her temple. She took in a long breath, then blew it out. "I knew he was going to take a big step toward his ultimate fate very soon. I should have known it would happen last night."

Was Amanda Lee talking about more than the vague suspicions we already had about Tim?

"Did your psychic vibes show you something concrete about him?" I asked, floating over to her.

"Nothing firm but, yes."

"A vision came to you before you got the news about Cassie?"

When Amanda Lee trained her tired gray eyes on me, I had my answer.

"So Cassie wasn't the only reason you'd been drinking," I said.

From the steps, Twyla peered over her shoulder, then faced back front, no doubt still listening.

"I only wanted the images to go away," Amanda Lee said. "They get to be too much sometimes."

"I can believe that." I hesitated to ask, but did, anyway. "What exactly did you see?"

"Tim, with his hands covered in blood. He was standing right in front of my closet, as real as the night itself, as I started to get ready for bed. After I noticed him, he went inside, and when I finally looked for him in there, he was gone. That was when I felt for certain that he wasn't a ghost who'd just entered your dimension or even a figment that my worried conscience had conjured up."

"It was a prescient warning," I said.

"Yes. To think, if you and Louis hadn't been at Tim's house, he could've truly hurt Nichelle. Or worse."

I took the route Louis would've. Optimism. "But now Nichelle is all the wiser to him."

Amanda Lee gazed at me like she wanted to catch my positivity by the tail and ride it. "She was in tears—angry ones—after Heidi called me and then brought her over here. Nichelle says she's never going back to him."

When Amanda Lee rested a veined hand against her forehead again, my sympathy stretched toward her. She was the same age as Suze, the same age as I would've been these days, and her sensitivity had taken its toll more than the years had.

"So many crimes to solve," she said. "Past and future. How are we going to get to them all?"

"Don't think about it now, Amanda Lee."

"I haven't forgotten about the others," she said.

She was talking about the murder victims she'd tried to contact before she'd gotten to me, the dead-and-gone people who might've been able to help her in solving Elizabeth Dalton's case, except she hadn't been successful in linking to them.

Their fates had bothered me, too. Were they somewhere in Boo World? Could they be brought to peace if we found them and helped them with their tethers, just as we were trying to do for me?

Sometimes questions can haunt, too.

"I wonder how many Valium pills are still in the bottle," she said, laughing a little. "It's been a while since I took any."

Twyla turned all the way around from her spot on the steps. "Cassie used to tell me about downers. She used to take that shit in life, and it did her more harm than good." She got a guilty cast to her essence. "Also, I tried some bad stuff when I was alive. It's, like, not the road to go down for Amanda Lee, Jen."

I'd done my share of toking, so I wasn't one to talk about recreational helpers. But Twyla was right.

Amanda Lee was giving me an ashen smile. "You wouldn't happen to have any hallucinations on tap, just like you'd give to Tim, would you?"

Twyla frowned.

I looked at Amanda Lee, with her reddened eyes. I couldn't stop her from taking a pill, but I could control a hallucination.

"Any requests?" I asked.

As she smiled in relief, Twyla kept watching us. I responded before she could bitch at me.

"I'm giving her just one."

She shrugged, going back to guarding.

Amanda Lee was already prepared. She stared ahead, like she was imagining a picture in her head, then folded her hands in her skirted lap. "When I was a girl living in our Greek Revival home, we had a lawn that swept down a hill. It was massive and emerald green, like an ocean that ruffled in a spring breeze. I would sit on the porch and watch it . . ."

I was already all over it, lifting my hand to touch Amanda Lee's face softly.

We're on a porch where tall columns hold up the sloping roof of our house. A spring wind brushes through the bright Southern sky, the smell of grass and hay soothing us. From next door, where a paddock spreads, a neighbor's horse runs free, its hooves drumming on the ground.

In front of us lies a sea of green ruffles, blades of grass whistling in the wind, making us think that life could always be this easy if we just let it flow. . . .

I backed out of Amanda Lee with a mild *pop*, bobbing in front of her, looking into her hazy eyes. Her smile was docile, grateful.

"That's what I needed," she said. "Now I can handle what today brings."

I saw in Amanda Lee what *I* must've been like after taking a drag off a joint, sitting for hours in the same chair in my apartment, letting the world go by and not letting it hurt me.

One time, I thought. This was all I would give Amanda Lee.

"I already called Ruben, just after I heard from Heidi," she said contentedly, sinking down in her swing. It creaked as it swayed. "He already had some information that a cop friend gave him about Tim's background, but he wants to come over, anyway. Nichelle should be informed about it. He isn't sure that she's aware of his past."

Why was I getting an unsettling vibe about this info

Ruben was bringing? "Why didn't he give it to you over the phone?"

"He wanted to talk to Nichelle face-to-face, probably to make certain she understands everything about the man she chose to be with. Besides, I invited him over for breakfast. I believe he likes to be coddled when he's under the weather."

My dad was like that, too. Maybe a lot of men were. "I have a little news for Ruben when he gets here. It's about my bracelets. I was at my death spot yesterday and I saw an image showing that I was wearing them when I died. Can Ruben do any of those CSI tests on them to see if they have DNA or whatever from the killer?"

"We'll ask him. I'm sure he'll have a way to accomplish that." She locked her sleepy gaze on me. "If you were wearing them when you died, then . . ."

"Then it was the killer that placed the bracelets in the car. I didn't take them off and put them there."

In back of us, Twyla made a shivery sound. "That's heinous."

"Tell me about it," I said. Tim wasn't the only cruel game player I was dealing with.

Amanda Lee breathed in deeply, like she was still in Virginia, smelling the fresh air as a girl, surrounded by clusters of leafy trees instead of the California mountains. Maybe she needed to cool out after that sick piece of news I'd just given her.

"Jensen," she said. "Are you ever going to discuss Tim's dream with me?"

"Yeah." Louis and I had already dissected the imagery while we'd been observing Tim this morning, but I was sure Amanda Lee would have her own takes on the symbolism.

So I told her about encountering the abyss, the chessboard with the white team that had claw marks on their casings, plus the blood-coated members of the red side who all wore my ghostly hallucination face. I told her about the white mother queen, the forklift, the red queen who'd ended up in a scarlet puddle over the chessboard. Then there was the part where Tim had bitten me, wallowing in my bloody taste.

"So I came out of the dream with this," I said, pointing at my arm.

"We'll have to keep our eye on that. Twyla, does there happen to be anything like a ghost doctor in your dimension?"

Twyla let out a massive laugh that Amanda Lee probably couldn't hear.

"She says no," I said to Amanda Lee. I coasted onto the swing next to her. "You know, earlier, I was feeling like I created something awful in Tim. I kept thinking that I'm the one who brought the lightning to Frankenstein's monster."

Amanda Lee gave a heavy sigh like those I remembered from my friends after a room was already enclosed by the fog of pot.

"We can argue all night about whether people like him are born this way or made," she said. "Nature versus nurture. Don't take either one upon yourself."

She sent me a smile that told me I was only doing my best to help others, and I accepted it.

"So," I said, moving on, "what do you think about that abyss in the dream?"

She rested her arm on the back of the swing. "It had to be another reference to the subconscious. That's one interpretation down."

I stole a glance at Twyla, who was fascinated with seeing Amanda Lee as mellow as this.

"He sure is big on the subconscious symbolism," I said.

She was off and running, but in a far less General-like way. "Then there's the chess game. Usually that imagery would mean our little monster is utterly focused on something in his life, and it's shutting out everything else around him."

"Like he's focused on Nichelle?" Since all the red pieces had been brunette, that might make sense. She'd been a part of his game.

"That could be," she said. "What's interesting, though, is that generally, if your king piece is under attack, it could mean you're being stifled by a female presence in your life."

"Again, that brings Nichelle to mind. But Tim's king wasn't under attack."

"Not when you got there. He might have fought that battle before you arrived, based on the claw marks on his casings. Then you saw how he got rid of that mother queen without much consideration. He wasn't about to be stifled by *any* woman on that board."

"Especially the red one . . ." She'd had the worst of it, becoming that pool of blood.

Twyla was tapping her booted foot on the steps, like

she was itching to turn around and engage with us but knew that she had the responsibility of keeping watch for not only a surprise visit from that dark spirit, but Tim, too.

Amanda Lee sighed. "He certainly did control that board."

"Is it significant that he was dressed in white?"

"I believe so. He's a good guy in this. Don't they say that all villains are heroes in their own story?"

Good point. "One more thing—the chessboards I've always seen had black pieces against white, not red."

"Blood. He dreams in blood."

I discovered I'd been floating off the swing, and I brought myself down. "Do you really think he would've gone through with strangling Nichelle if we hadn't stopped him?"

"She seems to think so." Amanda Lee glanced in back of her, at the shaded window.

I shivered off a chill, then said, "How about that forklift in the dream? At first, it seems like a connection to Tim's warehouse job, but Louis thought it might have something to do with needing help clearing out the junk from Tim's psyche instead."

"He'd already done that by jettisoning his mother."

"Maybe he needed to get rid of me, too." Yikes. "And maybe he needed to do it with *all* those pieces that had my anonymous face with brunette hair, so that's why he started doing away with that team."

"He also might have been combining you, Nichelle, and the other brunettes he covets, especially since you'd been controlling him during that hallucination, just like *Nichelle* mentally and emotionally controls him every day. That's why he grouped you together."

Twyla lost her discipline, and she stood, turning around to us. "How about the ick factor in that dream? You skipped over that."

Amanda Lee's arm fell from the back of the swing. "Is that Twyla? I can hear her as if she's on a radio that's not quite working."

Twyla started talking like someone who was trying to communicate with a person who didn't speak English. Of course, when you yell at them, we all know that they automatically understand you more.

"I said, there was a part of the dream where he totally came on to the red queen. Did he do the nasty to her or something?"

Amanda Lee evidently did hear that. "We've seen a thread of seduction in both of Tim's dreams. It's his fantasies being mixed in with the surreal. In his first dream, he was going to make love to the neighbor in the bathing suit. In this dream, he sexually came on to her again, but he got further this time." She paused. "I've seen pictures of his mother online, and she used to be a brunette."

Ick, indeed.

"Why did Tim wig out after he nastied the red queen?" Twyla yelled.

"Because he was being judged by the others," I said.

Amanda Lee added, "Being looked down on is a button he doesn't like pushed."

"His chessboard, his rules . . . his world," I said. "Nobody disobeys, and if they do . . ."

Amanda Lee put a hand to her neck. "Off with their heads."

All of us let that soak in. Nichelle's throat had almost suffered similar consequences.

"What it boils down to," I said, "is domination. He needs to be successful at it."

"His board," Twyla repeated, softer now, "his rules."

"And he came to play." I floated over to Twyla. "When I escaped from him, he was upset that I didn't want to play anymore. Just like a boy who didn't understand why I was taking my ball and going home."

"He's no boy," Twyla said.

When we heard a car turn into Amanda Lee's driveway, Twyla sprang into the air and rushed forward with me right behind her.

It couldn't be Tim, but we weren't about to take that risk.

A mint Dodge Aspen—the kind of ride my dad would've dweebed out over back in the day—cruised past the bank of oleanders where Heidi's car was hidden. It continued toward Amanda Lee's door. In the window, an older man wearing a Padres cap brought the car to a stop, then cut the engine.

"Ruben," I said to Twyla.

As he climbed out, he stifled a cough. He was a walking billboard for San Diego, wearing a rumpled blue Chargers shirt and jeans with black sports sneakers. Also, he was shorter than I remembered as he limped toward Amanda Lee, who'd stood from the swing to greet him.

I hadn't seen him walk before, so I hadn't noticed

the limp. Had he gotten it during the car accident Amanda Lee had mentioned?

"Morning," he said to Amanda Lee when he got to the porch. He'd tucked a clasped folder beneath a muscled yet loose-skinned arm, and he carried a computer pad in his other hand. "Sorry to seem so eager for breakfast."

"I'm flattered you rushed over here," she said, still so chilled out that she was like Amanda Lee on Opposite Day. Seriously, if you put Buddha in her body, this was what you might get.

But, as laid-back as she was because of the hallucination, Ruben wasn't even close. He was stone-faced and high-strung as he climbed the steps.

Amanda Lee caught on quick, and she moved aside, making room for him on the swing as they sat down.

Twyla hovered next to me. "Bad, bad vibes here."

A slight electric rattle in the air hadn't escaped my notice, either. I think it was coming from the tension that Ruben was putting out.

He placed the folder in Amanda Lee's lap. "Copies of my notes. I'm sure there's more to come."

Oh, what I'd give to have hands so I could simply comb through those papers myself.

The best me and Twyla could do was slide into the slim space behind the porch swing, looking over Amanda Lee's shoulder.

But it was like Ruben couldn't wait for her to read, and in his hurry to talk, he coughed, coning his hand over his mouth and turning aside his head. Then he started up. "We've got a real winner here. I talked to a friend in the department downtown to get this information. I was his training officer, and he owed me one because I saved his ass—pardon me—*rear end* after we cornered a perp while we were on patrol. Armed convenience store robbery. I had a good shot and took the bastard down before he could blow away my boot."

When Amanda Lee gave him a curious look, he said, "I mean to say 'blow away my trainee.'"

"I see."

He tapped the folder. "My buddy came through for me late last night after checking around with other professionals, mainly those in Buffalo Falls, Montana, where Tim grew up."

Amanda Lee couldn't restrain herself anymore, and she shuffled through the papers so fast that they were unreadable to me.

"Hey," Twyla said, but I nudged her, my elbow going right through her essence. Still, she got the hint.

"My God," Amanda Lee said, dwelling on one particular legal paper with Ruben's scrawls on it.

"That's right," he said. "Tim Knudson has a sealed juvie record, and it ain't exactly for stealing candy from the corner shop. He's been a sociopath ready to make his debut at the bastard ball for years."

19

At Ruben's pronouncement, I felt like I usually did in Tim's dreams—nauseated, with the world tilting on its axis and swaying back and forth.

When the wound on my arm started to pound harder, I pressed my hand against it. Red glowed between my fingers. Was my essence reacting to Ruben's news? Or was my injury worse than I'd realized?

Amanda Lee noticed my discomfort and, without attracting Ruben's attention, she took her phone out of a skirt pocket, placing the device on the arm of the swing. I connected with it, feeding off the charge.

Unruffled, she said, "Why don't you give me the short version, Ruben? Why was Tim in juvenile hall?"

"He set a fire at a neighbor's house when he was nine, back in Montana. A man a few houses down noticed Tim loitering near a girl's window on the same block. She was in Tim's class—a good kid with good grades, one of those angels in braids." Ruben pushed up the brim of his cap, revealing a fine sheen of sweat on his forehead. "She'd made it clear that she didn't care much for Tim, and he repaid her by setting the trellis outside her room on fire. Her father and some neighbors were able to douse the flames before it did much harm, but Tim was hauled in for it. He told his counselor that the girl was stuck up and she deserved a scare."

Amanda Lee hadn't looked any farther through the folder. "All that because he perceived that she'd jilted him?"

"Talk about an angry kid, huh? But before you start thinking that he ran around like *el diablo* all the time, Tim did have male friends he got along with. And some of the girls reportedly thought he was cute. He was caught several times by the jungle gym teaching some of them how to, uh . . ."

"French kiss?"

Ruben cleared his throat. "I was going to say 'get to second base.' That's what we called it back in the day."

I thought about the red queen in his dream and how she'd given in to Tim's seduction. Had he always fancied himself a ladies' man?

Ruben was talking again. "A few times, Tim was sent to the principal's office for harassing other girls. He even switched schools, moving from one town to another—three different campuses in two years. His mom, who was single, would pull him out whenever the staff 'got on his case' too much."

"Enabler," I said. Based on all the bitching Mama Knudson had been doing in Tim's dreams, I wasn't terribly disposed to liking her, anyway.

Twyla had been drifting to Ruben's other side this

whole time, extremely curious about him. She might've even been digging his Padres cap, dying to flip it off his head because it'd be funny.

I attempted to snap my fingers at her, failing, but she was back into the conversation, anyway.

Ruben fired up his computer pad, and me and Twyla quickly backed away from him. We didn't want to accidently suck battery energy from it and tip him off to our presence.

"I know you've seen Tim's Facebook page," Ruben said, navigating the device. After a minute, he said, "But here's a picture from the page of one of his sister's childhood friends. It took a little digging." He handed the pad to Amanda Lee.

Me and Twyla rose to the eaves, pasting ourselves there, twisting and peering down at a photo that Amanda Lee had enlarged.

The image was old, with Tim as a kid, probably when he was about nine. He wasn't bad looking, with the same buzz cut, wearing a mini sheriff's uniform, holding a wide-brimmed hat with a silver star shining on his chest. A gun belt hung from his waist, a holster with a fake revolver at the side of his skinny body, his face freckled, his eyes wide, like he was waiting for the flash to go off. Even back then, I didn't see much in that gaze of his.

It had to have been Halloween, because the little girl next to him was garbed in a fairy princess gown with a crown, diaphanous wings, and a wand. She was way shorter than Tim and, like him, she had light eyes with golden lashes and blond hair, but her smile barely existed, like she didn't want to be there. Another fairy princess stood next to her, a redhead.

A woman stood in back of both blond children, her hands on their shoulders, almost like she was keeping the kids firmly in place. She wasn't wearing a costume, just a cream jacket with a pink silk top underneath, her dark brown hair in a side braid over her shoulder. She was probably in her early thirties and fashionable in a way that told me she was a couple of years behind the curve, but still decently put together.

Amanda Lee pointed a shapely nail at her. "Mother Knudson. Francesca, right?"

Ruben nodded.

Amanda Lee allowed her finger to linger over the woman's brunette hair, emphasizing the detail to me and Twyla. Then she moved her finger to the young blond fairy princess. "Is this Tim's sister? I haven't seen her in his pictures."

"Yeah, Francine," he said. "She's four years younger. The other princess was her best friend."

"What about a father? Tim never mentions him on his social media."

Ruben chuffed, and it was partly a cough, which he covered with his hand again. Then he said, "The father, Edvard, was literally out of the picture for years. The mom kicked him out of the house when she was pregnant with Francine."

Me and Twyla asked, "Why?" in stereo.

After Amanda Lee asked the same to Ruben, he said, "He was a well-known ne'er-do-well. Everyone in the neighborhood was aware of how he drank too much at the bars, picking up on women who passed through town. He was a laborer, a handyman, so there were a few house calls involved, too. As you can imagine, there was lots of fighting at home."

"So Tim grew up in a household fraught with ugliness."

Another nod from Ruben. All I could keep thinking was, *"Just like your father!"* from Tim's dreams. And what Ruben said next only hammered that home.

"Reportedly, Mom would get on Tim's ass . . . I mean, *case* all the time because she didn't want him to follow in his father's footsteps. But he did. He was caught drinking once by a well-meaning deputy in Buffalo Falls who tried to take Tim under his wing after the dad left home. My local friend had a good chat with him. He said Tim was half drunk when he was brought into juvie, although he started getting real good at hiding it after that."

"He was nine at the time?"

"Yup, but I've seen worse, Amanda Lee, and we're not even close to the end of this story."

I chimed in. "Don't tell me—Tim completed the violent offender triad. Fire starting, and also bedwetting and cruelty to animals."

"Ew," Twyla said.

Amanda Lee lackadaisically followed through on my comment. "Are there any violently deceased house pets involved with Tim's background?"

"Not quite, but in the juvie records, his mother did mention that Tim had a fascination with hunting down squirrels and dissecting them to see what they were made of. She thought his curiosity was normal for a kid, that he might be a burgeoning scientist or something."

"Talk about willfully blind."

"*Loco*, I know."

"Did he . . ." Amanda Lee fluidly motioned with one of her hands. "This is so indelicate, but we did just mention slain squirrels, so . . . Did he wet the bed at an inappropriate age?"

Ruben gave her an appraising glance. "You got it. And no wonder he did. His mother was a piece of work, and anyone would probably piss their sheets with her around—" He held up a hand. "Forgive me. I can be blunt."

"You go right ahead, Ruben." Mellow as a sundown— that was our Amanda Lee.

Ruben seemed to get more comfortable in the swing. "Well, as you saw," he said, gesturing toward the computer Amanda Lee was still holding, "Tim was an older brother, and when the mother had Francine, she began getting paranoid about her boy."

"Because she feared he would become like his dad."

"You could say that. You see, the family lived in a small house with only two rooms—one for the mother, one for Tim. And when it came time to move the baby out of Mom's room, she didn't want Francine and Tim in the same space, so she figured out a solution. She put him in the only available place with privacy."

Me and Twyla looked at each other.

"The basement," I said, images of Tim's first dream hitting me. A furnace. A window. A TV for his entertainment.

He'd literally been kept in a damned basement.

Amanda Lee had heard me, and when Ruben started telling her more about Tim's living conditions—which were no surprise to us—I felt ill again.

Why had I left Amanda Lee's phone on that swing? It might've helped me feel better. Also, my arm was thudding red again. I really needed juice.

As we continued hanging upside down from the eaves, Twyla leaned over to whisper, "Have a snack." She pointed to an outlet in the stucco wall, and even though it was on the other side of the porch, I didn't have much of a choice but to relocate.

Yet I could still hear the discussion as clear as day over here, as Ruben continued.

"The mother was afraid Tim would be inappropriate with Francine in a room of their own, so she kept them separated in what I suppose she thought was a better way. After Tim was taken into juvie and counseled, everyone could tell how bitter he was about being banished to the basement. There was a lot of anger toward his mom because of that and also because he blamed her for throwing out his father. Overall, Francesca Knudson is a control freak, and Tim resented having to obey her. He got away from her as soon as he could."

"How?" Amanda Lee asked.

"I did a little research of my own to find out that, on the day he graduated from high school, he drove down to San Diego, kept his nose clean, and even tried to go to community college. He dropped out, which is understandable since he can't hold down jobs, either."

Hey, I'd been on and off with my own college career, too. What of it? Then again, I wasn't exactly a raging-temper freakazoid like Tim, so I let it go.

"You research quickly, Ruben," Amanda Lee said with a smile.

"Social media is a gold mine for a PI." He grinned. "Tim likes to share, and I filled in the blanks he left with information you already told me and with public records."

"You'd think a person like him would want to be more private."

"He doesn't think there's anything wrong with him. And, I hate to say it, but we live in a world where people share what they just had for lunch. Who holds back anymore?"

Amanda Lee accepted that. "And what about Tim's mother?"

"She's living with Francine and her family in Buffalo Falls."

"Francine sounds like a mother's girl."

"By all accounts she is, and Tim's the bad egg." Ruben pointed to the folder that was still on Amanda Lee's lap. "But it seems he's made an effort to be good in some respects. It could be to win his mom's approval."

Oh, how Tim probably hated his need to do that, I thought. And, unfortunately, he took out his frustrations because of it on the female symbols in his dreams . . . and Nichelle this morning.

Ruben said, "I found out that Tim has applied for the sheriff's office over the years, as well as the SDPD."

"An attempt to shine up his reputation? Or is he merely a police junkie?" Amanda Lee asked.

"Could be either. He had no shot, though, so he ended up in jobs that he probably considers below his aptitude. This isn't for you to broadcast, Amanda Lee, but I made a call to his supervisor at work, pretending to be a landlord doing a reference check. His boss isn't allowed to give out detailed information, but reading between the lines, I got the feeling Tim's on shaky ground at the warehouse, and it might not be long until he doesn't have a job anymore. Again."

"A stressor," I said to myself from the other side of the porch.

Both Twyla and Amanda Lee gave me quizzical looks but didn't pursue it. I'd have to explain later, because I'd already gone on to my next thought—Ruben had mentioned something I should've been looking for in Tim's dreams: a grandiose attitude, which was a marker of an inadequate personality. I wondered if Tim did wield one at work, if he showed everyone he was too good for his menial job. Hell, I already knew he had a seed of the grandiose in him—not everyone sees themselves as a chess king.

Ruben retrieved his computer pad from Amanda Lee and shut it down. "He's had short, tempestuous relationships in the past, according to a couple friends I was able to contact off Facebook. It seems Nichelle was the lucky one who got him just at the right point, while he neared the end of his fuse."

"It's a good thing she's getting out while she can."

"Relationships like this never turn out well. And if

she is tempted to go back to him, just have her read about Dominique Dunne. She was an actress from the eighties who had this type of boyfriend, and he ended up strangling her in front of her own home."

That's right, I remembered that. She was in *Poltergeist*, and she'd seemed too together to be in this type of relationship. Even Twyla must've recalled her, because both her Robert Smith side and Cyndi Lauper side were slit-eyed and serious. She looked at me, clenching her jaw.

But, at that moment, the door opened, and we ghosts shifted at the sight of Heidi sticking her head out.

A long brown ponytail flapped over her sweat-shirted shoulder as she checked out Ruben. "I thought I heard a man out here, but I knew it wouldn't be Tim."

"No, dear," Amanda Lee said. "This is Ruben Diaz, the PI I was telling you about."

Heidi came outside. She wasn't a big girl—in fact, her baggy gray sweatshirt swallowed her up—but she walked with the confidence of a giant this morning. I would've, too, if someone had gone after Suze like Tim had with Nichelle. I would've been ready to beat anyone down.

She shook hands with Ruben, who'd stood up, proving to be not much taller than she was.

"Thank you," she said to him. "We really owe you."

Amanda Lee cleared her throat, and when Heidi glanced at her, my associate subtly shook her head.

No fees, she'd said before. Her journey to absolution was still rolling along.

As Heidi glanced around the property, probably to see if there were any signs of me, she tucked her hands up into her sleeves. But this time, it didn't seem like she was retreating into herself as much as making fists, in case Tim did come around. Meanwhile, Twyla hung above her from the eaves, her petticoats swishing down as she took stock of this human.

"Nichelle just woke up," Heidi said. "She's still in bed, staring at her phone like she wants to listen to all the voice mails Tim left."

"I thought she turned the phone off," Amanda Lee said in her even tone.

"It's back on." There was a trace of anxiety in Heidi's own voice.

"How many messages from Tim?" Ruben asked.

"We're up to nineteen now."

Ugh. When I got back to that pain in the ass's house, I was going to suck all the life out of his phone so he couldn't use it. Or maybe Louis and Randy were just letting Tim incriminate himself by giving Nichelle ample evidence of harassment.

Ruben asked, "Is Nichelle planning to pursue a restraining order against him?"

Amanda Lee held the folder to her chest. "She'd have to build up to it. There's no sign that Tim attacked her—he'd only started putting his hand around her neck when she fled. She didn't think it'd be worth calling the authorities right now because it might set him off even more."

Heidi said, "Ruben, if you could talk to her about it, that'd be great. And I'd love if you would let her know that calling him back again, even to tell him to leave her alone, is just rewarding him for all the messages he's left."

Could a ghost adopt a human? Because Heidi had *awesome* written all over her.

"I'd be glad to," Ruben said.

Amanda Lee was already on her way inside, holding the door open for Heidi and Ruben.

Me and Twyla shrugged at each other, knowing that Amanda Lee wouldn't allow us in, no matter how buddy-buddy we were getting to be. She'd ghost-proofed her main house with everything from salt—as ineffective as it was against seasoned ghosts—to smudging and incantations.

A person needed their own haven, and she'd given the casita over to us, after all.

But after both her guests went inside, she whispered over her shoulder, "I'll open the kitchen window," then shut the door.

I raised an eyebrow at Twyla. "Sounds like the lady is leaving a gap for us."

"Like, an on-purpose chink in her armor. Aw."

I unplugged from the porch outlet, my injured arm still throbbing a little as we flew around to the side of the house.

Amanda Lee was true to her word, cracking the window enough for Twyla and me to cozy up to the sill and hear what was going on inside. She even left a battery-operated radio there for me to glom on to so I could energize.

Aw was right.

I could see Nichelle sitting at the kitchen table in the sloppy long-sleeved shirt and pants she'd pulled from the closet on her way out of her house. Her dark hair was in a haphazard side ponytail as she slumped in her chair across from Heidi, shoulders bowed. Ruben had taken off his cap, revealing his sparse gray hair, sitting between the girls while Amanda Lee whipped up bacon and pancakes at the stove.

The sizzle and smokiness of the bacon made Twyla and me lay our heads against the stucco wall. The smell wasn't as heavenly as that pizza had been last night for me in my fake body—ghosts never quite got to that point in these forms—but it left a yearning that couldn't be denied. Even the muscle-head lookiloos by the pool and the others around the property closed their eyes with the aroma.

Ruben had just finished telling Nichelle all about her lovely boyfriend. She had been listening in stunned silence the whole time, never interrupting.

As Ruben and Heidi waited for her to respond, Amanda Lee poured some batter on the griddle. She seemed occupied, but she was obviously very tuned in.

"You okay?" Ruben finally asked Nichelle.

She nodded mutely, and Heidi reached across the table, holding Nichelle's hand. Nichelle grasped on to it.

"How could I've been so dumb?" she asked, her voice a croak. "I knew about the stuff I could look up about him online, and it was easy to think he would grow out of all that, but the fire? Juvie? The basement? So, so dumb . . ."

"Don't say that," Heidi whispered.

Twyla snorted. "I'll say it."

"And you were doing so well," I muttered.

Inside, Ruben coughed, but I think it was more out of being ill-suited to this touchy-feely stuff than his sickness. He pointed to Nichelle's phone waiting on the table.

"May I?" he asked. "I'd like to check Tim's messages so you won't have to."

"Please," she said.

Most gladly, he went for the phone as Nichelle wiped her teary cheek against her sweatshirt at her shoulder. Ruben began listening to the voice mails, and as I detected them in the air, they sounded like your basic, *"Baby, come on. What was the big deal? It was just a bad dream. . . ."*

"When I met Tim a few months ago," Nichelle said over his tinny phone voice, "I thought he had an edge. I was in the mood for someone dangerous, and there he was, in front of the Leviathan, getting off that motorcycle like he owned the world."

The Leviathan was a super-seedy bar near Solana Beach. Real Dean and I used to joke all the time about stopping there for a drink, but its reputation had put us off.

Across the kitchen, Ruben listened to more messages. *"Okay, baby, I'm starting to get pissed here. Call me back."*

Nichelle went on. "Things happened so fast, and I've never had that in my life before. In case you haven't noticed, I'm not exactly Miss America, and I've been told a hundred times that I'm too passive-aggressive to ever make a man happy. Guys never come on to me strong, like Tim did. I liked his confidence and determination. He liked that I was so into him. We had one date, two . . . and I thought, 'I've found my perfect match,' so we moved in together, but Heidi was one of the people who asked me what I was thinking."

"I was looking out for you," she said.

"And I should've listened. You knew I was jumping into something too quick, and obviously, with Tim, there's a reason he put us into high gear. Any sane girl wouldn't have him. They would've known better."

"Nich . . ." Heidi said, squeezing her friend's hand.

On the phone, Tim went on. *"It'd be in your best interest to call, Nichelle. Right away. Seriously."*

She rested her elbow on the table, leaning her face into her hand and covering her eyes. At the stove, Amanda Lee used the spatula to scoop the pancakes onto a plate. Ruben was still listening to the phone, frowning, and every once in a while, accessing it to get to the next message.

"Stop fucking with me, Nichelle. . . ."

"Dammit," she said into her hand. "You would've thought that all the fights we had would tip me off. But, no, I thought we were passionate, and passion is love. The sex was amazing after each fight, and in my mind, I thought it just meant he cared. Our battles were only foreplay."

"Don't be so . . ." Heidi began.

"No, don't softball this. My judgment sucks, Heidi. The minute things started going sour with Tim I should've had the same alarms shrieking that you did. I should've never blown you off, because you were right. It took seeing him with that look on his face this morning to make me hear the warnings. Now he won't stop calling me. What the hell do I do?"

Rubén paused in accessing another message. "We'll find a way, Nichelle. Tim's building a case against himself real quick, for one thing."

"Will I have to move out of the state or get another identity or . . . ? Just listen to me. Am I paranoid or what?"

As Ruben brought up another message, he didn't say a word, instead locking gazes with Amanda Lee as she brought plates and syrup to the table.

"*Nichelle,*" said Tim's voice on the phone. "*If I have to drive around town looking for you, I will. And I'll start by going to Heidi's, even if you told me you're not there. I'll tear her fucking place apart if I have to. . . .*"

When Amanda Lee brought the food to the table, Ruben stood from his chair, limping out of the room and nodding his head toward the hall. Amanda Lee left the girls alone and followed him.

Twyla whispered, "Louis and Randy are going to keep Tim from leaving the house, right?"

"That's the plan." Even if I should've plugged in somewhere first because my arm had started beating again, I began to back away from the window. "But I can't just sit here wondering what Tim's going to pull. I'm going over there."

"What about your arm!" Twyla yelled as I conjured a travel tunnel.

"It'll hold," I said, praying I was right as I blasted into the arterial pink tube and bolted away.

20

When I saw Tim sitting on his sofa, everything seemed okay. Just another typical day staring at the TV, waiting for Nichelle to return a call that would never come.

Then again, his posture was unnaturally still, and he had one flip-flop on and one off, the second one resting on the carpet near his bare foot. Shivers consumed him, his teeth chattering. But the troubled expression on Louis' face *really* told me that something was off.

"Randy's trying to give Tim a hallucination," he said as he stood at the foot of the sofa while that ever-present soundtrack from the TV blared. Baseball, of course.

I glanced around to locate Randy, but Louis and Tim were the only other entities around.

"You don't see Randy out here because he's melded with Tim's mind," Louis said, giving me the curious eye, like I should've already realized where we ghosts went during a hallucination and dream-digging.

No doy, Jensen. "I should've known that. If I hadn't gone inside Tim, how else would I have been vulnerable to his dream attack last night?" But . . . "I just thought we went inside a human only if they're willing to be possessed."

"No, although, in that case, we take over their entire bodies—we're not merely interacting with their psyches. But that's neither here nor there." Louis' dark eyes brimmed with caution. "Tim's been so agitated today that he's been unconsciously blocking us from entering him. The only reason Randy made it in was because Tim was distracted, running around and preparing to leave the house so he could go out and look for Nichelle. He let down his shields, and Randy's been in there for ten minutes now. I'm watching to see that there's no trouble. Ten minutes is a long time for a hallucination."

"Tim's got some of my power making him stronger," I said. "He could probably withstand hours of hallucinations before his body and mind break down."

When Tim's lips parted and his gaze went foggy, I tried to lighten things up.

"Still, it looks like whatever Randy is doing is working."

Tim's eyes went totally sleepy, and Louis and I smiled at each other. But just as quickly, Tim's gaze flew open again. On the TV, the crowd roared as a player hit the ball to the outfield.

Score: Tim 1, Randy 0?

Louis rubbed the back of his neck. "So you can see how we aren't getting anywhere."

"Tim's been fighting a hallucination that's supposed to be calming him down."

"You got it."

I wafted to the top of the sofa, near the fish tank, which bubbled away like this was the happiest do-dah day ever. "Then, all in all, these hallucinations are doing no good. We're wasting our time."

"Not necessarily. Tim hasn't gotten out the door to hunt down Nichelle yet. Also, in spite of that extra strength, his body's bound to get stressed, so the visions will hopefully wear him down. We ghosts can recharge, but he won't have that luxury. The more successful we are at occupying him with hallucinations now that we made it inside of him, the weaker he should get."

I leaned closer to the guy's face. "I'd hate to go into another dream when he falls asleep. Please tell me that's not in the plan."

"It'd be great if we could just *keep* him asleep."

Again, there was no long-term solution at hand.

I chased off the blues. "In case you think that it was a bad thing when Tim was harassing Nichelle with those phone calls, those'll at least give her ammunition against him, if she ever needs it. Amanda Lee's PI is trying to gather enough information to build a case against him, too."

"That might also save his future girlfriends grief if he can be identified as a stalker."

I thought of what Ruben had told us earlier. "I feel bad for Nichelle. She's in the unfortunate position of being the girl who was around at the exact wrong time with Tim. All his frustrations built to a boiling point while he was dating her. I just hope she doesn't become his permanent fixation."

"Right." Louis floated over to the TV, laying a hand on it. The screen screamed with snow, canceling out the baseball. "And that's why I've got to be ready to go in when Randy comes out. We need to keep these hallucinations going for her sake."

"I can tag in afterward." It was better than surrendering to my urge to do something vicious to Tim, like scratching him or leaving welts that would make him hurt.

When Randy did come out of him ten minutes later, it was with a flying pop. Louis was all set, swooping away from the TV and to Tim's face with no lag time. He touched his cheek hard, preparing to enter. Already, Tim's teeth began clicking together with the chill we ghosts were bringing.

As Louis started to sink toward Tim's face, Tim's features took on Louis' ghost ones; they misted and melded together into one frozen expression for a brief hypnotic instant. Then the hazy vision disappeared, and Tim went back to being his saucer-eyed, hallucinating self.

Randy had air-stumbled toward an outlet, plugging in, his sailor hat over his brow. "I tried to put the wise guy to sleep, but he's hard-boiled. And it's like a storm-toshed ship 'n there!"

"He was drinking beer earlier, wasn't he?"

"Yeah."

The first dream I'd gone in with Tim had been a wild ride, too.

"I wonder," Randy said, "if he was this blank durin' one of them scary hallucinations you gave 'im."

"Doubtful. When I showed him that fake, formless face in the window reflection yesterday, he reacted pretty strongly. I know that because we started in the front of the house and ended up with him cowering on the floor of his bedroom." Man, it'd been satisfying to see Tim huddling at the side of the mattress, afraid of me.

"I tell ya, with the com-for-ble thunnerstorm images I gave 'im, most people'd be curled in the corner of their seat by now, snoozin' off."

"Well, we're not dealing with Sleeping Beauty here."

Me and Randy settled in while Louis conducted his hallucination. After he came out, we took turns going into Tim like he was a revolving door. I sent him images of spring in a prairie, hoping it would appeal to his Montana roots. Not quite. Louis and Randy tried bayou effects, tranquil desert scapes, and nature trails, but they all kept Tim sitting up straight on that sofa.

All we were trying to do was wear him down enough so that he'd be useless, too tired to look for Nichelle. We were also trying to give Amanda Lee and Ruben time to come up with a better plan than a restraining order, which I knew didn't always keep mad boyfriends away from their exes.

When I emerged from Tim after attempting a new approach—creating a Mozart symphony in him without any images to distract him—Randy took my place again. I plugged into the outlet by the screen door, the TV flickering right along with the lights because I was drawing more and more juice. That had to be because of my arm wound, which kept beating red, not getting any better.

When would it start really healing?

Louis had gone outside, probably to do the ghost version of pacing and trying to hit on a better idea than this. And after he slid in through the space between the screen door and wall, he had a pensive expression on him.

"Odd how the world goes on outside while we try to stop it in here," he said. "Down the street, someone's using one of those machines that blows leaves around. Next door, Mrs. Cavendish is cleaning her pool in her bathing suit. In back of us, someone's watching soap operas."

I smiled, leaning my head near the wall. "You took the time to check out Mrs. Cavendish's hot cougar bod in a bathing suit?"

If Louis could've blushed at my comment, I'm sure he would've. His skin remained the same cocoa tone with a cast of gray.

"I'm not too sure of what a cougar is, but Mrs. Cavendish does present a lovely—"

Out of nowhere, a streak of blackness shot out of the hallway, straight for Tim on the sofa.

As I pasted myself against the wall, I thought I could identify a dark . . .

Blob?

Before Louis or I could react, the thing nailed itself into Tim's skull, making him bolt to his feet, yelling and scratching at his face, leaving agitated red streaks.

"Louis!" I unplugged from my socket, but he'd already flown forward as Tim's frantic maneuvers stopped and he fell back to the sofa, the dark blob and

Randy both crashing out of Tim at the same time, flying across the room in a whirling tangle.

I saw what happened next in slow, horrific motion: Randy arching away from what could only be the infamous dark spirit from Wendy's, sailing across the room, as white as paper and as limp as air. He flew up and over the fish tank, falling and skidding just above the carpet and coming to a halt right before the kitchen counter, then lying completely still.

"Randy!"

I zoomed toward him as he stared up at me, his gaze almost a void. But there was still ghost life left in him as he whispered to me.

"Time . . . loop . . ."

With a jerking shock, I remembered what the dark spirit had done to Cassie yesterday, taking a handful of her and shoving it into itself, weakening her just like this and bringing her too damned close to the limbo I'd once been in.

Had the spirit done the same to Randy after they'd emerged from Tim? Everything had happened so fast that I hadn't seen it.

I forgot I couldn't drag him to an outlet, and when I reached for him, my hand passed right through his *bzzt*-ing essence with a snapping whimper.

"Shit!" He was already flickering. "I don't know if Amanda Lee can pull you out of a time loop like she did for me!"

As he slid a hand toward the wall, stretching out, mere feet away from the outlet, I wished I knew that prayer Wendy had used on the blob to chase it off . . .

A loud sparking sound made me turn around to see that Louis and the dark spirit had been going at it, hammering at each other with hardened essences. As I cemented my fists, too, I saw Tim out of the corner of my gaze, his arms over his face to protect himself from the mayhem as cold air whooshed around the room.

When the dark spirit yanked itself from Louis, it fell back toward Tim, circling around his head, then paused midair to split into two blobs, just at it'd separated its essence at Wendy's.

As its first half charged at a taken-aback Louis, its other part summoned the electricity in the room, materializing fully in front of Tim so he could see it.

But it didn't appear in its dark shape. It looked more like . . .

Cassie?

I couldn't move as I watched. It was just like she'd come back to us, her ponytail waving in the air like wheat in the wind.

"Tim," she said. "You're under attack by a haunting, and I need your help so *I* can help *you*. On the shelf, those little cast-iron statues. Go!"

Oh, crap. Iron. Poison.

Thank God Tim just stood there like the asshole he was.

"Go!" the creature roared with a reedy, electric voice, filling the house with new malevolence.

Tim sprinted for the shelves above the dining table where the fairy-tale souvenirs waited. Snow White and her dwarves, all suddenly weapons against us.

I almost went after him, but seeing "Cassie" had stymied me. *It isn't her,* I kept telling myself. It was the dark spirit using the essence that it'd stolen from Cassie yesterday.

Once I got that in my head, I revved up, putting Tim in my sights. Then I rushed toward him, screaming through the air as I aimed to the side of the dark spirit to get to the shelves before Tim did.

Cassie . . . *the thing* . . . grew bigger as I flew toward it, its eyes widening into a glare so intensely evil that fear ripped through me. Its Cassie smile was just as hellish.

Not her. Not my dead-and-gone friend at all.

The dark spirit hardened its arms into what looked like spikes under those paisley blouse's sleeves, and it aimed one at me as I kept coming.

Was it hoping for an impalement?

I angled toward the ceiling just in time, bringing around my hammer arm, arcing it down—

"Swing at the air!" Dark Cassie yelled to someone who wasn't me.

My instinct forced me to change course, jetting away from Dark Cassie again, back toward the ceiling. When I saw Tim below, blindly swinging around a cast-iron dwarf, I wanted to laugh.

Dark Cassie materialized again so Tim could see her. "Keep on going!"

Then the entity popped back to spirit form, but in the few seconds it took for it to dematerialize, everything happened in a blink: Louis and his own dark spirit fighting, inching dangerously close to Tim. The dark spirit using its hammer fist to bat Louis away, making him spin into the path of Tim's swinging statuette.

Iron.

Poison.

Tim bashed the dwarf through Louis, making him freeze and go pale in the air, part of him dissipating.

Like a rock, he dropped to just above the floor, hovering, unmoving.

Oh, God.

As Dark Cassie loomed in front of me again, I glanced at the equally wounded Randy oozing toward the outlet, and I started losing hope.

But hope grew eternal again when I saw that, in all the excitement, Tim had dropped his phone close by Randy, only an inch away, and Randy had seen it.

While Louis lay still, ashy and bewildered, Randy reached the phone, resting a pale hand on it.

Then he began . . .

Talking to it? Was there a Ghost 9-1-1 he was calling or something?

I didn't have time to wonder what was going on with him because the dark blob had come over to join fake Cassie, and they weren't attacking me. They were just facing me, giving me awful, baneful leers.

Why weren't they coming at me? Why just sit there staring like they were enjoying the clear terror on my face?

Because they're feeding off it, I thought. *It's making them stronger.*

Now that the air was still, Tim tossed the dwarf statuette to the ground and sprinted to the front door, leaving it open as he burst outside. I almost went after him again, but Dark Cassie moved to block me.

"Let him go," the creature said, but instead of using a demented version of Cassie's voice, it sounded more like a corrupted man—a tone that reminded me of steel nails running over asphalt.

Was that supposed to scare me? Well, it pretty much did, but I wasn't about to show it. I cut my fear off from them.

Thwarted, Dark Cassie rejoined with the black blob, becoming one entity again, stronger, darker. Now the single being hunkered over me, pointing a knifed fist at my throat.

"It looks like you're intent on going back to a residual haunting phase in that forest," it said in its ice-inducing voice. "That's what's going to happen if you insist on running off from me."

But if I stayed, Tim would escape. Then again, if I ran, I would leave my friends in danger, just as Louis was sliding toward the nearest power outlet and Randy was drawing power from touching that phone. He'd finished talking to it and thuds of color blipped through him every so often. Yet it wasn't happening fast enough.

"Why're you helping Tim?" I asked the dark spirit, buying time. Maybe soon, Randy would be powered up enough to join me. But what if the dark spirit had taken a handful of Randy earlier? Was that why he was so slow to recover?

Had it done the same to Louis when I wasn't paying attention?

Then another thought—when the dark spirit had

stabbed me at the séance over a month ago, had it taken a piece of *me*? I didn't think so. How had I somehow escaped that?

The only thing I was sure about was that stealing part of a ghost's essence allowed the spirit to impersonate different personalities, like Cassie's.

The creature kept staring at me, moving up and down as it hovered, but I still didn't give it my fear.

Finally, it answered my question. "Why wouldn't I help Tim when he's just like me?" Now I could see swirls in its dark essence, like it was rearranging itself.

Malignant electricity was slicing over me in this thing's quiet presence, and I thought part of it had to do with the way it was keeping me on a string, making me anticipate the moment it would finally attack.

Sadist, I thought. How appropriate for the monster that'd been Wendy's dad in life.

Through the open front door, the unstable roar of a motorcycle trying to start growled through the air, then sputtered to death. I glanced over at Randy, who smiled faintly at Louis as his buddy struggled toward the outlet.

They'd obviously disabled Tim's bike earlier. Score: Tim 1, Randy 1. Tie freaking game.

When I heard a female voice from outside call Tim's name, I wasn't sure what to make of it. But the dark blob . . . I swore I saw it smile in its blackness.

"When I was inside of Tim," it said in its screeching, low tone, "I couldn't resist quietly meddling. I suggested a diversion that might keep him away from Nichelle for a time, so you can thank me later for that. But I told him something rather helpful, too."

What was it talking about? Whatever it was, I didn't like the sound of it. "How did you know where we were—" I started to ask.

"Can't you feel me outside open windows, Jensen Murphy? I love to watch and listen to you. I've been doing it for a while, biding my time. Didn't you feel me?"

An army of shivers needled me as an opening appeared in the dark spirit's face. A bigger smile, crooked and foreboding.

From the depths of my memories, I heard a cackle.

"Stop! Please! Why're you doing this?"

The mask, the ax . . .

I jerked with such force that I sank toward the carpet, shivering, my arm injury beating feverishly as I looked into the anonymous form of my killer.

"Are you hurt, little girl?" it said, looking down on me as I stayed low to the ground.

Can't be happening, I kept repeating, avoiding the truth as my arm pounded ten times worse. *Can't be happening. . . .*

It continued. "I guarantee you're not as hurt now as you were that night. And, damn, but you're a far better fighter than you were then, too. I caught you so easily in those woods, but then again, I got better and better at catching all my girls. Practice makes perfect. But I'll give you this—you escaped what *they* ended up getting from me."

I could barely speak. When Randy groaned from across the room, he expressed my terror more than I could.

Flicking a gaze to my friends, I saw that Randy was still gradually adding color from the phone's charge, slowly, so slowly. Louis' own essence was shaking as he reached for the outlet . . .

The dark spirit clucked his tongue. "Poor baby. Are you embarrassed for your friends to hear how you died? You certainly don't like to hear about it yourself, do you? *I* like to hear it, though. Haunting you with the details was all I thought about in that place they kept me in for what felt like an eternity."

Weaker, weaker by the second. My arm was sapping me. So was my newly awakened horror.

Now that I was at the moment of truth, I *didn't* want to hear everything about how I'd died. But I couldn't get away from it, either, pinned by my concern for my friends . . . and, whether I admitted it or not, a compulsion to know all, no matter what my common sense was telling me.

"I don't know where I was sent after I died," the dark spirit said in that scratch-steel voice. "Maybe hell? A holding cell? A dark tube that allowed me and millions of cursed others to skim the perimeter of life so we could watch and yearn and hope for a way in?" He laughed. "Looks like I found one, thanks to Amanda Lee Minter. She all but invited me back here, never knowing that I was watching you. Waiting to see you again."

I was gathering my quaking energy, my will. Finally, I said, "I didn't put you in that place."

"No, someone else did. Does that make you feel better, to know I stopped killing girls after *I* was killed?"

It laughed like rusted nails being twisted around a tight hole. "But I'm baa-ack. Someday I'll express my appreciation to your psychic friend. I like that woman. I worship her in all her righteous ineptitude. How wrong were the two of you to think I was after Wendy Edgett, of all people? Yes, she's wonderful, fresh, young meat, but I like the blondes so much more." My killer leaned down close enough to me that I smelled old blood. "I like *you*."

Its words flipped a switch in me, making me think . . .

No, it couldn't be.

"Is that you, Dean?" I asked, meaning fake Dean, fear edging the question.

The thing hesitated, and I almost barfed ghost-style. It couldn't be him. . . .

But then it laughed in its serrated way until the water in the fish tank rippled.

What a stupid thing to have said. No, this couldn't be Dean. I was still in ghost form and didn't have that pseudo-body that I had whenever fake Dean was with me. But this creature had sounded as arrogant as Dean was, and it'd assumed another form, too, just as fake Dean liked to do.

This wasn't the devious spirit I'd come to kind of like.

As the creature kept laughing, I saw that Louis had recovered way faster than Randy, who was only barely past pale. Even though Louis wasn't as gray as he should be yet, he'd already pulled out of his power source, creeping toward the front door that Tim had left open.

He was going to see about Tim. . . .

Randy gave me a nod, like he was telling me to keep the dark spirit talking.

I went on. "How many girls did you kill?"

The thing smiled widely again, opening up its essence. "Fifteen, if we're talking about pure kills."

Fifteen, just like me. "What do you mean, *pure kills*?"

For the first time, I saw the semblance of a face in the darkness, but I closed my eyes because I could only recognize the mask—the hag's mouth, wrinkled skin, piercing blue eyes. The face that had killed me.

My energy drained out of me a little more, like the spirit was devouring my fear from only feet away. My arm thudded even harder, each tremoring beat a fast pulse of electricity out of my essence.

"What I mean," it said, "is that I only count the bloody kills. Those were the times when my ax blade would actually hit one of my little darlings in the head and I'd see a brief, lovely look of surprise on her." The spirit held up a handlike appendage to its temple. " 'Gee, am I really dead?' That's what she'd be thinking as she realized she'd just been snuffed. But you?" Even this thing's chuff sounded twisted. "You were only my fourth kill, and I was still in that first stage of excitement. You flinched, moved out of the way, and I missed your sweet spot on the way down. The blunt side of the blade got your head in a place that did you in, anyway, but you died without that beautiful spray of blood that I love to see and feel."

How much more could I hear? Whatever my limits, I wasn't going to let this thing win.

"But you inspired me, Jensen Murphy. You saved me a lot of cleanup that night and in the future. You were a learning experience, because I ended up dragging you to my van and cutting you the fuck up there. I already had the plastic lining in place for your remains, so I started on you right away, while I was still in heat."

This isn't me he's talking about, I kept thinking, trying hard not to picture what he was describing. *Not me.*

"I was so high off your blood," he said, "that afterward I took those bracelets of yours, wiped them off nicely, then removed my costume and pretended like I was just an average Joe in the forest at night. The car you drove was unlocked, so I left a calling card, just to see if anyone noticed I'd been there." He laughed. "'Fraid not."

I didn't tell him that, in the time he'd been gone, *CSI* had taken over the world. He couldn't have been careful enough, and we were going to finger him.

"I got even better after that night, cleaner," he said. "I nearly perfected my art until . . ."

The spirit halted, smiling widely again, lifting its blobby hand and shaking what looked like a finger at me.

"You thought I was going to tell you how I died."

"I don't care."

"I think you do. And I'm going to let you wonder. I'm also going to let you imagine all those other girls whose chopped limbs got consumed by a lye solution, just like yours. Burning the bones was always fun, too. You're not the only one who likes to give out nightmares, you know."

My temper took me over. "I do that for damned good reason. Don't you dare compare yourself to me."

Don't you dare make it seem like I haven't made any difference.

"Now there's the feistiness I was hoping for. You know what I'm going to do with you, Jensen Murphy?"

"Kill me again?" Fucker.

"Yes, in a way." The spirit grew larger, trying to intimidate me. "I'm going to chase you again and again, because that's what floats my boat. I'm going to haunt the shit out of you. I'm going to make you wonder where I am, when I could appear, and I'm going to eat your fear like it's a feast until I get tired of it. And when I do get tired, I'm going to move on to the other girls I killed, because there're still a few in this dimension. None of them have taken up with a vengeful psychic like you did, though, so congratulations—you won the grand prize of being my main love interest!" It sighed. "This *is* kind of like first love, isn't it? And I did love you when I was watching you in the woods, at that party, Jensen Murphy. I loved every part of you after I cut you up."

I'd been saving all the energy I could, just for a moment like this. And when I focused electricity on that cast-iron figurine Tim had dropped, making it fly through the air and right through the center of the spirit, the creature flinched back from me with a cry.

"Bitch!"

As it darted its blobby hand out, I knew it wanted to grab a piece of me like I'd seen it do to Cassie.

But I was prepared.

I jetted out of the way, and Randy must've seen what my plan was, because he'd gotten strong enough to crawl to an outlet, and he was pointing at the iron dwarf, too, helping me to move it.

The figurine felt so much lighter with Randy's aid as we manipulated the iron through the dark spirit's essence, making the creature scream in pain as, little by little, its insides began to dissipate.

But after it dissipated, where would it go? I didn't know, but it sure as hell wouldn't be here.

When it started laughing, weakly this time, I braced myself for one last attack. But it just kept fading away, dust to dust.

"Remember," it said in its last moments. "I'll be watching you!"

A cold wind screamed around the room as the thing disappeared.

Me and Randy dropped the figurine to the floor, and I flew over to him.

"Are you all right?"

"A lil' worse for the wear, but still dead 'nuf." He closed his eyes and rested his head near the wall. "I called Amanda Lee to git over here, but you need to go to Louis. See what's keepin' 'im . . ."

Shit, Louis had been gone for a while. I didn't know how long I'd been held up from chasing Tim, but I didn't want to let the asshole out of my sight for any more time.

I whisked through the front door and outside to the driveway, whirling around, trying to find a sign of Tim or Louis. All I saw was Tim's abandoned motorcycle.

Who'd been the female who'd talked to him out here? Where'd they gone?

I flew to the backyard, but there was nothing. And when I saw Mrs. Cavendish's empty pool yard over the fence, I got a very bad feeling. It got even worse when I went to the rear of her house and found the door open.

I streamed in through her kitchen, hearing an animallike sound. I found Louis—why was he so pale now?—on the tile floor, inches from an outlet that he was reaching for, and I got that sick feeling in my pit.

"Keep . . . going . . ." Louis said with effort. Dammit, he'd left Tim's house too soon.

But too soon for what?

I drifted low along the floor, so very quiet, gradually realizing that the sound I was hearing wasn't exactly weeping.

It was the sound of deranged delight. And it was coming from Tim.

He was kneeling on the floor, staring at his clean hands, which he'd raised in front of him. He was staring at them like there was blood on his skin while he hunched over Mrs. Cavendish, whose still gaze was fixed on the ceiling, her mouth open in a silent scream.

21

The lights flickered as Louis slumped by the outlet, drawing too much power from the fuses as he lowered his head. "We were too late. . . ."

The smell of breath mints traced the air as Tim rocked back and forth by Mrs. Cavendish, his hands still in front of his face as he stared at them. A shroud of silence pressed the oxygen from the room, weighing over me, and my arm was throbbing harder, like steps in a funeral procession for Mrs. Cavendish.

I didn't ask Louis what'd gone on in here, or if her wrangler had escorted her to the glare yet. I only rose up from the floor and inched into Mrs. Cavendish's family room, decorated all over with framed landscapes of the sunny sea. Next to her, a coffee table was overturned, spilling travel magazines and potpourri over the carpet.

My essence quaked, sputtering in disappointment and failure. Tim had fulfilled all the promises of his bloody dreams. Worse yet, that dark spirit, my killer, had helped him, just as if he'd wanted to make Tim into an apprentice. Back in the other house, he'd said, "*I couldn't resist quietly meddling. I suggested a diversion that might keep him away from Nichelle for a time, so you can thank me later for that.*"

Was *this* the result of his interference? But he'd also made another comment.

"*I told him something rather helpful, too. . . .*"

What had he meant by that? Because murder didn't fit the definition of *helpful*.

When Tim smiled, laughing softly to himself, I wondered if he'd gotten high from killing Mrs. Cavendish. Just to be sure, I reached out, touched him, using my empathy even if it was the last thing I felt for him.

Hands around her neck, squeezing and squeezing, her eyes glassy, full of terror, confused and begging. Choking, gasping . . .

Mom's face?

Nichelle's?

A rush of adrenaline pumping the heart. Alive, so alive!

Pulling away from her, having the power of death over life. Fun. That was such fun . . . !

I shoved out of Tim, retreating to the kitchen, weaker now, my arm like a flashing beacon. He shivered like he was in the middle of an ice storm, but he still had that smile on his face as he kept rocking over her.

I wanted to maim him. No, better yet, I wanted to ignore the consequences fake Dean had said there would be for killing him and just do it.

But all my choices didn't matter worth a shit when

Mrs. Cavendish made a final, tiny throttled sound—she hadn't been dead?—and a misty stream of gray rose out of her eyes. . . .

I could only stare as she officially gave up the ghost.

She floated over her body, a pearly gray middle-aged woman in a white mesh bathing suit cover-up, looking at her new hands, just as Tim had looked at his—almost like she didn't recognize that they were a part of her. She ran her fingers over her arm, then traced her palms down her torso, and I didn't know if it was because she was realizing she was dead or if she was getting used to the fact that she'd be in this outfit for the rest of her ghost existence. Her long brunette hair was in disarray, probably from her battle with Tim, and when she saw him kneeling in front of her deceased body—the one she'd taken such pains to maintain in her cougar years—she fisted her hands, then let out a blood-stopping scream.

Too bad Tim couldn't hear it. Too bad I couldn't even go over to comfort her because, at that moment, a familiar, beautiful gray shape fogged out of the ceiling, like it'd traveled right through it, and wafted like a veiled bride toward Mrs. Cavendish.

When she saw the wrangler, her scream cut off. Then she stumbled backward through the air.

"No," she said. "No, no, no . . ."

I had to help her. "This is your reaper. It only wants to escort you to the real afterlife."

Mrs. Cavendish finally noticed I was there. She screamed again, this time at the sight of me, then Louis. Then, clumsily, she flew toward the rear of her house where the door was open, her scream drifting back to us, fading a little more with every passing second.

All that was left was Tim, the wrangler, Louis, and me.

The reaper didn't seem to mind Mrs. Cavendish's rejection. Instead, it gravitated to Tim, its veils flowing as it reached out and used its twiggy fingers to rake down his face, almost like a cruel, curious stroke.

He gasped in agony, because the wrangler had combed over the same red streaks that he'd put there himself when he had scratched his face after my dark killer had shown up at his house. Now he scrambled away from Mrs. Cavendish's body, coming to a stand, holding a palm over a cheek. With his other hand, he rubbed an arm. Then he started pacing back and forth while never dragging his gaze away from his victim.

Had Tim just woken up from his killing glee? Did he realize now that he was in trouble?

The wrangler paused above, then circled around him, sending a veiled glance to me and Louis. Deep in my essence, I knew what it was thinking.

He'll get his. Don't worry.

A sense of peace should've come over me, but it didn't. Hatred was hanging through me like parasitic moss, and the wrangler must've known that, because it slowly shook its head, discouraging me from doing anything to him on my own, then drifted back to the ceiling in reverse, absorbed into the plaster, leaving a faint shadow of its outline before it disappeared altogether.

The only sounds I could hear were Tim's heavy

breathing while he paced, plus the thud of his sneak-ered footsteps. As my own beating essence—the wound on my arm—ran a race with his rhythms, a random thought came to me. He must've grabbed the shoes outside, before he'd tried to start his bike. Right before he'd come inside to murder Mrs. Cavendish. He wasn't crazed.

My hatred of him swelled.

"Jensen," Louis said in that thin, wounded tone. "Don't do it. Don't put a mark of darkness on yourself by going after that monster."

I stayed silent.

"The wrangler even warned you," Louis said. "I saw it with my own two eyes. The universe must have a plan for Tim. Let it happen."

He came off like fake Dean when he'd warned me about acting like a god. But I had the power of a god over a dung beetle like Tim, didn't I? And he was right here, pacing, nervously brushing a hand over his hair as he panicked and probably thought about how to dis-pose of the body.

"What else did you see with your own two eyes?" I asked Louis. "How did this happen?"

Grayness cut with faint color washed through him, thanks to the power outlet, but the fight with the dark spirit had still sapped him. I didn't even have to ask if that thing had taken a chunk out of Louis and put it into itself during their fight because the answer was clear.

"I'll tell you after you plug in," Louis said. "You're not looking well."

I glanced at Tim wearing a hole in the carpet, and I knew that I'd need all the energy I could get to deal with him. So I slid to an outlet above the kitchen's Formica counter, near a big blender. Space-age machines were all over the place, but Mrs. Cavendish wouldn't be using them anymore. There was also a ceramic bowl filled with keys nearby, a patchwork purse, and two clean glasses on the counter.

I started to electrify myself, ready to spring at Tim at a moment's notice.

Louis seemed satisfied with me now, although he kept monitoring Tim, too. "Mrs. Cavendish . . ." He trailed off and soberly corrected himself. "Margaret. She told Tim to call her Margaret when she saw him trying to start his motorcycle and went over to ask if she could help. He'd called her Mrs. Cavendish, and she'd told him that only her middle school students had called her that before she'd stopped teaching and went into online education consulting for herself." He paused. "When she found out Tim didn't have Triple-A for towing his bike to a garage, she offered to use her card to get someone out here. He thanked her, and she said that's what good neighbors do, then asked him in for lemonade while she made the call."

"Was she . . . ?"

"Inviting him in for another reason? I don't think so, but I think Tim did. He popped one of those breath mints he's always carrying into his mouth while she got ready to pour lemonade." Louis lethargically indicated the glasses on the counter. "I was strong enough to follow them inside at that point. Tim was already worked up from the dark spirit, and he started getting insistent about borrowing Margaret's car instead of having his bike towed."

"So he could go and find Nichelle, just like he'd threatened to."

"Yes."

Had Tim snapped then? Had he given in to my dark killer's suggestion to kill his neighbor?

I asked, "Did she refuse to give him her car?"

"Yes. She was nice about it, and Tim began sweet-talking her, but in an aggressive way. She got nervous and asked him to leave the house."

Oh, no. That had probably been the start of the nightmare for her, because Tim's dreams and fantasies had been much different from this reality. In his mind, she would've given him anything, a car, her body . . .

In the family room, Tim stopped pacing, like his panic had finally subsided. He flexed his fingers, another hazy smile tipping the corners of his mouth as his gaze caressed Mrs. Cavendish's body.

Was he remembering what it'd been like to kill her?

I hunched on the counter, wanting so bad to pry a picture off the wall and send it across the room, decapitating him.

Louis went on. "I hadn't juiced up enough over at the other house, so the trip over here made me tired. I wanted to go into Tim's head to see if a hallucination might calm him, but I needed energy. I couldn't even throw a lamp at him, not after that dark spirit took a piece of me."

I closed my eyes, not just in pain for Louis, but because I didn't want to talk about my killer. It was too soon.

Deal with this first, I thought. *Then . . .*

Then I didn't know what.

Louis looked as sick as I felt. "Tim was barely containing his rage by then, and Mrs. Cavendish started running toward the back door to leave. He went after her, grabbing her arm, telling her that he was going to use her car. That she couldn't deny him that."

"His board, his rules," I said, tracking Tim while he got to his knees in front of the body.

Louis continued. "Tim had that look in his eyes. Coveting. Anger. Aggression. A hint of those fantasies we saw in his dreams."

I knew what was coming next and steadied myself for it.

"He took Margaret by the hair," Louis said, "then dragged her into the main room." His voice broke. "He started pulling down her cover-up, groping her, telling her to shut up because he'd seen how she flaunted herself in her backyard, knowing that he was watching. But Margaret was a fighter. She kneed him so hard in the groin that it stopped him, but not long enough, because he put his hands around her neck and squeezed." Louis rested his head in his hand. "There still wasn't a thing I could do but plug in and try to knock something off the couch nearby to distract him, and I did manage that."

I saw a yellow throw pillow on the floor, next to her body.

"He didn't notice," Louis said. "She choked for minutes on end and then . . . It got so, so quiet. And you know what he said to her afterward?"

"Do I have to know?" I whispered as I watched Tim staring at Mrs. Cavendish.

Louis said it, anyway. " 'I thought you liked me.' That's what was running through his head after he killed her. Not *I'm sorry* or *What have I done?*"

I'd never imagined Tim would be like some of the fiends I'd read about. A male chauvinist rapist? Was that what an expert might call him? He couldn't fathom how a woman might ever want to deny him. He would even try to explain the attack away by saying something like Tim had said.

"He didn't expect her to fight back," I said. "When she did, he just wanted her to cut it out. He panicked, and that's why she's dead. But, even if this was a mistake, he realized afterward that he's got a taste for this."

Maybe even because my dark killer had implanted that in his psyche, encouraging what was already there, finally sending him over the line?

Tim was reaching out a hand to Mrs. Cavendish's hair now, and when he began fluffing the strands over her shoulder in a style that Nichelle or his mom might've worn, that was the last straw.

"Don't touch her," I said.

Summoning energy, I rolled it into a bolt and hurled it toward one of the sea pictures, batting it off the wall, sending the frame toward Tim and smashing him in the face.

He fell backward, his hand over his nose. When he took his hand away, it was covered in blood, and he could make only a yawping sound while getting to his feet. He was so off balance that he leaned over Mrs. Cavendish's face in the process, dripping blood onto her, adding insult to injury.

But he'd added even more than that. Trace evidence.

I got ready to fling another projectile at him because the more blood he left here, the better.

"*Jensen*," Louis said.

"It would only be right," I said, my voice trembling. "Didn't you see him? He was going to pose her body, making it into Nichelle's or that picture I saw of his mother with her side braid. If we went into him right this second, we'd see a lot of sick new fantasies he's conjuring up."

But I didn't want to see anything more about Tim Knudson. I wanted him erased.

Just as I was choosing which picture would look good up his ass, there was a rattle at the front door.

The knob, twisting.

Tim took off toward the kitchen, going for the ceramic bowl on the counter, grabbing Mrs. Cavendish's purse, and fleeing for the back door. At the same time, the front door opened and Amanda Lee walked through, trailed by Twyla, who floated just above her.

"Randy said you two would be in here. . . ." Amanda Lee froze at the sight of Mrs. Cavendish.

Out front, a car started. Tim must've run around to the driveway to take Mrs. Cavendish's vehicle.

"Go!" I said to Twyla, who was at full energy. "He's getting away!"

She didn't hesitate, darting back outside as the squeal of tires hit pavement.

I unplugged from the outlet, even though my arm was still giving me fits, beating, beating. Louis could stay here and tell Amanda Lee everything, but I wanted to go with Twyla to catch Tim.

I still wanted to give him more than a bloody nose.

Zooming out the door, I sputtered on the street, seeing that Twyla and Tim were already gone. I thought of bringing up a travel tunnel for speed, but that wasn't smart since I didn't know the destination . . . unless he was going to Heidi's house.

But he couldn't be that dumb. He might've even been making a run for the Mexican border, and we had to get the cops over here quick so they could start pursuing him. Dammit, the minute that Louis or I saw what was going on, we should've manipulated a phone to report a killing, but we'd been trying to sort out the murder.

I went back inside, admitting I wasn't going to be fast enough for a car until I charged up more. Besides, I could be useful here . . . "The only witness to Mrs. Cavendish's death was a ghost," I said. "We need to tie suspicion to Tim before he makes it into Mexico. He had a nosebleed over the body, but it'll take too long—"

"To have his blood analyzed so he can be identified and charged by the authorities," finished Amanda Lee. "I can lie and tell the police that I saw Tim leaving the premises. It's close to the truth."

I had a better idea, and it was totally gross, but it was for justice's sake.

"Amanda Lee," I said, "just call 9-1-1."

Then I went about my business. I sailed to Mrs. Cavendish, settling next to her and bowing my head, apologizing to the universe. Then I fortified myself, pressing my hand on her face.

Once, I'd possessed a willing person. Gavin. He'd invited me in, and since there was no one at home to keep me out of Mrs. Cavendish's body, I filled her up with my essence and—

Oh, God, it was stiff and colder than hell inside her body, like I was wearing a wet suit that'd been soaked in icy water. I couldn't even move her head to look around.

I was a rubber mummy.

I heard Amanda Lee gasp, long and harsh. Louis called my name again, but he would understand what I was doing soon enough.

It took everything I had to manipulate Mrs. Cavendish's hand, raising her fingers enough to dip them in the blood Tim had dripped onto her face. I reached over to the marble surface of the table that had probably been knocked over during her struggle with him. Then I forced that hand to write:

T-I-M K-N-

It was too difficult to get any farther than that, and I let Mrs. Cavendish's hand trail down in a streak of blood to the carpet. Then I erupted out of her with a jarring *thunk*, shuddering in the aftermath.

"I'm so sorry, Mrs. Cavendish," I said, heading for

the outlet again. The red pounding on my arm had spread farther, making me slightly numb.

Amanda Lee was off the phone, and now she yelled at me, the mellowness from today's hallucination utterly kaput. "You didn't have to go that far, Jensen! *I* could have grabbed her hand and written his name on that table!"

"And I probably could've manipulated her hand to do the same thing," I said. "This way it looks like *she* did it. On *CSI*, they totally would be able to tell if someone moved her body, and we don't want to screw with the chain of evidence or whatever."

Louis was merely shaking his head as he kept powering up. "Yes, this way, the detectives will only wonder why she was moving after she died."

Was *CSI* that good?

"But first," I said, "they'll be wondering why she wrote Tim's name, and they'll get busy investigating him."

Louis clenched his jaw.

No time to argue. Now I had to charge up even more since going into Mrs. Cavendish had wasted me. While I did that, Amanda Lee called Ruben, even though chances were incredibly slim that Tim would find Nichelle at her house since she and Amanda Lee had no obvious connection. Then she went outside to wait for a patrol car. After I heard sirens, I couldn't wait around anymore.

"Louis, I'm strong again. I'm going to try and catch up to Tim and Twyla. She might need help."

"She can handle him, Jensen. Just rest some more."

I looked at Mrs. Cavendish. I hadn't done enough.

Streaming out the door, I headed for the freeway, hoping I could find Tim traveling southbound, driving toward the border with Twyla in pursuit. I even remembered the blue car parked in Mrs. Cavendish's driveway, so I could identify it.

But things weren't that easy. Ghosts—especially wounded ones—aren't as fast as cars, and as hard as I tried, I couldn't find the one I was looking for. My arm kept slowing me down most of all.

My frustration came to a head: Tim, the dark spirit, the injustice of how this universe worked.

I started to run out of steam, skidding over to the side of the freeway, close to Mission Bay, where the water spread like a gray tarp under the overcast sky.

Why couldn't ghosts have unlimited energy? How unfair was that? I screamed at the injustice, just as Mrs. Cavendish had screamed when her ghost had seen her dead body. I almost started to cry, but I was *too* full of rage.

This had to be *someone's* fault. I mean, who put monsters on earth to kill innocent women in the first place? Who just sat back in whatever cosmic throne they'd made for themselves and watched it all happen?

I knew of one entity that saw all the pain go by and had the power to do more about it than he was doing, and I couldn't hold back from screaming at him, too.

"Dean, you son of a bitch, don't just sit there watching this happen! Do something! Stop that bastard!"

And while he was at it, why couldn't he deal with my own dark killer, wherever *he* was?

All I got in return was silence, except for the metallic roar of the cars on the freeway, the squawk of seagulls as they winged over me.

I shoved a middle finger at the sky, to wherever the star place was. "Is this fun for you, to see humans and ghosts and all us lesser beings thrown into chaos? Do you eat our pain, just like my killer wants to eat mine?" Then I went for a shot below the belt. "Do you want me to belong to him instead of you? Because that's what he wants. . . ."

A whooshing vortex enveloped me as I spun skyward, pulled to a familiar plane.

The star place.

I had a body up here, so I panted and took in all the air I needed as I stayed on all fours, braced on that invisible floor that held me up from the purple, star-dotted sky around me. Out of the corner of my eye, I saw a few glowing bodies suspended in the near distance—male and female, comatose and sublimely tranquil. Then I saw the standing white lotus pool sending up a pale glow.

A glare spot? A temptation to go into the light.

"Be my guest," fake Dean's voice said on my left. "I won't stop you from going with your wrangler and taking that next step."

As I moved, I winced. My arm keened like someone had taken a chomp out of it. And someone had.

I held my hand over the injury. "I didn't come up here for that. You heard what I was saying down below."

"Yeah, you're pretty angry. At me, of all people."

I almost told him he wasn't a person. "You could've stopped Tim."

Fake Dean had his thumbs in his belt loops, so casual, so careless. But then I saw the hurt in his eyes just before he closed his lids, opening them again and showing me the same cool cat as before.

He grinned. "There can't be darkness without light, and vice versa, Jenny. I can't stop darkness from operating."

"You're colder than I thought."

He didn't answer. Had I hit a bull's-eye in him?

"Somewhere on the earthly plane," I said, shakily rising to my knees, "there's a killer on the loose. He wants to find his ex-girlfriend and hurt her. Hell, he wanted to hurt *her* earlier in the day, but someone took her place in a massive way. We can't let him get away with that."

"But he might get away. That's the way of the world. It's been like that since its inception, since the gods used humans in their games with each other, since man coveted another man's piece of hunted meat. Someday, when everyone goes too far in their appetite for destruction, it'll all end, but they have a ways to travel, Jenny."

He was talking like he knew much more than he always claimed he did. He *had* to have the power to interfere with this one little thing. Why wasn't he giving in to me?

Reading me, he said, "I don't make exceptions. They tend to snowball. I've spent a lot of time learning risk management, believe me."

This was going nowhere. There had to be something I could do. But how far would I go?

I thought of Tim's bloody dreams, his fantasies that had starred all those brunettes who substituted for his mother. He'd seen his domineering mom's face as he'd strangled Mrs. Cavendish, and I knew he would take his frustration in not being able to control her and Nichelle out on a lot more women if he wasn't stopped.

"He's going to get good at hunting," I said to fake Dean. "He's dreamed about it." I thought of Tim's first dream: the chase through the forest, the woman screaming for mercy. He'd wanted to hunt and kill all along, and he'd gotten the chance for the last wish today.

"You're taking it too personally," he said. "You're relating Tim to your own murderer."

"And why wouldn't I?"

"You shouldn't."

Fake Dean dropped the cool act and walked over to me, getting to his knees and looking into my eyes. He gently removed my hand from over my wound and replaced it with his own.

Warmth and serene energy rushed into me, and I held back a content moan at the relief. And the desire.

I strengthened my voice. "You know that I met my killer today. Did that give you a thrill?"

"No." He held my arm tighter. "It slayed me to watch it happening."

I spoke before thinking. "Are you hoping my dark killer is going to push me into your arms? Was that your plan all along?"

"Jenny . . ."

"No—let me answer that. There's no light without darkness and there was nothing you could do to interfere."

"I wish you actually understood that. Do you think it gave me happiness to see that abomination taunt you today?"

He sounded tortured, gripping my arm harder. I almost melted into him, and I might've if I didn't always suspect that he was playing one of his games to capture me.

"My killer's also going to haunt me," I said. "Isn't that rich? He's going to make sure I'm always looking over my shoulder. It *is* almost enough to make me want to go into the glare, but there's that whole thing about me wanting to kick my killer's ass before that happens."

Dean smiled. "That's the spirit."

"Oh, you approve?"

"I do. That thing is off licking its wounds and building itself back up again, but I would banish him back to wherever he came from, myself, if . . ."

"You were allowed to. I know." I reveled in his dizzying touch some more. "Can you at least tell me why he doesn't have a wrangler who recaptures him and takes him back to wherever he came from?"

"Amanda Lee invited him back into this dimension. It's up to her to put him back. The wrangler already did its job once, and it's not its fault this one got away."

"Sounds very bureaucratic, wherever it comes from."

I breathed, letting his touch pulse through me. "Today, I thought that dark spirit might be you. He used Cassie's façade from when he reached into her yesterday." I stopped, then said, "Did that thing get a part of me, too, back at the séance when it stabbed me?"

"No." Dean smiled. "It was new to this plane back then, and it only learned recently that it could steal essences."

"Can we regular ghosts do that?"

"You can't."

At least he could tell me that. "You like to switch your appearance, too. It sort of made sense that the dark spirit might be you, for a minute."

"Dark spirits aren't what you humans refer to as the devil, but they're still deceivers."

"You're not?"

"Oh, I am. But I'm not altogether dark or light."

When he took his hand away from my skin, his imprint stayed behind, like I truly belonged to him.

I looked at my wound and it was gone.

"Sometimes more light than dark," he said, smiling again.

How I wanted to give in to that smile. . . .

But that's not why I was here. "It seems that a creature with more light in them would want to stop a killer."

"Jenny . . ."

"What about a trade?" What was coming out of my mouth? "What if I said I'd go along with your reindeer games if you'd just do this one thing for me?"

He tilted his head, narrowed his eyes. "Are you offering yourself to me?"

Now that the words were still ringing in the air, I couldn't take them back. Actually, I didn't even want to.

"Yes, I am," I whispered.

22

Fake Dean began to glow at my yes.

His skin became as ethereal as the stars he'd collected all around us. His eyes darkened with pleasure, affection . . . whatever it was that an entity like him felt.

And I basked in that glow. It wasn't only because he resembled my old Dean—to tell the truth, I was sick of comparing the two when they weren't the same at all. I had developed some kind of bizarre relationship with this entity. He made me feel, and I could believe that he wanted me for the sake of me.

But that didn't mean I would become just one of his stars.

As he cupped my face in his hands, I almost gave myself over to him, though. His light brown eyes . . . they promised a beautiful, perfect world where pain and loss didn't exist. The world of his seduced stars.

I wrapped my fingers around his wrists. "Before I promise anything else, I want to hear you tell me that you'll bring Tim Knudson to justice."

"And what about *your* killer?"

"Why ask when you can't do anything about it?"

He gave me a touché look, but then his gaze took on the darkness around his irises that meant there was something much deeper and complicated going on inside fake Dean. I burned with the want of him. Damn it all.

"You told me yes," he said. "But you didn't really mean it, did you?"

"I did. Just not in the way you were thinking." I lowered his hands away from me. "You want me? Okay then. It would be for a night." What was I doing bargaining with him? And offering a night? Damn, I sounded like a skeez.

He laughed. "One night. Unless I'm mistaken, weren't you the one asking for a favor from me?"

I boldly went where no one probably went before. "Also, I want to know your name."

For a flaring second, his irises expanded all the way, two burnished suns, temptation blazing in him like he wanted to agree to everything I was asking for.

"If I give you my name," he said, "I give you too much power."

"What would I do? Use it against you?"

"It's been done before."

In his eyes, I could also see all the years this entity had lived, could see eons of coveting and collecting and having his heart broken because this was all there was for him—a continual fight against eternal boredom.

As well as the need to survive.

I don't know why I did it exactly, but I touched his

face with my fingertips, feeling skin, the bristle of stubble, alluring warmth. All so real in the glow of the stars.

He smiled, and I knew in my heart it was sincere, aching, needing. But then he took my hands away from his face like I'd done to him earlier.

"No deal," he said. "There'll never be a deal like the one you want, Jenny. You see, I'm into this little thing called self-preservation, and everything you're asking for goes against that."

His rejection twisted inside me like a drill making me bleed drop by drop. Why, though, when I wasn't supposed to care for him?

He helped me to my feet, and when I wobbled, totally unbalanced by my reaction to him, he slung an arm around my shoulders, walking me over the invisible floor that held us up above the stretching expanse of purple and stars.

"If there's one thing you really should learn about this dimension," he said, "it's that you never overplay your hand with an entity who's more powerful than you are."

That drill in my chest began to hollow me out. This was starting to sound like a dismissal. Was he about to send me back to the earthly plane now, empty-handed? And why did it matter more than it should've?

We stopped over a cluster of stars miles below us, so far away that I couldn't make out their bodies as much as their glows.

He pointed to them. "My newest bunch. I brought them here nearly twenty years ago in your time. I haven't had any new ones since. These came in a cluster—a traveling group of bons vivants who had so much joy in life that it took me two of your decades to experience everything they had to offer. In the star world of their suspended minds, they keep living the good life over and over again, for as long as they want to. They kept me happy for a long time."

Once, he'd asked me to stay with him here, just like this group. He'd wanted to give me never-ending happiness in a limbo where I wouldn't remember my death or the pain of my old life, only the good. He'd even admitted that he would feed off my happiness until he got bored and wanted a new star.

"Why're you showing them to me?" I asked.

"Because I want you to know that you were the first ghost who caught my attention in a while. You, however, won't be the last."

That drill inside me finished its job, leaving nothing behind but total emptiness. I didn't know how I'd let fake Dean become this important to me. Hadn't even known that hearing him say something like this would matter.

"It's okay," he said, squeezing my shoulder. "We can still be friends."

He was imitating what my old Dean would've said if he'd actually broken up with me and our relationship hadn't just faded away over time and distance.

I stepped back from him. "Is this fun for you?"

"That's what you think I'm doing, having fun?"

"Yes. And all I wanted was help in making the world right. . . ."

"You wanted to make *my* world wrong. And that can't happen, Jenny."

So this was it. I was on my own, along with help from my friends. Us against the world.

I fought back the sinking pierce of disappointment that threatened to rush up from my chest and into my throat, tightening it.

"You need to let me go now," I said.

Was that sadness in his eyes again? Couldn't be. Not from an entity that could only concentrate on his own needs.

"I see what's going on here," he said. "You're jealous that I'd like to move on from you. But you can't tell me that you were the ideal relationship, so what else do you expect from me?"

"Stop it with the games. If you're trying to *make* me jealous, I don't have time for it." I motioned downward, to wherever the earthly plane was. Focusing on that instead of what was going on in my heart was so much better. "Let me go so I can get on with my responsibilities."

He closed his eyes in what looked like pain, then smiled, the gesture barely there.

"I truly wish you good luck then, Jenny," he said softly as the floor circled open like a swirling hole beneath me.

As I fell back to my dimension, my body turned to electricity and air, my heart going invisible. You could even say I didn't have a heart anymore—at all.

At least he sent me to above Tim's house, as the afternoon burned off with a gray cast into an equally colorless evening.

I wouldn't think about him, I kept telling myself. Too many things to do. Too many lives to vindicate . . .

But I kept thinking, anyway.

As I descended, I noticed how, below me on the neighborhood street, the cops were at Mrs. Cavendish's, blocking the area with yellow crime scene tape and patrol cars, authorities going in and out of Tim's house. Neighbors had gathered outside the barriers, their arms crossed over their chests as they traded the news about Mrs. Cavendish and the suspect, Tim Knudson.

Amanda Lee was one of the crowd, even while standing apart from them. She *almost* blended with her Southwestern gypsy gear and the gray streaks running through the front of her red hair. I could tell she was listening to everyone talk around her, picking up vibes and sorting through them. The ghosts hovered around her like they were waiting for her to give them some direction.

I floated down and down, wanting more than anything to go to them as my nonexistent heart told me one more time to forget about fake Dean.

When the ghosts saw me coming toward them, they yelled, "Jen!"

As I came in for a landing, I saw that Randy looked better than I'd expected, along with Louis, even though both of them seemed off in some slight way. Scott was even here, now that we knew the dark spirit wasn't after Wendy. Someone had fetched Old Seth, too, and it looked like he'd gotten over his mourning period for Cassie, because he was floating closer than anyone to Amanda Lee, his cowboy hat pushed back on his head, as if it made him hear the human gossip better.

Every one of them, including Amanda Lee, checked out how colorful I was, thanks to my final encounter with fake Dean. But, as usual, none of them commented right off the bat, and I was glad for it.

Of course, my essence buzzed dully with the hurt that I couldn't quite shake, but I'd get over it soon. Really.

Amanda Lee walked over, gazing pointedly at my healed arm, then away from me, back to the onlookers. Taking out her phone, she pretended she was having a conversation on it while chatting with us, just to cover our discussion. "The police are onto Tim, and it isn't only because I tipped them off and they found his name written in blood on the table. A neighbor saw him getting in Mrs. Cavendish's car and escaping from her house."

"He doesn't have much luck with neighbors and committing crimes, does he?" Strike two for him, since he'd been caught by another neighbor when he was nine, when he'd set that fire.

"True," Amanda Lee said. "So they're searching his house and are looking for him on the roads. I've already been interviewed, as well, since I discovered Margaret's body."

"What reason did you give them for being in her house?"

"I was truthful. Mainly." She shrugged. "I said I

know Nichelle, and I was going over to her home to pick up clothes because I was harboring her from Tim. Where the story changes a tad is that I 'heard' Margaret scream and went over to see why. They told me I was fortunate Tim didn't attack me, as well, but little did they know that I was perfectly safe."

She sent me a confident glance that told me she knew that me or one of the ghosts would always come to the rescue. I would sure try, even if we would have to do all our heroics on our own, without help from something more celestial, like fake Dean.

Pushing him from my mind again—how many times would I have to do that?—I asked, "Are they interviewing Nichelle about Tim?"

"Yes, they already did at my home."

Wow. I guess I'd spent some time in the star place, much longer than I'd realized.

Amanda Lee said, "Nichelle didn't hold anything back from them. She was able to tell her story to someone who can actually put him away now." Amanda Lee touched her turquoise necklace. "I only wish it hadn't come to this."

"You and me both."

A beat passed, loaded with regret. What could we have done to stop Tim from getting to Margaret Cavendish, though? What hadn't we tried?

Randy, Louis, Scott, and Old Seth air-ambled over to us.

"D'ja tell her?" Randy asked. He was the same old joyful sailor, but there was a slowness to his voice. And why not, when a part of him had been stolen?

Scott was clearly excited to be on active duty. Leave it to a cop's son. "Twyla's still got to be on Tim's trail somewhere out there," he blurted out. "There's still hope that she'll bring him in."

Amanda Lee was light-years ahead of this conversation, and she looked me over but good. "I hear you met your killer today."

Right to the point. The chill-out Amanda Lee had definitely worn off and the General was back full force.

"Yeah, meeting him was the highlight of my week," I said.

"Randy told Louis everything, and Louis told me." Amanda Lee fiddled with her necklace as she still held her phone to her ear. "How are you doing?"

"Peachy. We got along famously, you know? He was even kind enough to give me a heads-up about haunting the shit out of me."

"Maybe something can be done when Ruben has the opportunity to take a close look at your bracelets. He'll be sending them out to a lab he uses. I was able to pick them up from Brittany's office today before Randy called me with your SOS."

"Even if we lucked out and IDed my creep," I said, "what good will it do? He's dead, and we can't exactly arrest him." I surveyed the crowd. "You probably know that he can impersonate ghosts he draws essences from, so he could be anyone we run into in this dimension."

Louis said, "We'll have the advantage of feeling his bad vibrations if he comes face-to-face again with us, Jensen. That's going to help us know when he's around."

Even Louis sounded more bummed out than usual, compliments of the dark spirit.

Amanda Lee gave me a reassuring smile, like everything would be fine and dandy. I was about to tell her what fake Dean had said about her being the one who would be responsible for sending the dark spirit away, but then she walked toward her car down the street, still focused on what we could do for Nichelle.

This would be a conversation for another time.

We ghosts followed her, and after she got into the Bentley, we hovered outside.

She rolled down a window and still pretended to talk on her phone. "If you all come in, we can brainstorm on our way back to Nichelle."

Old Seth backed off. "Sorry, ma'am. I'm not much for tight squeezes."

He was a big cowpoke and would probably take up half the backseat. The friction between ghost essences might even create sparks all over the place.

As he held out his hand to the rest of us, he bowed. "Be my guest. I'll take the air, if you don't mind."

We were fine with his offer, so Louis and Scott went to hover in the backseat, me in front, and Randy stuck near the roof, looking down on us all as Amanda Lee started the car. Old Seth raised a hand in farewell outside, watching us leave.

As we traveled down the neighborhood streets, palm trees and pastel houses under the gray-flannel-dulled sky, Amanda Lee said, "So Tim went after someone else because he couldn't have it out with his girlfriend."

"Or his mother," I said.

Randy talked down to us. "Whass next for 'im then?"

Scott said, "The police catch him, and justice will be done. That's what my father would've told me when he was on the force." He smiled. "I like to think he's on heaven patrol now, itching to lecture me about driving too fast and staying out too late."

Ghost. A.D.D.

Back on track. "It's not that I don't believe the police will catch up to Tim before he hurts someone else, but . . . What if Tim evades them? What if he gets a chance to hurt someone else before all is said and done?"

Amanda Lee gripped the wheel. "Serial offenders become more arrogant with each attack, so he might get bold if he doesn't get caught."

Didn't I know it. According to my killer, he'd gotten so good at what he did that he deserved a gold medal or something. The only thing that was keeping me from being totally depressed about him hunting me down again was the fact that someone had busted him and the world had been freed of him.

Had being the operative word.

I said, "Tim discovered today that killing excites him. His psyche has known it for years, but he con-sciously realizes it now. He'll have a craving to get the same rush he felt today. What if he makes it across the border, to a place where no one is up on the news, and he strolls into a bar? He's going to see a brunette in Mexico, and she'll become another red queen for him."

Randy's sailor tie was wagging back and forth with the motion of the car. "Twyla's *got* to find him."

"And when she does?" I asked.

Louis said, "She'll have enough brains to manipulate a phone to get in touch with the cops and Amanda Lee."

"If she don't kill 'im first," Randy said.

God, I hoped she wouldn't. Even obnoxious Twyla didn't deserve a dark mark.

"And then . . . ?" I asked.

Scott scooted up toward Amanda Lee's seat. "We let the cops do their duty. I told you that."

"Then he'll simply go to jail, if he's even convicted?" I asked. "Let me give you a different scenario—he gets put away, but there's this thing they call parole, and if his behavior is good, then he gets out."

Louis asked, "But what if he's rehabilitated in prison?"

Amanda Lee shook her head but didn't say anything.

"What worries me most," I said, "is that Tim might get some guidance in steering clear of the law, and it'll take a while for him to get caught. My killer's still around, and what if he decides to train Tim? He seemed to enjoy doing that today, egging him on, giving him ideas. And even if my killer doesn't do that, Tim's cravings aren't just going to go away."

I could feel the sympathetic vibrations from them all over the car because I'd brought my killer up.

I looked each ghost in the eye. "Since Tim wants to kill, he needs to know without a doubt that he's going to get hell for it. That's what we should've done with him in the first place."

"We tried that, didn't we?" Scott asked.

Louis stared long and hard at me. "I think Jensen's talking about something else. Something along the lines of Pavlov's dog?"

"And *Bingo* was his name-o," I said.

Louis' voice became more animated. "Classical conditioning. A learned response to stimulus. When Tim gets those bad urges, we'll give him a shock—even more of one than we were giving him with suggestions to his psyche."

"These shocks," I said, "would be physical, not mental. Mental didn't work with him."

We all kept our thoughts to ourselves the rest of the way to Amanda Lee's, but I already had a firm idea of what I wanted to carry out with Tim if or when Twyla found him: the kind of justice that would lock him away for good, whether it was in a jail cell or his mind.

Amanda Lee pulled into her posh Rancho Santa Fe neighborhood, the streetlights awakening to fight the gloom. She finally spoke.

"All I can tell you is this—if I could have had a moment with the woman who'd killed my Elizabeth, I wouldn't have waited for the police and the courts to give Farah justice. I hope the shocks you give Tim are worse than the ones his victim had at the end."

Her words resonated with Louis and Scott in the backseat, because they stayed deathly quiet. Randy nodded from his spot on the ceiling, and I knew where he stood.

Amanda Lee rounded a corner, then slowed down as a barrage of misty forms sped right at us.

"Hey!" Scott yelled as Amanda Lee swerved to avoid the lookiloo ghosts.

When I got a better view, I saw that the two muscle-heads who'd been playing cops and robbers near Amanda Lee's pool were sailing alongside the car now, yelling unintelligible words and pointing up ahead to the side of the street.

Amanda Lee slammed on the brakes because, there, near the curb eight houses down from Amanda Lee's place, sat a blue Prius with a TEACHERS HAVE CLASS bumper sticker on the fender.

We idled in the middle of the street. Amanda Lee's eyes were wide, her hands slipping off the steering wheel as she motioned toward the car.

She was having a psychic vibe. "It's Margaret's," she whispered. "How did Tim know where Nichelle is?"

I recalled my dark killer's words. *But I told him something rather helpful, too. . . .*

Had this been the second suggestion he'd made to Tim? He'd told him where Nichelle was being kept, and that's why Tim had been so on fire to steal Mrs. Cavendish's car?

But if the car was here . . . where was Twyla?

I squeezed through a gap in the window, zooming toward Amanda Lee's house, where the front window by the door was shattered, a porch chair lodged in it while the curtains blew around the chair and silence rocked the air. More lookiloos were hovering near the damage and waiting for us, including the turn-of-the-century man in his straw hat and fancy pale suit, plus one of the Native Americans dressed in the rough white shirt and short pants he'd probably gotten from a mission.

"Hurry," one of the muscle-heads said. "That Tim dude just bashed the window in and went running inside and—"

That's when the screaming started.

23

I needed to get inside—but, dammit, Amanda Lee had ghost-proofed her home.

The screaming continued just as Scott, Louis, and Randy flared up to the porch, stopping cold at the door.

Tim's voice was muffled through the shattered window. "Shut the fuck up, Heidi!"

Heidi. But what about Nichelle? Ruben?

Behind us, I could hear Amanda Lee's running footsteps, and I turned to her.

"Don't!" I yelled. "If you go in there, he might hurt Heidi or you."

"Where's Ruben?" she whispered, the porch lantern casting a shadow over her face. "Nichelle?"

"I don't know, and I'm not gonna know if you don't lift those incantations and the smudging that're keeping us out."

Her hands were shaking as she held her phone and her keys. "I think I have to be inside to erase those . . ."

Great. "Then you'll have to go in . . . quietly. We'll be

waiting on the threshold for you to finish." I motioned to her phone. "Let's wait on any calls, though."

She raised her eyebrows at first, then took my meaning. We needed the cops eventually, but would they arrive before I could Pavlov our killer, making one final attempt to reprogram him in case he ever roamed free again? I had to look at the long-term game here, not the short-term. I had to try to fix him and hope the attempt didn't backfire.

Amanda Lee didn't stand around. She strode forward, shoving her phone in a pocket of her skirt, then carefully mounting the porch steps. Holding her breath, she inserted a key into the lock, slowly turning it, closing her eyes when the key clicked home.

We all held our almost-breaths now, waiting to see if Tim had heard, but he was still busy telling Heidi to shut up somewhere that sounded like he was near the back of the house.

She stopped screaming.

Had Tim hurt her? And were Nichelle and Ruben with her? If that was the case, then why was Tim still in the house yelling at Heidi?

I ghost-crossed my fingers, bobbing in the air impatiently as Amanda Lee's hushed anti-incantations carried to us.

Scott said, "Ruben could've rung 9-1-1 when Tim shattered the window. The heat could be on their way."

The Native American lookiloo floated forward, his English stilted but good. "He did not use his phone, or a gun." The ghost had as many wrinkles as Ruben on his dark, grayish complexion, and the reminder of our PI made me even more anxious.

Where *was* he? And Twyla?

The man in the turn-of-the-century suit coasted up to the side of the Native American. "We were listening and watching the humans through the kitchen window when this happened. I know we were supposed to be waiting around the rest of the property, just in case Tim showed, but we figured what were the chances that he was gonna connect Nichelle to Amanda Lee?"

During this confession, the Native American had meandered off, going around the corner toward the back of the house, where I was sure he'd be looking through the kitchen window, keeping tabs on the situation.

Anyway, it was clear that the lookiloos had been listening in on conversations after I'd left today. That didn't mean I was going to let them know everything else about the case—especially what I suspected my dark killer had implanted in Tim's head to get him here.

The suited man continued. "After we heard the front window smash, Tim was inside before any of us knew what was going on. We couldn't even *get* inside."

"The house is protected from spirits."

"No joke." He was thrilled to be a part of this—I could tell because he talked with his hands a lot and totally enunciated his words. "To continue, Ruben was in the john, and I think he left his piece in there when he took a piss. He didn't have it when he left with Nichelle."

Was he talking about leaving a gun in the bathroom?

He continued. "He didn't need it, anyway, 'cos he

ran out the back of the house, and without his phone, too, 'cos he was moving too fast with Nichelle to grab it from the kitchen. Heidi was taking a nap, however. When she heard the commotion, she ran to the kitchen and grabbed a knife and her phone from the counter. Tim found her, and she must have decided to hold him up in the kitchen so Nichelle could get away. Heidi started calling the police, but Tim slapped that phone away first, then she told him that she was the only one home. He didn't believe her, and that's where we are."

Amanda Lee was still working on those incantations and smudging. How many had she put on the house? Shit.

"Tim didn't find the gun?" I asked.

"Not that I know of. He's only been around the house with Heidi in tow, trying to find Nichelle. He ain't doing a careful search."

"And what about Twyla?" I asked. "You know the ghost in the eighties getup? Is she with Tim?"

The three remaining lookiloos shook their heads, and my essence sank.

Had Tim lost her during the car chase? Or had something worse happened?

"Okay," I said to the lookiloos. "Why don't you scout around for Ruben, and if you find him and Nichelle, make sure they get somewhere safe. We're going in to help Heidi."

"Me, too," one of the muscle-heads said, flexing his humungo bicep.

"No." I paused. "You know what might work to distract Tim from Heidi, though? Rapping."

"Like Pitbull?" said the other gym rat. This one was so bulky that his arms were permanently curved at his sides.

When he started rapping like the Sugarhill Gang, I waved him off. Jeez, new ghosts.

The guy in the old-time suit grunted. "She means *rapping*, you dip. You know, knocking? Like ghosts do?"

I pointed toward the side of the house. "Knock on the kitchen window, just enough to get Tim's attention. Don't overdo it—and I'm not kidding. He already had a run-in with the paranormal today, and he's going to be wired up enough as it is."

The man in the suit took charge, heading back first, the gym rats following.

It occurred to me that none of us had ever exchanged names or death stories. So much for ghost etiquette in these hurried times.

Focusing again, I realized that Amanda Lee was still doing her house cleansing, and I listened for any more screams. Nothing. I prayed that the raps would consume Tim's attention and give Heidi a few minutes of safety.

Finally, Amanda Lee finished, rushing out of the door and not stopping. "You have five minutes before I call the cops, so do what you need to do!"

We rushed inside, but Louis was the one who slowed us all down.

"He'll recognize our cold wind, Jensen, so we can't go fast and stir up the atmosphere."

Always with the caution, but he was right. I knew we should get the lay of the land first. We also wanted to keep Tim here for the cops while easing into our plan for retooling his urges, which hopefully wouldn't take all that long.

Shocks in general never did.

I forced myself to slow as we all advanced on the kitchen. The first thing I saw was Heidi in a chair facing us, three cell phones on the table in front of her: Nichelle's, Ruben's, and her own? She had a bloodied lip as she looked out of the corner of her eye at something behind the wall.

It had to be Tim.

If he wasn't near her, that was a good thing. Louis obviously thought so, too, because he stopped Randy and Scott near the brink of the room.

Tim's voice was ravaged. "Fuck, look at this. You made me bleed."

"The shattered window cut you, Tim," Heidi said levelly.

The sound of a paper towel roller banged through the air. Then a rapping followed.

Bang-bang-bang.

"There it is again," Tim said. "Is there a basement where Nichelle could've hidden? Tell me, you bitch. I've looked everywhere else."

From the expression on Heidi's face and the messiness of her ponytail, I had the feeling that Tim had dragged her around by the hair to do a quick search.

"Most Southern California houses don't have basements, Tim," she said.

Maybe every place had a basement in Tim's mind. He'd grown up in one, still lived in one, as far as his subconscious was concerned.

I crept to the entrance, peering around the corner to find him holding a knife—probably the one Heidi had grabbed. He was standing at the evening-shaded kitchen window, inspecting the area around it, probably to see what was making the knocking sound. He had cuts on his arms and legs, and the red-blotched paper towel he held to his face with his other hand told me that he'd staunched a decent amount of blood.

I remembered his blood on Mrs. Cavendish's skin. *T-I-M K-N-* It was satisfying to know that he'd sealed his fate with his bleeding, and I wanted to seal it some more.

Shaking, I held back the need to scream up to him, materializing so fast that it'd make him crap his pants. But what good would that do? Haunting methodically was better—especially the kind I wanted to try, shocking him out of his nasty cravings. And we had one more chance at it.

But our inaction right now made me feel sidelined, just like I'd been all my life. Watching everything pass by, reacting instead of acting.

Tim leaned against the wall near the window, where one of the muscle-heads' faces peeked in from the falling darkness. I made a cutting gesture through the air. *That'll be enough rapping, thank you.*

He disappeared.

Tim blotted more blood from his arm while staring at Heidi, tapping the knife against his thigh. He was wearing shorts, his skin exposed, and I wished he would shred himself. That's just one of the reasons I didn't cuff the knife away from him yet. The other was because he'd know we were here if I did it.

Slowly, slowly, the haunting would creep up on him, then—bam. He'd be done for.

"You never liked me," he said to Heidi accusingly.

She kept her tongue, her gaze straying to a pueblo cookie jar on a counter, like she was thinking of hopping out of her chair, grabbing it, and bashing it over Tim's head. Join the club.

But . . . patience.

Tim added, "Everyone tries to shit on me at some point. But you did it right away, Heidi. You poisoned Nichelle's mind against me."

"Tim, I never disliked you." She kept her hands on the table, so calm, so collected. "I love my best friend as much as you do. You know what it's like to love. You get protective."

She was trying to relate to him, and that's why she kept using his name. She wanted him to see her as a person, not a thing to hurt.

But he wasn't buying it. "I know Nichelle's been here. Her phone's right there on the table."

"I wish I could tell you where she is, Tim, but I don't know. She gave me her phone when she dropped by my house this morning and took off. She said she'd get a disposable one from a convenience store so she wouldn't have to listen to all your calls coming through. I agreed because I wanted to monitor them."

"Why?" he raged.

We ghosts revved up, but Tim had only lifted the knife in her direction from across the room.

Heidi remained smooth. "I was worried about you, Tim. I was thinking of ways I could help you to make you less upset. I was going to call you to discuss things."

He walked away from the window, tossing the bloodied paper towel aside. When he approached her, his knife at his side, he raised his other hand, reaching for her brunette ponytail. He had the same smile on his face that he'd had when he'd touched Mrs. Cavendish's hair postmortem.

Louis and Scott buzzed hard, right along with me.

But Randy went for it, pointing to a phone on the table. It dinged.

Heidi looked up at Tim, and when he grabbed for the phone, she swallowed and took a deep, subtle breath.

He accessed the screen, reading it, then slammed the phone down. "What the hell is this?"

Randy gestured to the phone again and it dinged once more. He grinned at me, Scott, and Louis, but even if it was cheeky, it wasn't the same kind of Randy grin as before.

When Tim took another look at the screen, he shoved the phone off the table, and it clattered to the floor.

I couldn't help myself—I moved to the phone and saw what was bothering Tim so much.

Texts from . . . Mrs. Cavendish?

Can I get you anything from the store?

Just checking if there's anything from Japan in mail. Just a package from . . . someone. ☺ Thanks again for looking after house while gone.

I'd have to learn this trick of conjuring old texts from the air.

Tim laughed nervously, brushing his hand over his hair as he moved to the counter. He stabbed the point of the knife at the tile and twisted the blade.

Just as he yanked the knife back to him and started toward Heidi, Randy sprang into action, whirling in front of her, blocking her.

Tim cringed, sensing the disturbance in the air and, ridiculously quick, he turned and grabbed a pan off the stove.

Cast iron?

He swung it toward Randy, catching him full in the torso, making him dissipate through his middle and drop to the floor with a muffled, "Unngh!"

Tim was laughing, and it made me only angrier, boiling inside.

"I hate that cold wind," he said to Heidi. "There were ghosts in my house today. Crazy. I can't even believe it, but I'll tell you what—I'm carrying around iron from now on since it makes the wind go away. I even used a crowbar from Mrs. Cavendish's trunk on some wind when I was laying low in a parking lot after I throttled her. And you know what? No more wind after that!"

Was he talking about attacking Twyla with the crowbar after she'd caught up to him? Was that why she wasn't here?

My hatred burned, and I gestured toward Tim's wrists, manipulating the electricity in the air and jerking the pan and knife away. They clattered to the ground, and Tim backed up, hitting the refrigerator and cowering against it. Meanwhile, Randy was on the floor crawling toward a power source, clutching his hazy middle, the dissipation creeping up and down, eating him away. When he reached Nichelle's discarded phone, he drew energy from it.

Scott, Louis, and I moved in on Tim, but I got to him first, surging forward, sucking to his skin, sliding under it. Hallucination time, Pavlov style, starting with my image of a jail cell.

Around us, the walls turn gray and stark. A cell with bunk beds, a steel sink, bars blocking the opening.

We run for those bars, grasping them with our hands, shaking them and trying to get out. The cell begins to shrink around us, smaller and smaller, unless we're getting bigger and bigger . . .

It all stops, and the sound of clanking keys makes us glance to the left, where a woman in a skintight guard uniform approaches, her keys hitting her thigh, her dark hair long and braided over her shoulder.

Mist scrambles her face.

When she stops in front of us, a smile comes through the mist. Inviting. Tempting.

Our blood shivers, then pounds to life. And when she reaches to the front of her blouse, ripping it open to reveal luscious breasts, we salivate.

"Do you want me?" she asks in a low, seductive tone.

"Yes," we say.

"You can take me. You can take anything you want, Tim."

She strolls toward the bars, holding her breasts in her hands, massaging them. "Take me, baby."

Our hands grasp through the bars, but she steps back, away from us.

"What are you doing?" she says cruelly, closing her blouse. Suddenly, she's holding two glasses of lemonade instead. "I didn't invite you in because I wanted you."

Our temper seethes, burning through us, bathing our sight in red.

"I thought you liked me," we say through our teeth, rage licking at our nerves, making us clench the bars.

She smiles and hands us a lemonade, but we grab her wrist instead, pulling her into the bars. She drops both glasses and they shatter.

We bend and pick up a shard with one hand. No one is going to mess with us. She'll see that we can't be controlled or fooled like this.

As we raise the shard to cut her—

I pulled out of Tim, but only enough to zing him with a bolt of my energy.

Bad dog.

He started, shocked. He began to quiver with the cold and the full-body electrocution. Looked like the power he'd bitten out of me during our last dream was gone.

I went back in and introduced the image of Mrs. Cavendish. . . .

We are in our backyard, looking through the slats of the fence that separate us from Mrs. Cavendish. She's lying on a

*lounger in her bathing suit again, worshipping the sun,
mocking us with her toned, tanned body.*

She sees that we're peeping, smiles, crooks her finger at us.

*"Come over, Tim. I'll call Triple-A for you, but really
what I mean to say is that I'll bang you silly. Please?"*

*We climb the fence, landing on the other side, heading
straight for her, our lust high and taking us over.*

*But she rolls off the lounger, grabbing a towel to hide her
bareness. "What're you doing?"*

Anger explodes in us, but . . .

*A tiny shock jolts us, like a loaded memory of a sensation
we'd just felt a minute ago, and we startle.*

We shake it off, reaching out for her neck—

I busted out of Tim again, drawing on all my energy
and doing the same thing as before.

Zzzzt!

He jerked with the jolt this time, quaking as he fell
to his knees.

I was about to go in again when I heard Louis' voice
banging through my perception.

"The cops are here!" he yelled. "Let's give this up to
them, Jensen!"

Tim had stumbled to his feet, swaying and shivering, wildly looking around. But Heidi was already
gone, along with the knife that'd been on the floor. She
obviously hadn't wasted a moment when he'd gone
into a spacey state that she couldn't have understood,
but she'd been as smart as always and motored out.
Scott was gone, so he must've flown out with her.

I was weaker from giving Tim the hallucination and

the shocks, but fake Dean's touch had filled me up with a lot of excess juice. Also, there was the little matter of motivation.

I could go all night with this.

"I'm not leaving yet, Louis," I said. I wanted to make Tim hallucinate and then shock him until his brain was fried. I couldn't seem to stop the need for it.

"Jensen . . ." Louis said as the sirens got louder.

Bummer. I merely pooled the rest of my energy and materialized to Tim in a swan song. For now.

"Hi," I said to him with a little wave.

Tim started to scream, but then it choked off. Did he . . . recognize me?

Had my killer showed Tim my image? Or did Tim know me from his dreams?

When he squashed that scream and started to smile, it reminded me of the leer on that granny mask in Elfin Forest, and I knew that my dark killer had shown my image to Tim, just for kicks.

He laughed, crazy and not altogether there, then sprinted out of the room.

I took off after him. I liked a chase. The cops would probably get him first, anyway.

Still, as the sirens screeched louder, I kept thinking, *Fry him.* It wasn't the same as killing. Why hadn't I thought of it before? Create a vegetable who couldn't murder. And it wouldn't be killing on my part—it wouldn't be wrong.

Tim was taking the long way, running past Amanda Lee's pool, circling back to where he'd parked Mrs. Cavendish's car eight houses down.

Would the cops know about the deserted Prius?

I guessed not, because when I tracked Tim there, he ducked inside, avoiding a patrol car that tore down the road to Amanda Lee's.

He fumbled with the car keys, taking them out of his shorts pocket, as I easily slipped through a cracked window, intending to jar the keys away from him.

When I manipulated the air to slap the keys from him, he fought me, managing to get the keys in the ignition and start the car. And when he burned off in a scream of tires, I realized that he didn't want to just get away.

He wanted to take out a few cops while he was at it.

As I was about to blast into his head, seeing if I could control him into stepping on the brakes, something nebulous and gray materialized about a hundred feet in front of us.

A ghost?

As we hurled closer, Mrs. Cavendish and her mesh cover-up body came into clear view, and she was leveling a glare so lethal on Tim that even I froze.

Her glare turned into a full-throated roar as she opened her mouth and let out a banshee yell that nailed through my essence. Tim shoved his hands over his ears, cringing, the car squealing to the left where a streetlamp pole loomed.

Closer . . .

Closer—

With all the strength I had left, I shot out of the same window I'd come in just before the car crunched into the pole and something exploded from the steering wheel. As I hovered nearby, the engine hissed, split down the middle. Tim didn't move.

His ghost didn't emerge, either, and that meant he was still alive.

He was there for the taking. But I wasn't just seeing Tim in that car. No, I also saw *my* killer. Yeah, I could fry his brains like Picnic 'n Chicken, letting out all my frustration and anger on both of them.

I could make a difference in this world, all right. A big one.

There was a commotion down the street as cops ran toward us, but all I really saw was Mrs. Cavendish floating with purpose toward the car.

She stopped by my side, locking her haunted, dark gaze on me. In her eyes, I saw the need for the same justice I wanted with my killer. A personal reckoning that would untether her from this dimension.

But then I remembered our limits as ghosts. They cramped inside of me, unjust and unfair. Why couldn't we take care of our own business instead of leaving it to something else?

Helpless. I'd never felt more helpless and enraged.

Mrs. Cavendish stared at Tim. "He deserves a painful death."

I couldn't let her, but what *could* I do? "You're a new ghost and you don't know what it means to kill a human."

"Nothing's going to stop me." An anguished smile pulled on her lips as the cops arrived, surrounding the car with their guns drawn. "I was just about to meet a man who was stationed in Japan in the army. We'd been writing to each other for years, and I was going to fly out next month. I hadn't dated anyone since my husband died years ago. This man was my new future, but that's not all Tim took away from me." She gestured to herself. "I never thought this could happen to me. He violated something I never thought could be touched, and it wasn't just my body."

"I thought the same thing after I was killed."

"Then you understand why Tim Knudson should suffer like I did."

When she moved forward, I wanted to reach out and grab her arm to stop her but I couldn't, so I only said, "Darkness is going to come to you, and you don't know where your wrangler will take you after that. I'm pretty sure it won't be a good place."

"Are there any good places left now?"

As Tim stirred in the front seat, I said, "Do you even know how to kill?"

"I've been practicing." Mrs. Cavendish had an answer for everything.

Without any ceremony, she gestured to a garden spike in a neighbor's front yard and made it fly straight toward Tim's head. It impaled him in the temple, his head dropping forward onto the cushion that'd come out of the steering wheel.

I fisted my hands, not only because I feared for Mrs. Cavendish, but because I wished I'd been the one who felt good about killing him, wished I could've done it with my own murderer.

When Tim's ghost spun out of the window, he was flummoxed, turning around and around to see where he was. When he saw Mrs. Cavendish, he stopped, then started to laugh.

She laughed, too, but she sounded way scarier.

Then a wrangler skyrocketed out of nowhere, but it wasn't gentle—Tim had already been judged, like Farah Edgett had. It whipped its arm out like a lasso and encircled his neck, burning his skin, making it steam. He caterwauled as the creature brutally dragged him under its bridal veil, almost like it was devouring him.

As me and Mrs. Cavendish stood there in awe, it lingered, gazing at her, ruefully shaking its head.

Then it dispassionately sank into the street, its gray veil belled up, almost giving us a view of what was underneath.

But not quite.

As the cops ran around and went about securing the crime scene, I glanced at Mrs. Cavendish, seeing that a big dark X was oozing from the front of her essence. She looked down at it.

"It was worth it," she whispered, and my essence moaned.

What was going to happen to her? Why couldn't she just have her reckoning with Tim?

From behind us, a familiar voice sounded.

"No, duh, it was worth it."

I whipped around to find Twyla, a little grayer for the wear, but in one piece.

I went to hug her, but then remembered that I shouldn't even bother. Still, happiness abounded.

"Where were you?" I asked.

"Hanging out with the Brat Pack at the Hard Rock. Where do you, like, think I was? I thought I had that wastoid Tim cornered in a parking lot, but he felt me or something and grabbed a crowbar. Messed me up, too, then he drove off again. Bu-ut, since I was near a gob of cars, I sucked on a battery for a while. Then this bohunk guy came to pick up his Porsche, and I was like, *Yow*."

No words. And it wasn't just because of what Twyla had said. I kept looking at Mrs. Cavendish's *X*.

It could've been me. . . .

"Psych!" Twyla said, making a flicking motion at my head and recapturing my focus. "Kidding about the bohunk. It took a while for me to recover, then I wasn't sure where to go, so I looked on the freeway again for Tim, then came back here. Looks like I missed most of the fun, too." She faced Mrs. Cavendish. "And, like, gag me out the door, that last part was nasty *gross*, you Terror Train! Job well done."

Mrs. Cavendish didn't seem to mind Twyla's weird dual-sided look. In fact, the woman smiled at her, as if Twyla reminded her of a student who needed guidance.

I left them alone to bond, because Mrs. Cavendish would need it. Plus, I had a few other loose ends to tie up tonight.

And I wasn't just talking about how Heidi, Nichelle, and Ruben were doing.

24

After I'd made sure that Nichelle, Ruben, and Heidi were a-okay, all my core ghost buds except for Louis had gone over to Wendy's and gathered outside her window in the courtyard while the fountain trickled happily.

Even Mrs. Cavendish was here, hovering over the wall next to Twyla, who'd adopted her in the place of Cassie. I guessed it was one of those *pay it forward* things I'd heard of recently—Cassie had helped Twyla transition into Boo World so Twyla was going to do the same for "Marg," as she'd taken to calling her.

I was up by the window with Scott as Wendy leaned out of it. The recent gloom had worn off, bringing the moon out, and it shone over the pink streak in Wendy's black hair. When she'd first seen our ragtag flock, she'd pointed us to the fuse box and listened to our tale of our big adventure, asking a million questions.

We hadn't told her everything about Tim, though. Why did a kid like her need to know? She had enough to handle. But we could tell her the good parts.

After the storytelling and juicing up, she said, "I know how it feels to have your house invaded by a killer, just like Amanda Lee and her place were." Her eyes were dark and troubled, because I'm sure she was remembering when Farah had lived in the mansion with her . . . and when that dark spirit had made its way through it, too. "At least Louis and Old Seth are with her to put everything back into place."

Old Seth had missed all the action, just like Twyla. That's what you got for being a slowpoke.

"Where's everyone else?" Wendy asked me.

"Heidi took Nichelle home with her, and Ruben's also with Amanda Lee. She's cooking him soup or what-have-you to make him feel better about leaving the house with just Nichelle. He wanted to grab Heidi, too, but she was in another room and he didn't have time to get to her."

We'd skipped over the details about Ruben and Nichelle's escape. They'd run to a neighboring house when Tim had first gotten to Amanda Lee's. No one had been home, so they'd scooted to another one. Unfortunately, the next closest neighbor was a ninety-five-year-old woman who didn't have her hearing aid in, and after she let them inside, it took a minute or two to explain themselves so they could use the phone for the cops.

Scott was watching Wendy with his dreamy gaze. "They're all cool now. Even those lookiloo ghosts who've been hanging around Amanda Lee's went off to find something more amusing, now that the party's over."

"I'm sure there's a lot of counseling in everyone's future," Wendy said. "I should know about that. Gavin's been making me take some sessions on Skype."

When I looked confused, Wendy added, "Remember where you talk on the computer and see the person at the same time? You'll get comfy with the new millennium eventually, Jen."

Everyone laughed, even Randy, who lived so deep in the past that he'd probably be getting his butt downtown before the sun rose so he could hunt down his old girlfriend's love letter in the rocks where he'd taken a fall and died. Old habits were hard to kill.

Speaking of killing . . .

I glanced at Mrs. Cavendish. Marg. That's what she'd told us to call her, as soon as Twyla had started doing it. She stood out from the rest of us because of that fluid X on her chest, and she still looked stunned, even with Twyla trying to cheer her up in her own quirky way.

I wasn't sure if regret had set in for Marg, but I did know that I would've done the same damned thing as she'd done to Tim if my own killer had been alive and I'd had the chance to give him his just deserts. It wasn't fair that Marg would exist with a mark now for taking the place of karma.

As she tried to smile at me, I smiled back, sending her a thumbs-up. Yeah, I'd been ready to fry Tim myself, and giving that power up to Marg had left me restless. But now, more than ever, I was going to bring right to the world.

Or maybe all I could manage was *my* world.

Scott looked at me like, *Can we tell Wendy about who the dark spirit really is now?*

We'd been putting that off after the small talk, so I nodded, letting him take the reins. It felt like I'd been talking all night and day with no downtime.

"Guess what?" he asked Wendy.

She trained that dark gaze on him, and he reached out to clip her under the chin with a finger. Of course, he didn't quite succeed. All he did was make her shiver, but she smiled a little, amused.

"You can come out of your castle now," he said. "That dark spirit? It's not your pop."

She wrinkled her brow. "It's not?"

Twyla finally sounded off. "It's Jen's killer. Like, talk about a situation not improving all that much."

Wide-eyed, Wendy turned to me. "Your killer broke through the portal?"

I sank against the wall. "Long story. Short version? You don't need to worry about it coming after you."

Not unless my killer decided he wanted to attack the people I held dear in life—and Wendy had become one of those. Wendy and Suze and . . . whoa, even Amanda Lee, with all her faults. Ruben was in the running, too.

Fake Dean's face crossed my mind, but I shut it out. He wasn't human, anyway. Not in any capacity. Even so, my essence fizzed at the thought of him.

Wendy noticed my preoccupation, but Scott brought her attention back to him.

"You can walk around outside now, have some fun."

"I've got my computer to keep me busy," she said.

But she was just kidding with him, because her cheeks were flushed with the good news. Then she frowned. "Gavin'll probably make me go back to school now, but I suppose that's okay. You don't do squat for work right before summer break, anyway."

"Things'll be boring without you," Scott said.

"Aw," said Twyla from the cheap seats. But it got a faint smile from Marg.

Scott gave Twyla a shut-up look, and Wendy glanced at all of us in turn, even Marg. Wendy had asked about the X and we'd had to tell the truth about it, so Wendy was already being extra nice to her.

"Does this mean you're not going to come around now that I don't need protecting?" she asked. "Because, Jensen, I'm still working on your fake boyfriend stuff. You'll still need help with that."

She seemed so hopeful. Why crush her heart by telling her I'd never see fake Dean again?

Why crush my own?

Besides, I hadn't given the details about the "breakup" to anyone. It wasn't worth the effort.

"Yeah," I said to Wendy. "We'll sure be around."

She and Scott exchanged cute looks.

When the sound of the garage door opener buzzed the air, all ghost eyes went to me. Gossips. But Wendy had only the vaguest clue about the level of strangeness my relationship with Gavin had reached.

"Looks like he's back for the night," she said. "Gavin's been getting out more and more. I don't know where he goes, but he seems kind of smiley when he gets back."

Suze, I thought. She made Gavin smile, and evidently it lasted long after he got home from the pub.

God. Someday my friend would have to know everything about Gavin, *if* they continued to see each other. And I was afraid the bearer of bad news would have to be me. Fake Dean had taunted me about wanting to tell Suze, but I actually didn't want to see her disappointed. Not when she'd been that way for most of her life.

Randy was watching Marg, and I saw him trade looks with Twyla, too.

"Whaddya say we have some fun?" he slurred, pushing his tilting sailor cap in place. "I know a good pub to show Marg. . . ."

"You do know a few," I said.

Twyla had already risen above the wall, waving Marg to come with her.

"Have we got a world to show you," she said to the new ghost. "And you're looking foxy enough to attract some male ghost attention in it, even if we can't, like, fool around with each other."

She gave Marg directions, then said a quick goodbye as two travel tunnels sprang into the air. They went through them and disappeared.

Randy waited for a moment, grinning at me. And, even though it wasn't the same grin I was used to, I loved to see it on him.

Who cares if a dark spirit has part of me? he seemed to be saying. *I'm off to paint the town red.*

He busted into his tunnel, too, leaving me with the tentative lovebirds. Through Wendy's open door, I heard Gavin's boots pound up the stairs, then down the opposite side of the hall.

"Still not talking to him?" I asked Wendy.

"I'm making him suffer." She didn't look happy about it, though. "I'll go to him tonight to tell him the news about the dark spirit. In a while."

"I can tell him about it first. If you want."

"Would you?"

I nodded, rising up to the entire window. But as I slid through it, something caught the corner of my eye. A movement in the trees. A formless flash.

My killer? No, there was no negative energy around.

I hesitated to think of the other possibility, because to think of fake Dean would be to hope, and to hope would mean disappointment.

But it couldn't be him, either. I didn't have that solid phantom body he gave me when he was near.

When a cat jumped out of the tree, I shut all my optimism down. Instead, I thought how pathetic it was that I was a ghost who jumped at horror movie clichés. Nice.

As Wendy and Scott murmured to each other, I went through her room, took a left in the hall, and found Gavin's door gapped, like he'd left it that way in case Wendy wanted to stop by.

I peeked inside to see him lying flat on the bed, the TV on, his eyes closed. Was he sleeping?

I slipped into the room, flattening myself above him so that I looked straight down at him.

Yes, he was smiling, just like Wendy had said he'd be. And he'd gone right to sleep, his thick lashes dust-

ing his cheeks, his cupid-bow mouth giving his tough
face a sense of peace.

I wished I could have some of that peace. Wished I
knew for sure what was making him smile.

Aching, I touched his skin, going deep into him, my
psyche body landing softly in the dream he'd already
put in motion.

Before, he'd dreamed of fire and dragons and death,
punctuated by creative machines and monsters and
emotional anarchy. But now . . .

Now his subconscious was a simple tank of flowy
blue water, and I was outside the glass of it, watching
him float, tranquil and placid, his arms stretched, looking like the angel he'd believed I was at one time.

To my right, a stairway stretched, and I took it,
climbing up and up until I reached a sundeck, where a
bright sky swallowed the sound of palm fronds in the
wind. Waves languorously rolled upon an unseen
shore, and there Gavin was in a swimming pool, floating on his back.

I was standing behind two beach chairs, and someone was sitting in one of them. It was only when Gavin
lazily stopped floating in the pool and swam over
with that smile still on his face that I realized who it
was.

Suze stood, handing him a towel, smiling, too.

I pushed out of the dream before I could see any
more of it, snapping out of him with a small, gentle
break. Hovering over him, my essence hummed.

I felt his happiness, and Suze's, all the way through

me. And when I glanced up to see that he'd taken down those pictures he'd drawn of me as the hellbitch, I smiled, myself.

Floating above him, I lingered, watching over him.

Truly becoming his angel again.